Praise for the Novels of Sasha Lord

In My Wild Dream

"Lord scores another win with the fifth in her Wild series. . . . Lord's vivid prose, vibrant central characters, and fast-paced plot should satisfy fans of historical romance who don't mind a side order of magic."
—*Publishers Weekly*

"Sweeping readers into a magical and romantic world is what Lord does best. Her memorable characters and fine writing style lure you into her powerfully imaginative stories and keep you spellbound to the end."
—*Romantic Times*

Beyond the Wild Wind

"Intriguing. . . . The story line never slows down . . . a delightful romance." —*Midwest Book Review*

"*Beyond the Wild Wind* is another bold adventure in Ms. Lord's Wild series . . . action-packed [and] emotionally charged." —Romance Reviews Today

"Intense emotions and searing sensuality flow from Lord's powerful prose. The author has the ability to create characters whose passions ignite the imagination, and her talent for vivid storytelling increases with each new tantalizing tale."
—*Romantic Times* (4½ stars, top pick)

Across a Wild Sea

"Lord is a grand mistress at blending the reality of a medieval romance with magic and myth to create a story with the essence of a fairy tale and the drama of a grand epic. Those who love Mary Stewart will savor Lord's latest."
—*Romantic Times*

continued . . .

"Ms. Lord's richly woven historical draws readers into a vivid world of court politics, hatred, jealousy, greed, and erotic passion. With multidimensional characters and a stunning love story, you can't help but be thoroughly captivated by this reading pleasure." —*Rendezvous*

"A superb historical romantic fantasy that combines medieval elements with a fine adult-fairy-tale-like atmosphere. . . . The exciting story line blends the fantasy elements inside a well-written historical tale that showcases Sasha Lord's ability to provide a wild read for her fans." —The Best Reviews

In a Wild Wood

"Dark and filled with potent sensuality and rough sex (à la early Johanna Lindsey), Lord's latest pushes the boundaries with an emotionally intense, sexually charged tale." —*Romantic Times* (4½ stars, top pick)

"This exciting medieval romance is an intriguing historical relationship drama . . . cleverly developed support cast." —*Midwest Book Review*

Under a Wild Sky

"Sasha Lord weaves a most imaginative tale."
—Bertrice Small

"Stunningly imaginative and compelling."
—Virginia Henley

"Lord's debut is a powerful, highly romantic adventure with marvelous mystical overtones. Like a lush fairy tale, the story unfolds against a backdrop brimming with fascinating characters, a legend of grand proportions, and magical animals."
—*Romantic Times* (4½ stars, top pick)

"Ms. Lord's debut novel was a surefire hit with this reader, and I eagerly look forward to the next book of hers featuring characters from *Under a Wild Sky*."
—*Rendezvous*

**Also in the Wild series
by Sasha Lord**

WILD ANGEL

SASHA LORD

A SIGNET ECLIPSE BOOK

SIGNET ECLIPSE
Published by New American Library, a division of
Penguin Group (USA) Inc., 375 Hudson Street,
New York, New York 10014, USA
Penguin Group (Canada), 90 Eglinton Avenue East, Suite 700, Toronto,
Ontario M4P 2Y3, Canada (a division of Pearson Penguin Canada Inc.)
Penguin Books Ltd., 80 Strand, London WC2R 0RL, England
Penguin Ireland, 25 St. Stephen's Green, Dublin 2,
Ireland (a division of Penguin Books Ltd.)
Penguin Group (Australia), 250 Camberwell Road, Camberwell, Victoria 3124,
Australia (a division of Pearson Australia Group Pty. Ltd.)
Penguin Books India Pvt. Ltd., 11 Community Centre, Panchsheel Park,
New Delhi - 110 017, India
Penguin Group (NZ), 67 Apollo Drive, Rosedale, North Shore 0632,
New Zealand (a division of Pearson New Zealand Ltd.)
Penguin Books (South Africa) (Pty.) Ltd., 24 Sturdee Avenue,
Rosebank, Johannesburg 2196, South Africa

Penguin Books Ltd., Registered Offices:
80 Strand, London WC2R 0RL, England

First published by Signet Eclipse, an imprint of New American Library,
a division of Penguin Group (USA) Inc.

First Printing, January 2008
10 9 8 7 6 5 4 3 2 1

PUBLISHER'S NOTE
This is a work of fiction. Names, characters, places, and incidents either are
the product of the author's imagination or are used fictitiously, and any resemblance to actual persons, living or dead, business establishments, events, or
locales is entirely coincidental.
    The publisher does not have any control over and does not assume any
responsibility for author or third-party Web sites or their content.

To God, and all who serve You faithfully.

Thank You for helping me find my path
and for leading me toward the
fulfillment of my mission. May all who
know love, know Your blessing; and
may all who are searching for love find
Your guidance.

*God, love and milk
make you strong.*

—Julian, four years old, 2002

ACKNOWLEDGMENTS

Many thanks to my wonderful friends, who contribute their own particular brand of research to my books. Lynn, may you live under the rainbow. Maureen, may the thunderstorms of life excite and thrill you. And Joan, may the mountainside calm you.

Prologue

France, Early Eleventh Century

Mangan O'Bannon's brave Scottish heart thundered and his muscles pulsed with power as he swung his broadsword and buried its deadly edge into the trunk of a tree, then sank to his knees and dropped his head into his hands.

A soldier lay dying at Mangan's feet. The man moaned, his face contorting in agony. As the pain spread he screamed, a long, inhuman howl, until his lips drained of all color, his head lolled to the side and his lifeless eyes stared out over the battlefield.

From dawn till dusk Mangan had fought on this field. Again and again he had swung his sword, maiming, mutilating . . . killing. The sun had risen, climbed over the noon apex and slid down toward the horizon, yet still he and his men had fought the French until now, leaving the meadow covered with dead and dying bodies.

"Why?" Mangan whispered. "Why have we fought this war? Why have these brave men died? French or Scot . . . those who have fallen and those who remain . . . why are we here?" He looked up and saw the mangled body of one of his men. That man would never go home. He would never see his two sons grow to manhood or hear the sweet words of his wife welcoming him back.

Mangan rose and yanked his blade free, his thumb absently caressing the inlaid hilt. Several lengths away stood his horse, Sir Scott. The animal's head hung low in exhaustion and the reins trailed onto the ground. The horse was draped with a rich caparison and an equally expensive saddle. Jewels winked in the setting sun, and golden threads shimmered as the horse took several labored breaths. Two flags were mounted on the back of the saddle, one for Scotland and one of his family's crest. Both still fluttered in the breeze, mutely proclaiming both Mangan's status and his loyalty to his king. If he had fallen, a Frenchman would have cut down the flags, but since he still stood, the flags symbolized his victory.

Mangan walked over to his fellow soldier and touched his arm, but the man's flesh was cold. Fury surged through Mangan's soul, and he strode abruptly toward Sir Scott and vaulted aboard, then kicked the stallion's sides. Sir Scott's head rose and he surged forward.

They made their way across the field, stepping over dead bodies and weaving in and around wounded men. Mangan stood tall in the stirrups, and his eyes blazed as he took in friend and foe, the land a twilight graveyard littered with thousands of bodies, French and Scot often indistinguishable.

A few men stood or rode their horses as he did, taking in the vast waste, listening to the torturous moans of the wounded and seeing the vacant faces of the dead. They were fellow Scots, but even so they steered clear of one another, knowing that battle lust often made soldiers into murderers. Until morning, when they could gather in their tents and see one another in the light of day, it was best to avoid fellow soldiers after a battle such as this.

Mangan knew because he had survived many such battles.

He slowed his stallion and peered down at the corpse of a young man, not even five and ten. He jumped down, recognizing one of his pages. He would tell the boy's father that his son had died a courageous death and his family should be proud. But French and Scots blood melded in sticky pools . . . black, blond and red hair lay matted against too many faces. No nation could claim victory on this field. No leader could cry out triumphantly and brandish Scotland's flag over the field in glory.

Mangan staggered back under the weight of his guilt. As streaks of yellow and gold laced the far horizon and the setting sun reflected a glorious display across the sky, Mangan cast a haunted gaze through the lengthening shadows, seeing only pain and destruction.

He was the son of the great Earl of Kirkcaldy, heir to one of the richest and most powerful fiefdoms in all of Scotland. Mangan O'Bannon, a warrior whose prowess with the sword was known throughout the country and beyond. A leader of armies, a man who remained boldly victorious in battle despite all odds. Nine and twenty years old and brashly handsome, he was as politically astute as his father. He was a king's man who had carried Scotland's banner with courage and pride.

Until today.

Mangan sheathed his sword and stared around him in horror. No victory. No surrender. Just death.

Army followers began creeping across the field like shadowy specters from the underworld, stealing a ring here . . . a jeweled dagger there. One took a rock and smashed a dead man's teeth to knock loose a gold filling. Although Mangan had seen them pillage many times before, he had never felt such heart-wrenching despair at their avarice.

A sudden fight erupted between two female marauders as the women grappled over a silver chain one had ripped from the neck of a fallen warrior. They screamed and scratched, then tumbled to the ground and rolled over each other as their legs kicked and their hands struck. Then one woman plunged a knife into the other's side and sprang to her feet, cackling with glee.

Such were the spoils of war, the results of political greed.

This field was located in French territory, but the Scottish king wanted it for himself. He had instructed Mangan to lead an army of a thousand men into battle to claim the land for Scotland. And now the landscape was blanketed with thousands of dead souls whose lives would have no everlasting meaning.

Where was God? Where were compassion and kindness? Where were truth and justice in this senseless struggle of king against king? Why were they fighting over a tract of desolate land? Why were they dying for something as nameless—as faceless—as power?

The agony in Mangan's heart made him weak. He had contributed to this carnage. He had led a thousand trusting men into battle and allowed them to be massacred. The names of his soldiers echoed through his mind, and at each name the pain in his heart twisted deeper. The men should not have trusted him.

He had failed everyone—his father, his mother, his country . . .

Mostly he had failed God.

The dying sun blazed, drenching the field in red just before it sank beneath the horizon.

Mangan remounted his horse and flung Scotland's flags to the ground. As his soul keened in mourning, his heart heavy with agonizing guilt, Mangan reined his horse around. Then he left the battlefield, intending never to return, and began a long journey in search of solace.

Chapter 1

Scotland, Thirteen Months Later . . .

Brother Mangan of St. Ignacio Abbey gripped his long-handled spade and attacked the earth, churning a hard patch of ground into a moist and inviting bit of earth in which to plant seeds. Sweat dripped down his face, and his arms shook with fatigue, but he did not slow his pace. Instead he drove his spade deeper and more furiously, as if his physical efforts alone could erase the pain in his soul.

Brother Bartholomew, abbot of St. Ignacio, watched him from the shade of a willow tree. Mangan had come to him over a year ago and begged for admittance into the cloistered monastery in order to cleanse his heart and absolve his sins.

At first the abbot had welcomed him. Mangan's turmoil had been plain to read, and his desire for redemption real. Mangan had immersed himself in the monks' daily devotions and embraced their customs. His communion with God had been sincere and the goodness struggling to break forth clearly apparent.

But something was still missing.

Despite having spent the required year within the

monastery before pledging his life to the church, Mangan still seemed unsettled. It was not that he did not pray, for his worn robes bore proof of the hours he'd spent on his knees. It was not that Mangan did not understand God's word or know God's book, for he did. In fact, Mangan had a special sense of God that awed the abbot. Mangan could look into a person's eyes and understand that person's soul in a way that Brother Bartholomew wished for himself. Perhaps Mangan's gift arose from the horrors he had witnessed, or perhaps from something deep within his soul that had always been a part of him.

Mangan paused in his labors and looked up at the church spire, mouthing words that the abbot assumed to be prayers. It was high noon, and the monks always gave thanks at this time.

Brother Bartholomew walked forward with Mangan's sword in his hand.

Mangan's shoulders tensed as he heard a soft footfall and he spun quickly, his hands clenched around the handle of the spade. As soon as he saw the abbot, he averted his gaze and relaxed his grip while taking a deep breath. He did not want to look at the sword. It reminded him of that last battle . . . of all those dead people.

"My approach startled you," the abbot said as he stood at the edge of the tilled ground and smiled at Mangan.

"I am always pleased to see you," Mangan replied, although still he did not look up.

The abbot smiled more broadly, aware that Mangan's answer had been a clever evasion. "You still react with the instincts of a warrior."

Mangan glanced across the fields to where the other monks had returned to work now that their prayers

were done. The sight calmed him and he smiled ruefully. "You are here to talk with me about my vows,"
he suspected.

The abbot's smile faded and he nodded. "You are
not ready." He dug the sword's tip into the earth and
stepped back as the hilt wavered back and forth between them.

Mangan could not help it. He stared at the blade,
his hand trembling as he remembered the feel of the
hard steel against his palm. "I never want to use that
again," he said harshly. "Why do you bring it to me?"

"You must make peace with yourself before you
can make peace with God."

"That is why I am here," Mangan answered, his
voice rising with anger.

The abbot shook his head. "No, that is why you
must go. Your journey does not end here. You have
learned much with us, and we have learned much from
you, but the restlessness in your soul persists. You
have contained the fire, but it smolders within."

"No," Mangan denied. "I am ready. I want to be
ordained."

The abbot nodded. "I knew you would answer in
such a way, and I prayed for guidance, both for you
and for me." He clasped his hands together and
pressed them against his lips. "In His merciful kindness, God answered me."

"What did He say?"

"He said that you must embark on a holy quest."

"A quest? For what? Why?"

"Many years ago a young monk was asked to clean
the relic room. He wanted to do it well, so he removed
all the relics from our church sanctuary and placed
them carefully along a bench near a window. He
scrubbed the chamber for two days until it shone. He

then began replacing the relics in the chamber, taking care to treat each one with the respect it deserved. But one was missing."

The abbot paused, remembering. "The young monk was inconsolable. The relic was the only remaining piece of baby Jesus' blanket. Despite our assurances that God would forgive him, the monk left St. Ignacio, pledging to find and return the relic."

Mangan frowned. "You have no such relic in the sanctuary."

The abbot shook his head. "No. The monk never returned."

"Perhaps he stole it."

"I never suspected the monk. In fact, I assumed he died during his travels. But I recently heard that several religious relics were sold to a merchant at a southern port. I would like you to travel there and determine whether Jesus' blanket was among the items sold."

"And if it was?"

"Then bring it home and I will accept your final vows."

"And if it is not there?"

"Allow God to guide you in your journey. Follow your heart and it will lead you home when you are ready."

"Is that all you ask? If I do this, will I experience the peace I have been seeking for the past thirteen months?"

The abbot smiled again. He noted the bulging muscles of Mangan's broad back and the tension in his handsome face, but he also saw the haunting loneliness deep within Mangan's green eyes. Mangan needed to find a missing piece, but Brother Bartholomew was not certain whether it was a piece of Jesus' blanket or a piece of Mangan's own soul.

Two seasons later, a Gypsy family traveled through a Highland forest en route to an ailing relative.

Ashleigh's tinkling laughter filled the greenwood, causing birds to trill and squirrels to chatter as if they shared her gaiety. Her parents grinned at each other, pleased by the young woman's obvious pleasure after so many days of exhausting travel. An exotic beauty of six and ten, their daughter was accustomed to the excitement of the Gypsy camp and had been sullen when her mother and father had set out toward her mother's homeland to visit an ill grandmother Ashleigh had never met. They had traveled fast, rarely pausing to enjoy the landscape they traversed, and Ashleigh was in sore need of a moment's diversion.

"You are laughing at my mistake, young Ashleigh?" her mother questioned, her dark eyes narrowing as she jumped down from the wagon seat and waggled a finger at her. "I should punish you for your insolence!"

"You are not a full-blooded Gypsy like Father," Ashleigh reminded her. "You do not live by the rules of vengeance; thus you must grant me full pardon." She, too, jumped down and stretched her back. Then she walked up to the paired gray horses and patted each fondly on the neck. "You did well, Franco," she whispered. "And so did you, Francis." She placed a kiss on each of their muzzles and smiled when they butted her back.

"And you are only half-Gypsy. The other half ought to be a lady," her mother responded. "Therefore, somewhere inside your soul, you should have *some* manners." She laughed at Ashleigh's affronted look and handed her daughter a length of rope.

"Let me show you how to do it," Ashleigh replied as she began looping the rope deftly around her delicate fingers. Since she had always lived like a Gypsy, she knew no other way. The members of the camp feasted together, sang together and practiced their skills on unsuspecting peasants in carefully orchestrated feats. Sometimes they stole; sometimes they presented plays. Ashleigh's father was a magician whose shows drew large crowds and much coin, which they shared among everyone in the camp. The people of their extended family protected and helped one another. As far as Ashleigh was concerned, there was no better way to live.

"Look carefully," she intoned, as if she were practicing before a much larger audience. So far her parents had not allowed her to do the more complicated tricks in front of others, but she was determined to show them that she was ready. Perhaps by the time they returned to camp, her father would let her create her own show.

She flourished the rope in grand style, even batting her large, black-fringed eyes in imitation of her mother's mannerism. Her father laughed uproariously and leaned against the wagon wheel to watch her antics.

Ashleigh threaded the rope through the fingers of one hand, then extracted a slim knife with the other. "I will cut the rope," she said dramatically, and appeared to slice it in half. "See?" she said, brandishing the supposedly cut ends of the rope.

"No, no," her father complained good-naturedly. "That was a good piece of rope. Why did you cut it in twain?"

"Oh, my," Ashleigh answered, and her youthful lips

turned up in an impish smile. "If it is so important, I will fix it for you."

"But how, young miss? You have already destroyed it."

Ashleigh giggled at her father's acting and rapidly began twisting the rope in a knot. "Watch carefully," she cautioned. "Especially you," she said, glancing at her mother.

Her mother groaned and put her hands on her hips. "You have turned into a bit of a spoiled brat," she said fondly. "But such a clever one, I can only thank the stars for such good fortune."

Her father slid his hands around his wife's waist and pulled her close for a kiss. "If she grows up as lovely as her mother, she will doubtless cause us more grief with her looks than with her magic tricks."

Glancing at her daughter's blossoming figure, Mary nodded in agreement. "Much too pretty. It would have been wiser to lock her in a convent than to teach her your Gypsy tricks."

"Pay attention," Ashleigh scolded, ignoring her mother's lament. Raised as a Gypsy child despite her mother's highborn status, she knew nothing of rules and restraint. Her mother had long ago forsaken such restrictions herself and run off to be with her Gypsy lover, and she had instilled a passion for all things wild and wonderful in her daughter—which both pleased and worried Mary.

"See?" Ashleigh commanded as she twitched the rope. "I have knotted the ends like so . . . Now . . . pull them and . . . the rope is miraculously restored!" She snapped the rope and it was, indeed, all in one piece.

Mary sighed. "How is it that she can perfect that trick and I cannot?"

"Her fingers are smaller than yours, my dear," Romil answered. "Besides, she has a gift. Her ability to manipulate objects surpasses even my own."

"Not possible," Mary said. "You are the acknowledged master magician in our caravan. Romil, the master magician. 'Twas what first attracted me to you."

He laughed and kissed her once again as their daughter folded the rope and began practicing other tricks her father had shown her. "If I were to die today, I would be happy because I have known your love," he said with a smile, causing Ashleigh to groan in disgust.

"Ach, you still know how to make your wife feel loved, even after seventeen years," she said. He grinned and slid his hands up her back, but she pulled away and sighed. "I am concerned about my mother. I hope she will receive me after all these years. 'Twas only happenstance that I overheard her name mentioned at that play we did for a French noble, and learned that she is ill."

Sobering, he let her go and nodded with serious concern. "I know her acceptance means much to you, Mary. We have already traveled for over a fortnight in Scotland. You know I would do anything for you, even return with you to your homeland for good, if it would please you. Ashleigh should meet her grandmother and learn about your side of the family. Perhaps even stay with them for a while."

Mary smiled softly and placed a hand upon her husband's shoulder. "Ashleigh is a happy child. Being a Gypsy is all she knows, and I pray that her love of life will last forever. She does not need the trappings of my old life, and neither do I. You have already done much to fill me with joy, and I have never regretted leaving that world behind and joining your beautiful, carefree life. You gave me a lovely daughter, a

sturdy wagon." She waved at the colorful vehicle behind her. "And a comfortable bed." She smiled and
winked over the head of their black-haired daughter,
who was fiddling with a cup and a cloth, turning the
cup upside down so that bubbles floated upward. The
trick was done to simulate boiling water without a fire,
and it always made the crowd gasp.

Ashleigh glanced up and flashed her parents a
frown. "I, for one, have no desire to meet your family,
for my only wish is to become a master magician like
Father. Any mother who could cast aside her own
daughter for loving a man as wonderful as Father has
a rotten soul. I know I will despise her on sight, no
matter how ill she is."

Mary smiled sadly and touched her daughter's hair.
"It is not so simple, Ashleigh. My mother had little
choice."

"Ashleigh, we will not speak poorly of anyone in
the family," Romil added, "whether they acknowledge
us or not. I insist you treat your grandmother with
respect when we reach her home. You have much to
learn about family love."

Romil began unharnessing the horses from the
wagon. Both animals were an unusual smoky gray with
flaxen white manes and tails, and were a source of
great pride to the family. Ashleigh had learned to ride
on them, and treated them as friends.

As Ashleigh flushed and looked down, her father
walked over to her and touched her on the shoulder.
"You must not allow anger to prevent you from seiz-
ing opportunities. Your grandmother is an important
woman, and she has endured much in her life. You
would learn from her if you would open your heart."

"How can you defend her when 'twas she who rejected you?" Ashleigh cried.

"As your mother said, events are not always within our power to change, and they are not always easy to explain. There are times when one must accept and learn to adapt." He turned from Ashleigh and glanced at his wife. "Mary, why don't you set up camp and start the fire? We will not make it much farther tonight, and this glade seems secluded enough. I want to teach Ash how to disappear. She will need the skill if she attracts the wrong kind of attention during a performance."

"Will we reach Dunkeld by the full moon? I am anxious to see Mother."

"Because we must stay off the main roads to avoid attention from any who would seek to prevent our visit, it will most likely take at least two days longer, perhaps even three."

As Mary nodded and began gathering wood, Romil drew Ashleigh aside and showed her one of his most precious possessions, a piece of highly polished metal hinged on one side that could either form a sharp angle or lie flat.

"Place it like this," he instructed his daughter. "Then, with a flick of your wrist, open it like so."

Ashleigh gasped with delight as her father seemed to disappear. She clapped and dashed behind the metal plate. "I cannot see you from the front!" she cried. "What a wonderful trick!"

" 'Tis called an illusion, and is a secret for only our Gypsy family. Never share our tricks with anyone."

"No," Ashleigh replied as her eyes narrowed. "It is only for us. I will never betray our secrets."

"And never use them to harm another," he reminded her.

"Of course not." She laughed and skipped to the other side of the clearing. "Why would I?"

Chapter 2

A sound in the forest caught Romil's attention, and he looked toward his wife. Mary had paused and was also attempting to see through the trees.

"I hear riders," Mary said as Romil stepped beside her.

"They should be traveling on the main road," he replied as he, too, peered through the forest, trying to see from whence the riders came. As Gypsies, they were always vigilant, for many people distrusted their presence, and in this unfamiliar land they were even more cautious.

"We are far from the worn path," Romil assured her, but he drew his short sword as the hoofbeats drew closer.

"They are coming toward us," Mary warned as she stood behind her husband. "What purpose would cause them to ride so far from the road? Do they travel in secrecy? Do you think they know of our presence?"

"Most likely they are other wary travelers like us," Romil replied. He cast a look over his shoulder and saw his daughter playing with the disappearing plate. Already she had figured out how to move the hinges so that she seemed to disappear before his very eyes.

The sound of the horses grew louder, and Mary and Romil looked nervously at each other. The horses were traveling too rapidly for simple travelers. Mary quickly removed her favorite locket and wedged it between two of the wagon's floorboards in case the approaching riders were bandits set on stealing their valuables. The other items in the wagon had little worth, so she hoped the men would leave them be. She looked behind her and smiled nervously as Ashleigh slipped behind the plate.

"Stay there," Mary cautioned. "Do not come out."

Ashleigh peeked over the top and frowned. "But—"

"Do as your mother says," Romil commanded, and Ashleigh huddled back down with a sigh of frustration. Her parents were always acting overly wary, forever protecting her from strangers as if something terrible would happen if their watchfulness waned. Someday soon she would have to tell them that she was nearly grown and their protection was no longer necessary. She already knew enough magic to tantalize a crowd and earn her own coin, and she had received three offers of marriage from young men within their camp. She could ride as well as anyone, and was skilled at obscuring their tracks whenever they needed to hide from the authorities. She even knew how to gather edible plants and prepare them in appetizing dishes.

Suddenly six horses thundered out of the trees and galloped into the clearing where Mary and Romil were standing. The leader raised his hand and yanked his steed to a halt as the other riders instantly followed suit. Three of them wore chain mail under tunics emblazoned with a red and silver insignia, and their weapons were shiny, their horses well kept. The other three were dressed plainly and carried no weapons, yet their faces bore bruises, as if they had recently come from battle.

Mary shivered and pressed close against her husband. " 'Tis the insignia of the king's first cousin," she whispered. "My mother made me memorize all the symbols so I would know how to address the nobles."

"Will he know your face?" Romil whispered back.

"I don't think so . . . He barely noticed my mother, and I doubt any of his men would remember me."

The leader, a massive man bulging with muscle, leaped down from his mount and advanced upon them with his sword at the ready.

"Why do you go here?" he demanded, his voice thick with angry suspicion.

"We are only Gypsies passing through," Romil answered. "People of the land, like some of you," he added, waving to encompass the other men's utilitarian clothing and lack of adornment. "We certainly meant no trespass. By what name shall I call you, great warrior?"

"I am Douglas of Tiernay, nephew to the laird of this surrounding land, and not a man who is easily duped. You say you are a Gypsy, and I know that Gypsies are always up to no good."

"Oh, noble sir, we are truly innocent. We are traveling to the far side of the mountain on our way to Dunkeld and have no intention of disturbing you or your people."

"The other side of the mountain?" the leader asked, his voice rising. "Why? What business do you have near the castle?"

Romil looked at Mary, who gazed back at him with concern. Given her mother's highborn status and connection to ancient royalty, she dared not tell the full truth. Alliances were complicated in this land, and ever shifting. Whatever she said might make their situation worse. "We are traveling to visit an ailing relative," she replied. "We will move on if our presence displeases you."

"You speak our tongue with a natural brogue," the man snarled. "I think you are a local wench. Your hair . . . your skin . . . you are no Gypsy. You must be a spy." He drew his sword and pointed it at the pair. "What do you know? Who sent you to glean secrets from the village?"

Romil stepped back and pushed his wife behind him after assuring himself that Ashleigh was still hidden behind the mirror. "We are not spies, for we are only simple people. We know nothing of secrets."

"Then tell me the name of the relative you seek."

Mary averted her gaze as Romil tried to think quickly, but his pause was taken as proof of his guilt, and Douglas's eyes narrowed with distrust.

Another armored man swung down and assessed the pair. "Do not try to fool us," he warned. "We have already reminded the villagers of their rightful allegiances with a small example of what will befall them should they not follow the laird's commands. Although this mountainside town does not lie within the shadow of the castle walls, its people are beholden to Laird Geoffrey of Tiernay. He placed this village here to enrich his coffers. Perhaps through you we will demonstrate the seriousness of his demands."

One of the simply dressed peasants tried to intervene. "They be strangers to this land, not part of our local disputes. We already understand and have pledged our word as well as our hands to Laird Geoffrey. Let them travel through to visit their ailing relative and none will be the poorer."

The leader glanced at the man. "Are you willing to break your promise of allegiance so soon, Branan McFadden? Are you shielding a spy, or perhaps assisting in their journey?"

The man shook his head and dropped his gaze. "No, milord. I apologize. I just thought . . ." His voice trailed off as Douglas's angry gaze bored into him. "I am loyal to my laird," he said fearfully. "I shouldna have spoken so rashly."

Douglas of Tiernay stepped forward and yanked the man off his horse. "Prove your devotion. Kill them." He turned toward Romil and Mary as an evil smile spread across his face.

Mary gasped and looked at her husband in horror while the two other peasants blanched.

Ashleigh . . . Mary mouthed.

"Stay where you are!" Romil shouted, hoping his daughter would know the words were meant for her.

The mirror wavered, and Romil took a quick step toward the men to distract them from where Ashleigh was hidden. "We mean you no harm," he pleaded. "We will move on immediately and leave your forest untouched. We know nothing. We saw nothing. We know naught about your secrets, but wish only to visit my wife's mother."

A third armed man swung one leg over his horse's neck and grinned lecherously at Mary. "You will not leave untouched. In fact, unless you tell us who it is you claim to be visiting, I think we will have to teach you a *special* lesson."

Romil's hand clenched and he raised his sword. "Leave my woman alone," he warned.

"Or what?" The man laughed as he pulled his broadsword free and hefted it in his hand. "You will attack me with the piddling piece of steel you call a sword?" He jumped off his horse and landed on two feet, then joined the other men already facing Romil. "Hand the wench over and perhaps we will let you go after we have had our fill of her charms."

"Mercy," Mary whispered to her husband. "Why are they doing this? They are my countrymen. Perhaps I should tell them . . ."

"Men are men, no matter what land they call home," Romil growled. "This has nothing to do with your mother, and naught will halt them now." He edged back, then pushed Mary toward the trees. "Do as I say," he murmured; then he shoved Mary's back and shouted, "Run, Mary! Run!" He lunged forward and brandished his sword in front of the leader's face, then ducked as the man roared in anger and swung his massive weapon at Romil's head.

Mary stumbled, then took three running leaps toward the forest before the second man jumped forward and tackled her legs, flinging her to the ground. Mary crashed to the earth, her temple grazing a stone half-hidden in the grass. Stunned, she stared across the field and beheld her daughter, eyes wide in terror, huddled behind the disappearing plate.

Ashleigh started to rise. "Mother?"

"Stay," Mary whispered. "No matter what, stay hidden."

Not hearing Ashleigh's soft voice, the man yanked on Mary's ankles and dragged her back to the center of the field, where Romil was desperately defending himself against Douglas and his man while the peasants cowered from the melee. Romil fell to his knees, then struggled to stand while the men attacking him laughed and jeered at his efforts. "Do you have any idea who we are?" one said. "You are no match for seasoned warriors. Give up and cry mercy!"

Douglas chuckled and flicked his wrist, easily disarming Romil. He wiped the back of his hand across his nose, then reached for Mary's hair and pulled her upright. "You would give up your life for this?" he said as he shook her body at Romil, then tossed her toward one of his companions. "You fool! No woman is worth your life!" He turned and grasped the bodice of her dress, then ripped it down to the waist.

"*She* is," Romil growled. "Ever since the moment I laid eyes upon her gentle face." He lunged forward, his hands raised toward the man's throat, but the other warrior swung his sword and smashed Romil's knee, nearly severing it from his body. Romil toppled to one side, howling in rage and fury. "Mary!" he shouted. "God forgive me for failing to protect you! I am no warrior, merely a man of tricks and illusion! I should never have—"

"Romil!" Mary cried as the man holding her flung her to the ground, flipped her skirts up and tore her underlinens. "Say no more. I love you for who you are."

The soldier slapped Mary's face. "With a face and body like yours, you could have wed a real man like me."

Mary yanked her head away from his and spit in his face. "He is a man worth tenfold more than you."

"Mary," Romil whispered to his wife as he stared into her beautiful eyes, tears filling his own. Douglas stood over Romil's crippled form as he tried to crawl toward his beloved. Out of the corner of his eye Romil saw the man raise his sword once more.

"No regrets," Mary answered softly as Douglas plunged his sword into her husband's back and impaled him to the ground. She flinched at the sound of steel scraping bone and tears poured from her eyes as she saw death wash over Romil's face. Her love . . . the man she had fled across the country to be with, leaving behind all riches and connections just so she could sleep in his embrace. They had had seventeen wonderful years together . . . years of love and devotion that had enriched her heart and made her whole.

She went limp as the man above her yanked her legs apart, mounted her and thrust inside her. Even if she had known that it would end like this, she would not have changed anything. She looked up at the blue sky and saw a fluffy white cloud that was shaped like wings. *Please,* she prayed to the heavens. *Do as you will with me, but take care of my child.*

Endless pain followed. Over and over again the three men used her. She heard them call one another by name . . . Douglas . . . Tory . . . Curtis. At first she struggled, but when the men beat her she stopped resisting and only repeated her silent prayers that they would not find Ashleigh. God help her, she wanted to die, but she couldn't abandon her daughter. No matter how much it hurt, she had to make sure Ashleigh remained safe. Her head lolled back and she stared toward where Ashleigh was hidden. There was no sign of her. Like her father, she had already perfected the illusion. Ashleigh had disappeared.

The men continued for hours, not caring that the woman's mind had already separated from her soul. Limp and unresisting, Mary suffered their humiliation, no longer aware of their brutal attack. The three soldiers forced the peasant who had spoken in the Gypsy's defense to partake in their game, threatening him with a knife to his neck if he did not do as they said. Then, once it was over, they laughed and slapped the man on the back, telling him that his wife was safe from similar sport as long as he continued to cooperate so well.

Branan buried his head in his hands. "How could I do such a thing?" he whispered. "How will I ever erase my sin?"

Douglas laughed. "Do not let such scruples weaken you, peasant. Might will always prevail." He waved toward the two bodies lying in the clearing. "This could happen to anyone . . ." He paused and leaned close to the peasant. "Don't forget. It could have been your own wife—Eva is her name, is it not? Let this be a reminder should anyone in the village disappoint or betray Laird Geoffrey of Tiernay."

Branan shuddered.

Douglas stood up and tied his breeches, then faced the others. "I think I've made myself clear. Your village needs our benevolence, does it not?"

The men nodded.

"You should thank the laird for his willingness to offer it to you. Located so far from our castle, your village is without protection. Think of what could happen to your families if my laird is not assured of your allegiance. All will prey upon your wives and daughters, your homes and fields, and you will have no defense against them. Do you understand?"

"Aye," one replied

"Aye, milord," said another. "We be returnin' to the village so we can explain t' situation to the elders. They will spread the word amongst t' others."

Douglas mounted, then urged his horse forward until its hooves stood next to Mary's head. With an abrupt kick of his spur, he yanked on his horse's reins and forced the creature to rear high. The horse neighed and twisted his head in anger, then landed on the ground with a sickening crunch, its hooves crushing Mary's skull.

The leader backed his horse away and looked down at the dead couple. "Yes," he agreed pleasantly. "Go back to the village. I trust I will not have to visit again to ensure your obedience. These are strangers, but it could have been you . . ."

Two of the villagers nodded, their eyes haunted with fear, while Branan wrapped his arms around his waist and huddled in the dirt.

With a quick motion of Douglas's hand, he, Tory and Curtis rode out of the meadow. Silence descended in their wake.

"Branan," one of the peasants said hesitantly.

"Go," Branan answered. "I canna return home . . . I canna see my wife after what I've done." He leaned forward and vomited.

"You had no choice," his friend consoled. "If you had not done wha' they demanded, they would 'ave killed you, or worse, hurt yur own wife." He looked over his shoulder to where the soldiers had pulled up and were staring back at them, impatient for the others to join them.

Branan shook his head as he flung his knife aside and clasped his head with his hands. "How will I ever face her?" he cried. "How will Eva ever forgive me?"

Douglas yanked on his horse's reins and made the beast rear once again. "Leave Branan behind," he called out from the tree line. "Today he cries like a woman, but tomorrow he will be a man. He will remember the feel of an unwilling woman beneath him and will crave the sensation." Douglas smiled, although his eyes remained cold. "Your Eva will seem dull and lifeless in comparison."

When Branan heaved again, Douglas turned away

in disgust. "Peasants," he grumbled. "Weak and sorrowful excuses for men. Come," he called to the two others as he pulled his sword free once more. "Let him walk home. Or need there be more lessons today?"

With one last pitying look at Branan, the others mounted their horses and turned them away from their friend, following Douglas and his henchmen back toward the village.

Chapter 3

Behind the disappearing plate, Ashleigh huddled in terror. She had heard everything, but seen little. All she knew was that her father had been badly hurt and her mother had been raped.

Ashleigh's head swam, and denial rushed through her thoughts. It hadn't really happened . . . her parents were unharmed. It was all a trick her father had conjured up in order to frighten her into obedience.

She blinked as a flash of light glanced off a bit of metal lying in the grass. The man had flung his knife aside and it had come to rest in front of her. She stared at the small blade, her mind oddly blank. The world seemed to be spinning around her . . . spinning around the sharp blade as if it were the focus of fire, water, wind and earth . . . all twirling around that small piece of pointed metal.

Around the knife. Cast in front of her by fickle fate.

She could still hear her mother's cries . . . her father's desperate pleas..

It wasn't real. Nothing seemed real.

She picked up the blade and rose slowly to her feet. Her heart thundered and she could not think clearly. As if in a trance, she stepped out from behind the plate and walked up to the huddled man. His back was toward her, and he seemed unaware of her presence.

Ashleigh glanced at the blade again. Although roughly hewn, it was wickedly sharp. She vaguely heard a raven caw from high above her, and she looked up as a black shadow crossed the sun. Dark and beautiful . . . wings spread like a paired quiver of black-tipped arrows. The shadow swooped over the man, and Ashleigh felt the whisper of death brush her cheek.

Whose soul was the raven seeking?

Ashleigh looked at the man kneeling before her. He had hurt her mother. He had used her mother's body, been a part of the horror that had resulted in her mother's death.

Ashleigh raised the blade. The man should die.

Suddenly he looked up, twisting to see behind him. His eyes widened as he saw a woman. The sun's rays formed a halo around her black curls, and her face was cloaked in darkness. Sunlight glinted off an object in her hand.

"Take me," he whispered. "Take me quickly, vengeful angel, for I have sinned and cannot live with the suffering in my heart."

Her eyes blank, her mind still reeling in shock, Ashleigh plunged the blade into the man's chest and watched with a strange detachment as he groaned in agony and crumpled to the ground.

For two days she crouched behind the plate.

After the man's blood had soaked the ground, Ashleigh had returned to her hiding place. Occasionally she looked out at the three dead people. Mother . . . Father . . . peasant. Her senses were overloaded. The agony of her parents' deaths reverberated within her—the sounds, the smells, the sights. Her mother's eyes, glazed with pain. Her father's leg, nearly severed at the knee. The sound of her mother's skull cracking. The feel of the blade in her hand. The smell of blood . . . and then the smell of death. By the next day her muscles had ceased cramping. Her tears had long since dried. Pangs of hunger and thirst did not plague her. Even the natural urges had faded away, leaving her numb to all feeling.

No remorse for murdering a man. No grief for the loss of her parents. Not even the simplest understanding of those events.

Times of laughter faded from her memory; only horror filled her thoughts.

After the first two days she faced the realization that she was still alive. She could hear her own heart thudding and smell the stench of her own urine. When had she urinated?

She shivered in self-disgust. She should not be thinking of cleanliness and base needs—not when her parents were lying unavenged in an open meadow. She should not think of anything but punishing those who were responsible. It was the way of the Gypsies, and her father's people had survived for centuries because everyone knew that a Gypsy always avenged a wrong against one of her own. They had only themselves, and therefore they acted with single-minded focus to exact revenge and ensure justice whenever a Gypsy was involved. It was the way of her people, and she was bound by duty to fulfill her role.

Yet she couldn't. She didn't want to think of anything.

Birds circled down from the sky and began plucking at her parents' flesh. Franco and Francis grazed in the meadow, occasionally nickering at her, but she couldn't bear to touch them. Not now . . . not when they reminded her of her parents.

Another day passed, and Ashleigh's body began to war with her mind, forcing her by necessity to begin the simple acts of living again. She washed in the stream and drank from its refreshing depths. She picked a few berries, ate one, then dropped the others to the ground, leaving them forgotten. When a short summer rain drenched the meadow, she slipped under the sheltering branches of a tree and watched until the sun peeked out again.

Along the streambank she found wild carrots, which she dug up, washed and ate. A fish swam by, and she thought about catching it, but then it was gone and she closed her eyes and cried. She flung the carrot greens aside, wishing she were in the heavens with her parents, wanting desperately to escape the agony of life. But her body refused to die.

Her muscles ached, and the stench of the rotting bodies permeated the glade. Soon roving foxes and assorted vermin began tearing at the carcasses, and she could no longer deny that her beloved parents were dead. Grief surged through her as she watched the forest creatures. Then, finally, came anger.

Waves and waves of intense, all-consuming anger.

"No!" she screamed. "No! You can't die!" Her voice echoed around her, magnifying her pain. *No . . . No*, echoed across the meadow, a furious and helpless wail.

"What am I supposed to do?" she cried. When one of the foxes paused and looked at her, she got up on her weakened legs and stumbled across the meadow, waving her arms and shouting, "Go away! Leave us alone!"

Then denial returned. Time and again she thought

that it was all an act and her father would stand up and announce that his death had been a marvelous magic trick. If she stared at him long enough, she could convince herself that her father's chest was moving up and down, as if he were simply sleeping.

But he never got up, and no breath escaped his gaping mouth.

Once, the raven flew down and landed on her mother's face, then twisted his head to stare at Ashleigh, his gaze questioning.

Grief flooded her heart, and she collapsed on the ground and wept again, her shoulders heaving with heart-wrenching sorrow. "What do you want?" she screamed. "Will you take me, too? Are you death's herald?"

The raven merely cocked his head.

"Go away!" she screamed again, and the raven rose into the air. But then he came back, still looking at her with a strange intelligence that pierced Ashleigh's grief and made the agony of her loneliness all the more acute. Again and again, Ashleigh would chase the bird away, but he always returned as if he were intent on completing some mysterious mission.

A large black raven. Black like death. Black like her mother's hair. Like her own hair.

Ashleigh watched the raven with narrowed eyes. Anger replaced grief once more, and she hefted a stone in her right hand. How could this have happened to her family? What evil spirit had infused the men on horseback, to make them torture and kill her beautiful parents? She raised the rock and sent it whistling through the air, striking the hapless bird.

It fluttered, unable to rise, then squawked and screeched as it flip-flopped in the grass.

Shame filled Ashleigh, and she knelt next to the

raven, crooning softly, hoping he would not die. He had been her only companion these past days, and she did not want him to leave her. She needed a friend, even if it was just a bird.

She heard voices. Voices coming through the trees.

The raven struggled upright, his beady eyes already forgiving her with an understanding that seemed to come from deep within his soul.

Fear and loneliness rippled through Ashleigh as she swept up the raven and placed him in the crook of a tree, then spun around and crouched in the bushes. The voices frightened her. She wanted comfort, yet she trusted no one. What if these people were the same men coming back? What if they intended to hurt her just as the men had harmed her parents?

"It were o'er that way," a man said. "Beside the low meadow."

"Hmm," the man's companion replied, his voice deep and familiar.

"Branan McFadden never came home. He might still be there."

"Aye," the companion murmured. "He be afeared to go home ta Eva. If'n she ever found out . . ."

"The elder told us ne'er to talk about it," the first man reminded the other. "As long as we do as he says, our village will be safe."

The first man grunted in agreement. "Nothin' will come out of me lips."

Two men emerged from the trees and entered the clearing, unaware of Ashleigh hidden behind the greenery. Her overwhelming emotions began to coalesce, and her heart hardened with hatred. These were the men who had watched her mother's rape. These were the men who had done nothing to save her father.

As the two approached, one gasped and fell to his knees in front of his dead friend. "He must have killed himself," he moaned. "Auch, Branan . . ." The stench from the decomposing bodies made him gag and he placed his hand over his nose. "We wouldn'ta told anyone."

"Mayhap God struck him down," the other man argued, his voice shaky as he looked up at the black raven that stared down at them from the tree. "Branan helped rape that woman." He crossed himself and backed away. "I want t' go. I don't want t' be near the dead . . ."

"He had no choice. You said that yurself when we told the elder." The man rose and stared sorrowfully at Branan's body.

Across the meadow Ashleigh felt her anger grow and red spots speckled her vision. She hated them! They were the cause of her misery, and they must suffer just as she was suffering. They had had a choice. They could have stopped the torture. They could have refused to follow the leader. Their compassion was only for their dead comrade. Her heart thundered with all-consuming rage. She wanted to kill them . . . murder them just as they had murdered her loved ones.

It did not matter who had struck the final blow. All were responsible. All should pay.

A flash of the peasant's face just as she had plunged the knife into his body raced across her mind. He had almost looked relieved.

Ashleigh's breathing increased, and she clutched the knife tightly. She would not kill these men so quickly. She would make them endure days of horror before she released them from this world.

"What will we be doing with Branan's body?"

"We canna bury it in sacred ground if he killed hisself. We'll have ta' burn it w' the others."

The peasant nodded. "What about Eva?"

"Don't tell her anythin'."

"Aye. That'll be best."

One man climbed into the wagon and began rummaging through the belongings, tossing various items out onto the ground, including small gourds and bags of unfamiliar powders. "Lot of things here that have no use," he mumbled. "Odd people, those Gypsies. Wonder what they used this for?" He held up a spoon with a hole in the center. "Here are a few pots and pans that have seen better days . . ." He tossed them aside as well, then placed some kindling inside the wagon. "Help me w' the bodies. Douglas said ta ensure that no evidence remains."

After they dragged all three bodies into the wagon, one of the men struck a flint and set the kindling afire.

The other man spied two gray horses grazing at the far end of the meadow and went to collect them. As he led them back to the clearing, he patted their necks. "Don't want to kill the beasts," he said. "I don't be thinking the soldiers would notice if we kept them. 'Twould be a shame to waste such fine horseflesh."

The other man jumped out of the back of the wagon. He sent several more sparks flying onto the wagon's bench and watched the wood smolder. "Aye, you have the right of it. Keep the horses."

The wagon caught fire, and flames began licking the sides. They watched it for several minutes, taking care to pull brush away from the flames so that the forest would not ignite. Then, with a nod at each other, the men led the horses out of the clearing and headed back the way they had come.

Ashleigh rose and glared after them. "You will be punished," she vowed. "You will die. All of you will die. Nothing and no one will interfere. May God help and serve me, for I will have my rightful vengeance."

Then, as she watched flames engulf the wagon containing her parents' bodies and the remnants of her formerly happy life, she began plotting her revenge.

Chapter 4

Three days later, cold, tired and hungry, Ashleigh stared blankly at the sky, loneliness and despair filling her soul. So many losses . . . so much pain. She wrapped her arms around her waist and rocked herself, wishing they were her mother's arms.

She had already begun her revenge. Using the skills her father had taught her, she had played tricks upon the villagers and cast them into chaos, yet her heart still felt empty. Would her misdeeds make any difference? Would frightening the villagers bring her solace or return her parents?

Despite trying to stem them, tears once again flooded down her face. Looking into the stream, she saw her black eyes reflecting back at her like windows into her stormy inner tumult. Every day she alternated between overwhelming sorrow and all-encompassing rage. Dashing the tears from her cheeks, she clenched her fists. "No!" she screamed as she grabbed handfuls of damp grass and earth and flung them at the trees where the raven watched her.

His wing had only been bruised and he could already fly again, but he did not fly away. Instead the creature remained nearby, his intelligent eyes peering at her with a strange fascination that made Ashleigh's stomach tremble. It was as if he knew something about her that she did not, and he made her uneasy. Yet he had become the one constant in a life that suddenly made no sense.

Screaming at him as if he could understand her, she raked her fingers through her hair, ripping out strands and grinding them into the mud. "I do not deserve to be alive! I do not deserve to have a full belly!" she shouted. "Not when my parents lie burned and rotting in the forest, scavenged by beasts and eaten by beetles."

Using her toe she drew an ancient Gypsy symbol for death in the dirt. "I will not leave this mountain, until my vengance is complete. I will kill the peasants who watched my mother's torture, and then I will murder the soldiers who killed my father." Her breathing increased, and she felt her throat constrict. "Not just them," she hissed. "I will kill more. I will kill the entire village and all the inhabitants of the soldier's castle. I will kill them all!" She rose and walked over to the stream. "I know how to poison their water. I can contaminate all the wells and send everyone to their graves. Every last soul . . ." But her voice trailed off, and misery brought her back down to her knees.

As her shoulders wilted, her rage died. Thoughts wavered, and her mind could not discern real from imagined. She felt anger, yet she could not seem to focus her thoughts. She heard her mother's voice, but her mother was no longer on this earth. She wanted her parents, yet she could not recall their faces. How could she forget, or was it a trick of her mind that had temporarily erased them from her memories?

She huddled in place, miserable and afraid.

Her gaze paused on a moderately sized plant growing along the streambed. Its smooth green stem was spotted with red dots like droplets of blood. Fine, lacy leaves shielded clusters of small white blossoms.

Hemlock.

As if in a daze, Ashleigh strode through the water and plucked the plant from the earth, then crushed a leaf and smelled its rank odor. All she had to do was drop it into a well and wait while all the inhabitants drank from the killing depths. And what about herself? Should she drink from the tainted water as well?

She pressed a hand to her lips, wishing her father were there to scold her for her evil thoughts. The need for vengeance waged a battle in her soul. Her parents had taught her to love and respect all the creatures of this earth, but how could she forgive this mortal deed? She hated everyone . . . hate permeated her soul with such force that the blood running through her veins felt like thick sludge. If her father were here, he could wash away her hurtful thoughts and hold and protect her. Without him . . . without anyone, why should she continue?

The raven swooped down from the tree and landed on her shoulder. His talons gripped her firmly but without puncturing her skin, and Ashleigh turned her head to stare into his face. Black eyes . . . pointed black beak . . . he was both beautiful and frightening.

He leaned forward and plucked one leaf from her plant and held it in his beak.

"Drop that," Ashleigh commanded weakly as she reached for the poisonous sprig, but the raven twisted his neck and dodged her hands, then hopped down to the ground.

"You stupid beast!" Ashleigh shouted as she clutched the rest of the plant in her hand. She splashed after him until she reached the far edge of the streambed, whereupon the bird flew up into a tree and perched on a high branch.

Ashleigh sank down, then lowered her head into the water with her cheek pressed against the smooth stones lining the bank. As she closed her eyes, water swirled around her, drenching her hair and stroking her throat, allowing only her face to remain dry. "Will you now abandon me as well, black raven? Leave me as everyone else has?" she whispered.

She held on tightly to the rest of the hemlock. Every part of it was deadly . . . the root, the leaves, and the tiny blossoms. Three or four plants dropped into the well would be enough to ruin the water, but images of young children running up to dip their ladles into a poisonous brew made her ill, and she suddenly heaved, then vomited into the flowing stream. Other birds . . . little rabbits. Mothers and fathers. All would drink from the tainted water.

She could not do it. She could not be responsible for so many deaths. Despite the overwhelming despair that left her entire being rigid and cold, she could do nothing. She had murdered once—killed the man named Branan—and guilt simmered within her soul. Helpless and weak, she huddled in the stream and pressed the poisonous plant to her face, trying to dredge up the courage to chew it. She fingered the root and crushed it against her breasts, wishing it could replace her broken heart.

She plucked a blossom and tucked it behind her ear, but as the frigid water swirled around her, her shivering hands could not secure the sprig, and the white petals fell like shimmering rain. The tips of her fingers were tinged blue and her teeth chattered uncontrollably, yet she had no desire to climb out of the stream.

As her muscles grew weaker, she slid deeper into the current until half her body was immersed in nature's flow, her hair trailing through the water. With her free hand she clutched a rock to keep from sliding completely into the water.

Help me, she cried silently not knowing to whom she prayed. *I'm sorry. I have done wrong. I have no courage to continue living. I am nothing . . . I am lonely and scared, and I don't know what to do. All I know is that I need someone . . . to tell me that all will be well again one day.*

Gradually her shivering slowed and a warm lassitude began to fill her. Why fight anymore? Why harbor anger and resentment? Why long for something that would never be? It was so much easier to let Mother Earth engulf her within her watery embrace. Maybe there . . . beyond all this . . . she would no longer feel alone.

Her eyelids flickered open briefly, then closed, and water swirled higher up her neck. She wanted to sleep. The water was no longer cold. It felt soothing.

Her hand on the rock opened slowly, and the other holding the hemlock relaxed. As the current caught the sprig and sent it swirling downstream, the current tugged at her body, moving it inch by inch into deeper water.

Mangan pulled his horse to a stop and let it drink from a stream as he gazed at the mountain ahead. It was not a tall mountain, not like the massive peaks he had seen in France two years ago when he had fought for the king. This mountain sloped gently uphill and was embraced by a ribbon of road that circled its base and was eventually lost to view as it swept around the far side. Along the road were several clearings, some containing cottages and gardens and others holding herds of sheep. Halfway around the mountain was a small village, complete with a church and a windmill.

It appeared to be one of the outlying villages that some lairds were establishing to realize more profit. Although they were not located in close proximity to the castle, like most villages, they were designed to be self-sufficient and often had their own churches, priests and governing clerics or group of elders.

Mangan smiled. The village was exactly as the old man had described, and it might signify the end to his quest. If he found the relic here, he could return to the monastery and take his final vows.

The year he'd spent at the monastery had been a time of deep healing and even deeper reflection, and this year had been a journey toward tranquillity. Brother Bartholomew had understood what Mangan had not . . . that he needed more time to find serenity. He now understood that his communion with God was incomplete, and that his faith required him to continue his quest before presenting himself to his maker and the monks of St. Ignacio.

Mangan sighed. He did not know if he would ever find the lost blanket. So many times he had believed that he was only one step away, yet always he had been disappointed.

Still, his failure had shown him the path toward salvation. Wandering the countryside had finally brought him some measure of peace. His meditations helped him to understand himself. Although he still carried his sword, he wanted to celebrate life, not bring death.

Perhaps, in time, he would also absolve his guilt.

For now he was content to wear the robes of a novice. Instead of a life of cloistered celibacy, he remained searching . . . searching for a well of strength from which to draw . . . searching for answers to questions he himself did not understand.

For nearly a year Mangan had traveled with only his stallion, Sir Scott, for companionship. Guided by his faith and always seeking knowledge, he had done as the abbot had asked, locating clues to the whereabouts of the holy blanket. A fortnight ago an old man had told Mangan about a church on a mountain in the deep interior of Scotland whose presiding priest had collected numerous relics for his small perish. The old man said that the sanctuary appeared to contain riches more appropriate for a laird's church or a monastery than a small chapel. Mangan wanted to determine how such a small church could obtain so many relics, and whether any of them could have been stolen.

Mangan glanced up at the blue sky with its soft white clouds. He was getting tired. His quest had been long and his heart was sad. He needed answers, for he feared that the longer his soul remained empty, the harder it would be to find eternal peace.

Sir Scott suddenly lifted his head and snorted at a trail of white blossoms that drifted down the stream near where he was drinking. Mangan frowned, recognizing the deadly hemlock plant. He yanked on the horse's reins and backed him away from the water, then leaped to the ground to peer upstream.

A woman's body lay half submerged, caught in an eddy formed by a pair of branches. Perched beside her was a black raven.

Caw! Caw!

The bird's cry echoed through the forest, galvanizing Mangan into action. He plunged into the stream. Something profound rippled through him . . . a surging need to save this single soul after having killed so many others. She was not just one person; she symbolized everyone. Every agonizing death . . . every blood-curdling scream or gurgling last breath was abruptly fused into one, and Mangan's soul split open. Pain, rage, guilt . . . even the remnants of forgotten love . . . burst through his body.

He had to save her. His own life—his broken heart and his yearning soul—demanded it.

"No!" he bellowed as he reached the woman and yanked her from the frigid water, then dragged her to the bank and up onto dry land. "You will not take this one! She will be mine! Mine to save, mine to hold!"

He flipped the woman onto her stomach and pounded her back. Water gushed out of her mouth, but her body remained limp and unresponsive.

"No!" he cried again, his anguish compounded. Her one, motionless body was more horrible than a field of bloody corpses. Turning her onto her back, he bent to breathe life aganist her blue lips.

Still, she did not wake.

He pounded her chest frantically, wanting to awaken the heart that beat beneath her ribs. He needed to feel the thrust of her blood pulsing in her wrist and see the rise of her chest as her lungs expanded.

He breathed into her mouth once again . . . kissing her more intimately than the deepest, sensual meeting of lips. "Breathe," he pleaded, pressing his ear to her chest. "Beat. I will give my life for yours. Please . . . please, my angel."

One thud. Then a gasp, and she suddenly arched up and coughed.

Tears fell from his eyes as he turned her over once again and held her as she vomited more water, then struggled to draw her next breath.

"Help," she whimpered as she clung to his knee.

He leaned close and drew the hair back from her face, laughing and crying as the blue tinge of her lips faded and pink flooded back into her cheeks.

She shivered uncontrollably, unable to say more, yet she looked at him with endless desperation, making his own heart ache. Her fingers touched his eyes, caressing the tears that flowed down his cheeks. She tried to shake her head, but he pulled her close, cradling her face in the crook of his neck. "Don't talk," he whispered. "Just breathe. Live."

She wrapped her arms around him, her body so cold it burned, yet his flesh was warm and dry, and that warmth seeped into her. Her shivers wouldn't stop, and her teeth chattered, but still she clung to him. To this stranger.

You came for me.

Aye. I will never leave. You are not alone. You will never be alone.

Her shivers began to slow, and she lifted her head to stare into his eyes.

He stroked her face and kissed the tip of her nose. "Who are you?" he whispered. "What is your name?"

"I am called Ashleigh," she answered, her voice soft and thready. "Why did you save me?"

He brushed a wet tendril from her face. "Because you are a precious angel and God placed me in your path."

Ashleigh stared at him curiously, her gaze flicking

over his face. "But that would mean He placed *me* in *your* path as well," she whispered.

"Indeed," Mangan replied, then pulled her body close and leaned his head against hers.

Mangan drifted in and out of sleep, his hand resting against the woman's back. She had stopped shivering and had curled against him, wicking his warmth, yet replacing it with a sensation that was immeasurably precious. For once he had saved someone. His bloodied hands had brought forth life, not death. Without knowing it she was his salvation, and he gave her his heart, freely and completely.

Darkness had fallen, and stars twinkled in the night sky. The half moon cast a soft glow across the glen, its cool light complementing the dancing orange flames of their fire. A sense of peace soothed Mangan. He smiled, relishing the softness of his angel's skin, and the weight of her in his lap.

He took a deep breath and leaned back against a tree, letting his body relax. Finally, after years of restless nights, Mangan fell into a deep and dreamless sleep.

Chapter 5

The sound of a woman weeping woke Mangan the next morning.

He frowned and rose to his feet. "Miss?" he called, looking for her. "Ashleigh?" She no longer lay next to him, and he felt her absence keenly. "Do you need assistance?"

Ashleigh froze at the clearing's edge, terrified that the man had come from the village. She had woken to find herself wrapped in his embrace and had slid out from under his arm and crawled into the bushes. She had gathered her things and was about to sneak away when his voice startled her.

Biting her lip to hold in her tears, she pulled her disappearing plate off her back, where she had devised an ingenious way of strapping it in place, and wrapped it around herself, making herself invisible. Then she waited, hoping the stranger would go away.

"Miss? Have no fear. I am a holy man. Is something wrong? Can I help you?"

"Stay where you are," Ashleigh commanded, her voice strained. "Are you from the village?"

"No. I am a traveler. I . . . I am the one who pulled you from the stream."

She nibbled a fingernail, debating. He did not look like a villager. Peeking around her mirror, she could see that he was dressed in brown holy robes, belted by a plain hemp rope. His face, though, seemed far too handsome for that of a holy man. Too handsome and too young. "You . . . you might be one of their friends, dressed in some sort of disguise," she accused.

Mangan shook his head. "I can sense that pain fills your soul, but please do not direct it at me. I am a humble man on a religious quest. My only friends are my horse and my cross." The bushes shook, and then she seemed to magically appear before his eyes. He blinked several times in disbelief and rubbed his eyes. He must be more tired than he thought if he was seeing a woman take form out of thin air.

He smiled toward where the figure still hovered in the dark. He spread his hands wide, his palms up. "I am traveling on a mission for God. Why are you out here in the woods all alone, crying? What has caused you such misery that you were driven to taste the bitter bite of hemlock?"

"I never meant to harm myself," Ashleigh lied, "and I am not crying." She continued angrily as she wiped her hand across her nose, "My father told me never to cry."

Mangan nodded, his eyes kind and compassionate. "I don't like to cry, either," he said. "But I do admit that I feel sad, for that is the first step toward relieving the pain. I feel anger and hurt. Sometimes my soul feels like it is overflowing with misery. Is that how you felt yesterday?"

"You don't know anything about misery," the woman answered bitterly. "You are a monk. What agony have you endured? Sore knees? A poor meal?"

Mangan had been a man of war, accepting death

and destruction as necessities of battle. He knew pain. But what could have made this young woman feel so helpless? What agony had sent her into death's embrace?

"Where is your home?" he asked her.

"Here," the woman replied. "I live on the mountain."

He pulled a piece of jerky out from a packet within his robes and tore it in half. On the mountain? What an odd choice of words. Most people would say "in the village," or "in a farmhouse," or "in a cottage at the top of the hill." "Are you hungry?" he asked her shadow.

There was a lengthy pause in which he heard the squawk of a bird and the chatter of a squirrel as well as the rustling of leaves overhead. Finally she answered.

"Yes."

"If I swear upon my Bible not to harm you, will you come out and share a meal with me?"

"Perhaps."

Mangan hid a grin and turned to rummage in his bags for some corn cakes as he listened to the young woman take a few hesitant steps into the clearing. When he turned back, he stared at her in shock.

No mortal being should be so beautiful. Last night he had hardly noticed her features. He had wanted only to chase away death's grip. But as he gazed upon her today, his heart thundered with new emotion. She was like a dark angel who had somehow lost her way. Her coal black hair fell down her back in rippling waves, framing her alabaster face with feathery curls. Her large, black-fringed eyes were deep and sensual, yet burning with an inner fire that made them shimmer with rich intensity. And her lips . . . red, moist and curved downward in the saddest of expressions.

Reddened tracks trailed down her cheeks where her tears had left streaks. So beautiful, yet so miserable.

He swallowed against the sudden dryness in his throat and handed her a corn cake.

A squawk from the high reaches of a tree startled him. "He is a very loud raven," Mangan stated.

"Yes. He won't leave me alone."

Mangan glanced at her, hearing an unspoken emotion in her voice. Was it fear? Loneliness? Grudging acceptance of the strange bird's unwelcome company?

A tear rolled down her face and she dashed it away. She stared at Mangan defensively, seeking to hide her vulnerability. "He doesn't bother me, at least not much. I've gotten used to him."

"Ravens are wild animals, rarely tamed by human hands, and they are quite intelligent. Don't refuse his friendship, for I have seen even stranger alliances. My mother has a small pack of wolves that listen to her sing. She cares for them deeply."

"Wolves? She must be an interesting person. You are lucky to have a family. I do not." Her voice cracked, and the sadness fled from her face, replaced by rising anger.

"I'm sorry to hear that," he said soothingly. "When did your family pass away?"

The young woman shook her head and lifted her hand toward the heavens. "If there were hope and justice in this world, they would still be alive." The raven flew up and began circling in the sky as if thrown there by the tip of her finger. "I'd rather not talk about it."

"Very well. You told me last night that your name is Ashleigh," he replied. "I am Mangan O'Bannon, a monk recently come from St. Ignacio Abbey."

She looked at him through her lashes, and her

cheeks flushed. He was so handsome with his dark hair and swarthy skin. His eyes were green, a light springtime green that looked striking against his tanned face. A lock of hair fell across one brow, giving his benevolent expression a hint of wildness that was at odds with his priestly robes. "Mangan," she said slowly. "You are truly a monk?"

"Yes."

"I . . ." She paused, and tears filled her eyes once again as she instinctively leaned closer to him. "My mother believed in God. She told me about men like you. She said you listen to and help those who are in need of solace. I . . . have done something . . . and I . . ."

Mangan's heart skipped a beat, and for a moment he felt paralyzed by her sad gaze. Her need seemed to filled the grove, and he had the same instant, insane desire to pledge himself to her that he had felt last night. He wanted to tell her that he would love and protect her, ensuring that no one would ever harm her. His hands twitched, and he had to clench his fists to hold them back from reaching out to touch her face and pull her into a loving embrace.

If he had wanted to hold her as a priest, he would have opened his arms to her. He would have offered her simple confession and anointed her head with oil. But a slumbering emotion stirred deep within his soul, and he knew he could not touch her. He had believed his year in the monastery had prepared him for the celibate life he was seeking. He had thought he was beyond such primitive urges. He could not let his base emotions supercede his faith and dedication. She might be beautiful, but wanting to touch such beauty was forbidden.

He had saved her, but he had no right to claim her.

She took a step closer, a plea in her gaze. "I am frightened and feel so helpless. If you are a man of God, then you can help me. Can you tell me if I am doing the right thing?"

He couldn't resist. She needed him, and he wanted to help her in any way he could. He opened his arms and gathered her close, feeling her shoulders shake as she sobbed against his chest. He could feel her cold flesh through her threadbare cloak as she pressed against him. Her gaunt body was so light and thin, it felt as if a strong breeze could knock her to the ground, yet underneath the fragility he sensed an admirable resilience.

"Shush . . ." he whispered. "Nothing could be that terrible." *Lord guide me,* he thought, for she was more temptation than he could resist.

She clung to him, her fingers fisted around his robes. "Please help me," she cried. "I don't know what to do or who to turn to."

"I'm right here," he answered as he pulled her tighter, trying to ignore the press of her breasts against his chest. "I will help you." She needed his comfort, not his passion.

She looked up with her fantastic black eyes, and he saw a hint of midnight blue at the centers, like the backlit depths of a dark sapphire. She touched his cheek, her fingers trembling. "Will you?"

His breath shortened and he became light-headed. She overwhelmed him . . . made him forget everything. He wanted to bury his hands in her hair and pull her lips closer . . . to kiss her tears away and tell her he would save her from the world.

She pulled slightly back, her gaze flickering over his face, and he gazed at her as ardor warmed his blood. Such wide, dark eyes. They reminded him of a lost fawn's. Her chest rose and fell with quick breaths as she held his gaze, and her heart thudded so strongly he could feel it.

Something shifted inside her, as if for the first time in weeks Ashleigh felt hope. She saw love and conviction in his gaze and felt the power of his strength through his robes. He was the answer to her prayers.

"I will," he promised, heat rushing through his body.

"Mangan," she repeated, so softly he had to strain to hear. Her hands trailed down from his cheek to his broad shoulders, and she looked at him in wonderment. "How is such a strong man also a monk? I thought men of the cloth were scholars. Are you not a warrior?"

Her words hit him in the gut, and he abruptly pushed her away. He could not react this way to a child in need. It was wrong. "I was once a warrior, but now I am a novice monk," he said firmly, more to himself than to her. "I seek to bring a criminal to justice and demand he pay for his crime against God by returning the object he stole back to its rightful owner."

A bell rang in the distance, its insistent clamor carrying across the mountainside.

Ashleigh frowned, anxiety suddenly tightening her face. She stared at the sheathed sword tied to his stallion's saddle and looked at him with rising concern. "What kind of criminal do you pursue? Only one thief, or are there others?" she asked, doubt beginning to hold sway. Perhaps he was not here to help her, but rather to capture her. Perhaps the townsfolk had already raised the alarm about her antics and had sent this man to stop her. Anger replaced hope, and her jaw clenched.

"I would confront anyone who sought to harm innocent folk but I am searching for a particular person
with a special item," he said, then turned and stared
down the road. "What is that bell? Does it come from
the village?"

"Oh," Ashleigh replied, casting her eyes downward
and drawing her cloak closer around her shoulders.
How could she have believed that he was here for
her? That in rescuing her he meant to save not just
her body but also her soul? She squeezed her eyes
shut and drew in a deep breath. She was still alone.
He was not going to help her. Her face grew guarded
and withdrawn.

"It sounds like a distress call from the church,"
Mangan surmised. "Is it ringing for you? Is someone
wondering where you were last night?"

Ashleigh shook her head and stepped farther away
from him. "No," she murmured. "Nothing like that."

His gaze swung back and he looked at her curiously,
surprised by her sudden reserve. "Then what?"

Ashleigh jerked her chin toward the village. "You'd
best find out for yourself," she advised.

He reached for her hand, but she shrank away. "I
promised to help you first," he answered. "You must
tell me what has caused you such grief."

She shook her head, then forced a teasing grin to
her lips. "Just a personal matter," she said lightly.

"Ah," he answered, feeling oddly deflated. Probably
a sweetheart's quarrel. Of course a beautiful angel like
her would have a man. Not that it mattered to him;
in fact, it was better that he knew she was spoken
for. Perhaps God was warning him not to stray from
his path.

"Don't worry about me," Ashleigh said as she
wiped the remaining tears from her face and smiled

brightly. "Hurry and see what is wrong in the village. I will be fine."

He frowned, sensing more behind her words. It did not seem right that such agony only moments before was suddenly replaced by apparent gaiety.

The bells pealed incessantly, distracting Mangan from pursuing her suspicious change of behavior.

"Then if you are truly all right . . ." he murmured.

"I am. Go."

He looked at her one more time. Dark smudges underneath her wounded eyes overshadowed her thin cheeks. She looked exhausted. Exhausted but determined.

"Do you want me to come back?"

"No." She laughed, flicking her hair over her shoulder, but her voice seemed artificially high. "I will deal with my problems and you can deal with yours. Continue on toward the village, and I wish you Godspeed."

He nodded and swung up on his horse. When he looked back toward where she had been standing, to his amazement, she was gone.

Frowning, he spun his horse around and galloped up the mountain road.

Ashleigh waited until he rounded a corner, then folded her disappearing plate and strapped it back in place behind her. What a fool she had been to believe that help had arrived. She was alone, and no one was going to save her. If she wanted justice, she would have to win it herself.

She smiled grimly, thinking of the disarray her tricks had already caused in the village. Two days ago she had finally found the home of one of the peasants who had been with the soldiers. Franco was in his stable, and she had stolen the horse back, leaving a skunk in his place. She had then painted a red mark upon the stable door and underneath a small stick figure of a man.

The villager had become terrified, thinking that the horse had been transformed into the skunk, and he had holed himself up in his cottage ever since, afraid that he, too, would be turned into a four-legged creature if he dared to venture forth.

A guilty conscience was easily aroused and twisted to one's favor, Ashleigh had discovered.

His reaction had inspired her, and yesterday she had played many small tricks upon the man's household, thereby feeding the family's rising fear. The man deserved to sleep poorly at night. He deserved to believe that the devil had come for his soul. If not for him, her family might still be alive. The man's secrets made him susceptible to her manipulations, and Ashleigh had every intention of making him suffer a long time.

She would have her revenge. After she was through with him, she would find the other men and send them cowering in the dark, too. And then once she had located all five of them, she would find a way to destroy them all completely.

But first she intended to torture the one man she had already located. Killing her first victim so quickly had been wrong. He had not suffered enough, and she would not make that mistake again.

Last night, she had experienced a moment of weakness, and she would not allow despair to control her destiny again. She would not die.

The memory of the monk's arms holding her whispered through her mind. For one moment she had felt safe . . . loved. Her hopelessness had been cast aside, replaced with peace and security. His green eyes had made her think of springtime bursting forth after a harsh winter.

But such thoughts were absurd. He was no savior.

She would exact revenge.

Earlier she had caused complete pandemonium at her victim's farmhouse, and now that she had collected herself and stopped crying, she intended to go back and hide behind her plate so she could gloat over the chaos.

She mounted Franco and sent him trotting through the trees toward the village center. A squawk from up above indicated that the raven followed.

Chapter 6

Mangan rode hard, galloping past several cottages whose inhabitants were in an uproar, waving their hands and shouting at one another. One man fell to his knees, his hands clasped to the heavens while his wife ran in circles and yanked on fistfuls of her own hair.

"Good Lord," Mangan mumbled as he passed several outlying abodes. "What could have happened to cause such upheaval?" He abruptly reined in and looked at one farmhouse in surprise. Three sheep were standing on the roof of the cottage, *baa*ing in distress.

"How did those sheep get on the roof?" he called out.

The farmer crossed himself and rolled his eyes. " 'Twas evil spirits! I am cursed!"

Spying a section of bark recently rubbed off a sturdy branch nearby, Mangan surmised that a system of ropes had been used to lever the sheep onto the roof. He frowned and urged his horse closer.

" 'Twas not evil spirits, but instead the clever hand of man." Mangan replied.

"Me milk casks!" the man wailed. "The milk, 'tis bloodred! I will surely die tonight!"

"Red?" Mangan leaped from his steed and strode over to the casks, picked one up and peered inside. Sure enough, the milk was tinged red, and Mangan jerked back in shock.

"Ya see?" the man cried. "Evil spirits have come down and cursed the village. Turned me milk into blood. The evil started two days ago, and now 'tis spreading all over."

Mangan looked at his hands. A fine rust-colored dust coated his fingers. He looked at it suspiciously, then spit on his palm. The spittle instantly turned red.

"Oooo-eeee!" the man wailed even louder. " 'Tis spreading onto your flesh!"

"Your milk is fine," Mangan told the man. "It is only colored red with henna."

The man shook his head and pointed to the sheep. " 'Tis terrible spirits. I know it. You be a monk? Can you save us from this devil work?"

"I am a monk, but I think that this is more the work of a trickster than the devil."

"You don't know what goes on here. 'Tis a curse, I know it. Go to the church," the man pleaded. "Help dispel the evil."

Suddenly a child ran from the back of the house, chasing something that floated in the air. Right behind the toddler came his mother, dashing around with a broom, trying to squash the floating object. With a roar of anger the farmer picked up an ax and began swinging it to and fro, narrowly missing his own son.

"Have you no sense?" Mangan shouted as he tore the ax from the man's grasp. "Why do you fight bub-

bles with an ax?" Mangan questioned in disgust.
"They are causing no harm."

"I must save me family," the man growled as he
lunged for his tool.

"I am Mangan, a monk, and I am here to help you."

"Aye," the man agreed as he abruptly collapsed in
a shaking heap, his voice trembling with fear. "We be
needin' a man o' God. Our village is cursed, and our
own priest does nae know what to do."

"Thrice you have said this, and thrice I do not believe it. This is the work of someone who intends to
cause mischief, not an evil spirit bent upon cursing
your village."

"You cannae say that until you've lived in our
homes. Things are wrong here. We are being punished."

Suddenly curious, and wondering if the man's words
were related to his quest, Mangan took a step forward.
"Punished? By whom and why?"

"By God," the man answered, and he turned away
to grip his child by the hand and gather his frantic
wife and hustle them back into the cottage, away from
the mysterious bubbles.

What sounded like a giggle caused Mangan to look
toward the trees. He peered through the leaves, listening intently. It could be another child chasing bubbles, or it could be the person responsible for making
them. "Come forth," he commanded. "Show yourself."

Ashleigh clamped a hand over her mouth and men-
tally berated herself for laughing aloud, but it had
been so funny seeing that man chasing bubbles with
a double-edged ax! What a fool! After such a terrible
night it felt good to smile again, even if at another's
expense.

She stealthily pulled the set of rings down from the trees where she had tied them, and removed the pitcher of soapy water she had balanced to drip slowly over the rings. The summer breeze had cooperated perfectly, and the steady flow of bubbles had made the inhabitants every bit as nervous as she had hoped.

"I hear you," Mangan said as he started walking his horse toward her. "I will recommend a lighter punishment if you reveal yourself immediately and stop terrorizing the people of this home."

Ashleigh glared at him through the leaves, remembering the feel of his broad shoulders and muscled arms. He no longer looked kind and compassionate. His face was tight and angry, and fear rippled through her. If he caught her he would imprison her at the very least, kill her at the very worst. And if he discovered that she had murdered a man . . . Either way she would be unable to exact her revenge upon the men who had killed her mother and father.

Suddenly the raven that persisted in staying with her burst into flight and swooped through the trees, sending a rabbit scurrying for cover. The bunny raced underneath a log, then changed its mind and dashed out of the woods and headed across the farmhouse clearing before it ducked underneath the cottage steps.

Mangan, too, had watched the rabbit, and he shook his head in disgust, annoyed that a simple animal had made him draw his weapon. He remounted his horse, cast one last look over his shoulder and rode the rest of the way to the village.

Ashleigh gaped in astonishment as the raven fluttered back to her, his wise eyes staring into her own. "You saved me," she whispered. "You flushed the rabbit on purpose to distract the monk."

The raven tilted his neck, his beady eyes bright as he ruffled his feathers and preened.

"What a clever little beast," Ashleigh whispered as she touched his head and patted his beak. "I don't know why you have chosen to befriend me, but . . . I don't mind." Glancing toward where Mangan had disappeared down the road, she pressed her lips together and lifted her chin. "Together we will exact my revenge, and that man can do nothing to stop us."

She followed Mangan to the edge of town, where the villagers were shouting and shaking their fists, then slipped off her horse and tied her mount to a tree in a place where it was unlikely to be seen. She drew her cloak over her head, picked up a staff and crouched down like an older woman using a cane, taking care to stay away from where Mangan was greeting the village leaders. Her mother had often acted like an old woman when she begged for coins, and Ashleigh remembered the mannerisms and imitated them well. Using her staff, taking halting steps and keeping to the edge of the crowd, she began stealthily looking at faces, searching for the other of the men who had attacked her family.

"Where is your overlord?" Mangan was asking as the villagers bombarded him with tales of woe. "Shouldn't he send some of his soldiers to protect you?"

"Our overlord is otherwise occupied," a village elder replied. "He does not like to be bothered with the concerns of his peasants. Besides, the fields have not been burned and the herds have not been stolen. As far as our lord is concerned, there is no need for alarm."

" 'Tis his duty to protect his people." Mangan insisted. "If one farmer is being unfairly besieged by some trickster, he should investigate."

"He has greater worries." answered the village elder, who was stooped and gray and whose eyes bore signs of anxiety. He is cousin to the king, and must remain focused on politics and war. We are only a small outlying village. Our affairs are not nearly as important as the fate of Scotland."

"What about your priest?"

"Recently, he has abided with Laird Geoffrey."

Mangan nodded and looked over the crowd. It was a common enough answer. There was no reason to become angry, yet he struggled to remain calm. Why should nobles force men to kill and maim others in return for more land when their leaders did not bother tending their own? Such senselessness was exactly why he had undertaken his quest.

As a monk he could travel as he wanted and help those in need. No one but God could tell him where he must be or what he must do, and this village was clearly in need of his assistance. If he helped them, then perhaps he could gain their trust and they would allow him to view the relics of the church.

Goose bumps rose on his arms and he turned, scanning the populace for the source of his disquiet. He had sensed something similar at the farmhouse. It was as if someone were watching him. Everyone he saw seemed genuinely agitated, but he felt as if something were left unsaid. Their faces looked too frightened, too tight with worry. His gaze swept the shadowed visage of an old woman, and he thought for a moment that her focus was all on him before she ducked her face and moved out of his line of vision.

"Have you had trouble before?" he asked, still wondering if he had mistaken a flash of ire in the woman's hooded expression. For some reason he had felt the weight of her gaze even though he could not see the lines of her face. She disturbed him, and he scanned the crowd, hoping to find her again.

"Nothing like this," the elder answered. "Nothing so . . . unnatural. We are a peaceful village. We keep to ourselves and cause our lord no concerns. We till our land and pay our tithes. We need you to exorcize the evil spirits and help our village return to normal. Please promise that you will stay and help."

"I will stay for a few days," Mangan assured him. "I will find the source of your trouble and bring harmony back to your people."

The elder grasped Mangan's hand and kissed his fingers. "You will see," he said. "The fates have brought you here to us. We thank you." Then the man turned to his people and held up his hands for silence. "Hear ye all!" he cried. "This man has come from God, yet he also carries a sword. He is a warrior monk, a person who can fight both man and supernatural beast. He has vowed to stay among us until the evil spirits have been vanquished! I declare a day of holiday for all the villagers wherein we shall welcome this man and show him our gratitude. We shall eat and drink and make merry, for our savior has come!"

Mangan shifted uneasily in his saddle, uncomfortable with the man's declaration. He was far from a savior. He just wanted to ease his own guilt by helping others and completing his journey. He carried the sword for defense, but he had no desire to use it ever again. Certainly not to chase after an irritating trickster.

*　　*　　*

Ashleigh's annoyance grew as the feast continued. While the people enjoyed food and ale, she was forced the crouch underneath her cape and refuse the succulent food. As her belly rumbled, her anger flourished. The villagers were already acting as if Mangan had saved them and all was as it should be. The wives who had shuddered in fear this morn were now laughing and dancing with their friends, and the husbands who had raced to the village in response to the church bells were now drinking and cavorting as if they had no concerns.

All her efforts had been wasted, because this man—this monk!—had arrived and promised to help the villagers.

She hobbled closer and peered at him through the shadow of her cowl. Once again she thought he was too handsome to be a monk. A monk should appear innocent and sublime, not devilishly good-looking. This man had strong cheekbones and lashes longer than she had ever seen on a man. His frame was large and solid, obviously well honed by years of hard work, and he moved with a confidence that belied the meek subservience required by men of the cloth.

There was also something about the way he watched the people. He scanned the villagers constantly, as if always on the alert for an attack. His body was coiled tight, ready to spring into action at the slightest sign of danger. Even his eyebrows swept up, then down— full, dark and striking, his gaze far too worldly-wise for a man who had spent his life behind the cloistered walls of a monastery.

Yet, as far as she could tell, the villagers saw nothing amiss in him. The lasses talked to him respectfully without any hint of flirtatiousness, oblivious to his masculine charms. They saw only his exterior—his

robes, his shuttered face, his slow, deliberate movements. The men treated him with the honor due a
leader of the church, seemingly unaware of his rigidly
restrained power.

Ashleigh looked away in confusion. Perhaps she was
the one imagining things and he was, indeed, a simple,
honest man. Perhaps she was seeing danger and deceit
in every face because of the horrible way her parents
had been murdered. The monk radiated strength of
purpose, not might of arm. He was a monk, not a
soldier.

"Woman," one of the elders called out to her.

Ashleigh ducked her head and turned away, trying
not to be noticed.

"Woman!" the man repeated sharply. "Come and
rub the monk's feet. He has traveled far and deserves
the solace of oil massaged into his tired muscles."

Ashleigh shuffled to the right, deliberately ignoring
the man's command. She had no intention of touching
that monk! Besides, she needed to make the most of
this opportunity to see all the villagers and find the
other culprits. Soon this stranger would move on, and
she would be left with the yawning sense of undeliv-
ered justice.

A heavy hand descended upon her shoulder. "Old
woman, your ears must be failing, for I have called
you twice. Come." The villager pushed her gently but
firmly toward where Mangan was seated. "Remove his
boots and apply this precious butter to the soles of
his feet." The man looked meaningfully at her. "We
must thank God for his presence, and we want to
ensure that he stays to help us resolve *all* our
troubles."

"I will find out who is responsible for the mischief
today," Mangan replied, glancing briefly at the woman

who was trying to wiggle out of the villager's hold, then staring at her intently. The curve of her shadowed cheek . . . the arch of her smooth neck . . . could it be Ashleigh? If so, why was such a lovely girl dressed as an old beggar woman?

"Aye, that is good," the man answered. "Eogan Fergus, my firstborn son, has received the worst of the curse, and the fear runs so deep in his blood that he will not leave his home. 'Tis his milk that turned to blood and his sheep that flew onto the roof. My name is Eo'Ghanan Fergus, and I offer me home to you. I will provide a warm bed and ensure that you receive the best off our plates, while you ask for God's grace to protect us from the evil that surrounds us."

Mangan smiled and stretched his foot toward the woman, who had finally ceased her struggles and was being urged to kneel at his feet. His calves did ache, and a good rub would be much appreciated. Besides, it would give him some time to determine who she was without making his interest obvious. "I am honored that you would relinquish your bed for me, but I am happier in the forest," he said. "I can concentrate on my devotions when I am among the trees, and I sleep better adjacent to a stream, but I will take you up on your offer of food, for I must restock my supplies. However, there is one thing I would greatly enjoy."

"Anything, Brother Mangan."

"I would like to see your church, for I have heard that your priest has collected many important religious artifacts. I am on a journey to visit churches throughout the land."

Eo'Ghanan shook his head. "We have but a small chapel, built by our own hands. If ye be seeking something grand, ye must go to our overlord's castle. He has a mighty church, I am told, a church whose coffers are enriched as our lord prospers. That church may contain relics, but I warn you that our lord does not receive strangers easily. It would be best to speak with our priest before approaching the castle gates. He should be returning here within the next several days. Until then you are welcome to meditate within our simple chapel whenever you wish."

Eo'Ghanan nudged the old woman. "Treat our guest well, crone," he cautioned, "or you will receive no ration tonight. You must be new to our village, and I expect you to prove your worth if you wish to remain. Do you understand me?"

Mangan placed a protective hand on the woman's head and looked reproachfully at the elder. "I am certain she will do her best. Pray, do not withhold sustenance from one in need."

As Eo'Ghanan walked away, Mangan leaned back in his chair and sighed, momentarily forgetting about Ashleigh. One more church . . . one more clue, but still no closer to finding the relic he sought. It had been the same every place he went. *No, not here, but why don't you try there?* Mangan was beginning to doubt he would ever find it, even though he knew such a lack of faith was sacrilegious.

Ashleigh hesitated, aware of Mangan's temporary distraction. If she scrambled away, Eo'Ghanan might seek her out and confront her, thus exposing her disguise. But if she took her time and rubbed the monk's feet well, the villagers would gradually come by and greet Mangan, which would give her a golden opportunity to see everyone and possibly find the last of the peasants from the meadow. She had already discovered that the man who had stolen Franco was called Eogan.

She peeked up at Mangan's face. His eyes were closed and he was breathing deeply, as if he were already half-asleep. *Good. Let him doze, and I can surreptitiously watch the villagers as they celebrate.* Slowly, drawing each motion out as long as she could, she unlaced his boots as she sneaked glances around her from the shadow of her hood.

Mangan twitched. He was trying to act relaxed and calm, while inside he felt a strange, unsettled anxiety at the woman's touch. How was he to confront her if she was, indeed, the angel he had rescued? How could he account for meeting her without betraying her attempted suicide? As a monk he could not reveal her secrets, and certainly her flirtation with hemlock was something she would not wish others to know.

Trying to ignore her, he turned his thoughts back to his quest. His arrival here was similar to his arrival in many villages. He was often accosted as a savior and begged to help the beleaguered pastors with their hapless flock. Sometimes the peasants wanted his prayers to increase their harvest or bring needed rain. At other times the people needed his intervention between two warring clans, and he acted as a mediator to help settle disputes.

This village's problem, although a bit more dramatic than the others', was no different. Someone was causing trouble, and he was here to end it. So why was he so anxious? Why was he more interested in one woman than all the other villagers?

The woman's hands brushed his ankle and he twitched again. She was unlacing his boots so slowly that he was tempted to lean down and help her, especially since her touch was sending unwelcome shivers up his leg.

"This is unnecessary," he said to her, trying not to sound gruff.

The woman did not answer. She finished unlacing the boot, then gripped the heel and tugged.

He moved his foot up and down, assisting her, until the boot finally slid off. Mangan smiled. It did feel good to have his foot free of the constricting leather, but, taking pity on her when he saw her hands tremble, he used his toe to push the heel of the other boot off.

Ashleigh frowned, wishing she could have spent more time with his boots. Now that they were off, she had no choice but to pull his socks free and start rubbing his bare toes. She had seen her mother massage her father's feet, but she had never touched a man so intimately before. *Focus,* she reminded herself. *'Tis just a monk's foot. He is not even a real man!*

She rolled down one sock, then the other, and was surprised by the coarse hair she felt along his calves. Her own calves were slender and soft, with only a downy touch of hair. She paused, intrigued, and brushed her thumb across his lower calf. 'Twas also much harder than her own leg, more so than even her father's. More muscular and solid.

Ashleigh bit her lip, fascinated by his leg. She shifted her hands down to his toes, pulling and wriggling them until several cracked. Then she took a bit of the butter Eo'Ghanan had left her and rubbed it between each of his toes. He had big feet. Big, strong feet with calluses from riding. She was surprised he had ridden so much, for she thought monks stayed within their monastery, venturing forth only to complete specific missions.

She caressed the calluses, sensing his soreness by

the way his foot jerked slightly. Bending to her task, she rolled her thumbs over the bottom of his foot as her fingers stroked the top, smoothing the muscles and working the area between his bones. She could feel the tendons flex and quiver before she coaxed them to relax, and as she rubbed his foot's lower arch she felt his entire body shudder.

Mangan instinctively pulled back, then gritted his teeth and returned his foot to the woman's hand. There was no question that she must be Ashleigh, for he was reacting to her as he had responded earlier. Her touch felt like the caress of a lover instead of the impersonal massage of a beggar woman. Memories of making love to countless women as his army marched through foreign lands flickered through his mind before he forcefully quashed them. Passion was behind him. He had forsaken such pleasure as penance for his years as a warrior.

God must be testing him. These urges had been brought to life when he rescued the dark angel, but he must remain strong enough to control them. She was not at fault; he must flush such emotions from his thoughts. He must face his fears and conquer them before they overtook his soul.

Yet, unable to endure the torture any longer, he leaned forward and gripped her hand with his. "That is enough," he said, his voice oddly husky even to his own ears.

"Your other foot . . ." the woman mumbled.

"Leave it. I will tell Eo'Ghanan that you did well and I am refreshed. I will seek the answers to the chaos in your village and set everything back to rights, and perhaps then whatever pains you will be mended. Now please go and get some food for yourself. You must eat and gather strength."

Ashleigh yanked her hand out from under his and hid it in the folds of her cape. For a moment she had forgotten that he was here to find and stop her. Could he know she was the one causing the trouble? Could he have pierced her disguise when all the others had not? She could not trust him. He was aligned with the enemy, and because he had vowed to help them, he deserved her animosity just as much as the others did.

She pulled the hood of her cape tighter around her face and dropped her voice low, making it crackly and old. "Ye shouldna be fiddlin' with the spirits," she warned. "This town is cursed, and the longer you remain, the more the curse will rub off on ye."

Mangan struggled to contain his unexpected physical reaction to her touch as he tried to concentrate on her words. "There are no evil spirits here," he answered, curious about her conviction.

"Is that so?" she answered as she rose and backed away from him. "Ye feel nothing wrong around ye? Nothing . . . disturbing?"

Mangan, too, got to his feet. His thighs twitched and he was forced to concentrate on his breathing. He closed his eyes and rubbed his forehead, feeling the onset of one of his headaches. Ever since that last battle he had been plagued with intense headaches that made his temples pound and his head throb. "Ashleigh, you must not allow fear to cloud your judgment," he explained as patiently as he could. He opened his eyes, then looked around in confusion. She was gone.

Ashleigh pressed against the wall of the church and hid behind her disappearing plate. Her Gypsy band had always relied upon people's fears and superstitions to reinforce the effectiveness of their magic. It was the people's own inability to accept the unexpected that made tricks seem fantastic and other-worldly, yet this man was unimpressed. He had seen through her feats and called them pranks. He was cautioning the villagers and easing their terror. He had even seen through her disguise. In effect, he was ruining everything!

She truly disliked him.

Chapter 7

Near midnight the last of the villagers staggered home and collapsed into their beds. After his foot massage Mangan had retired to the church and tried to cleanse his thoughts through prayer, emerging only when the moon was high and the village quiet. He could not shake the unease that filled his heart.

He had not found baby Jesus' blanket; he had found nothing.

He had been on this quest for nearly a year, and never before had he felt so discouraged. Furthermore, he was confounded by the intensity of the villagers' fear. Although he knew that uneducated peasants were often afraid of what they did not understand, he was surprised that they were so quick to assume that evil spirits were among them.

He walked slowly through the silent village and untied his horse from the post adjacent to the blacksmith's abode. Sir Scott nickered at him and he gave him a pat on the neck as he removed the feed bag from around the horse's nose. "At least they fed us well," Mangan murmured as he swung up and reined his mount, then sent him walking down the moonlit road. His horse nickered again, and Mangan gave him another pat.

He rode for a few minutes until he heard the burbling of a stream, then angled his horse off the road and located a clearing. Moonlight shone through the trees and reflected off the water, giving the scene a nighttime radiance.

The stallion suddenly pricked his ears and stared into the darker recesses of the clearing. He whinnied and stomped his foot as a black raven flew from a low tree branch.

" 'Tis only a bird," Mangan soothed his horse. "You've seen plenty. No need to act nervous about that one." He swung down and pulled the saddle and bridle off the horse, then gave him a final pat on the rump before setting him loose. He then untied the belt around his robes and started to remove his heavy clothing in preparation for his midnight devotions.

Ashleigh woke with a start as the raven burst past her face in a swooping flight from one branch to another. She had been resting on a bed of leaves underneath the sheltering branches of a tree at the edge of a clearing. She sat up quickly and bumped her head on a branch before catching her breath in surprise. Mangan stood several feet from her sleeping place, his back to her as he stared into the stream.

Panic infused her, and her heart skipped a beat. She scrambled to her feet and picked up a stick, willing to fight to the death to remain free, but Mangan did not turn around. He had untied the belt around his robes and now tossed it to the side, seemingly unaware of her presence.

As his robes fell open he yanked off his boots and socks, then pulled the robes over his head, shucked off his shirt and pants and threw them over a nearby rock. When he stood straight, his naked form was silhouetted against the moonlight.

Her fear forgotten, Ashleigh stared at him in awe. She had felt the muscles of his calf, and had leaned against his broad chest, but nothing had prepared her for the chiseled perfection of his entire form.

He reached into his saddlebag and withdrew a flask. Then, as Ashleigh watched in rapt attention, he knelt at the edge of the streambed and lifted his arms up toward the stars. Muscles rippled in his arms and across his shoulders, then down his back, finally swelling over his taut buttocks. Bare, naked strength . . . pure masculine power.

He began to chant in Latin in a low voice. He took slow, deep breaths and widened his arms as if he were trying to encompass the entire heavens above. His voice soothed her, made her forget her rage. His very presence drew the anger from her heart, then tickled the void with a new, heart-thudding desire. She was entranced, captivated by the glory of his body, his voice, his godly aura. She could not tear her gaze away despite the niggling guilt that told her she should not be watching him. She should not intrude upon his privacy.

But she did not leave the moonlit meadow, and she watched him as the fires of awakened passion licked at her belly and burned through her blood.

Mangan picked up the flask and reverently uncapped it, then poured a few silvery drops of oil onto his palm. The aroma of frankincense and ground orange rind wafted across the stream, then gently permeated the meadow and enfolded him in a familiar embrace. He inhaled slowly, then resumed his chant, his voice dropping lower as he concentrated on rubbing his palms together. This was where he had always found his greatest solace, in the comforting ritual of midnight matins.

Rubbing his oil-slick hands over his face, he inhaled again. This was his destiny. He was a child of God and was meant to devote his life to following the Lord's path. Standing, he dripped one drop on his right shoulder and let it run in a deliberate, agonizingly slow journey down his back.

May this represent my sorrow for all I have done to disrespect life.

He poured another portion upon his other shoulder. The oil paused, caught in the crease of his muscle, then suddenly surged over the bulge and raced down his back, trailing a glistening path over his buttocks and down his thigh.

May this represent the path I still must travel. May I remain true and obedient to God's will.

He then turned and extracted a sprig of myrrh from his bags. Using flint and a small oval striking stone, he set the myrrh smoldering and then laid it at his feet. The thin plumes of smoke circled his calves, then floated up his body in tender wisps before escaping into the night sky.

Take this smoke and let it represent the release of all that should not be. Let it guide me to righting the wrongs of this mortal earth.

The smoke trail flickered, then blew gently across the meadow on a soft breeze. Mangan closed his eyes, trying to merge with the smoke, trying to release his spirit from the confines of his human flesh.

But the peace of his prayers eluded him. The agitation that hovered at the edge of his consciousness flared to life. He felt restless and troubled. A dark angel had flown into his thoughts and set her black eyes upon his soul. Within his mind she mocked him, reminding him that his unruly thoughts proved he was still unworthy.

With a growl of frustration, Mangan opened his eyes and glared at the moon. "Are you testing me?" he called out, his voice echoing against the burbling stream. "Why now? Have I not shown you my commitment? Have I not forsaken all the pleasures that would turn me from the path of righteousness? I have left my fortune, my castle and my family. Why taunt me with a woman?"

Ashleigh gasped, startled by his sudden outburst. She could barely make out his words as his back remained turned to her, but she could feel his quaking energy as he clenched his fists and shook them at the sky. The power she had sensed was uncoiling, and she feared that once it was released he would be helpless to restrain it.

He gripped the flask and poured the entire contents on his head, drenching his hair with the fragrant oil. Then he ran his fingers through the slick strands and down his corded neck. With a quick leap he sprang up on a log that spanned the stream from edge to edge, and ran partway across balancing with effortless ease.

Ashleigh trembled. She could see his face now . . . his chest . . . his thick thatch of hair covering the male part of him that pulsed with vitality. He was no cloistered monk. He had quicksilver reflexes and acutely honed skills, yet his breathing was harsh and he clasped a beaded cross in his hand.

Wisps of burning myrrh wafted into the shadows,

touched and caressed her. She had a sudden urge to join Mangan and stroke his oily head, then trace the droplets that ran down his back. She clutched her hands around her arms and held herself tight, forcibly restraining her own body. He was the enemy! He was aligned with the men she had vowed to destroy. She could not succumb to the unwelcome desires of her traitorous flesh.

Mangan scanned the water, then looked across the stream to where his sprig was burning. Despite the lack of breeze, the smoke was still drifting into the forest as if it were being drawn there by some invisible force. A shiver rippled through him, and he felt his nether regions stir to life. He smelled more than the frankincense and myrrh. He smelled passion.

A woman. A woman who smelled as sweet as sugar but with eyes and hair as dark as the thickest, richest molasses.

A trick of the imagination, he told himself. No village miss would be out in the midnight hours. Certainly not a sad, frightened lass with alabaster skin and ruby red lips who sought to give her precious body to the cold caress of a forest stream.

He peered through the water and found the deepest pool on the lee of a log. Then, with hardly a splash, he dove in and immersed himself in one of God's greatest gifts—glorious, life-giving water.

Bursting to the surface, he gasped as the frigid stream sluiced off his oil-slick head and back but clung to his furred chest. The water refreshed him and instantly cooled his ardor. It was better this way. He must forget her, forget all women, cleanse the dark angel from his thoughts so that he could resume his quest and, ultimately, find forgiveness in the eyes of God.

* * *

The raven helped her escape into the forest before Mangan emerged from the stream. He swept down from the branches and landed on her shoulder, startling her from her intense fascination. Without the raven's interference, she would have remained crouched there even as the monk strode out of the water.

"You are a clever little beast," she whispered as she sped among the trees, the raven clinging to her shoulder and using his wings to maintain his balance. "Why ever are you helping me? One would expect you to fear me after I nearly killed you with that rock, yet you have chosen to stay and act as a faithful companion."

The bird rose from his precarious perch and circled up into the sky, his black form silhouetted against the moon.

Ashleigh shivered. "What kind of creature are you, *cairdean*?" she asked, using the Celtic word for *friend* that her mother had taught her. "You say no words, yet you speak to me. You have a vast forest, yet you stay nearby. Are you a spirit? A Scottish *aigne*? Or are you a messenger from the underworld, here to watch me in my misery?"

The raven cawed, then swept down to perch on the top of a large rock located on a steep incline. With two hops he abruptly disappeared through a moderately sized black hole in the granite about halfway up the incline. Ashleigh scrambled after him, first climbing several feet up, then ducking down and crawling through the small, dark space.

She paused, fascinated by the cave, and waited for her eyes to adjust. It was warm and sheltered from the wind. Just ahead she saw the raven's beady eyes as he half fluttered, half bounded into a thick collection of sticks and debris wedged into a ledge at the back. She also saw various shiny objects, ranging from steel spoons and rusty nails to lengths of chain and bits of cloth.

The raven made a soft sound in the back of his throat that sounded like a coo. Ashleigh smiled and held her hand out to him. " 'Tis a beautiful nest, Cairdean," she said, officially naming him. "Your home is like a Gypsy wagon."

The raven plucked a beaded necklace from the jumble and held it in his beak.

"You want me to have it?" Ashleigh asked, her sad face breaking into a hesitant smile. When the raven cocked his head and blinked rapidly, Ashleigh closed her fist around the necklace. "Thank you," she replied. "Thank you very much. You don't know how much this means to me . . . and this cave . . . you are a true friend, Cairdean."

Finding a soft pile of sheep's wool that she presumed Cairdean had stolen from an unsuspecting herder, and a few tattered remnants of blankets she guessed the raven had taken from someone's discard pile, Ashleigh made herself a bed far more comfortable than piled leaves and moss. Then, as the raven tucked his head under his wing and the heat of their bodies warmed the small cave, Ashleigh fell into her first restful sleep since her parents' death.

"I will set a trap," Mangan announced the next morning. He was speaking with five of the elders behind the closed doors of the church. He had requested a private discussion with the men under the assumption that someone from the village must be responsible for the mischief at the farmer's house. "Did anything unusual occur last night?" he asked.

Eo'Ghanan Fergus shook his head. "Not last night, but me son is still petrified, and dares not come out of his cottage for fear that the evil spirits will strike him dead."

"On another night? Before this all began?"

The elder glanced down and shook his head.

Mangan frowned. He sensed that there was more the elder was not revealing. "Is he engaged in a dispute? Perhaps with a neighbor?"

"No. They are good to one another, and their wives often sit and spin wool together."

"Has he trespassed upon another's home or property or perhaps upon his wife?"

"Heavens, no!" Eo'Ghanan exclaimed. "Eogan is a good, honest man who serves the community above his own personal needs. Even this past fortnight, he and Cormag O'Callaghan left the warmth of their hearths on a Sunday afternoon to look for their friend, Branan McFadden."

"What did he find?"

Eo'Ghanan shrugged. "Nothing. Only a campsite left smoldering by a careless traveler. Eogan would never place this village or anyone in it in jeopardy. He is a God-fearing man with five children and a wife of fourteen years." Eo'Ghanan glanced at the others and appeared to be about to say something, but then closed his mouth and said no more.

"Could Branan McFadden be the man responsible for the mischief? Could they have argued?"

The elder shook his head. "We believe Branan is dead."

"Why?"

Eo'Ghanan shuffled his feet. "Eogan said he and Cormag found his body."

"So you *know* he is dead," Mangan stated, then

watched Eo'Ghanan shrug and stare up at the church rafters. Mangan pondered his evasiveness. Could Eogan have harmed Branan? Since Eogan was Eo'Ghanan's son, was Eo'Ghanan afraid to tell the truth? "Did Eogan have a reason to dislike Branan?" he asked, trying to maintain a monkish demeanor in order to encourage Eo'Ghanan's confession.

"Absolutely not. They were friends—all three of them. Eogan believes Branan took his own life."

Mangan mulled over Eo'Ghanan's answer. In one village, within one sennight, one man was believed to have committed suicide and one woman had attempted the same. Could the incidents be related? "Eogan has how many children?"

"Five."

"Any of them daughters?"

"Aye, the oldest."

His heart sinking, Mangan nodded sagely. "I would like to meet Eogan's family," he said as he rose to his feet. "And I should speak with Eogan himself."

"Aye, you may do as you wish, but I promise that you will nae find the culprit within our midst. I will send everyone in the village to introduce themselves to you, but you will need to seek elsewhere for the source of our curse." Eo'Ghanan looked meaningfully at Mangan, but he had already turned away.

"My thanks for the food," Mangan said. "My saddlebags are overflowing with your bounty." He left the church and headed toward his horse, his head bowed in thought. There must be some reason Eogan's home and family had been targeted. Branan's disappearance coincided with the angel's appearance. Could they have been ill-fated sweethearts? Had

Eogan harbored anger at his friend because Branan had coveted Eogan's eldest daughter? Had there been a murder instead of a suicide, and Eogan was pretending to play tricks upon himself in order to gain sympathy?

Unless his meeting with Eogan's family revealed the truth, Mangan would have to hide in the outskirts of Eogan's farm and watch for the mischief maker to show himself. The entire situation seemed far-fetched, but Mangan had not slept well and his head was throbbing and he could think of no other explanation.

A messenger rode into the village and pulled his horse to a stop in front of Mangan. "You are the man of God for this village?" the messenger asked. His cheeks were still smooth and he seemed nervous.

"I am a monk from St. Ignacio," Mangan replied.

"Here," the boy said as he shoved a scroll at Mangan, then lifted his chin in a show of confidence. "I send my lord's response to your laird's missive."

Mangan frowned and unrolled the paper.

Laird Geoffrey, Your Offer is Most Generous and is Graciously Accepted. I am in Agreement with your Plans, and Express Interest in Forming an Alliance, since You have Demonstrated Adequate Resources for your Endeavor based on the Extensive Treasures You Sent with Your Missive. I Expect that Such was Only One Example of How you Intend to Reward your Loyal Followers. I have Been Assured that You have Already Gathered Support from Some Highland Clans, which will Prove to be an Asset in the Coming Events. Expect Delivery at the Half Moon, and Please Pre-

pare the Appropriate Accomodations for the Dig-
nitaries' Arrival the Following Fortnight.

> *Faithfully Yours,*
> *H.D.*

Mangan rerolled the parchment and tried to hand
it back to the messenger. "This is not intended for
me," he told the boy, but the youngster was already
turning his pony around.

"I must return immediately," the boy informed the
monk. "I was told that you would carry the message
to the next location."

Mangan shook his head. "Perhaps this is meant for
the priest presiding in this church, for it means nothing
to me. As I said, I am from St. Ignacio."

The boy shrugged as he started his pony trotting.
"I was told to hand it directly to the man of God in
the mountain village. I have done my duty and must
return for my coin." He waved and rode away, leaving Mangan standing alone with the scroll still in
his hand.

Mangan debated for a moment, then slid it into his
pocket. He would personally give it to the priest when
the man returned to the village. Since two more nights
would give rise to the half moon, he hoped the priest
would return shortly. It was exceedingly doubtful that
anyone else in the village would be able to read the
missive.

"Ooh," a young boy cried as he and another child
raced into the village center, then skidded to a stop.
Their dirty hands and guilty looks made Mangan assume that they had sneaked away from their chores
for a bit of fun. "Look at the monk's sword hilt," the
first boy gasped. " 'Tis inlaid w' gold!"

Mangan's eyes narrowed as the boy approached the stallion and reached out to finger Mangan's sword, exclaiming in awe over the intricate hilt. Mangan's hand instinctively reached for the second sword he always used to wear. Only when his hands encountered the hemp tie of his robe did he realize how close he had come to drawing a weapon upon two harmless boys.

The scroll forgotten, he strode up to the boys and glared fiercely at them. "Get away from my horse," he commanded. As they bolted, Mangan leaned his head against the horse's hide and closed his eyes. He should not have yelled at them, for 'twas only natural that they would be interested in his weapon. All boys were fascinated with instruments of war. Again, he was the one at fault. It was his reaction that was unnatural. A monk should not respond so harshly, especially regarding his possessions, and he should never turn to force when prayer and reason would suffice.

It was just that he was tired, and his body ached with pent-up frustration. He should be concentrating on the villagers' dilemma or on Branan's disappearance, but all he could think about was that he might see Ashleigh again if she was, indeed, Eogan's daughter. After almost two years of fidelity to God, his body was betraying him. He suspected that his dark angel was a young, innocent child mixed up in a bittersweet dispute between families. His desire to see her, to look into her exotic eyes and listen to her winsome voice, was sinfully selfish and lustful. He was supposed to be an introspective man of the cloth. If he could not control his emotions, he would fail the villagers and, in doing so, fail in his duty.

He sighed and opened his eyes, seeing a boy huddled in a doorway, staring at him with concern. Mangan forced a calm smile to his lips and mounted his horse. He must clear his mind and focus on the matter at hand, for as soon as he resolved this difficulty, he could leave the mountain and resume his quest.

And force his awakening passion back into submission.

Chapter 8

As evening approached, Mangan rubbed his forehead again and thought longingly of the dubious comfort of his cell in the monastery. After listening to Eogan's terrified ranting for the past two hours, the hard cot and cold floor of his previous abode were beginning to seem far preferable to sitting in this man's warm cottage and trying to stay measured and calm. He had met every one of Eogan's raucous children and had quickly discovered that Ashleigh was not among them.

Outside the cottage, equally uncomfortable, Ashleigh hid behind a row of bushes close by and eavesdropped on the monk's conversation through an open window. So far Eogan's version of how she had tricked him had been deliciously exaggerated, and Ashleigh couldn't help but feel proud of her handiwork. After only a few tricks she had successfully terrorized the first man on her list.

"The milk did not change to blood," Mangan explained as patiently as he could for what seemed like the twentieth time. "It was dyed red with a powder called henna. Women use it to color their hair."

Eogan shook his head and clasped his hands around his own shoulders, then commenced rocking back and forth in agitation. "Blood," he whispered. "Blood everywhere . . ."

Mangan rose abruptly and strode to the window. His eyes were drawn to the dark shadows behind the bushes, and he had an intense longing to head toward them. Perhaps, he reasoned, he wanted to lie down upon the soft earth and listen to the whisper of leaves in the breeze instead of sitting in this cottage interrogating this peasant. Or perhaps he simply sought the cool shade. He knew for certain that the man's words were too close to what he saw in his own nightmares, and he needed an escape.

Blood. Acres upon acres of bleeding bodies. I should have saved them.

A knock on the door startled them both.

"Eogan?" a man asked as he peeked his head around the doorjamb. " 'Tis Cormag. Might I come in? I heard there is a monk here who wants to speak with me."

Eogan jerked his head toward Mangan, but continued rocking. "I've been cursed . . ." he moaned. "The spirits have come t' take me soul away and cast it adrift in the fires of hell."

Cormag entered and nodded respectfully to Mangan. "We are grateful for your help," he said. "Poor Eogan cannae take much more o' this."

The headache that had simmered all day now burst into a full, blazing shaft of pain, and Mangan had to bite back a groan. Struggling to concentrate, he managed to ask, "Have you reason to dislike this man?" He motioned to Eogan.

"Merciful heavens, no," Cormag exclaimed. "He is one of me best companions, and was a great comfort to me after my wife died several years ago."

"What is it I hear about a horse and a skunk?

Eogan is not making sense. I count two horses in the stables, and his wife claims that they only have two horses, so why does Eogan state that the skunk now living in the hayloft is really a horse?"

Although Cormag averted his gaze and scuffed his foot, Mangan was rubbing his forehead and did not notice. "Dunno," Cormag answered.

Mangan glanced at him through his fingers. "No need to shout," he muttered. "Very well," he said as he motioned to the setting sun. "If you have nothing more to add, I will sit outside and wait to see what occurs."

"Do you need to rest, brother?" Cormag questioned. "Ye seem mighty tired."

"No," Mangan answered as he preceded Cormag outside and took a deep breath of fresh air, trying to clear the throbbing in his head. "I am perfectly fine."

A raven cawed from his perch on the cottage roof and Mangan winced in response. Such a loud, annoying noise! A flash of white caught his eye, and he looked to where a light gray horse was tethered to a hitching post. "Interesting animal." Mangan mentioned to Cormag. "I used to see many such beasts in France. Where did you come across one here in Scotland?"

Cormag smiled and lifted his hands in a show of innocence. "Found him wandering. No one claimed him, so I thought I might as well feed and care for him."

Mangan shrugged and turned away, already losing interest. The annoying raven was squawking even more loudly than before, and he had an insane desire to shout at it. Instead he clenched his teeth and walked with measured strides to the edge of the clear-

ing. "Good night," he said over his shoulder, then
entered the blessed coolness of the forest, leaving a
confused Cormag standing in the doorway.

With a gasp Ashleigh ducked down behind the bush
and prayed that Mangan had not seen her. Why was
he coming toward this side of the clearing? Why not
stay near the front of the farm? She reached behind
her back and started to set up her disappearing plate,
but the strap knotted. "Drat!" she whispered, then
clapped a hand over her mouth when Mangan's gaze
abruptly swung toward her hiding place.

Mangan took several steps toward the suspicious
sound, cautiously alert. It was possible that the trickster he was pursuing was skulking in the bushes
nearby. As he peered into the foliage, he spotted a
huddled form hidden amid the leaves. "Halt!" he
shouted as he ran forward.

Panicking, Ashleigh abandoned the disappearing
plate and dashed through the trees until she saw one
she could climb; then she began scrambling upward.
If she could get to the top quickly enough, he wouldn't
be able to see her!

Mangan instantly gave chase, leaping over the last
row of bushes and sprinting after the fleeing form.
"Don't be a fool!" he yelled. "It will go much easier
for you if you surrender!"

A branch cracked, and Ashleigh hung suspended in
the air for one moment before she managed to regain
her grip. She pulled herself up and scrampered to the
far side of the tree, trying to hide amid the thick
branches, but her hair got caught and she couldn't
move. Tears sprang to her eyes as she yanked, ripping
several strands from her scalp.

"I see you!" Mangan called out as he stepped

around the trunk, trying to get a better look at the person he was chasing. "Come down here immediately or I will shake the tree until you fall."

Ashleigh held her breath and looked upward. The tree was young and its trunk too narrow. Although she could climb a bit higher, she would not be able to get completely out of sight.

"Last chance!" Mangan yelled as he gripped the tree trunk and gave it a preliminary shake. "Come down and admit your guilt."

Ashleigh tried to get a foothold, but the tree wobbled and she lost her balance. "No!" she screamed as she teetered. She flailed her foot, trying to find a sturdy purchase, but as Mangan shook the tree once again the branch snapped. Crying out in fear, Ashleigh plummeted downward, crashing against branches and scraping through the leaves. In desperation she curled into a ball and squeezed her eyes shut, bracing for the impact of her body against the ground; then she suddenly tumbled into a male embrace.

Mangan braced to catch his culprit, then grunted in surprise as he caught her. Expecting a wiry young boy, he was shocked to behold someone light and softly feminine. He twisted her around and using his other hand brushed the hair from her face.

"Ashleigh?" He felt frozen, unable to comprehend who was in his arms. "What . . . ? Why . . . ?"

Ashleigh struggled to be free and managed to slide out of his hold, only to became imprisoned by his grip on her arm. "Let me go!" she insisted.

Mangan shook his head, glancing around in confusion. He had been chasing someone he thought might be the culprit, yet he appeared to have accidentally captured Ashleigh. "I was following someone who was hiding in the bushes . . ." he said as his gaze drifted

back to Ashleigh's blushing face, then was drawn
down her form. "You should be careful," he murmured. Her blouse had become ripped in her fall and
it gaped away from her flesh. Mangan's heart began
beating rapidly and he tried to tear his eyes away. His
mouth went dry and he could not say more. He tried
to focus elsewhere, but his mind remained stubbornly
blank, and he could not remember why he had been
chasing her.

Ashleigh looked at him dumbfounded, her head
spinning.

Mangan blinked, feeling awkward and unsure. The
swell of her breasts should not disturb him—he was a
monk and sworn to resist all temptations—yet he
could not glance away. Her flesh looked so soft and
plush . . . so round and succulent.

"I was just walking through the forest," Ashleigh
said hesitantly, sure that he would mock her excuse
for hiding in the fringes of Eogan's farmyard.

Instead he nodded, an unusual flush darkening his
skin. He opened his mouth as if to respond, but did
not say anything.

"Is everything all right?" Ashleigh asked. She
touched his head, feeling the heat at his temples.

He shook his head and pressed it against her cool
palm.

"You have a headache," Ashleigh surmised, her
own fears forgotten as compassion filled her heart.
"My father used to get headaches. Here, give me your
hand." She reached for his hand and held it in hers.
Then, using two fingers, she squeezed the web of flesh
between his thumb and forefinger. "His mother used
to do this to help his headaches, and my mother
learned it from her. Now I will do it for you."

As she leaned forward to press harder, Mangan's

gaze slid down the curve of her breast and he saw the frilled edge of her chemise. He moaned and closed his eyes, but the image was imprinted.

"Does that feel good?" Ashleigh asked.

He nodded and opened his eyes. "Go," he whispered. "Go now, while you can."

Her brow knitted and she looked at him, not sure what he meant. Was he warning her that he knew who she was, or was it something else? Something to do with the way his body was shaking and his hands trembling?

"Go," he repeated. "I must . . . I must stay and watch for someone . . ." His voice trailed off and he turned his back on her. Then he took a deep breath. "Thank you. My headache has eased."

Ashleigh nodded. She had an urge to turn him back around and stroke his forehead, but she, too, took a deep breath. It was a miracle he had not figured out that she was the person he sought, and she should not wait for him to think any harder. She spun around and slipped through the trees toward her horse.

Mangan listened until her footsteps receded, then gave a sigh of relief. As he picked up the odd-looking sheet of polished metal the girl had left behind, he shook his head in bemusement, then tied it on his horse's saddlebag so he could return it to her when he saw her next. Tonight's vigil would be good for him. It would provide the perfect time and place to reflect upon his unruly thoughts. No matter how lovely or how tempting she was, he could not give in to his base emotions. He had a duty and a quest.

Nothing else should matter.

Cormag mounted his stolen horse and took a quick breath, relieved that Mangan had not said more about the animal. It had been stupid to ride the beast over here, but he had been so proud of the unusual steed, he couldn't wait to show him off to the other villagers, especially Shana. He had asked Shana if she would accept his courtship, and she had shyly told him to ask her father, but he was nervous about her father's answer. If Shana's father was suitably impressed with Cormag's wealth, he might look upon Cormag more favorably. Nevertheless, he shouldn't have ridden the beast to a meeting with the monk. Fortunately the monk had accepted his story and hadn't asked more questions.

Cormag turned the horse around and frowned as a raven flew directly in front of him. He gasped and made the sign of the cross. A black raven crossing your path meant that something terrible was about to happen. He glanced around, his heart thundering. Eogan's afflictions frightened him, for if his best friend had been cursed for the reason he suspected, then he, too, could become cursed.

Anxiety and guilt set the hairs on the back of Cormag's neck to tingling. They had all merely followed their laird's commands. How was a poor, uneducated peasant such as he to know what to do when the laird demanded acts that Cormag knew were sinful?

As he rode up to what appeared to be an abandoned barn behind Eogan's farmhouse, he nodded to a man posted outside the rickety door. "Osgar," he greeted him. "Is all still proceeding as the laird instructed despite the haunting of Eogan's home? We should soon receive word of when the girl will be delivered and must have the barn ready to contain her."

"Have you brought your contribution?" Osgar asked, deliberately ignoring Cormag's statement.

Cormag passed the man a bag of iron nails.

Osgar nodded acceptance and took the bag, but his gaze shifted away. "This is wrong," he said.

"We have no choice," Cormag replied.

"There are always choices," Osgar answered. "God will hold us accountable for all our deeds."

As shivers rippled down his neck, Cormag reined his horse around, kicked his sides and galloped down the road toward his home, praying that God was not watching.

As she crouched in the dense forest Ashleigh smiled, her red lips curling up in triumph while Cormag rode past her hiding place. She had escaped Mangan and now she had found another of the villains she sought. As she looked up at the sky, she laughed. Everything was working out so well!

"You fool," she whispered as she mounted her horse and urged him to follow Cormag. "You came right to me. I came to play more tricks upon Eogan, but as luck would have it you arrived. Now I have found you, and I will make you suffer as much as he." The raven swooped down and landed on her shoulder, and Ashleigh stroked his glistening feathers. "Soon, Cairdean. Soon I will have my vengeance and all will be set to rights."

But even as she started out after Cormag, her thoughts drifted back to Mangan. She did not understand why she was drawn to his powerful body, nor why she sensed the faintest sense of vulnerability beneath his monkish facade. She did not know why he seemed to want to shelter and protect her, or why he had plucked her from the cold water and saved her life, but when he was near she felt his intense power and was soothed by its presence. She suspected that he maintained tight control over his soul, for though he walked softly and spoke quietly like a monk, he moved with a predator's grace.

He elicited strange emotions within her. Conflicting, confusing emotions that she could not untangle.

Chapter 9

Ashleigh followed the man on horseback until the sun sank behind the mountain and dusk overtook the land. She had left her disappearing plate behind and hoped that Mangan would not notice it, for she intended to pick it up after she determined where Cormag lived. When she was beginning to wonder how far away Cormag's home was, he finally turned off the road and headed up a rough path to another farmhouse. Unlike the first, this one had a small yard, and there was an unkempt air about the place. No flowers decorated the planters, and leaves were piled high against the log pile left untended from the past season.

A storehouse and chicken coop were located adjacent to the cottage, and there was a stable farther away. The man was in the process of unsaddling and feeding the smoky gray horse.

"My horse," Ashleigh hissed. "He has my horse." She swung off her mount and looped the reins over a tree branch. The horse had pricked his ears forward as soon as he had smelled his former companion and was acting a bit agitated. "Don't fuss," Ashleigh soothed. "I will get him back for us, and we will all be together again."

The raven fluttered and peered at the stable.

I will make that man suffer, Ashleigh silently vowed. *I will make him fear the very fire and water that he takes for granted.* She patted her pocket, where she had stowed a few items she had salvaged from her parents' wagon. The things this man had discarded as useless were the very ones her father had collected to produce his feats of magic, and she was ready to turn them against her enemy.

Pulling forth a stick her father had dyed, Ashleigh smiled grimly. When Cormag lit a fire in his stove, this dyed stick would produce eerie green flames and pungent smoke, a combination sure to frighten anyone.

Ashleigh bent over and raced around the edge of the farmyard then slipped through the front door while the man worked in the stable. Knowing she had little time, Ashleigh buried her stick in a pile of kindling near the stove, then spun around and located the man's cracked cup. She sprinkled some white powder into the cup, then searched for the jug of water she knew should be stored somewhere near the table. Sure enough, the man had filled a jug from the well and left it on the floor next to the table and bench. Grinning, Ashleigh poured the water onto the floor, then extracted a wineskin from underneath her blouse. She uncapped the wineskin, then added a few measures of rancid wine to the water jug. The wine was made from white grapes and was nearly clear, it had only a faint odor, which made it ideal for this particular trick. All the man had to do was pour the clear wine into his cup that contained the white powder, and the cup would immediately begin spewing foam like a devil erupting from the bowels of hell.

Ashleigh heard the stable door slam shut and footsteps approach the cottage. She gasped. He was returning too soon! She was looking frantically for a place to hide when she heard his exclamation of annoyance.

"Damn raven! Get away from me store bins! And me chickens! Auch!" His steps abruptly changed direction as he headed for the storage shed. "Begone!"

Ashleigh darted to the window, tumbled out, then sprinted for the trees, amazed once again at the cleverness of her newfound friend. Without him she might have been caught! Instead she hunkered down and smothered a giggle. Cairdean had opened the chicken coop and sent the chickens squawking around the yard in a frenzy of activity while Cormag raced to and fro, trying to gather them all up again. Ashleigh spied Cairdean perched upon the rooftop, his head cocked and his beady eyes watching the melee with what could be construed as amusement.

Finally the man collected his chickens, returned them to the coop and secured the latch, all the while grumbling at the raven. Then, with a final glare at the black-feathered beast, he stomped to his cottage and ducked inside.

Ashleigh whistled, and Cairdean immediately flew from his perch and landed on a branch near her. "You are wonderful! Now let's go watch him through the window." She smiled as the bird glided from tree to tree, following her as she crept closer to get a good view. "Watch," she whispered. "He is lighting his stove."

After a few false starts the man started a small fire. He then threw a bundle of kindling on the flickering flames and sat on his bench with a sigh. He reached for his cup with one hand while picking up the water jug with the other, ready to relax and take a deep draft of cool water.

"Shana . . ." he muttered as he raised his cup. "To the most beautiful woman in the village. May God bless me with a wife, for I'm in sore need of a woman. If Shana were here me home would be tidy, me dinner would be cooking and I'd be looking forward to a warm bedmate. Instead all I have is a measly fire . . ." He glanced at the fire and frowned. Intermixed in the orange and yellow flames were several flickers of green. He sniffed. Ashleigh knew it smelled awful . . . like the stench of burning flesh.

Turning from the fire, he poured water from the jug into his cup and prepared to take a deep swallow. Suddenly foam filled the cup, erupting from the bottom and spilling over the sides. Cormag shrieked in horror and flung the cup across the room as he leaped to his feet and sent the bench crashing backward.

A loud crack in the stove drew his terrified gaze. Leaping green flames engulfed the fire, dancing like ghoulish spirits upon the darkening embers.

"What?" Cormag gasped as he stumbled backward, tripping over the fallen bench and smashing his head against the table edge. "Ohhhh!" He rolled to his feet and tried to stand, but the stench made him nauseous, and he fell to his knees and vomited on the floor.

Gasping and retching, he clambered once more to his feet, gripping the table edge for support. Through a haze of green smoke, he saw a figure standing at his window. Black hair. Black eyes. A black raven on her shoulder.

His eyes rolled up in his head and he fainted dead away.

Ashleigh smiled, her eyes slanting in wicked glee.

Then she walked to the stable and tied a rope around her horse's neck, led him out and retrieved her second horse. "Franco and Francis. 'Tis good to have both of you back again," she whispered. As Cairdean flew above her, Ashleigh mounted and rode out of Cormag's yard, back to her forest hideaway.

Early the next morning church bells rang, startling Mangan from his steady perusal of Eogan's home. He had remained awake all night, using both his years as a soldier and his training as a monk to stay alert and ready throughout the nighttime hours.

The only thing he had noticed last night was the man sleeping in front of an old barn. After watching the man for several hours, he had concluded that the man was fixing the barn for Eogan's family in exchange for a temporary abode, for the man had hammered and sawed for hours, then fallen asleep in a bedroll after the sunlight had faded.

After the moon had risen and Mangan had spent many hours in meditation, he had felt God's forgiveness. God was not angry with him. To the contrary, Mangan felt closer and more understood by God than he ever had before. God knew his faults. He knew that the dark angel presented temptation to Mangan, yet he still accepted Mangan as his son. The dark angel needed his help, not his fear.

God understood and forgave. All would be well.

Mangan's brows drew together and he stood up. No one had come close to Eogan's farm, so why were the bells clamoring?

Eogan's wife peeked out the door, peered around the yard, then popped back inside. A clang announced her jamming a sturdy branch into the metal clamps that acted as internal locks—locks that were rarely used unless heavy winds threatened to blow open the door.

Mangan relieved himself, withdrew a piece of bread for sustenance, then mounted his horse and headed for town. It did not make sense. If someone had a grudge against Eogan, then all of the villain's efforts would have been focused upon him and his household. Why was someone else being targeted? Who was it this time? What was happening in this deceptively simple mountain village that would drive a person to such acts of revenge?

When Mangan arrived at the village center, he met the perturbed gazes of the elders. "Cormag," Eo'Ghanan informed Mangan immediately. "The devil came to Cormag last night and cursed him."

"The devil did not come," Mangan replied calmly. "Someone is—"

"Listen to his tale," Eo'Ghanan interrupted. "Cormag's fire cast dead spirits into the air, and his cup filled with the devil's own breath."

"Bring me to his house," Mangan commanded. "I will see for myself."

Eo'Ghanan led Mangan to Cormag's farmhouse, for Cormag himself refused to go back there. Once they arrived, Mangan looked around the yard and was surprised to notice the vast difference between this home and Eogan's. Certainly no one would begrudge Cormag his place. He had no possessions of value, and his land was rocky and untilled. One could surmise that Eogan's misfortune had been a result of jealousy, but there was nothing here that anyone would covet.

Then why had both Eogan and Cormag been attacked? He knew the two men were friends and had recently ridden together to investigate Branan's whereabouts. Could that be the link? But why would looking for someone outside of the village incite animosity within it?

Inside the cottage Mangan picked up the broken cup. He sniffed it, smelling the residue of poor-quality wine. "I'm thinking his delusions were exaggerated by the state of his drunkenness."

"He doesn't drink," Eo'Ghanan said. "Even before his wife passed away, he lived a pious life."

"Losing someone you love can change a man," Mangan cautioned.

"Not Cormag. He is a good man."

"Like Eogan?"

"Aye. Like Eogan."

"Don't you think it odd that two seemingly good men are suddenly being cursed by the devil?" Mangan questioned. "If they are so godly, then they should be protected by God's grace. That is, if you still believe that this is the work of a spirit and not a person."

Eo'Ghanan's gaze was troubled. He shrugged. " 'Tis not for me to understand. That is why He sent you."

"Well, I have found little here to help me," Mangan said. "We should collect his horse and bring it back to the village if no one is going to stay out here and feed it."

"Cormag doesn't have a horse. The stable is empty. He has only a mule, and it stays in the pasture. No need to bring it to the village, but I will send someone each day to check on the chickens and collect the eggs."

Mangan shook his head. "Cormag told me yesterday that he had recently found a gray horse. I saw it myself."

Eo'Ghanan opened the stable door and peered inside at the empty stall. "Ye must have been mistaken.

He was probably borrowing someone else's because his mule is so cussedly ornery."

Two horses missing. Two horses that the other villagers denied knowing about. If no one knew about the steeds, where had they come from? What was going on? "Show me which direction they went that Sunday when they discovered the traveler's untended fire. I would like to see what they found," said Mangan.

As Eo'Ghanan pointed up the mountainside, Mangan glanced around the unkempt yard, his mind racing. Never before on his quest had he felt this tingling excitement. He felt an energy here . . . something vibrating just under the surface, something important but unsaid. God wanted him to find something here. God wanted him to help these people.

It wasn't just Eogan and Cormag; nor was it only Eo'Ghanan and the elders. It was more. It was the girl who had massaged his feet—Ashleigh, the beautiful angel with wounded eyes. It was why an unknown assailant was plaguing these villagers, and it was why his last clue had pointed him toward this mountain.

Look higher, my son, the old man had said. *Look higher and deeper for the answer to your questions. Deep in the Scottish mountains.*

Mangan felt his heart pumping. Swinging up on his horse, he absently checked his sword, pulling it slightly out of the scabbard and then snapping it back in place in an unconscious habit. His green eyes glittered, and blood rushed through his body. Just as on the eve of battle, his senses came alive and he felt invigorated, yet this time there was no underlying guilt.

It was here. He felt it deep in his bones. What he needed . . . what he had been sent to find . . . it was here on this mountain. He felt energized and inspired.

"You must take care," Eo'Ghanan cautioned Mangan. " 'Tis dangerous for those who stray off the road."

"Dangerous? How so?" Mangan asked, his muscles already twitching with impatience.

"Be wary of other riders. I suggest that you turn a blind eye to any traveling highborn men, and it would be best to remain out of sight."

"Why would nobles travel off the road, and why should I avoid them if they do?"

Eo'Ghanan shrugged, his gaze skittering from Mangan's. "I can say no more."

"Indeed," Mangan replied. He stared at the elder man and tried to read his shuttered face. The man had spoken softly so that the others could not hear, and Mangan sensed that Eo'Ghanan did not want anyone to know of his warning. "Is the trickster a highborn noble causing the village's distress?" Mangan questioned quietly. "Could it be a son who is amused by taunting his father's people?"

Eo'Ghanan shook his head. "No. The problems here are . . . vastly different." Eo'Ghanan looked over his shoulder toward where one of the younger men was glaring at them. "Please, I truly can say no more without endangering my friends and family. Go . . . travel up the mountain and search for answers, for I cannot offer any here."

Mangan turned his stallion and pointed him toward the mountain, its trees, bushes, flowers and occasional rocky crags a testament to the beauty of God's creation. Mangan took a deep breath and let the awesome sight overtake him.

The mountain was calling him. He would follow an unknown, unmarked path and accept his destiny, for he knew it was waiting for him somewhere deep within this Highland forest.

Mangan kicked his horse and sent him cantering through the trees. He was ready. Ready for whatever God desired.

Chapter 10

Mangan rode for several hours, using a grid search technique he had learned in the army. Crossing back and forth was slow and tedious, but it ensured that he did not miss anything. He located several horse tracks, but they appeared to be old, and he discounted them as from highborn nobles' horses. Peasants did not waste iron on horse's hooves when they had many more important uses for ore.

Just as he was about to pull some food from his saddlebag, he heard a woman's voice up ahead. His hunger forgotten, he urged his horse forward and circled around a large, uprooted tree and a pile of jumbled rocks. If this area was considered dangerous, why was she up here? Who was with her? And then, a thought only partially formed, could it be *her*, the woman who had so easily penetrated his holy reserve and disrupted his thoughts? And if so, what a glorious sound. If in rescuing Ashleigh from the stream he had given her one more wonderful day in which to appreciate life, then he had fulfilled a portion of his duty.

He heard her laughing, and the sound sent shivers down his back. It was as lovely as tinkling springwater and as rich as cream. He pulled his horse to a stop and

held his breath, entranced by the sound. The desire to
see her was strong, too strong. She was temptation.

But even as he resolved to turn away, he swung
down and walked forward, remembering that he had
her metal sheet, which he was obligated to return. He
knew it was only an excuse, but he latched onto the
thought and ducked through the branches toward her.
Her black eyes had said something to him, yet he had
left without fully understanding. Perhaps if he saw her
again her spell would lessen. Perhaps God wanted him
to confront his fears. She would become just another
pretty face he passed in his travels, one he could easily
forget, as he had all the others.

He spotted a meadow. Glorious purple and golden
flowers shimmered through the trees, drawing him to
where she was frolicking. He heard her running steps,
then her giggles, and imagined her dropping to the
ground and rolling amid the flowers. His keen senses,
honed over years of brutal necessity, now allowed him
to visualize her actions in precise detail. The spin of
her heel—she was not wearing shoes—the swish of
her skirts.

She was talking, but he could not sense anyone else
nearby. Cocking his head, he concentrated. The birds
twittered evenly in every direction, and there were no
abnormal sounds of branches breaking or leaves crunching underfoot. He could not hear another's voice, nor
the cadence of another's breath. She was alone.

He ducked under a tree limb and stepped into the
clearing, then caught his breath in surprise.

It was Ashleigh, but she was *not* alone. She was
crouched on all fours staring into the soft brown eyes
of a spotted fawn, while the mother doe grazed several
feet away. As the fawn wobbled a few steps closer,
Ashleigh sat back on her heels and laughed.

"Here is another!" She giggled, holding out a clump of clover. The fawn stretched her delicate muzzle forward and nibbled the clover out of Ashleigh's hand. Suddenly Ashleigh bounded to her feet and raced around the meadow. The fawn gamboled after her, tossing her head and flicking her tail. The mother lifted her head and watched the pair, then twitched her ears and returned to grazing.

Darting left and right, Ashleigh kept just ahead of the fawn. She pulled her skirts up past her knees and leaped over a log partially buried in the grass, then ran as fast as she could straight through a clump of tall flowers, laughing as the petals tumbled around her and covered her hair in a fine mist of yellow pollen.

She shook her head and dashed a lock of hair from her face as the fawn scrambled after her; then she turned in search of another game, when she spotted Mangan standing at the edge of the meadow. She froze, her posture a tableau of shock.

"You must have a beautiful spirit if the creatures of the forest accept you as one of their own," he said softly.

The mother doe's head sprang up and she snorted. The fawn skidded to a stop and looked at Mangan with curiosity. Mangan remained still and unthreatening, waiting for Ashleigh's reaction, fearing that she would flee but hoping she would welcome him into her lovely playground.

"You . . ." Ashleigh breathed. "You found me."

The fawn darted sideways and raced to her mother's side, then picked her way awkwardly over the ferns as the doe scampered out of the meadow and into the forest.

"I made your friend leave," Mangan said. "You were having fun and I disturbed you."

"She will come back when she wants to."

Mangan smiled. "Good. It was nice to hear you laughing. The first time I saw you—"

"Why are you here?" Ashleigh asked. "Did you bring others?" She dropped her skirts and looked around nervously.

"Only me. I am searching for a campfire lit several nights ago."

"Have you found it?"

He shook his head. "I have found nothing."

Ashleigh's tension eased and she looked at him, assessing. "Nothing?"

He lifted his hands and shook his head again. "I am a poor investigator. Although I am searching for a man who holds a grudge against members of the village, I have come across only old horse tracks and a lovely young lass playing with a fawn. What am I going to tell the elders?"

Ashleigh smiled, and a rosy blush transformed her face. "You should tell them you found nothing and that they should search within themselves for the true culprit."

"Indeed I will, for I think you may be right. I sense there is more to this situation than a few harmless tricks. Do you know what is plaguing the village?"

Her smile turned into a full grin and she twirled around in a circle. Her black locks spun around her head and petals fluttered to the ground. "I am happy today," she said as she lifted her hands and spun faster. "Today is a good day! I don't want to talk about terrible things."

He stepped closer, entranced by her unrestrained joy. This young woman was a child of contradictory emotions, either desolate and hopeless or ecstatic and full of life. She climbed trees and gamboled in meadows. In contrast, he endeavored to remain calm and predictable, rejecting extreme emotions for fear they would recall the memories he tried so hard to forget.

She stopped, then teetered back and forth, dizzy from her spinning. She laughed as she tried to stay upright, but careened sideways in a collision course with Mangan. Unable, or perhaps unwilling, to move out of her way, he was forced to catch her, pulling her close against his chest as she collapsed in a fit of giggles.

Her lush body molded instantly to his, and she wrapped her hands around his neck. "Stop moving!" she scolded him.

"I am not moving," he informed her as he held her arms. "Your mind is spinning."

"They were not afraid of you, either," she replied.

He frowned, not following her meaning.

"The deer. They were not afraid of you, either. That means you must be a good man."

He stared down at her in bemusement. The sapphire blue centers of her eyes were brighter in the sunshine, and her long lashes looked soft and thick. "You are an odd one," he said as he carefully set her feet on the grass. She folded her legs and sat down. "You do not trust my robes, but you trust the opinion of a doe and fawn."

"Your robes are only clothes. They do not define the man."

Mangan lowered himself beside her, his face suddenly serious. "In my world a man is either a warrior or a monk, and one knows the difference by the way he dresses. But your words are wise and worthy of thought. 'Tis something my father would tell me."

"Mine, too."

"Why is today a happy day?" he asked her, trying to erase the sudden sadness that flitted over her face at the mention of her father. "What would make a young woman like you so full of glee?"

I recaptured Francis, my other horse, and found the second man.

Her lips spread into a saucy smile. "I found someone."

"Someone?"

"Aye."

"A man?"

She pressed the tip of her finger to her lips. "Yes. A man."

A cloud passed over Mangan's heart, and he turned away to stare across the meadow. This was foolish. He was a monk. He had just reminded her of his vocation, and now it was time to remind himself. She was a fresh young woman whom he did not know at all. Why should hearing that she had found a man upset him? "A man to marry," Mangan surmised, his voice flat and controlled.

Ashleigh's eyebrows rose. *Marry?*

" 'Tis a good thing," Mangan continued. "You should be under a man's protection now that your parents have passed away. It must be very difficult for you. Perhaps your husband can help you through this turbulent time."

"What would I do with a husband?" Ashleigh asked in confusion.

Not understanding her question, Mangan looked back at her and gently stroked her cheek. "You will find out. I pray that the man you choose will be good to you and treat you with gentle consideration."

"What is your meaning? What . . ." She paused and

stared into his eyes. Something flickered within the green depths. Hunger. Need. They intrigued her. "How should this man treat me?"

"Like a precious flower whose very scent brings beauty to his soul."

She trembled and her lips parted.

He touched her mouth, rubbing his thumb across the fullness.

"Will he kiss me?" she asked tremulously.

"Aye," he answered huskily. "Most definitely."

"Should I let him?"

"Yes, you should. You must. It will be your duty."

"How? How will I kiss him?"

"Open your mouth wider . . ." He pressed on her lower lip, grazing her teeth, and gently opened her mouth, moist and inviting.

Her tongue swept forward and she licked her lips, her tongue sliding over his thumb. Her breathing quickened, and the sense of dizziness she had felt earlier returned, only this time it was the rest of the world that spun, and only he remained still. She leaned closer, seeking his strength, drawn by his magnetism, remembering the sculpted lines of his bare chest in the moonlight.

She wanted to taste him.

She lifted her chin and closed her eyes. "Show me. Kiss me."

He wanted to. He could already taste the heady ambrosia of her welcoming mouth and sense the blazing heat of her wanton caress. He could see her midnight tresses splayed against the purple and yellow flowers as their bodies crushed the meadow grasses.

He shuddered and yanked his hand away. "God forgive me," he whispered as he rose to his feet. "You are an innocent and know not what you are doing, and I am a man of God who must remain pure of body."

Her eyes opened and she looked warily up at him.

"Why are you out here all alone?" he accused her as he sought to control his responses. His holy robes chafed his neck, and the belt felt unusually tight. "You should stay within the boundaries of the village where it is safe, not romp in the unprotected vales of the forest. Things can happen to girls like you if you do not take care to stay closer to home. I hear that many have traveled this way recently."

She frowned. His voice was rough and he looked angry. "Did I do something wrong?" she asked.

He shook his head. "No, my child. You . . . you are perfect. 'Tis I who am tainted. I must continue my search, while you must return to the village and wed your sweetheart. I . . . I cannot be near you anymore."

She rose and faced him, her gaze shielded. She had forgotten that he was searching for her. For a moment she had forgotten the horror of her parents' deaths and her vow of vengeance, and most important, she had forgotten that this monk had become her prime enemy. He was seeking her, and should he find out who she really was, he would ruin all her plans. No matter what odd feelings he generated in the pit of her stomach, she needed him to leave the mountain so she could continue undeterred in her revenge. "Why can you not be near me?" she asked.

"You are temptation." He took a step away from her, but his gaze remained locked on hers. "I think of you . . . I imagine you with me . . . 'Tis wrong, and I must repent my lustful thoughts."

She took a deep breath, noting that Mangan's gaze was immediately drawn to the swell of her cleavage.

She walked hesitantly up to him and placed a cautious hand upon his chest. He shuddered and stepped back, causing Ashleigh to gasp in surprise. He was reacting to her touch as a man reacted to a woman. Thrills rippled up her spine as his eyes flared.

Boldly this time she stepped after him, her head tilted at a coy angle. "Will you show me what I must know? Will you show me how to kiss, Brother Mangan? And after that what else will you teach me? I am not certain what happens between a man and a woman, and I should learn more before I agree to enter the marriage bed. Can you show me all the mysteries?"

"Stop. Do not say such things. Not to me. I am a monk. These are things that you must ask your mother."

"My mother is dead. Won't you help me?" She licked her finger, then pressed it against his mouth.

He grabbed her wrist with punishing force and shoved her backward. "Stop! 'Tis near blasphemy to act this way toward a man of God. Why do you tease me when I have confessed my weakness?"

Snatching her wrist free, she challenged him. "But this is where I came to think of these things, and you entered my private meadow. If you are not comfortable with me, then I suggest you leave. Leave the mountain and leave the village, but especially leave me alone."

His fists clenched, and he felt a surge of white-hot anger. How dared this woman taunt him and then mock his response? How dared she act so disrespectful toward a man of the cloth? "I offer my deepest apologies," he said through gritted teeth. "I will not trespass again." With the last of his control he managed to turn his back on her without exploding, then strode out of the meadow and snatched up the reins of his horse.

How had he gotten tangled in this woman's web? She made him think of things better left forgotten. She caused him to lose control of both his passion and his anger. He gripped the pommel of his saddle and swung up in a fluid motion, his muscles painfully tense with the effort to remain outwardly calm. With a quick backward glance toward where Ashleigh stood, he shot her an angry glare as he yanked his sword from its scabbard and pointed it at the sky.

His arm vibrated with coiled energy. A tall, solid tree stood next to him, and he had the urge to attack it with his blade. He wanted to expel his frustrations in the way he knew best. Hacking . . . swinging . . . using his sword as an outlet for his fury.

She returned his look, her black eyes glittering with unspoken emotion as a stray breeze cast a few strands of hair across her face. He was majestic, and her body quivered with awakened desire. He was no illusion; he was flesh and blood, and his weapon was made of pounded steel and inlaid gold. A flick of his wrist and she would be felled, yet his sword was not what frightened her. It was how he made her feel . . . something in his fierce gaze . . . something nameless hovering in the depths of his green eyes that nearly brought her to her knees.

Mangan struggled with his soul . . . his battle-hardened body warred with his beliefs. He wanted to attack, but he did not want to harm. Emitting a feral growl, he finally broke eye contact and sheathed his sword. In a battle of strength he would win against this dark angel, but in a battle of wills he surrendered. For all her small size and delicate features he felt powerless against her. Having no choice but to retreat, he thrummed his heels into his horse's sides and sent the stallion galloping down the hill.

As he left Ashleigh pressed her knuckles to her lips to still their trembling. Her own heart thundered, and her thoughts were in turmoil. His gaze had burned her, and his fingers had imprinted themselves upon her wrist. The sight of his raised sword had emblazoned itself on her mind, and she could see nothing except his challenging stance. He had retreated, but had she won? Or had she lit an innocent fire within her own heart that now blazed out of control?

If only she had not seen him that night. Not seen his naked flesh shining in the moonlight like that of a god of yesteryear. If only he had not held her close and infused her with a strange, intangible sensation that tickled her toes and made her feel light-headed. Had it been wise to play with something she did not understand?

And what about tomorrow? She was only a stone's throw from where her horses were tethered and her cave was located, and if he had not been so distracted he might have discovered them.

The raven swooped down and dropped a ball of string on the ground next to her. He had spent the day foraging and had returned several times with new bits of this and that. Ashleigh leaned down and picked up the ball, a sad smile stealing across her face. "Cairdean, you are a clever collector and a true friend." Ashleigh bounced the ball of string in her hand, trying to quash the sensations Mangan had aroused. She must stay true to her course. Her passion . . . her desire was nothing compared to what she must do.

Thinking over the tricks her father had taught her, Ashleigh began to develop a new strategy. Before refocusing on the peasants she had to remove Mangan.

He was too smart and had been too close to discovering the truth for her to ignore. Soon he would realize that she was the culprit.

She needed to do something that would scare even Mangan. Something that would make him depart immediately and forever. Something that would make him believe the land was cursed.

He was becoming more than just a nuisance. He was twisting her into knots and upsetting her balance. Each time she encountered him she was more helpless to resist his allure. In only a matter of time she would lose sight of her motives and beg to be held within his embrace.

He was a monk. He did not want this passion any more than she did. They were both trapped in an escalating torrent whose currents were too strong.

For both of them, there was only one answer.

It was time he left the mountain.

Chapter 11

That afternoon Ashleigh rummaged through Cairdean's piles, finding all sorts of oddities, then made
her way back to the burnt remains of her family's
wagon. A small set of clay jars lay tumbled about,
their outer surfaces charred. Ashleigh opened several,
and was relieved to find most of their contents
undisturbed.

She had noticed the cross Mangan wore around his
neck on a beaded chain. Made of steel and copper,
the cross was simple and elegant. Using some rancid
wine she could turn the cross into rust overnight, a
trick sure to fill a monk with fear. In addition she
would prepare some purple water by boiling cabbage,
then place some of his foodstuffs in the water and
stain them. Items such as celery and lettuce would
absorb the purple coloring and change from the inside
out, appearing to an unsuspecting person as a magical
transformation of green to purple.

Lastly, she created a stick figure with small branches
and string, then wrapped some filmy remnants of
clothing over the sticks to simulate clothes. If viewed
from afar and in the darkness of a moonlit eve, Ash-

leigh hoped the figure would look like a spirit floating in the air.

The sun was setting as she finished her preparations, and Ashleigh gathered one of her horses from the makeshift corral she had designed to hold them. She knew where he was camped. If all went well she would frighten him off the mountain tonight and be free to resume her revenge tomorrow.

But even as the thoughts ran through her mind, she felt an unusual tingling in her heart, something oddly similar to remorse.

She had killed one man already. Killed him in a fit of rage while her parents' blood still wet the earth and their eyes still glistened with moisture. She had not planned the act, had barely comprehended what she was doing as she thrust the blade into the man's chest. It had been an impulse she could not control, but now she was lucid. She knew what she was doing. Unlike before, when she had reacted without thinking, she was now methodically planning the destruction of the other five men, and something inside her cringed at her evil intentions.

Would her mother approve of her actions? Would she want her daughter to deliberately plan murder?

Ashleigh shuddered and took a deep breath. She was weakening when she must remain strong. No one would force the men to face justice unless she acted, and the monk was directly interfering with her plans. He must be removed—one way or another.

Ignoring the twinges of guilt, she swung her horse around and headed for Mangan's camp, found a secluded site near his campfire from which she could see him without being seen, and settled in to wait for nightfall.

Was he supposed to follow God's path?

If so, he was failing.

A dark cloud covered the moon, and the forest closed in around him. Even the gentle trickling of the stream seemed to taunt him as her name echoed within the water's flow. *Ashleigh . . . Ashhhhhhleigh.*

Mangan drew his cross over his head and clenched it in his palm until the copper wires dug painfully into his hand. Why were his emotions so turbulent? He knew nothing about her life, her goals or her ambitions. He did not know if she enjoyed music or dancing. All he knew was that she was a frightened, lonely young woman who had been orphaned.

He shook his head and drew in a deep breath. It didn't seem right. Her sorrow had been too deep, her feelings too raw for such a rapid recovery. How could she so easily forget her pain? His own horror still haunted him night and day. Was she truly so thoughtless, or was she hiding from her own emotions? His head started pounding as he recalled her answer. *Yes, a man*, she had replied when he had questioned her.

She must be burying her sorrow by running into the arms of a sweetheart.

He bowed his head, unable to face the truth that he wished she would run to him. He wanted to save her. He *needed* to save her.

In a burst of anger he flung his cross deep into the forest. "Why?" he thundered as he fell to his knees and glared at the black sky. "Why have our paths crossed? What cruel twist of fate have you cast upon me? Is this my punishment?"

Ashleigh was startled awake as his words reverberated around the campsite. She realized that she had fallen asleep and that the moon was already sliding down the far horizon past the midnight zenith. Something at her feet shimmered in the faint light, and she struggled to disentangle herself from her shawl to view it more clearly, but as she moved she accidentally knocked over her pot of rancid wine, drenching the object.

She gasped and snatched up the jar, then froze as Mangan leaped to his feet and shot a piercing glare into the darkness.

She pressed herself against the tree, desperately hoping he could not see her even as he drew his sword from its scabbard.

"Who goes there?" he said, the menace in his voice sending tremors down her back. "Think not to sneak upon me, for I am no easy target."

Ashleigh took a careful step back, sliding around the tree and clenching her eyes tightly closed. *Please, no,* she prayed. *Don't let him find me.*

Opening her eyes, she looked into the branches, hoping to see Cairdean, but for once her new friend was nowhere near.

She could just barely hear Mangan's stealthy footsteps as he moved from his campsite and entered the dense darkness of the forest. She clutched the tree behind her as her heart raced and her breathing quickened. Perhaps he would stop a few strides deep, give up and assume the noise had been a nocturnal creature.

His nearly imperceptible footsteps came closer, and Ashleigh tensed. She knew she should remain still, but her head was thrumming and she was dizzy with fear. He was coming, and she feared not only his sword but also his piercing green eyes and his powerful shoulders.

A breeze brushed across her face, and she caught her breath to hold back a scream.

Mangan paused. Years of training rushed through his limbs, and he held his sword in an experienced grip. No longer a monk, he was a warrior, a man with acute senses and merciless skill.

He felt someone nearby. He could hear breathing as a faint whisper amid the leaves, and the thundering heart of a trapped soul. Energy rippled through him, invigorating and exciting.

Ashleigh couldn't stop herself. She burst into full flight, fleeing deeper into the woods. She was smaller and lighter, and if she ran fast enough she might be able to lose him in the thickets. Nearly blinded with fear, she stumbled over logs and flailed through thorny bushes, urged forward by the sound of his heavy footsteps.

She bolted down a sharp decline, then tripped and rolled several feet, bruising her arm and ripping her hair. But as she struggled upright, she saw his shadow reach the top and start down after her. Crying now, using her hands and feet, she churned up the other side of the depression as decades of accumulated dirt and debris made her slip and slide backward as quickly as she scrambled forward.

"No!" she screamed as her clawing hands grasped a root. She yanked herself up, managing to get half-way up the incline and onto firmer ground.

Mangan leaped down the slope and reached for his prey, gripping the trailing edge of a dark cloak. Battle lust surged through his blood, and he had an over-whelming need to overpower and dominate, to master and claim victory. He would win this race through the forest. He would win and make his victim beg for clemency.

Ashleigh struggled out of her cloak and left it dangling in his hands. She bolted forward, then darted to the right, where a decayed and hollowed log lay in the darkness. She dropped to her stomach and wriggled inside, shaking her head as bits of bark and wood-eating insects fluttered down upon her shoulders. Holding her breath, she stilled, hoping that he would jump out of the depression and run straight over her hiding place.

Mangan slid once, then dug the toe of his boot into the soft earth, gripped a root and pulled himself out. He took several running steps, then paused to listen. Holding his sword in his right hand, he cocked his head and shrank down in a fighting stance. He glanced up at the trees, aware that someone could pounce on him from above, but no unusual shapes disturbed the shifting leaves. He scanned the ground, looking for a trail, but even his vision could not pierce the darkness for subtle signs of broken twigs or disturbed pebbles.

A sound in the distance made him jerk, and he almost shot off after it, but something made him wait. His prey was here. He could feel it. The person he sought was hiding nearby, breathing, pulsing . . . waiting for him.

He looked around again, this time moving his eyes slowly, searching for the clue he knew was there. A large boulder . . . a thin deer trail . . . a hollowed log. He smiled, one half of his lips curling upward. Padding forward, he moved with catlike grace and circled around to the other side of the log. Then, striking fast, he thrust his arm into the log and grasped the soft flesh hidden within, yanked her out, then flung her to the ground at his feet.

Ashleigh screamed and kicked. "Stop!" she shouted, but he gripped the edges of her blouse and wrenched her upright, then shoved her against a tree trunk.

"You again!" he hissed.

"Let me go!" Ashleigh screamed, pounding her fists against his chest and tossing her head back and forth as she tried to jerk free of his tight hold.

Repressed passion burst free, and blind desire engulfed his reason, setting loose the wild beast within. It was his dark angel, the very woman who had inflamed his ardor and become his obsession. She intruded upon his thoughts and made him question his sanity, and now here she was, at his mercy.

He tossed his sword aside, then twisted his hands in her black hair and pulled it back, baring her throat. Using his other hand he captured her flailing fists and pinned them against the tree trunk over her head.

Ducking his head, he bit her throat and sucked, filling his senses with the rich, womanly musk of her skin.

She groaned, the heady sensation of his lips making her weak and disoriented. She arched, drawing her head aside even as her body pressed closer. "Stop . . ." she whispered, her voice tremulous and thready. Nothing had prepared her for this assault. His intense seduction spread fire through her blood, instantly drowning her fear in waves of passion.

She gasped and his mouth swept up her neck to her lips. His heated kiss consumed her as his tongue plunged into her innocent mouth and took command of all her senses. The feel of him, the scent of him . . . his powerful body towering over her. His panting breaths, his whispered denials . . .

He devoured her, drinking her breath with the desperation of a parched man. "No . . ." he murmured even as he loosened his grip on her hair and slid his hand up her forearm to her soft palm. "What have you done to me?"

He lifted her, pulling her more tightly against his

body so she could feel the thrust of his cock through their layers of clothing. "I want you . . ." he growled. "I want you now."

"Oh, God," she cried as she lifted her arms around his neck. "Yes. Whatever you want, I will give you."

With an inhuman howl he thrust her away, sending her sprawling in the ferns. "No! You call upon God?" he questioned, his face twisted in agony. " 'Tis I who must seek his guidance!" He spun around, gasping for breath. He wanted her so badly, his body screamed for release. His chest burned and his stomach rolled with need, yet he had pledged to forsake bodily pleasures. "I must go . . . You are . . . You should not be here. I have a beast within me that I cannot control. I am too weak . . . too unworthy. Go! Go far from me and I will go far from here!" Grabbing his sword he stumbled away, guilt ripping through his gut like the dull edge of a rusty knife.

Ashleigh struggled to rise as he crashed through the bushes and disappeared into the darkness. What had happened? What had she said? One moment she had been running for her life, the next clinging to him for sustenance only he could provide.

She reached out, wanting him back, then covered her face as confusion welled from deep within her and tears began pouring down her cheeks. What had she done? He was the enemy!

She collapsed in a sobbing heap as her body quivered and her bruised lips trembled with the memory of his kiss. Everything was going so wrong!

She grabbed a fistful of dirt and flung it at the shadows. "What is happening?" she screamed. "What am I feeling? Why is he . . ." Her voice trailed off, and she stared up at the stars, imploring them for help. "All I want is to avenge my parents' deaths. Is that so wrong? Should I be punished with such unfamiliar feelings when all I seek is to right a terrible iniquity? Why put this man in my path? Why hinder my justice?"

As Ashleigh pleaded with the night sky, Mangan raced through the trees, his own soul twisted in agony. She could not be real. No woman could plunge her talons into a man's heart with so little effort. She was sent from the devil or flung upon the soil by an angry spirit. The villagers were right: Spirits were haunting their mountain.

Something white fluttered above his head, and he jumped back in surprise when he beheld what looked like a ghost hovering in the trees. Dropping to his knees, he cried out in fear. God was angry! He had failed in his duty and let the temptations of sin turn him from the true path.

The *ting* of his sword touching metal drew his gaze downward, and he saw his blade pressed against his cross half-buried in the earth. The polished copper reflected an eerie green, and the steel appeared old and corroded.

Clutching the cross in his hand and stumbling to his feet, he tore through the last row of bushes and plunged into the stream, submerging himself in the icy waters. "What are you trying to tell me?" he shouted. "Are you telling me that I am evil? That my past deeds have forever excluded me from finding peace?"

Rolling onto his back, half in and half out of the stream, he stared up at the moon, trying to still the trembling of his limbs. He was losing control.

He took a deep breath and focused on recalling a prayer. He had maintained strict control in the heat of the bloodiest battle. He had stayed calm even when his men's innards had spilled out onto the earth. No little black-eyed, black-haired woman, no matter how mysterious or how beautiful, should affect him this way.

She was a mortal.

He was a man of God.

Yet they were being drawn together by an inexorable force, and he was helpless to resist her lure.

Mangan sat up and climbed slowly out of the water.

Why had she been here tonight? Why had she been hiding in the bushes behind Eogan's home? Why did such a lovely woman wander alone on the mountain?

It must be her. She must be the culprit he was seeking, but he dared not confront her. If he were ever near her again, he knew he would be unable to control his passions.

He shuddered with pulsing need and shook his head to dispel his thoughts, flinging water droplets from his hair. His head pounded, and every muscle in his body ached. Gripping his sword, he buried its tip in the earth, then closed his eyes as he rested his forehead on the sword's hilt.

There was only one answer to his dilemma. Despite his suspicions he had no proof, and just as every general knew when to retreat, he must admit that he could not win this war.

He must leave the mountain and let the villagers solve their own problems without his help. He opened his eyes and looked up at the moon for solace, but all he saw was Ashleigh's alabaster face framed by her midnight tresses. Even the stars reminded him of the highlights in her eyes.

Knowing he had lost, he rose and began packing his belongings.

Down the road, another man of God pondered the path his life had taken. He sifted through the burnt rubble of a Gypsy cart and found human remains intermixed with household items. What had occurred in the village during his absence? He had been safe here for many years, but now evil was raising its terrible head, and he was helpless to stem the tide. Why did misfortune follow him wherever he went? What had he done to anger God?

His toe stubbed against something hard, and he leaned down to see what it was. His eyebrows rose, and he rubbed soot off a golden locket. He snapped it open and stared at the picture for several long moments; then he closed it and placed it in his pocket.

It was an expensive piece. And he had an affliction. No matter how hard he tried to tame them, he could not stop his fingers from stealing precious items.

Ashleigh galloped recklessly through the dark woods, tears streaming from her face. Since her parents' brutal murders, everything had collapsed into chaos. Her heart was in shambles, her emotions a jumbled mass of pain, confusion and anger. She wanted vengeance, but the desperation in her soul made her weak and weary.

Except when he wrapped his arms around her.

His strong shoulders kept the horrors at bay. A moment next to the stream . . . a brief interlude in the meadow. And now an earth-shattering meeting in the dark in which their mutual passions were fully exposed.

In each of those moments the pain had disappeared. His power had swept her fears aside and replaced them with soaring pleasure—a pleasure all too quickly dashed to the ground when he pulled away.

Had she won? Would he leave the mountain?

His face told her yea, but his body told her nay. He

wanted her. Part of him possibly needed her, but he
was a man of principle. He would not betray the code
of honor his robes demanded of him. She knew this.
She could feel the turmoil within him, and knew that
no matter how strongly he felt the attraction, he would
stay true to his path. Unlike the men who had violated
her mother, Mangan would not harm another person.
He would not force himself upon a woman, nor hurt
a fellow creature. It wasn't in his nature. He was good.

Unlike her. She was far from good. The fury inside
her was eating her soul and corroding her mind. Soon
the laughing child she had once been would be gone
forever. She would become an angry and bitter woman
with no friends, no family, no lover. A murderer with
a rotting soul.

Reaching the rocky cliffside, Ashleigh slipped off
her horse and climbed up into Cairdean's hidden nest.

I am not the murderer. They are. Those men.

Her face hardened. She did not need friends or lovers. She had proven that she could survive without
anyone. The moments in his arms had not been a
respite; they had been a diversion. Her only error had
been in wasting time playing petty tricks upon the
villagers instead of exacting her revenge in full.

Ashleigh curled into a ball and wrapped her arms
around her shoulders, then rested her head against
the bits of string and cloth scattered around the cave.
Mangan would leave. The energy between them was
too great for a man of his fortitude to deny. He would
flee just to avoid confronting her again.

Once he was gone she would do what she should
have done in the first place. No more tricks. No more
illusions. She would kill them all.

Chapter 12

The next morning, Mangan ate a cold breakfast, then saddled his stallion. He would do the courtesy of telling Eo'Ghanan and the elders that he was leaving. They would understand that he was on a quest and could delay only so long.

He paused as he heard a wagon roll down the road. It sounded as if it were being pulled by two draft horses and was accompanied by at least four escorts. Only highborn nobles would travel escorted, and, recalling Eo'Ghanan's admonition, Mangan waited until the entourage had passed before he mounted and walked his horse onto the road.

As he approached the village, he was surprised to see several people milling around the church steps. Their faces were anxious, and they appeared to be arguing amongst themselves.

"Brother Mangan!" Eo'Ghanan called out, spotting him. "What a pleasure! You are a gifted man, and we thank you most sincerely."

Mangan frowned. "What do you mean?"

"Last night, the spirits rested. There were no odd disturbances. All slept soundly and awoke with nothing amiss. Thank you for your prayers and your successful exorcism. We appreciate all you have done and encourage you to continue your journey."

"I did nothing," Mangan denied. "I—"

Eo'Ghanan laughed a bit too loudly and clapped Mangan on the back. "Such modesty is appropriate for a monk, but we would still like to express our joy and deep gratitude."

Mangan looked at him suspiciously; then his gaze swept the agitated villagers. Something was amiss. "Where is the wagon and escort I heard headed this way?" he asked.

Eo'Ghanan's eyes grew wide, but he shook his head. "No wagon or escort passed through here, brother. You must be mistaken."

Mangan glanced at the unmarked road, aware that any tracks had already been obliterated by a boy who was rapidly sweeping the road, sweat dripping down his dusty forehead.

"It is Sunday," Mangan said, trying to decipher the cause of the odd behavior amongst the villagers. "I would like to stay for Sunday services."

"That is not necessary. Our priest has returned."

"I would like to talk with him about my suspicions regarding the trickster in your village."

"Again, that is not necessary, for he has been told of all that occurred. You showed an interest in our small chapel. Surely you would like to travel on and see the laird's church?"

Mangan swung down and leveled a look at Eo'Ghanan. "I am a monk, and I am asking to stay for Sunday services. Would you deny me?"

Unable to refuse, Eo'Ghanan took the reins of Mangan's stallion and handed them to a young boy, then motioned for Mangan to precede him inside the church.

"Father Benedict," Eo'Ghanan introduced him. "Meet Brother Mangan, the man I told you about earlier."

A wave of animosity emanated from the priest, and Mangan stiffened in surprise.

"I do not like impostors deluding my people into believing in phantoms," Father Benedict said angrily. "There are no such things as false gods or evil beings causing sheep to fly or wine to boil. You should be ashamed of taking advantage of the uneducated and accepting their undeserved adulation."

Mangan's eyes flared, and something in his stance made Father Benedict step back nervously.

"I agree, Father," Mangan replied in a low voice. "I told them the same. I believe that human hands are behind the tricks that plagued the village in your absence."

Even though Mangan agreed with him, Father Benedict looked far from pleased. If anything he seemed even angrier. "And whom, then, do you blame? Have you pointed a finger at one of my good parishioners?"

Suddenly leery of voicing his suspicions to a man he was beginning to distrust, Mangan shook his head. "No. I have not fully determined whom the culprit is, but I trust you will continue to search after I have departed."

"Departed?" For the first time the priest appeared to relax.

"Aye," Mangan answered. "I intend to continue my quest this morn. I am on a holy mission to visit churches across Scotland. Eo'Ghanan Fergus mentioned that your laird's church might interest me."

Father Benedict flushed and turned away. "Then I apologize," he said, although his voice remained harsh and unfriendly. "I will say no more of your interfer-

ence in my village. You may stay for services and then
we will see you on your way. As for your request,
although I commend your quest, I cannot offer any
assistance. Laird Geoffrey of Tiernay's church is not
staffed and has not opened its doors in several years,
not since a fire destroyed it. However, once his son
marries"—he glanced back with a superior smile at
Mangan—"I will be appointed prior and will direct
the rebuilding."

"Congratulations," Mangan replied dryly, watching
Father Benedict turn away and mount the dais, then
light a candle in preparation for mass. "I hope that
such a happy event will occur soon."

"It will," Father Benedict replied. "Very soon."

Eo'Ghanan frowned at the priest, then motioned
Mangan away from him and toward the front row.
"Please join my family. Everyone is coming today.
Again, my sincere thanks to you for trying to help,
and after the service I will direct you toward the easi-
est route."

Mangan looked at him curiously. "Why are you suddenly not in need of my services?"

Eo'Ghanan reached across the pew to greeted Branan McFadden's abandoned wife. He became so involved in offering his support, he was unable, or
unwilling, to answer Mangan's question. Sighing, Mangan sat down and stared straight ahead. If everyone
in the village was coming to church, and if Ashleigh
was part of the village, she would also be attending.
Thank heavens he was seated in the front row, for
that meant he would not be able to see her.

Mangan clasped his hands in prayer and bowed his
head. He must erase thoughts of her from his mind.
She was a woman about to wed a young man. She
would be cooking at another's fire and sitting at anoth-

er's table. She would be undressing in another's home . . . sliding between another's sheets . . .

He groaned and pressed the heels of his palms against his forehead as pain surged forth, pounding behind his forehead like the crack of a hammer on an anvil. *Stop. Stop thinking about her. Think about where you must go now. Where should you search? Should you travel to the ruined church or seek elsewhere?*

Mangan tried to concentrate on the familiar Latin phrases of the mass, but his thoughts kept straying. Why had she been out in the woods at night? In fact, every time he had seen her she had been alone and unattended. Although peasant maidens enjoyed fewer restraints than highborn lasses, it still seemed odd that she traipsed about with such freedom. It gave her many opportunities to create mischief. He just did not know why she seemed bent on causing trouble.

He sneaked a glance behind him and scanned the rows. Where was she?

Eo'Ghanan looked at him questioningly, and Mangan dropped his head in a semblance of meditation. She had said that her parents had recently died, yet no one had mentioned such a tragedy, only that of Branan's disappearance. It would seem that such an event would be oft repeated, especially when the villagers suspected the presence of evil spirits.

Mangan's head snapped up and he stared at Father Benedict. The man was reciting the phrases one used in weddings, not those of a regular Mass.

Suddenly the doors opened and a heavily veiled woman was led into the church. The sound of her weeping echoed off the chapel walls, but none of the villagers appeared to notice.

A man rose from a chair that had been set in the

shadows, and he walked up to the altar to await the woman's arrival. Although the man was dressed in simple clothing, his stance betrayed his highborn status.

The congregation rose, and the woman was forced to kneel next to the man. Father Benedict shook water over them, cited the unbreakable vows of marriage, then pronounced them man and wife.

The woman's weeping escalated, and she flung herself on the dais, begging for mercy, but Father Benedict placed a quill in her hand and bade her to make her mark on a document, then waved to Eo'Ghanan, who rose and pulled her away from the altar and out the back door.

The man also signed the book, then nodded and left the church.

Mangan watched the proceedings with astonishment. Whereas arranged marriages were common in highborn society, and often the bride and groom did not know each other prior to their wedding, he had not expected to see such in the village chapel. Who was the man and where had he come from? And the girl? Had it been Ashleigh? Was this arrangement the source of her misery?

The mass resumed, and when it was over Mangan rose to his feet.

"Eo'Ghanan," Mangan said, placing a hand on the elder's shoulder. "Who were the two people wed today?"

"Just some travelers," he replied evasively. "They are already gone."

Mangan's face hardened and he struggled to hold his temper. "The bride was coerced. Could she have been the woman called Ashleigh?"

"No one by that name lives here."

"Would you lie to me?" Mangan asked, his low voice dark with menace.

Eo'Ghanan shifted back and forth, but shook his head again. "No, brother. I would not lie to a man of the cloth. The bride was not named Ashleigh."

"Then who was it?"

"I cannot say. Please do not press me on this matter, for I have no choice." Eo'Ghanan slid away, leaving Mangan standing alone.

"Did you appreciate my homily?" Father Benedict asked as he stepped off the dais.

"Indeed," Mangan replied. "Thank you for allowing me to attend."

"I would have preferred you did not," Father Benedict reminded him. "But since you were here, I would like to ask you to sign as another witness to the wedding. Since you are a monk, your signature will bear more weight than a peasant's will." The priest handed him the quill and pointed to the registry book.

Mangan stared at the priest. "Who was wed? You forgot to mention their names during your service."

"Did I?" Father Benedict replied. "How neglectful of me. However, I still request that you mark your name here to signify your witnessing the union."

Although the entire proceedings had seemed odd, it was true that Mangan had observed the service; thus he could sign the book. Taking the quill, he wrote his name, followed by the name of his monastery, on the line below Father Benedict's. Before he could read the names of the bride and groom, the priest snatched back the book and read Mangan's signature.

"St. Ignacio?" he asked, his face turning pale.

"Aye," Mangan replied. "It is a small monastery near the coast."

Collecting his composure, Father Benedict placed

the book in a chest and locked it with a large iron key. "I'm sure it is small, for I have never heard of it."

Mangan turned away, disgusted and disenchanted. The mass had been dull and lackluster, the wedding strange, and the absence of gaiety disturbing. But then, ever since he had ridden up this mountain, nothing had made sense.

Later that morning Ashleigh awoke feeling ill, her muscles cramped and the tip of her nose so cold she had to rub it just to make sure it was still there. Her stomach growled and her mouth was dry. The various roots, berries, and greens she had been able to find in the forest last night had not been enough to satisfy her. As she tried to stretch, Cairdean squawked and poked her foot with his beak.

"Augh!" Ashleigh grumbled. "You have more room than me!"

The raven reluctantly shuffled over, then fluffed his feathers and stared at her.

"Oh, all right," Ashleigh muttered. "I know it is your home and you are being kind to let me stay. 'Tis just that I am cold and tired and hungry." She glanced down at her blouse. "And dirty." As she crawled to the edge of the cave, her palm pressed against something hard and smooth. She lifted her hand and looked at the gold coin wedged into a rock crevasse. "Cairdean, this is worth something." Ashleigh wiggled it, trying to get it loose. "Is there nothing you don't steal?" The coin would not budge, and Ashleigh gave up with a sigh. "I only wish you could steal me some clothes, soap, a big washbasin and a huge length of soft cotton."

She reached the entrance to the cave and scurried down the cliff, then dropped onto the grass. "Since that is unlikely to occur, I suppose we ought to find a lake and some sand with which to scrub. I want to take a bath and clean my clothes."

But her thoughts kept straying to last night. She kept thinking of Mangan and his touch. His heat. His passion in the dark. He wanted her despite his religious calling. His need could not be masked, and it sent shimmers of excitement through her body that had nothing to do with revenge. Instead of forcing herself to focus upon the one thing she should be thinking about, she felt her mind spinning with new thoughts and desires. It was as if the vistas within her soul were suddenly expanding and fresh possibilities were unfolding before her.

Until a few weeks ago there had been only one choice, one world. She was a Gypsy, destined to follow in her father's craft of magical illusion. But what was she now? She was lost in her mother's land with no knowledge of how to return to her Gypsy camp. Instead of using her skills to beguile and amaze, she was using them to terrorize. She had no family and no friends other than a black-feathered creature that had inexplicably become her champion. She had done deeds that gave her nightmares, yet she felt compelled to do more. And lastly, her stomach was becoming twisted with a strange yearning she could not understand.

Yearning for a man.

Was she opening to new possibilities or being held captive to them? Was it her destiny to avenge her parents' deaths, and face a court's judgment should she be captured, or were there other choices? Could someone like Mangan hold the key to helping her see more? He was a learned man of the world. He was a man close to God. Once, he had offered to help. Might he still be willing?

She sniffed and shook her head at her ridiculous musings. It was far too late to ask for his assistance. She had lied to him and played tricks upon him. He would never trust her word against that of the villagers. It was best left as it was. He was her enemy and she wanted him gone.

Truly, why not rest for the day and take a leisurely swim? It might give her time to reflect and plan, time to clear her thoughts and soothe her trembling hands, for she hoped that after last night, Mangan would have left the mountain.

Ashleigh looked up at the sky for signs of smoke coming from Mangan's camp. No smoke. No morning campfire. He was most likely packing his belongings this very moment and preparing to ride away.

She lifted her lips in a semblance of a triumphant smile, trying to ignore the desolation that pricked behind her eyelids.

Chapter 13

Mangan rode out of the village, his war steed plodding with slow, deliberate strides. The steady hoofbeats should have been soothing, yet Mangan felt uncomfortably tense. Father Benedict had sent him on his way with a blessing from the patron saint of travelers, and the people of the village had smiled and waved to him after ensuring that his saddlebags were well stocked and his water gourd was full.

So why did he still want to find Ashleigh and discover why she had bothered Cormag and Eogan, or whether it had been her in the wedding dress?

He could forget about her and continue his journey by visiting Laird Geoffrey of Tiernay's burnt church. If he kept a steady pace he should reach the castle on the far side of the mountain within three days, according to Father Benedict's reluctantly given instructions.

A bird soared high in the sky, drawing Mangan's attention. Its flight was strong and graceful as it glided upon upcurrents, then dove downward in a dance of beauty.

Ashleigh was much like the black bird. Her glistening dark eyes and brilliant black tresses were like gilded feathers, and her solitary existence was like a bird's lonely flight in the huge, heavenly expanse.

His dark angel . . . alone on the mountain. Vulnerable and inexplicable. Why had his body and soul been cast into chaos by their chance meetings?

God was trying to tell him something, and he was obliged to listen.

He abruptly turned his horse from the road and guided him through the trees. Father Benedict had insisted that he stay on the road, but the need to find answers was too strong. He had to discover why his angel was trapped upon the mountain and why she was plaguing the innocent with her wicked ways.

It was his duty.

Ashleigh let the cool water soothe her tired muscles. The sun was pleasantly warm, and a soft breeze tickled the leaves on the trees, creating gentle music. Using a bit of cloth, she had rubbed herself with sand and scraped off all the accumulated dirt and grime and now felt refreshingly clean and relaxed.

Floating on her back, she hummed to herself, enjoying the peaceful moment.

Mangan, however, was hot, tired and getting frustrated as he and his stallion picked their way through thick underbrush and thorny brambles. His hand itched to draw his sword and hack at the foliage, but he forced himself to think rather than to stubbornly fight against nature. He saw a clearing up ahead, and suspected it bordered a loch. It would be much easier to travel around the edge of a body of water than struggle through the forest.

Angling his horse toward the clearing, he ducked under a tree and wiped the sweat from his brow, then glanced at the refreshing water. His heart skipped a beat when he saw Ashleigh floating in the center of the crystalline lake.

Slipping off his stallion and wrapping his reins around a fallen log, Mangan strolled forward and leaned against a tree, where he could easily observe her. For once he felt in control of their meeting, and he had no intention of losing his advantage.

"What would your new husband say to your romping unclothed in the loch?" he called as he casually crossed his arms over his chest.

Ashleigh flailed and sank into the shallow water. Then, as her feet found the bottom, she sputtered to the surface, sending a rippling wave crashing upon the shore. She wiped wet hair from her eyes and stared at him in shock, but after seeing his raised eyebrow, she abruptly sank up to her chin and cast him a withering look. "Turn away!" she commanded. " 'Tis inappropriate of you to watch me bathe!"

Mangan smiled and rested one foot on a rock, then leaned slightly forward and stared directly at her. "Who are you going to tell?"

"My father!" Ashleigh shouted indignantly. "He will come after you and . . . and . . ." Her voice trailed off, and she looked around in confusion.

"Your father is dead, or was that also a lie?"

"I would never lie about that!"

"What would you lie about?"

Ashleigh frowned, unsure how to respond. "How did you find me?" she queried.

"I am the one asking questions, not you." Mangan reached down on the ground and picked up a large piece of wet material. "Could this be the remnant of your skirt? And blouse?" Even he looked a bit surprised as he rummaged through the pile. "Are you truly wearing nothing at all?"

Ashleigh flushed and sank still lower in the water.

Mangan sat down on the rock and broke a branch from the tree. Pulling a small knife from his belt, he started to scrape the bark off the branch.

"I knew I shouldn't have taken a bath," Ashleigh grumbled.

"Excuse me?" Mangan asked, pausing in his whittling to look up at her.

"Nothing."

"That is a shame, because I was hoping you were ready to start answering some questions."

"What questions?"

"Are your parents truly dead?"

"Of course! I would never say that in jest!"

"What about the wedding today? Were you the unwilling bride?"

"Will you leave if I say yes?" Ashleigh responded angrily.

He lifted her wet skirt with the tip of his knife. "Such fragile material. It looks old and threadbare. I hope it doesn't tear easily."

"Don't do that," Ashleigh said sharply. "'Tis the only skirt I have."

His gaze hardened, and he looked at her with thinly concealed anger. "Are you married?"

"No!" Ashleigh shouted. "Now give me my skirt!"

Rising in fury, Mangan flung the piece of clothing at her and began pacing back and forth along the lakeshore. "Then who was wed today? What have you lied about? Why are you here? Are you the one who has been upsetting the villagers? And if so, why?" He paused, then turned to glare at her. "Why were you trying to drown yourself the day I met you, if not to avoid a forced marriage?"

"I'm not going to tell you anything," Ashleigh said

as she struggled to drag the skirt underwater and put it on. The material kept floating to the surface, making her feel like a frog on a sinking lily pad. "But I can assure you that I know nothing about a wedding. You can stand there and yell at me all day if you want, but I refuse to say anything more!" She met his glare and stuck out her tongue for good measure.

Mangan took a deep breath and looked up at the sky for guidance. He should know better than to argue with her. His cousin Istabelle was also an obstinate young lady, and the only way to get her to listen to reason was to approach her indirectly. Like his cousin, this woman might be more likely to respond to subtle coercion than outright force.

"You are being unreasonable," he replied gently. "I would like to help you."

"Ha!"

"Let me put it this way. If you want your clothes, you will answer my questions. I will give you one piece for every question you answer honestly."

"If you don't want me walking around half-dressed, then you will give me my clothes without taunting me with word games."

"Are you the one playing tricks upon the villagers?"

"Why do you care?"

"Are you? One question, one item," he reminded her.

"Maybe yes, maybe no. I heard them say it was evil spirits. Your question should be directed at them. Why do *they* fear evil spirits? If they were pure of heart, then they should be protected from the devil and have no such suspicions."

"That is not an answer," he said dryly. "If they have done something to you, I will help you, but if they are innocent you must leave them alone."

"I do not admit to doing anything," she replied, her lips curving into a mischievous smirk.

"Yet you do not deny it either." He rubbed his chin for a moment, considering. "The person who is perpetrating these tricks is quite clever, you know. Intelligent. Sophisticated. It is a person who has led a varied and well-traveled life."

Ashleigh's smile faded, and she looked at him with an impenetrable expression.

Mangan watched her face for a moment, then continued. "The person is trying to gain attention, almost as if he or she wants to create enough chaos so that others will take note."

"Why would this person do such a thing?" Ashleigh asked. "Why not just deal with the situation on his or her own?"

"Perhaps because she is frightened. She is alone and unsure of what to do."

"Then she is not as intelligent as you surmised."

"On the contrary, hesitancy indicates that she is contemplative and not willing to wreak havoc for no reason."

"There is a reason!"

"What reason would account for such animosity?"

Ashleigh held out her hand and wiggled her fingers. "I answered a question. Give me my clothes."

"You have not answered anything," he replied. "We are only talking about some other person who might or might not exist."

"If you don't hand me a piece of clothing, we will cease talking," she answered sharply.

He tossed her chemise into the lake in her general direction, trying not to react to the silky feel of the soft cloth. It was meant to press against her skin, to warm and protect her, and it smelled exotic and sensual—just like her. He did not want to stop the conversation, not only because he desired answers, but because he liked the way expressions flitted across her face and the way her eyebrows lifted as she talked.

Ashleigh breathed a sigh of relief as she successfully retrieved her chemise and jammed her arms through the soaking wet sleeves, then yanked it down over her breasts. Although the cloth was translucent it gave her some semblance of dignity, and she was able to start thinking of a way to escape. She spotted some reeds growing from the lake floor, and an idea began forming in her mind. She had lost her disappearing plate the day she had discovered Cormag's name and location, but there was more than one way to make it appear that she had vanished!

"That day Cormag and Eogan rode up the mountainside looking for Branan and discovered a fire, was it your campfire they found?"

"No."

"I need honest answers," Mangan said angrily as he waved a stocking in the air.

"I am being honest. I started no fire that day."

He tried to make sense of what she said as he watched the stocking swing back and forth from his fingers. She sounded so sure, and he was inclined to believe her.

Perhaps he was asking the wrong question.

"Had you met Cormag and Eogan before they searched for Branan?"

"Hand me a stocking."

"Answer me and I will give you both."

"Yes."

"Did they do something to you?"

"You owe me the stockings."

Mangan rolled them in a ball and tossed them at

Ashleigh, but they landed short, and she was forced to jump toward shore to catch them before they sank to the bottom of the lake. She looked at him accusingly. "You did that on purpose."

He shrugged. "It got you one step closer to coming out of the water."

She smiled slyly. "Do you want me to come out?"

Watching her carefully, he nodded.

"Then if you would please close your eyes, I will come out and cover myself with my blouse."

"I did not think you would agree so readily."

" 'Tis silly to stay in the water and get cold while I could be warm and dry on shore."

He closed his eyes, pleased that she was showing some sense after all. Perhaps she was not as stubborn and difficult as his cousin.

Ashleigh snapped off a hollow reed, put it in her mouth and sank under the water. Using her heavy skirt as a weight, she crouched down and walked along the lake floor toward the shore, using the reed to breathe.

"Are you coming out?" Mangan called as he listened for sounds of her emergence. A heartbeat. A sudden suspicion. "Ashleigh?" He opened his eyes and stared at the smooth lake in shock. She had disappeared!

"Ashleigh!" he shouted. Then, without thinking of the consequences, he kicked off his boots and dove in, going deep with a few, swift strokes. He swept his hands along the sandy floor, searching for her. She must have slipped under the water and drowned. He had to save her!

An unnameable emotion thudded through his soul as his hands continued to wave through nothing but algae and water grass, and he dove time and again through the murky water, searching for her. His dark angel . . . the woman whose eyes haunted his nights . . . it was not time to lose her. She could not die. Not now! He had saved her once from a watery death; he must again! He needed her. He needed to see her face relaxed and joyous. He needed to know she was safe and protected. It was a need deep inside his heart that had a hunger all its own. He was starving for her and knew that only she could sustain him. Only she could provide the intangible sustenance that would fulfill his spiritual and physical desires.

A laugh made him shoot to the surface and look toward shore.

"You dropped your cross when you raced into the water," Ashleigh taunted as she dangled the beaded chain from her fingers.

"You witch!" Mangan shouted as he lunged toward her, all warm thoughts wiped instantly from his mind. She was a manipulative trickster, and she would not fool him again!

"No, no, no," Ashleigh cautioned. "Come no closer or I will fling it into the deepest part of the lake and you will never find it."

How could he have ever cared whether she lived or died? She was the devil incarnate! How dared she threaten to lose his cross! He glared at her, fury making his body twitch uncontrollably. What he wouldn't give for a crossbow right now. He would string it tight and shoot a dart through her evil, conniving heart! "How did you do it?" he demanded. "How did you reach the shore without making a ripple on the surface?"

Ashleigh untied the disappearing plate from his horse's saddlebag and nonchalantly strapped it on her back. Then, with a wink, she wrapped it around her body and disappeared from his view.

He gasped, then narrowed his eyes and looked

closer. What an ingenious trick. The clever little lass—
he could throttle her with his bare hands!—she was
right in front of him, yet he could not see her.

"They killed your parents!" he shouted as comprehension dawned. Of course! How could he not have
realized the tie between the two events before?

It was Ashleigh's turn to gasp as she huddled behind
the plate. How did he know? He seemed to reach
inside her mind and pull thoughts out of her that no
one should be able to deduce. "No!" she yelled back,
then bit her nails as she awaited his reply.

"You are lying," he called out. "They killed your
parents, and you are seeking revenge upon them."

Ashleigh trembled. She could not trust him. He
could be one of them, trying to get her to admit that
she had murdered Branan. Guilt washed over her at
the memory, and she stared at her hands with fear.
How had her own fingers held the knife? How had she
lost such control that she had actually killed another
person? She bowed her head and held back tears, then
swallowed and took a deep breath. She must remain
true. An eye for an eye.

"You can't stay here," he told her, his voice low
and soothing. "You can't stay in the mountains forever. Winter will come. What will you do then?"

"I have a place to keep warm," Ashleigh replied.
"I even have a friend."

"Your raven," Mangan murmured, thinking back on
all the times he had come across the bird.

Ashleigh gasped again. He was a mind reader!
"How do you do that?" she questioned. "How do you
pluck thoughts from my head?"

Smiling smugly, he began wading toward shore,
careful that his motions did not create watery sounds.
"Magic. Just like you, I do magic."

"Humph." Ashleigh grunted. Her cousin read cards and used people's reactions to predict their future. It appeared magical, but was as much magic as her father's collection of conjuring tricks. "What am I thinking now?" she asked. "You can't see my face, so you have no clue."

He slipped out of the lake and crept up on her. Leaning over the top of the plate, he peered down at her crouched form. "You are trying to convince yourself that I am not standing next to you," he whispered just beside her unsuspecting head.

Chapter 14

Ashleigh screeched in surprise and leaped to her feet, knocking the mirrored plate to the ground, but Mangan's strong hand descended upon her arm and held her fast. "No, I don't want to chase you through the forest once again. We have had enough of those games."

"Stop touching me!" she shouted as she clawed at his fingers. "Let go of my shoulder!"

He swept her up in his arms and tossed her over his back like a sack of potatoes. Her wet clothing plastered itself to her legs and clung wantonly to her backside, making Mangan wince, so he reached down and scooped up her washcloth and the rest of her clothes, rolled them into a ball, then slid his feet into his boots. "You are a fool," he told her as he strode through the trees. "If you won't speak to me, mayhap you will speak to the laird of these lands."

"What do you mean?" Ashleigh cried. She wriggled and bucked, but his hold on her was too firm for her to escape.

"I am taking you to Tiernay Castle. Laird Geoffrey will see that you either speak the truth or are punished for your misbehavior."

Ashleigh twisted sharply and dug her elbows into Mangan's back. "I will not leave this mountain until my work is done." .

He spanked her. Hard.

She gasped and pounded her fists against his back. "Let me go!"

"For such an intelligent little lass, you are being stupidly obstinate. All you had to do was tell me the truth, and I would have ensured that justice was done. Now you . . ." He paused as he was forced to shift his grip and his palm cupped her hind end. It was incredibly soft, which made him more annoyed. He lifted his hand to spank her again, but she suddenly stilled. "Better," he commented, relieved that he did not have to touch her. "At least you learn from your mistakes."

He ducked under a tree branch and nearly ran into her gray horses. "Ahhh," he said. "The mystery of the horses has been solved. You stole them."

"They were mine! Those men stole them from me!"

"Is that why you harassed them? Because you lost your horses?"

"I am not so petty." She jerked and managed to slide off his shoulder and tumble to the ground on her hands and knees.

Mangan pressed his boot over her hair and ground his heel into the dirt.

"Augh!" Ashleigh shrieked as she tried to move. "My hair!"

Mangan bent over and gripped her chin. "Don't press me," he warned. "I have only so much patience, and you have already used up much of it."

Ashleigh jerked her head, tears springing to her eyes as several strands of hair were ripped from her scalp. His gaze bored into hers, and she felt captured not only by his unrelenting boot but also by the power of his gaze. A sense of futility filled her, and she closed her eyes in defeat.

Not trusting her sudden compliance, Mangan released her hair but wound his fist in the strings of her chemise. He yanked her upright. "Don't tell me, then," he snarled. "I care naught that you refuse to speak up in your own defense. I will bring you to justice and then wash my hands of you, for already you have caused me far too much grief."

She jerked back and the strings of her chemise snapped, causing the frayed edges to spring apart.

Both Mangan and Ashleigh froze.

A cool wind tickled through the trees, caressing her bare breasts and puckering her nipples. Ashleigh's throat constricted and she tried to move her arms, to clasp them around her nakedness, but her muscles wouldn't obey. She felt bound by invisible ropes, involuntarily displaying herself like produce at a market. Heat raced up her body, flushing her skin and darkening her nipples to a deep, luscious plum, yet still she could not move.

Mangan's gaze roved over her flesh. He was famished. Starving for her. His jaw trembled; his mouth went dry. To feast upon her . . . to drink from her breasts . . . He could see every tiny goose bump, each little nub encircling each pert point. He watched her quivering breath cause the swells to rise and fall, saw the dark shadow of her cleavage deepen, then open, as if inviting his tongue to explore her heat.

Only an angel blessed by the heavenly father could be so beautiful.

"Put on the cross," he commanded, his voice strangled and harsh as he held it out to her. "My cross . . . wear it around your neck."

With trembling fingers she slipped the chain over her head and felt the heavy cross thud against her chest.

"Leave it on. Always."

She swallowed and her legs became weak. The fever in his eyes engulfed her, awakening an answering need. "Why?"

"To protect you. To remind me that you . . . you are not my destiny." He unknotted the hemp around his waist and unwrapped his robe, leaving in place only his white cotton shirt and dark brown breeches. He then carefully draped the monk's robe around her shoulders. "Wear this, for your clothes are still too wet. Do as I say for I must bring you to the castle, but neither of us can risk a physical battle once again. Come willingly and I promise to defend you."

Ashleigh pulled the edges closer and sank into the garment's warmth. "You do not know what I have done," she whispered.

"I do not care."

As she stared at him, something intangible passed between them. She inhaled his scent, felt his heat. He was no longer her enemy; nor was he just a man who aroused her youthful desires. He was a soul. He was a man in pain, a man lost in confusion, struggling to find his way out of the murky abyss. A man who was willing to help her.

"You understand . . ." she breathed. "You know sadness."

"Aye. I know what it is to feel lost and alone . . . to believe that nothing can ever be right again."

Ashleigh touched the cross nestling between her breasts. "The church is where you have sought solace?"

"Aye," he repeated. "I know of no other path. In

my world one must be a leader of armies or a leader of souls. I no longer want to cause bloodshed. I do not want to bring destruction. I want to rebuild and renew."

"I have chosen a different path, for I want to hurt those who hurt me," Ashleigh answered, her eyes filling with tears. "Every night I feel the loss of my loved ones. Every night I long for their presence."

"Your parents?"

"Yes. I miss them."

He laid a hand on her shoulder and for once did not notice the softness of her flesh, only the depth of her sorrow. "You will find redemption with forgiveness."

For a timeless moment she searched the depths of his green eyes. "You have not forgiven yourself," she finally murmured.

He dropped his hand and smiled grimly. "No. I have not yet found such grace, but you are young and have not crossed the line into true evil. I will save you."

"What if I do not wish to be saved? What if I cannot be saved?"

"I will save you," he repeated as he took her hand and led her to her horses. He handed her the ball of clothing, then tied a rope around one horse's neck, leaving the other free. "I will bring you to the laird and he will ensure that justice is done. You need not risk your soul by dispensing judgment and punishment upon those who have wronged you. Let the men who are duty-bound to protect and care for you do what must be done."

"What about you? Why do you bring me to another when you offered to help me find and punish the men who hurt me? Do you rescind your promise?"

He looked at her wryly. "I lack the detachment necessary to fairly assess your situation. God placed you in my path to test my faith and to force you to seek a lawful solution to your situation. I intend to do what is right in both respects."

Ashleigh shivered, guilt making her feel unsure and anxious. She bowed her head. What would Mangan think of her if he knew the truth?

As she looked up, she saw Mangan staring at her. She lifted her chin. "I will go to the laird's castle and tell him what occurred. Perhaps once I know that the other men who killed my parents have been punished, I will find peace." She mounted her steed. "But, Mangan, there is more to my tale, all of which I am loath to admit. Must I tell everything?"

"Do you mean the tricks you played upon the villagers? Confession will cleanse your soul," he answered as he, too, mounted. "If I can help you admit your deeds, I can help you find forgiveness."

She shook her head sadly. The tricks were nothing compared to the true sin she had committed. "You say that you have not found forgiveness, either. Perhaps God wants *me* to save *you*."

His face became shuttered and unrevealing. "I am beyond saving," he answered, then gripped her lead rope, and they began the journey to the castle on the far side of the mountain.

They had ridden in silence for an hour when the caw of a raven made them both look up.

"Cairdean has found us," Ashleigh commented. Her clothes were dry, and she had returned Mangan's robe after pulling her blouse on over her damaged chemise, but the scent from his clothing lingered on her skin. She held up her hand, and the bird swooped down and landed on her wrist. He tilted his head, showing off a glittering swatch of fabric gripped in his beak.

Ashleigh held her palm out and Cairdean dropped the cloth into it. "Ohhh . . ." Ashleigh sighed as she admired the piece. "What beautiful workmanship. I could make a lovely dress from such material."

Mangan glanced at it, then pulled his horse to a stop. "Those are the king's colors," he said. "Where would a raven find a piece of a royal tunic or cape?"

Ashleigh rubbed its gilded surface, marveling at how the gold threads were interwoven with the purple ones. It would make a much prettier washcloth than the one she had tucked into her waistband. "Cairdean is more adept at finding shiny objects than a Gypsy." She grinned and placed her cheek against Cairdean's smooth feathers.

Mangan nodded, but a frown furrowed his brow. "Can your friend show us where he found that?"

Ashleigh laughed. "I cannot speak to him. He is not a trained pigeon. He comes and goes as he pleases."

"Have him fly off your wrist and we will follow him."

"Why? What does it matter?"

"I don't know. I . . . I sense that it does."

Ashleigh cocked her head. "You have instincts . . . intuitions?"

"No," he answered gruffly. "I merely assess the problem at hand and come up with the most probable conclusion. I am perturbed about the strange wedding, the warnings about traveling highborn men, and a wagon that the villagers deny seeing. Now we find a piece of royal clothing. Suffice it to say I am more than curious about how they are all connected."

Cairdean spread his wings and flew up into the sky, circled, then headed over the treetops.

"Come," Mangan demanded as he jerked on her lead rope. "We will lose him."

They trotted in between the trees as they attempted to keep Cairdean in sight. It soon became a game, and Ashleigh giggled as a flock of ravens burst into the air and swirled around their heads.

"Over there." She pointed. "Cairdean flies alone."

Sighing with relief, Mangan angled their horses and skirted around a bank of blackberry bushes, then paused when he once again lost sight of his quarry. "Where did he go this time?" he asked.

"To the right," Ashleigh answered. "Although I think chasing after him is ridiculous. 'Tis most likely he is searching for a mole to eat." Her dark eyes twinkled and she motioned for him to proceed.

Mangan lifted the corner of his upper lip. "You think I am odd."

"Yes, I do," Ashleigh replied, grinning more broadly. "But I am willing to play cat and mouse—or man and raven, as it may be—if you wish. It only delays our arrival at the castle and my subsequent interrogation. Look." She pulled an acorn from a tree and held it in her left palm. She rubbed her hands together, then closed her fists and presented them to him. "Where is the acorn?"

Mangan motioned to the right palm. "You switched it to the other hand."

Ashleigh opened her right hand and showed him an empty fist.

"Ahhhh. You tricked me and kept it in the left hand."

Ashleigh opened that palm, too, but there was no acorn.

Mangan leaned closer, as if he could not believe his eyes. "Where did it go?" He looked on the ground to see if she had dropped it, but Ashleigh reached forward and touched his ear, miraculously producing the nut.

"How did you do that?" Mangan asked.

"I normally do it with a coin," Ashleigh replied with a laugh.

Mangan chuckled and looked at her with a trace of fondness. "I don't believe I have ever met a woman as interesting as you. You may think I am odd, but you are more unusual. You can disappear before one's eyes and make objects move through the air. What else can you do?"

"Do you have a handkerchief?" Ashleigh asked as she carefully arranged her skirts and pulled the sleeves of her blouse down to her wrists.

Mangan searched his bags and produced a square of linen.

Taking it, Ashleigh wadded it up in her hand, then quickly tore it in half.

Mangan gasped and looked at her in shock. "Why did you do that?"

She folded the two pieces, then tore them again, all the while smiling at him. "Watch carefully." Folding it one more time, she ripped it a third time, then waved the pieces in her right hand in the air in front of him. "See all the pieces?"

He nodded dubiously. "I wish I didn't," he replied.

She then wadded them back up and pressed both hands together, blew on them, then opened her palm. The handkerchief slowly unfolded, whole and complete, without a single tear.

"Utterly amazing," he said. He reached for the handkerchief and looked it over carefully, seeing no visible signs of damage. "Such tricks are dangerous," he said seriously. "People in this country do not tolerate what they do not understand. You are not from here; I can tell by your accent."

"No. I was raised in France. Gypsy troupes like mine are common there."

"Not here. 'Tis too harsh a country for such nomadic people, but how is it that you know my language? You speak it fluently."

"My mother's family is from Scotland, and she taught me several languages, including yours. Actually, 'tis because of her family that we traveled to Scotland. She and her mother were estranged, but my mother wanted to make amends before my grandmother died."

"Did she?"

"No. We never made it to her home."

"Do you still want to find her?"

Ashleigh shook her head. "She cast away her own daughter. Why would I care to meet such a selfish woman?"

"Perhaps she had reasons you do not understand. Meeting her might heal some wounds."

"No," Ashleigh replied flatly. "I don't ever want to meet her. My father's people are my family."

"I spent time in France. I was not a friend to the French populace. I led armies across their fields and burnt their homes."

"Is that why you are sad? Because you feel so much guilt for what you have done? Most men have no remorse for having followed orders. They hurt people . . . mothers and fathers . . . without guilt."

"I *am* sorry," Mangan whispered, his eyes filling.

Ashleigh gently reached across their horses and took the handkerchief from his hands, then wiped his eyes. "It is not your fault."

"Aye, it is. I killed people. Women and children

were left without husbands and fathers because of me. Women like you."

She shook her head, but did not have words to comfort him, for her own pain welled forth and made her throat swell. She, too, had killed. She leaned forward and pressed her head against his chest, and he wrapped his arms around her, holding her close. They clasped each other, their horses remaining patiently still for long moments, until Mangan took a deep breath and gently pushed her away. "We have lost your raven."

Ashleigh smiled. "He sits on a tree just a few strides over there," she said, pointing to where Cairdean was perched on the gnarled branch of what had once been a thriving tree.

Mangan and Ashleigh clucked to their horses and walked forward as the second gray trailed behind them. A stench began filtering through the trees, and Mangan's face hardened.

He knew that smell.

Chapter 15

They came upon the carnage with a sense of horror. Two men and one woman lay splayed in heaps, their arms and legs broken and their faces twisted masks of agony. Trampled grass splattered with dried blood and bits of torn flesh made a gruesome bed for them, silent testimony to their long and torturous deaths.

Ashleigh screamed as her body started trembling uncontrollably. Memories flooded her mind—she saw her mother's and father's lifeless bodies merge with the faces of the dead, and helpless terror flooded her senses. She remembered the sounds, the sights, the smells . . . the faces of the men who had wrought such devastation. She remembered the flies buzzing around her mother's face.

"It was them!" she cried as she slid off Franco and stumbled over to the woman's body. "It was them! The men who killed my parents must have done this, too! I know it! Look, they crushed her skull just as they crushed my mother's!"

Mangan leaped off his mount and ran to Ashleigh's side, but she flailed her arms, keeping him at bay. "Those men did this," she screamed. "They must be stopped. How could anyone be so evil?" She turned to Mangan, her eyes begging for help. "Tell me," she cried as her voice cracked. "What would make one man torture and kill another? Why are these men killing people?"

Mangan's breath caught, and empathy welled within him. He dropped to his knees and opened his arms to her as she collapsed against him, sobbing hysterically. Questions rose, but he did not ask them. As she wept, he simply held and rocked her, repeating a silent prayer, pleading with God to show him how best to help her.

"Why?" she whispered, staring into his eyes after drawing a shaky breath. Her gaze flicked back and forth over his face, searching for answers he did not have.

"I don't know," he murmured against her hair pressing his brow against her head. "But I promise I will find out."

She pushed back and stared fiercely into his gaze. "Do you really? Do you really promise me?"

He grasped her face between his hands. "I do. Upon my honor I do. But you must guide me. Tell me what you remember of that day."

"All I know is that these men . . . these soldiers . . . tortured and killed my father, then raped and killed my mother. Three of them in addition to Cormag, Eogan and . . . and . . . Branan."

"The others—do you know their names?"

"Douglas." She paused as she shuddered and closed her eyes. "He was the leader. And Curtis and Troy or Tory, I think. I cannot be sure." Her tears slowed and her cheek rested against his strong chest. She felt soothed by his steady heartbeat. "They were soldiers."

"Were the men who attacked your family wearing royal colors like these men?" he asked, pointing to the purple-and-gold tunics on the dead men.

"No."

Mangan nodded, thinking. He glanced at the deceased woman, noting the elegant dress and expensive shoes. "Who would kill innocent travelers, and then murder royal guards? And a woman who appears to be a maid-in-waiting?"

Ashleigh looked up.

He stroked her drying cheeks. "Ashleigh, your family might have inadvertently stumbled into some plot involving the King of Scotland. Their murders may have been nothing but a tragic happenstance."

"Tell me," Ashleigh whispered. "Are my parents safe now? Is there truly someone above who wraps them in his arms and sets their souls free? I need to know that they are happy and at peace."

"I believe so. I believe that if you pray for happiness, God provides the opportunity for you to experience it. If you pray for heaven, he allows you the chance to enter it. Ashleigh . . ." He stroked his thumb across her chin. "Your parents *are* safe now. They are with God."

"Then what about me? What am I to do?"

"Find courage to live. Courage to do what is right."

"I want to stop those men and ensure that they never harm another person again."

Mangan nodded. "You said they were soldiers?"

"Yes. Three of them were."

"Then we must go to the castle and see if the laird can help us determine who is involved. As the king's cousin he will be more than ready to assist us, for once he knows that the king's guards and a maid-in-waiting have been killed, he will be anxious to investigate potential treason within his lands. With his help we should be able to find these rogues and punish them for their misdeeds."

"But what about me? Will I be punished for my misdeeds as well?" She recalled Branan's face and flushed with guilt.

"Because of your tricks?" Mangan asked, misunderstanding her. "Aye, you will be reprimanded, but I will stand by you. I will cast aside my robes and announce myself as Mangan O'Bannon, firstborn son of the Earl of Kirkcaldy. Laird Geoffrey will listen to my request for leniency, for I will ask for it upon his honor and upon the O'Bannon name. I swear that I will see to it that your punishment will be light, and if not I will stand in your stead."

She nodded, awed by his vehemence.

"Ashleigh, I must know everything. Do you understand?"

She bit her lip to still its trembling.

"What do you know of Branan?" he asked.

Her gaze dropped as renewed dread filled her heart. How could she tell him the truth? How could she admit her sin, yet still have his support?

Tilting her chin up, Mangan looked deep into Ashleigh's eyes, seeing her hurt and confusion, but not understanding all of it. He sensed there was something else, but that she was too fragile to explain more.

Ashleigh shivered. "I . . . I don't know what to say." She clung to him, terrified to speak but needing to tell him something . . . wanting to tell him all but able to reveal only part of her guilt. "I should have helped my parents. My mother, Mary . . . my father, Romil . . . I was so terrified . . . but I couldn't move. I hid while they did . . . did terrible things to Mother and Father." She clenched her fists and punched Mangan's chest.

"I did nothing! I let them rape and kill my mother!" She punched him again, then began pummeling and kicking him in rage. "I did nothing to help. I should have saved them!"

Mangan braced himself, accepting her blows. He felt her horror, absorbed her guilt. He understood her helpless futility and desperate need to right the wrongs of this world.

"Why didn't I die?" she cried. "I should have died with them! I should be lying in the grass, rotting away like these people . . . like my parents. Why am I being punished?" She slammed her fist against his chest once more, then collapsed in his arms. "Why am I alive?" she whispered.

"I can't answer you," he murmured against her hair. He held her close, familiar with her questions, since they echoed his own nightly prayers. "I don't know why certain people die while others do not, but I have had to accept that surviving is not a punishment. It leaves us with a duty. We survived because there is more for us to do."

Ashleigh lifted her face and looked at him. "What if I don't want to do anything more? What if my *more* is sinful? I am not like you. I am not called by some greater being, and I am no heroine. I am a simple Gypsy with a guilty conscience."

Mangan pressed his forehead against hers. "I am no hero," he replied. "Nonetheless, we are here by the grace of God. Perhaps we do not know why; nor do we know what he wants us to do, but we must accept that we are meant to do something."

Ashleigh pulled away and took a deep breath. "You must take me to the castle. You must help me tell the laird what happened and ensure that he punishes

Cormag, Eogan and the other culprits. Then . . . only then will I know my parents' souls are at peace."

He dropped to one knee in front of her, his hands sliding down her cheeks and over her arms, and then enfolding her hands in a warm, comforting clasp, which he held to his heart. "I swear to you that I will defend you. I will ask for leniency on your behalf, and ensure that your words fall upon caring and honest ears. I know there is more to tell . . . I can sense your turbulent heart. But I will stand beside you. Together we will find out what is happening on this mountain, and we will ensure that your parents did not die in vain."

She wrapped her hands over his. Energy vibrated between them, making their fingers tingle, yet they did not let go of each other.

They spent several hours preparing a grave site for the bodies, using his dagger to dig through the soft soil. Then Mangan offered a blessing on the souls of the two men and one woman, and they placed the broken corpses in the earth, knowing that their spirits were now free. As the horses grazed nearby and Cairdean watched from the treetops, Ashleigh and Mangan worked together in solemn silence, each absorbing the signifigance of what had just occurred between them.

Ashleigh glanced at Mangan as he tamped down the final pile of dirt with his boot. His powerful shoulders bulged and his back rippled with strength—strength that he was offering to her. Could he have secrets inside him and experiences that he had endured that would help him to understand hers? How had he managed to find a way out of the darkness? He was not filled with anger and rage. Instead he was compassionate and kind, seeking to assist others and spread goodwill among men.

She remembered the evening of her parents' deaths. They had been laughing together, a happy family ready to settle in for the night. Could she ever be happy again?

She shifted closer to Mangan, and he smiled reassuringly, as if he sensed her unease. She smiled back, hopeful for the future. Happiness was possible, and it would not mean she had forgotten her parents' deaths. In fact, by living her life well she would be celebrating their lives, for they had epitomized joy and thanksgiving.

Ashleigh plucked a few white flowers and tucked them behind her ear then took a deep breath.

Mangan stared at her beautiful face, seeing the relaxed lines and the softening around her eyes. She was so exquisite, like a fragile flower that stood at ease in the midst of a raging storm. The white blossoms in her black hair accentuated the pale flush in her cheeks, making her look like a shy bride.

How could she ever wonder why God would spare her? She was special; her spirit glowed with purity and love. He grinned to himself, seeing the glint of her mischievous nature as she twirled an acorn between her fingers. She was also an imp with a clever mind, and he had best keep a careful eye on her or she might play some trick upon him.

"Are you ready to go?" he asked.

She nodded and patted Francis on the neck before mounting Franco. "They are siblings," Ashleigh explained. " 'Tis rare for two foals to be born of the same mare and survive, but these two did. My mother helped nurse them with a bottle when the mare could not provide enough milk."

Mangan chuckled, realizing why she had been so adamant about regaining her horses, and why the other gray followed so obediently.

"They are gorgeous. They remind me of the white war stallions that do airs above the ground. Those horses are trained to leap and kick, spin and twist . . . They are incredible beasts, and worth a fortune."

Ashleigh shrugged. "We used them mostly to pull the wagon, but I often rode this one for fun. His name is Franco, and the other Francis. I would never sell them."

Mangan patted his horse as he swung up in the saddle. "This is Sir Scott. He managed to survive eleven battles with me. I, too, would never give or sell him to another."

They smiled, each realizing they had something in common.

"We will remain on the alert, for we do not know our enemies," Mangan said. "I suggest we stay off the main road and travel through the trees, even though the way will be longer and more difficult."

Ashleigh nodded in agreement, but cautioned, "Both the attack on my parents and on these people took place in the forest. These men do not travel merely by road. They seem to know the mountain well."

"Aye, and we do not. Did you see or hear anything when you were hiding out?"

"You were the only man I saw other than the villagers."

"I came across tracks," Mangan informed her. "They were from shod horses, which means their rid-

ers could be wearing armor. The sooner I get you to
the safety of the castle, the better I will sleep." Then
he clucked to Sir Scott and started through the trees.

As they rode, the pitch of the land gradually increased, and the trees became fewer and farther between. Instead of blackberry bushes and dense foliage,
there were grasses and tall fronds. The fronds were
tipped with dry pods that opened and released their
silky seeds into the air as their horses brushed past.
The golden seeds landed on Ashleigh's black tresses,
glittering like golden flakes on ebony waves, forming
a halo around her head.

She glanced back. "Why are you looking at me
like that?"

"You are beautiful. I think of you as a dark angel."

She laughed and shook her head, sending the pods
spinning in the breeze. "Then who are you? You, too,
have black hair. Perhaps you are God's warrior."

"I prefer not to call myself a warrior at all."

"But that is silly. You *are* a warrior. Just because
you feel sorrow for your deeds does not negate your
identity. You can be a warrior for God just as you
were a warrior for the king."

"I want to be a monk . . . a fully ordained monk."

Ashleigh's smile faded, and she studied Mangan's
too handsome face. Strong chin, intelligent brow.
Manly cheeks and a powerful, corded neck leading to
solid, broad shoulders. And lips. Full yet firm . . . she
had kissed those lips. She had felt his passion and
nearly drowned within his desire. Those feelings came
from him. She had not imagined them; in fact, she was
confused by them. She did not know if her feelings
grew out of her desperate loneliness, or from something her innocent body craved. It was true that he

made her stomach tingle and her breath shorten, but why? He made her feel as if there were a vista just ahead that would open her eyes to a glorious new world.

"Do you really want to be a monk?" she asked softly.

He shuddered. Her eyes were glinting in the sunlight, showing the thin line of sapphire around the pupil. White blossoms still nestled in her hair, and golden pods fluttered around her face with magical beauty. He wanted her. He wanted to lay her in the grass and slowly peel every layer of clothing from her body and make love to her in the brilliant sunshine so he could watch her body ripple beneath his caresses.

These were not the thoughts of a monk.

"Yes," he whispered, unaware of the desperate yearning that filled his voice.

"Why?" she asked as she pulled her horse to a stop. They had reached the top of the mountain, and a few steps farther would put them at the crest.

He, too, stopped and dismounted. "I want to erase my sins. I was a soldier and I killed many people. There was no glory or honor in my actions, and I cannot bear to see my reflection in the lake because all I see is their blood running down my visage."

"Won't God forgive you for your sin? Doesn't he bless those who ask for forgiveness? You told me that to be redeemed one must learn to forgive. Shouldn't you forgive yourself?"

A breath of wind rippled across the field, releasing the seeds of a thousand pods up into the air and sending them spinning in the currents. Some would land only a few feet away, while others would travel miles, germinating in fields far, far away.

"Come," she said, and took his hand. "Let us look

at God's country as Cairdean sees it." A seed became caught in Mangan's eyelashes, and she brushed it away with her fingers.

He groaned, feeling the sweetness of her caress and imagining it elsewhere, wanting to feel it lower, more intimately.

Hand in hand they walked to the top of the mountain and looked over the long, rolling valley. "Is this your Scotland?" Ashleigh asked. "Is this the land your God created?"

The view was breathtaking, and he clenched her hand tightly, unwilling to let her go. "Aye, this is God's land."

"Does God love his land? Love the creatures within it?"

"Aye," Mangan answered, pulling her closer so that their sides brushed against each other.

"Then God loves you," Ashleigh finished as she squeezed his hand.

He looked at her, stunned. Desire faded, to be replaced by awe. Who was this little angel who spoke as if the great Father communicated through her lips? Beautiful . . . in heart and soul. She could have scars upon her face and still he would think she was the most incredible woman on earth. "Perhaps," he whispered, "if you ask Him for me."

She smiled and her cheeks flushed. "Shall we ask together?"

She sat down. Still holding his hand she pulled him down beside her. As one they stared across the valley, absorbing the glory of nature. He thought about his past, remembering small things he had forgotten . . . a young girl who had thanked him for saving her mother from a tumbling pile of wood . . . a hungry man to whom he had given food and shelter. For so long he had remembered only the deaths. Sitting next to this woman, feeling her breath against his cheek, he began to remember life.

Little rabbits scampered about. A seven-point buck moved cautiously across a lower meadow, his antlers magnificently displayed. Occasional gusts of wind brushed over the grassy fronds and shook the treetops, sending leaves fluttering and seedpods spinning.

Ashleigh prayed for him in her own way. She did not know the intricate chants; nor did she know the solemn Latin phrases, but she understood his need, and she felt the emptiness in his heart. She wanted to help him heal.

She traced the veins on his wrist with her fingertips, then brushed his palm with her thumb. She took a deep breath, seeking to draw the pain out and send it floating up into the heavens, where it could slowly ebb away and leave him whole once again.

And while she concentrated on him, her own heart began to mend. Her anger eased and changed to sorrow. It was right to feel sad. She missed her parents. But it was time to release the fury and accept her loss. She would bring the men to justice, but if she lost her own soul to anger, the men would claim her as well.

She leaned her head against Mangan's shoulder, and he wrapped an arm around her to hold her close. The sun sank over the horizon, casting rippling waves of purple and pink through the clouds, and still they sat next to each other. And slowly, ever so slowly, they began to feel a measure of peace.

Chapter 16

A day later they reached the outskirts of Laird Geoffrey's castle. Sitting low in the valley, it was made of gray stone and was surrounded by a vast, cleared expanse of grassland, which Mangan informed Ashleigh had been formed by a huge flood many generations ago.

"Laird Geoffrey's ancestors built this castle in the center of the valley because stones were plentiful and the land had already been cleared. However, I fear that one day another flood will pummel the castle and cause significant losses."

"It seems unwise to build in such a location."

Mangan shrugged. "The Tiernays had little status then, and had to be thankful for what they could obtain from the king. Since then, however, they have gained power and prestige via marriages and commerce. The current laird is the king's cousin, and is rumored to be one of his closest advisers."

"You know much about the highborn families. I have never been inside such a castle," she said, urging her horse nearer to his. "The closest I ever came to a castle was once when I was five or six. We entered the courtyard because our troupe had been hired to perform a play, but my mother started to cry and we left."

"Why did she cry?"

"I think because she remembered her mother and the life she lived before running off with my father."

"Yet she never talked to you about that life?"

"Very rarely. What about your parents?" Ashleigh asked.

Mangan scanned the walls and perused the high towers. "I am not impressed by Laird Geoffrey's castle, because I have seen a castle much larger and more majestic," he answered softly.

"Where?"

"The place where I was born." He untied his hemp belt and drew off his monk's robes. Carefully folding them, he placed them reverently in his saddlebag and withdrew a ruby signet ring, which he slid onto his small finger. "I am the son of an earl. My familial castle, Castle Kirkcaldy, is many times grander than this one, and my father Brogan O'Bannon, many times more powerful." Mangan glanced ruefully at Ashleigh. "I trust you will still wear and protect my cross?"

"Yes," Ashleigh answered. "Are you certain you should—"

"Discard my robes?" Mangan answered for her. He touched the hilt of his sword and sat up straighter in the saddle, then took a deep breath and stared at the tops of the trees. They swayed gently in the breeze, and light trickled through the branches. A squirrel sat very still, its tiny paws clutched around a pinecone, yet every few seconds its tail twitched upward. "I cannot run from myself forever," he finally answered.

She watched emotions whisper across his face and the shadow of pain cloud his eyes.

"You did not dream of becoming a monk as a child," she surmised.

"No," he agreed. "I wanted to be a great warrior and an honorable leader. I wanted to make my king proud. I wanted to prove myself worthy of being my father's son."

"Yet you feel you failed?"

He dragged his gaze away from the squirrel and smiled sadly at her. "Aye. I failed at everything."

Ashleigh blinked rapidly, trying to hold her tears at bay. This man's agony somehow made her own tragedy seem smaller . . . as if their shared sorrow were diminished because they both had endured so much. Her calamity had been catastrophic, a sudden shattering of all the happiness and security she had always known, while his was long and drawn-out, a lifetime of feeling inadequate and lost.

Cairdean swooped in front of them, his black feathers gleaming against the blue sky. Ashleigh pulled her horse to a stop and glanced nervously at Mangan. "The raven crosses our path."

Mangan also halted his steed. " 'Tis your own friend that flies nearby, not an ill omen. You are letting your superstitions guide you when your mind must stay calm." But he, too, looked at the castle with apprehension. A strange tightening filled his chest—what he used to feel on the eve of battle.

The raven landed on a tree branch and cawed, then swiveled his head and fixed a beady eye on the castle ahead. The squirrel chattered in anger, then scurried down the tree trunk and disappeared into the underbrush. Both Ashleigh and Mangan stared at Cairdean, then at each other.

"Come," Mangan said, forcing his voice to remain steady and reassuring. "All will be well. Our delay only makes us nervous. 'Tis a castle and laird like any other." But he was frowning at the castle. "There are men fortifying the walls," Mangan remarked. " 'Tis odd."

"Why?" Ashleigh asked, only partially interested.

" 'Tis time to shear the sheep."

"So?" Ashleigh commented as she tried to collect her black tresses into a semblance of a braid, then smoothed her skirt.

"So, the men should be working in the corrals, helping to collect the wool and prepare it for cleaning, or working on the church Father Benedict said has not been rebuilt since a fire. It is not a time to set able-bodied men to work on unnecessary additions to the castle walls."

"Perhaps they are not unnecessary," Ashleigh replied.

"Ho, there!" a man shouted from around a bend in the road. "State your name and business!"

Mangan dropped his reins and spread his arms wide. "I am Mangan O'Bannon of Kirkcaldy Castle, and I seek an audience with your Laird Geoffrey of Tiernay ."

"You travel with no contingent," the man replied. "I do not believe your claim."

"I spent the previous year in a monastery and have spent the past many months traveling Scotland to view her many churches."

"Ha. Do you claim to be a monk? You bear a sword upon your saddle!"

" 'Tis a dangerous world, even for a man of God," Mangan answered, as he had many times before.

"Who is the woman?"

"A lass traveling under my protection."

The man came forward and looked at both of them

with obvious distrust, but Mangan stared back un-
flinchingly. His instincts were making his blood thunder, and he had the urge to draw his sword and teach
the pup a lesson, but he clenched his fists and left his
sword sheathed.

*Why is there a sentry on this isolated road? What is
he supposed to be watching for?*

"I will escort you to the castle," the man replied,
"but you will ride in front of me."

Mangan's eyes narrowed, but he picked up his reins,
squeezed his horse and nodded for Ashleigh to join
him.

"Lovely little tart." The man smirked as he rode
behind them and leered at Ashleigh's buttocks. "I'll
give you a pence for a quick tumble with her."

Mangan spun his stallion around and caused Sir
Scott to rear up and neigh angrily as Mangan gripped
the hilt of his sword and drew it half out of its scabbard. "If I draw this blade any further, you will not
see tomorrow's sunrise," he hissed. "I suggest you
keep your comments to yourself and not force me to
prove my words."

Ashleigh gasped and forced Franco between the two
men. "I have heard much worse," she murmured to
Mangan. "I am a Gypsy. Such phrases have no power
to hurt me."

Mangan yanked his gaze from the frightened sentry
and focused on Ashleigh's beautiful face. His hand
slowly released its grip on the blade, and he allowed
it to slide back into the scabbard. "I vowed to raise
my weapon only when there is no other choice, but I
will lift it to protect you, should he insult you again."

The sentry averted his gaze, and Mangan nodded.
"Good. It appears that you understand my warning."

He turned Sir Scott back toward the castle and resumed walking him up the road to the massive gate.

After a brief pause in which Ashleigh stared at Mangan's rigid back in surprise, she clucked to Franco and followed after him. The unexpected flare of Mangan's anger had shocked her, and revealed something about him. His monk's robes had not changed him; they had only banked his warrior's fire.

Above their heads Cairdean cawed again, and this time his warning cry echoed over the forest, sending creatures diving for cover.

As Mangan and Ashleigh rode up to the gate, Mangan's jaw clenched tight with the effort to keep his face impassive. Every one of his warrior instincts told him that they were riding into danger, yet ever since meeting Ashleigh he wasn't certain he could trust his emotions. Although he no longer wore the robes, he would gain strength from the lessons he had learned as a monk. Force would avail him nothing. He must continue to use his head, not his sword.

They entered the courtyard under the intimidating stare of many soldiers braced along the wall. The soldiers' clothing looked worn, and they were too high up to distinguish the insignias on their tunics, but their weapons were shiny, and Mangan had no doubt that the men knew how to use them well. "Has there been trouble in these mountains?" he finally asked, indicating the state of preparedness as he and Ashleigh dismounted.

"No," the man answered shortly.

"Then why—"

"Save your questions for the laird," the man interrupted him. "I must return to my post. The groom's boy will take your horses, and I will send a housemaid to inform the laird of your arrival. In the meantime stay within the courtyard, and do not interfere with the workers. They are on a strict schedule and will be punished if you slow them down."

"May I await word from your laird within the church?" Mangan asked carefully, although his teeth were set with anger. He had never been treated with such disrespect, not as a highborn heir, a warrior, nor a lowly monk. Taking a deep breath, he reminded himself that faith was the most powerful weapon against the ill-mannered.

"I suppose so," the man answered. "But don't expect too much. The laird never enters the church and has not repaired it since the fire."

"When did the church catch fire?"

"Ten years ago. No one knows how it started, but ever since then it has been abandoned. I doubt any other than Father Benedict have trodden its flagstones in many years."

Staring at the crumbling walls and noting the birds flying in and out of holes in the roof, Mangan nodded. "I can see that. However, it is still a house of worship, and I'd like to spend a moment there."

"It will be more than a moment," the man answered smugly. "The laird is busy and rarely bothers to grant audiences to lesser men."

Mangan ignored the taunt, turned and ushered Ashleigh into the church, then shut the half-rotted door behind them.

"He was so rude!" Ashleigh exclaimed. "I thought you said your name granted you some prestige."

"He is an underling and knows nothing," Mangan replied as he glanced at the blackened walls, his face drawn in a frown. "This doesn't feel right. I wonder if someone deliberately set this church afire."

Ashleigh watched him for a moment, her head tilted in curiosity as he paced around the church, examining under the dusty pews and behind fallen stones. "Why would someone do that? Who would gain from burning a church?"

Mangan grunted. "Nonbelievers. People with angry hearts."

"Even if someone does not agree with your beliefs, they have no cause to destroy such a precious place."

As Ashleigh turned away and poked her toe into a pile of charred debris, Mangan took a moment to stare at her. Her innocent statement so perfectly mirrored his own thoughts. His heart skipped a beat as her angelic features reflected her inner beauty . . . A shaft of light highlighted the shape of her generous lips . . . then danced along the curve of her cheek. He was inexorably drawn to her and had to forcibly halt his arms from reaching out to her.

He began sifting through the remnants on the altar as a means of changing the focus of his thoughts.

"What are you looking for?" she asked him.

"A relic," he answered. "I have been on a quest to find a relic that disappeared from the monastery that offered me sanctuary. That is why I was traveling to the mountain village when I came upon you."

"A quest? How noble."

He harrumphed. "Well, I have yet to locate the relic."

"Surely you don't think it is in this decrepit church?"

"No." He sighed. "I doubt I will ever find it. Perhaps the abbot knew my quest would be futile. He may have sent me on this journey because he knew I would come to doubt my future as a monk. Regardless, the laird should not have allowed this sanctuary to become so . . . so . . ." He waved his hands, unable to express his frustration. "If a man does not respect God, then his subjects will also become disrespectful. Once God's word is tarnished, then the people have no guidance other than martial law, and force alone will never control an entire populace. Believe me, I know."

Ashleigh frowned, mulling over his statement. "You speak like a man who cares for his people."

"Of course I care. I care for all God's children."

Ashleigh pursed her lips and put her hands on her hips. "Mangan, if your people are so important to you, why did you leave your home and deny your inheritance to enter the monastery? It would seem that you could do much more for your people as their overlord than as a wandering monk." When he ducked through a doorway and was lost to sight, she followed him into a small chamber, frowning in frustration because he wasn't listening to her. But when she saw what had caught his attention, she gasped. It was a small anteroom with an arched doorway and rows upon rows of intricately carved stone shelves. The workmanship was superior to anything she had ever seen, and she brushed her fingers across the carvings in awe. There were angels and vines interwoven together along the edges, and the shelf ends were finished with elegant scrollwork, but the ledges themselves were bare.

"A holy chamber," Mangan informed her. "This is where a church's valuables and special relics would usually be stored. Someone must have removed them before the fire."

"How fortunate."

"Hmm," Mangan replied, his tone revealing doubt. "Or the fire was set to mask a theft."

Ashleigh perused the dirty chamber, seeing bird and

mouse droppings and what appeared to be years of
dust and debris. "Could someone be that awful?" she
asked, but Mangan was staring at a Latin inscription
carved into the stone wall above the ledges.

" 'To love Him is to love all others,' " Mangan
translated for her as he touched the stone. " 'And to
love all others is to worship Him.' "

Ashleigh shook her head. "One cannot love all others," she said sadly. "I do not love the men who killed
my parents, and you do not love even yourself."

Mangan stroked the stone once again, rereading it.
He nodded, agreeing with Ashleigh, even though he
wished it were not so. "I am a sorry man," he said
softly. "I cannot care for my people if I can't lead
them in righteousness. I have masqueraded as a monk,
yet I cannot follow the simplest of commands engraved in the humblest of sanctuaries."

"You are not masquerading," she answered. "You
are on the path to becoming a monk. You are kind
and generous. You listen to people and make fair
judgments. You seek honor and justice. The only reason you removed your robes today is so that the laird
will listen to our tale."

"Is that true?" he asked, glancing at her lovely face.
Emotions welled inside him. He wanted to hold her
close and bury his nose in her hair. He imagined how
she would look with her belly filled with a child . . .
his child. Rounded and beautiful, his dark angel glow-
ing with inner radiance. He imagined her in his family's church, where he had been baptized and where
his children—should he have any—would be baptized.
Where his parents had expected him to be wed before
he informed them that he had relinquished everything.

He had hurt them, especially his father. Mangan was
their only son, and his father loved Castle Kirkcaldy.

He had raised Mangan to cherish and protect her lands at all costs. Mangan closed his eyes and took a deep breath. He, too, loved his home's golden walls and endless acres. He loved the caves and the forest, the hillsides and the valleys. Would he ever return? Would his father ever forgive him for casting aside his inheritance?

In some ways he and Ashleigh were so similar, but in others so different. She was a Gypsy following the road of trickery, stealth and opportunity, while he was a highborn heir traveling the road to simplicity, purity and poverty. She was open and without pretense, seeking to remain close to her family; he was solitary and withdrawn, abandoning his mortal father in favor of an immortal one.

Yet when he was with her he felt no guilt. When she smiled at him his soul radiated with joy and his turbulent thoughts settled into simple needs and desires. He stood strong and at peace, knowing his duty was to protect and care for her, to make her happy and see her smile. He saw truth in her gaze and knew that she saw him for who he was, and he could sense that they abided by similar codes of morality and justice despite their differing methods of achieving them.

He felt he could tell her things he could barely admit to himself. What made her so unique? It was not just her appearance, for although she was beautiful, he had seen many beauties in his life. It was not only that she had endured tragedy, for he had seen many women weeping over their dead. It was the part of him that was lonely . . . the part of him he always tried to ignore. The essence inside that reached for her as if it already knew her and recognized that she was the answer to his emptiness.

He chuckled in self-deprecation as he looked up at

the bare rafters and shook his head at his own thoughts. "I am not so certain I will still make a good monk." He smiled as he saw from the corner of his eye that she was frowning. His chuckle faded into silence and he sighed. "I don't know who I am or who I should be anymore. I feel as if I have to start all over once again."

"You are confusing me," Ashleigh replied.

"And you are confusing me," he agreed. "Come." He motioned. "Let us forget my last words and prepare for our audience. I hear someone approaching."

Chapter 17

"Laird Geoffrey has consented to see you," the soldier announced, his expression conveying his annoyance. "He bade me to escort you to the great room while a maid directs the woman to the kitchens."

"She comes with me," Mangan replied. "Her tale is of importance to the laird."

The soldier frowned. "That is not what—"

"I am Lord O'Bannon, and I have had enough of your insolence." He turned to Ashleigh. "Stay behind me and remain silent until I ask you to speak."

Ducking her head and wrapping her arms around herself to still her nervous shivering, Ashleigh nodded.

They trekked across the courtyard and entered the castle. Again Mangan was struck by the military state of preparedness in the castle. Two sets of guards manned the door, and several soldiers were posted throughout the room. Two lean hounds bayed in warning as they entered, while the laird and a younger man seated beside him at a long, scarred wooden table observed their approach.

The dogs rushed toward Mangan and Ashleigh, then growled and showed their teeth until a hound master hustled forward and looped a rope around their necks and yanked the dogs away.

"They no' be likin' strangers," the hound master explained.

As he talked his lips parted, showing a partial set of broken, yellowed teeth that made Ashleigh shudder. The dogs spun and lunged at their master, who was forced to kick them back into obedience, then drag them yelping and squirming to the far side of the room. "They don't appear to like anyone," Ashleigh commented under her breath, but pressed her lips together in silence when Mangan cast a frown over his shoulder.

The next moment his eyes widened as he recognized the younger man at the table. Mangan placed a hand on Ashleigh's arm to warn her to say nothing.

"Milord," the laird greeted Mangan. "And?" he added, his eyebrows lifting as he took in Ashleigh's ragged but colorful clothing and the beaded chain and cross around her neck.

"Greetings, Laird Geoffrey of Tiernay. I appreciate your gracious hospitality at our unanticipated arrival. May I introduce Ashleigh, daughter of Romil?"

The laird nodded at her and replied smoothly, "I am honored to welcome a member of the O'Bannon family, especially one as renowned as you, Lord Mangan. My cousin, the king, speaks highly of your skill in battle, as well as of your brilliant military strategy. To what do I owe the pleasure of your appearance at my home so far from your own?"

"This young lady has come to seek justice for murder. I speak on her behalf."

The laird took his time perusing Ashleigh's form, his gaze lingering on her bosom and taking note of her bare feet. "The woman is a peasant," he said dismissively. "Probably a Gypsy. Anything she has to say is most likely a lie."

"I saw evidence with my own eyes that supports her claim," Mangan stated firmly.

"Why should my father believe you?" the younger man snarled.

Mangan's eyes flared, and he stared at the young man as Laird Geoffrey placed a restraining hand on his son's arm.

"Excuse my son's brash demeanor," Laird Geoffrey interjected. "He means no disrespect to your name or honor. 'Tis just that it was recently Jordan's wedding night and he has not slept much."

Mangan's lips thinned in anger, but he tilted his head in nearly imperceptible acknowledgment. "You were the man at the village chapel yesterday morning," he stated to Jordan, who appeared to be no more than ten and nine and likely more familiar with lounging in a chair than riding a horse. Compared to Mangan's muscular body, Jordan's looked thin and slight.

"What do you know of the wedding?" Laird Geoffrey asked with a hooded expression.

"Only that the lady appeared distressed, as is often the case in arranged marriages. I trust that she is settling in well?" Mangan glanced around the room, looking for other female household members, but saw only a few maids.

"So it seems . . ." the laird replied after a moment.

"Will I have a chance to offer her my congratulations?" Mangan asked, becoming aware of an undercurrent of tension in the room. Something seemed amiss, and he reached behind him for Ashleigh's hand.

She gripped it tightly and tugged to get his attention. "The soldiers who attacked my parents," she whispered, "they looked like these guards . . . same tunics and insignia."

Mangan's muscles tightened, and his sense of unease escalated into certainty. Something foul was going on in this castle. "Laird Geoffrey," Mangan said as he turned back to face the table. "On our journey here we came upon two royal guards and one maid-in-waiting who had been ambushed and murdered on the far side of the mountain, their bodies left unburied. Ashleigh's parents were similarly killed, and she narrowly survived. Based upon her observations, three of your soldiers may be responsible."

Laird Geoffrey rose to his feet and leaned over the table to stare into Mangan's face. "These are serious charges," he murmured softly. "You are speaking of treason, for killing a royal guard is tantamount to attacking the king himself."

"Aye."

"You suspect some of *my* soldiers have done these terrible deeds?"

"Ashleigh can provide names and can identify the culprits. I trust you to mete out fair punishment."

Laird Geoffrey's gaze slid to his son's and he smiled. "Indeed. I will ensure that everything is set back to rights. Have you told anyone else of your suspicions?"

"We came directly to you."

Standing fully upright, Laird Geoffrey slapped the table with a flash of jovial good humor. "Excellent. Why don't you retire to a guest chamber and rest while I assemble my soldiers and begin the investigation? I presume you would enjoy a warm bath and a hearty meal?"

Mangan bowed. "Many thanks, Laird Geoffrey."

"The Gypsy," he said, his voice dropping with derision, "may await our pleasure in the servants' hall, as long as she promises not to fill her pockets with any of my household valuables."

"I prefer that she come with me," Mangan answered, tightening his hold on Ashleigh's hand. "As you are my gracious host, I trust you will accommodate my request," he added.

Delectable smells wafted from the kitchen. Ashleigh's stomach grumbled loudly enough for both men to hear.

The laird smiled. "Very well, I understand. Why don't you allow the housemaid to bring you each to a bedchamber, and perhaps she can find the lass some clean clothing."

"I don't trust him," Ashleigh stated as soon as they were in an upstairs room and the maid had closed the door behind them.

"I don't either," Mangan replied as he swiftly searched the room, finding that the windows were too narrow for escape and the only other door led to a servant's bedchamber.

"His men killed my parents."

Mangan turned around and held her shoulders in order to stare down at her face. "I am not so certain they were rogue soldiers. They may have acted upon his orders. His son was wed in the chapel under very unusual circumstances, and neither man offered the bride's name, which I find highly suspicious. I suspect the lass was kidnapped and forced into a political alliance."

"But why?" Ashleigh asked. "The laird is already a powerful man, is he not?"

"Perhaps he seeks more," Mangan replied as he let her go and started pacing around the room. It would make sense in light of all that was happening. Eo'Ghanan had warned him that the highborn men traveling through the woods were dangerous. Presumably they were dangerous because they were moving in secrecy and the laird had demanded that any witnesses to their presence be silenced with a sword.

Ashleigh's family had simply been unlucky.

But what of the royal party? What had brought them to this place? A sound outside the door made Mangan pause. He approached the door and pressed his ear against the wood. After listening for a moment, he took Ashleigh's hand and pulled her to the far side of the room. He bent and brushed his lips over her ear.

Initially she jerked back, but Mangan held her close. "Listen carefully," Mangan whispered. "They are eavesdropping on us."

As his breath rippled over her ear, Ashleigh shivered. "Why?" she whispered back.

"Because the laird and his son are at the core of this plot. We must escape from here and find a lord whose loyalty to the king is unquestioned. Only then will Tiernay's plot be exposed, and you will obtain justice for your parents' deaths."

Ashleigh's dark eyes searched his. "If he is plotting against the king, he will do anything to prevent you from exposing his plans."

Mangan breathed in her scent. He pulled her closer, pressing the tips of her breasts against his muscled chest. "We can reveal nothing of my suspicions."

"Nothing? What can I say? What will you do?"

He brushed his lips across the delicate curve of her ear. "You and I will leave the castle together—tonight."

A shiver ran up her spine and made her weak. "When?"

"After dinner, when all is dark. Until then, do nothing to arouse their suspicions."

He stared at her, recognizing the fear tempered with trust that lay buried behind her deeply colored eyes. She believed in him, and her belief awed him. Her lashes were wet with unshed tears, and her cheeks were flushed. He touched the bridge of her nose, then cupped her cheek in his hand. Her face felt hot against his cool palm.

"Will your God protect us?" she questioned.

"How can I answer that?" he replied as he caressed her neck. "God's plans have mystified the greatest scholars, and I doubt we will ever understand Him. However, I do believe He watches over us and gives us the chance to do what is right at several crossroads in life. If we take the right path and don't squander our opportunities to show faith, courage, forgiveness and charity, then He will be pleased with us."

"I want to kill the rest of them. I want to murder the murderers. You would say that I am walking down the wrong path, wouldn't you?"

He tilted his head and kissed the top of her forehead, then inhaled deeply. Her scent was intoxicating. He wished she knew that he would not leave her while her soul still struggled against itself. He had been there. He had had blood on his blade and had faced demons in the night. He would never let her walk down the same road. He would stand by her and help her find the light to guide her back to happiness.

"God always honors His promises, as will I."

He closed his eyes and kissed her forehead again, feeling her hair brush across his closed lids. Their bond had already been forged, and he would not allow anything to break it. If it became necessary, he would lay down his life for her.

The fresh innocence in her gaze . . . her impetuous mischievousness. She was a child cast into an adult game of murder, intrigue and political power. But he was no youth, and he understood the royal court and the battlefield. Perhaps God had placed him in Ashleigh's path just for this moment . . .

She wrapped her arms around his shoulders and laid her head against his chest. His heartbeat thrummed, and she felt his powerful muscles ripple with suppressed power. He was going to stay. He was going to honor his promise. Wonderment filled her heart as his arms wrapped firmly around her. This powerful man . . . this man on a holy quest . . . had paused to help her.

She looked up and touched a lock of hair that had fallen across his brow. "Why?" she whispered. "Why do this for me?"

"I had everything. A castle, prestige, wealth . . . My equals as well as my subordinates held me in high regard, but I discovered that there was something still missing in my life. I went to the monastery to find that elusive secret, and I almost did find it."

"Almost?"

"Almost. Not quite. Not until I sat on that mountaintop with you." He smiled, half of his mouth curling up and a small dimple appearing in his cheek. "I thought I understood God's path for me, but I realize now that I do not. All I know is that He brought you and me together and is asking me to help you, so here I am." His grin grew and he brushed his thumb over her eyebrow. "Let God guide me in the path of His choosing." Sliding his hand up her back and into the thick wealth of her hair, he pulled her head back and angled her toward him, then touched her lips with his.

As she felt his kiss, the last rays of sunlight burst

through the narrow window and infused the room with multicolored brilliance. His mouth felt firm and warm, evoking peace and tranquility, yet sent her mind spinning into chaos. His arms were powerful and muscled, yet she felt his vulnerability. Passion was mixed with something indefinable . . . something she could not name.

He tasted her lips with his tongue, touching their sweetness and savoring the delicate juncture at the corner of her mouth. "Dark angel," he whispered. "I am beginning to believe that you bring me as close to heaven as I will ever come."

She pulled back, her gaze flickering over his face. She touched his lips, then the place where his dimple had appeared for one brief moment. "So serious," she murmured. "I—"

A sudden knock on the door interrupted them, and they both froze.

"Milord?" the housemaid asked through the closed portal. "I have ordered your bath and brought the lass some clothes. May I enter?"

Ashleigh looked at Mangan, then at the door.

He took a deep breath, disengaged her arms from around his neck and pushed her back one step. "Don't forget," he cautioned. "Show no evidence of our suspicions."

Chapter 18

The overdress was pale lilac trimmed with silver embroidery and white ermine. The matching handworked silver girdle had tiny purple beads interwoven between the metal links, and the long strands of the belt ended in tufts of more white fur. A large tub was placed by the fire, and several boys poured pans of hot water into the tub, filling it near to the brim.

"Would ye like me to stay and help you?" the maid asked Mangan respectfully as the last of the boys departed. "I'd be pleased to assist with *whatever* needs you may have."

He shook his head as he smiled at her insinuation.

The maid looked dubiously at Ashleigh. "I can help scrub yer back," she started to say, but Mangan waved his hand in dismissal. "No. I do not want assistance. Miss Ashleigh will provide for me."

The maid shrugged and turned away. "As you wish, milord. The evening meal will be served after the sun drops o'er the horizon."

Ashleigh glanced out the narrow window, suddenly feeling shy. As the maid closed the door, Ashleigh stroked the gown's soft material and picked up one of a pair of silken stockings. She knew what to do with these, but there were several other garments to be layered over the chemise that confounded her. How was she to put all those pieces of clothing on without assistance? A fluttering at the window caused her to look up, and she beheld Cairdean landing on the window ledge. "You are such an intelligent beast," Ashleigh said with a smile. "How do you always find me?"

The raven emitted a soft trill quite unlike his normal caw. He swiveled his head and trained a beady eye on her, then fluffed his feathers in agitation as Mangan approached.

"You don't like it here, do you?" Ashleigh asked the raven. She glanced over her shoulder at Mangan. "I will wait in the servant's chamber while you bathe," she offered.

"No, you may go first. I will step into the side room and plan our escape while you freshen up."

As he closed the door behind him, she took a deep breath and peeled off her ragged clothing, shivering slightly as a gust of wind slipped though the window and brushed over her bare body. The tub looked incredibly inviting, and she leaped in to avoid the breeze, only to shriek in surprise at the steaming hot water.

Mangan flung open the door and rushed inside. "Ashleigh!" he cried, then caught his breath. "I . . . I thought you were hurt."

She squealed and sank deep into the tub, sending water sloshing over the sides. As he continued to stare at her, she sank down even farther, leaving only the tops of her shoulders and her head above water.

"I . . ." Mangan stuttered, trying to drag his gaze away but unable to move. As if frozen in stone, he stared at her wide eyes and watched the steam caress her blazing cheeks.

Ashleigh clasped the cross she still wore around her neck as if it could ward off his heated gaze. " 'Twas just the hot water . . ." she whispered.

"Yes . . ." he stammered. He had bidden her to wear the cross as a reminder to himself that her flesh was forbidden, but his feelings were changing. Her body was forbidden only if he chose to continue his path of celibacy. What if that path was the wrong one? Her own lips had said nearly as much. She had questioned his motivations and doubted his goals. Perhaps she saw more clearly than he did.

He walked forward and stared down at her. Her pale flesh shimmered underneath the water, and tendrils of her long black hair floated upon the surface, partially shielding her from his view. "You are beautiful."

Ashleigh bit her lip and drew her knees up as she tried to shield her breasts. "Shouldn't you go? Don't you pray at this time?"

"No. My prayers have been answered."

"I thought you prayed until well past sundown."

He noted a thin bead of water trickling across her temple and down the curve of her jaw. "Not tonight." He picked up a bar of soap and reached into the tub to grasp her ankle. "Tonight I will help you bathe, then dress."

Ashleigh trembled as his strong fingers wrapped around her foot and lifted it only inches above the tub's rim. The water sloshed again, sending a small wave splashing over the side and soaking the front of Mangan's breeches. "Such assistance is not necessary," Ashleigh whispered, terrified by her own response to his caress.

"You know how to put on all the garments the laird has provided?" Mangan asked with a raised eyebrow.

Ashleigh gasped as his fingers rubbed the soap around her toes and massaged her delicate instep.

"Do you?" he asked again, secretly smiling at her reaction.

"No," she replied as a sense of bliss rippled up from her feet and landed in the center of her abdomen.

"Does that feel good?"

"Ummm . . ." she answered as her head lolled back and rested on the tub's rim.

"You have lovely toes," Mangan murmured as he slid his fingers in and around each individual appendage.

"Mother called them piggies."

A smile broke across Mangan's face. "I think they are far too beautiful to be named after a fat and dirty barnyard beast."

Ashleigh slanted a look at him through her eyelashes. "You smiled again. I like it when you smile."

Mangan tilted his head and looked at her with consternation. "Are you deliberately confusing me, or does your mind normally wander at will?"

"You are too serious and rarely smile."

"I smile."

"A smile of satisfaction or a look of triumph is not the same as smiling with humor."

"I don't find your naked body and exquisite toes humorous."

Ashleigh grinned as she wiggled her toes and splashed a dab of soapsuds on his shirt. "You should."

He frowned. "I just left my prayers to come over and save you, and you tease me with thoughts of pigs?"

"This little piggy went to market . . ." Ashleigh wriggled her large toe against his chest, leaving a wet mark.

Mangan gripped the offending toe and soaped it, sending delicious shivers up Ashleigh's leg.

"This little piggy stayed home." She tried to move her second toe but could not wriggle it independently. Instead she accidentally slid her foot under his shirt and untied it.

Mangan grasped the foot and shrugged off the garment, then flung the shirt over a chair, where it would not get wet. "Are you speaking of this toe, now?" He dipped his hand in the warm water, then rubbed her second toe between his thumb and forefinger.

Ashleigh giggled and tried to jerk her foot out of his hand, resisting the temptation to stare at his bare chest. Like rocks along the shore, his muscles looked smooth and solid, and she had an urge to knead them with her fingers.

"Not so fast, my darling angel. I have to know the rest, for you have intrigued me."

"The next little piggy had roast lamb . . ."

"What a lucky piggy," Mangan murmured, his lips curling up in a true smile as he watched Ashleigh's eyes dance with happiness. "Did he have it with potatoes and carrots, or did he get the slop from the master's table?"

Ashleigh laughed. "You are impossible! Of course he did not get the slop. He is a precious pig and gets only the best!"

"Ahh . . . I see that now." Mangan picked up the soap and swirled it around the entire foot, rubbing his calloused hands over its soft hills and valleys. "This is a shy piggy, for it curls just slightly underneath the other."

Ashleigh leaned forward to peer at the offending toe, unaware that the water level abruptly sluiced down her throat and swirled into eddies around the sides of her breasts.

Mangan swallowed and struggled to maintain the smile on his face. The beaded chain hung between her breasts. His cross . . . against her flesh.

"You are making fun of my feet," Ashleigh complained as she tried to pull her foot away from his hold.

"Not at all. They are lovely piggies. What happens next?"

She leaned back once again and bent her toes back and forth. "The next little piggy got none."

"None? Why deprive the little creature? Give it some shepherd's pie or some bread and wine."

"Those would not rhyme, Mangan," she admonished.

"I could make them rhyme. This little piggy had bread and wine, and *this* little piggy is all mine."

"I was wrong. You do have a sense of humor."

His smile faded, but his eyes twinkled. "I never had a use for humor before."

"Not having humor is like not having fun, or not knowing tricks, or not playing jokes upon another. Humor is the essence of loving and caring for one another. My parents were always teasing each other."

Mangan pressed her foot against his chest, staring at the strong bones and the lithe curves of her lower calf. "I do recall my mother laughing with my father."

"That is a sign of love."

"I was always told that I was a serious boy. I guess that is why I thought the priesthood was the best place for me."

She wriggled her foot, sliding it into his armpit.

He jerked and almost toppled into the bathtub.

She laughed and tried it again, but this time he held

her foot firmly and frowned with mock seriousness. "Now stop this foolery and tell me the final chapter of the piggy's edifying epic. What happens to the last one?"

Her face slowly shifted as she stared at the wet curls of chest hair plastered against his body. Three rows of taut muscles graced his abdomen, and his pectorals were hard and tight. The urge to touch him grew stronger. She had seen his back in the moonlight, seen his buttocks clench and ripple with every movement, but now he was facing her and she saw even more. His manly nipples were hard and firm, and she was tempted to kiss them. She had a strange desire to grip his neck and pull his head down to lick them . . . She took a breath and dropped her gaze. "It goes wee-wee-wee . . . all the way home," she answered in a mere whisper.

"Home?"

"Yes . . . home. It rhymes with the second piggy."

"Where is home?" His gaze traveled up her leg to her bent knee, then down her thigh as it wavered beneath the rippled surface of the water.

Ashleigh's mouth went dry, and for once she had no reply.

"I think I am beginning to guess where home is," he said quietly as he slipped his hands into the warm water and grasped her hand where it lay folded across her chest.

She tightened her arms, nervous yet oddly excited by his shuttered expression. Then suddenly, without warning, he pulled her completely under the water.

"Agh!" Ashleigh exclaimed as she flung her arms wide and flailed her feet. She swallowed water, then sputtered and coughed and struggled upright. Shoving the mass of her wet hair aside, she then wiped the water from her eyes and peered angrily up at where Mangan was calmly observing her frantic efforts.

"Why did you do that?" she shouted as she tried to splash him with a quick smack of her hand across the water's surface. "You dunked me!"

Mangan laughed and turned away. "It was fun. Now get out and let's enjoy the laird's supper before we head back to the forest."

Gaping with astonishment, she had no choice but to obey.

Chapter 19

It took them several attempts to get Ashleigh dressed, but in the end she looked like a true angel. Mangan, however, was feeling anything but holy. Wishing he were wrapped in the voluminous folds of his robe, he had to adjust himself in order to hide evidence of his arousal from Ashleigh, although Cairdean's accusing look through the bars on the window made him acutely aware of the ineffectiveness of his efforts.

Just as the sun sank behind the horizon and red streaks faded from the sky, Mangan opened the door to escort Ashleigh from the room. An armed guard stood at attention on the far side of the hall and rapped the floor with his lance as soon as the two exited.

"I'm surprised the door wasn't bolted from the outside," Mangan murmured, but motioned for Ashleigh to precede him down the hallway and to the stairs that led to the great room.

As soon as they entered, Mangan noted that more guards now lined the hall. Several additional soldiers had arrived and were positioned every few feet. Father Benedict and a decorated soldier were also present. Mangan nodded to the priest, then approached the laird. "You appear to place a high value on military vigilance," he said, glancing pointedly at the guards.

"Two of my men have just returned and reported finding three fresh graves."

"Indeed," Mangan agreed. " 'Tis as I stated."

"I am concerned about who might have killed them, then attempted to hide evidence of their crime."

Mangan stood up straighter and stared stonily at Laird Geoffrey. "What are you insinuating?"

"I find it odd that these royal guards were murdered at the same time that you were traveling the roads. Your prowess with a sword is renowned. But I'm sure the mystery will be solved shortly." Laird Geoffrey's cold gaze held Mangan's.

Mangan's hand twitched and he nearly reached for his sword, but a movement on the stairs caught his attention, and he turned to see a woman slowly enter the room, followed by an impatient Jordan. Her face was streaked with tears and her head was bowed, yet she moved to the table with gentle grace and curtsied to the gathered assemblage.

"Lady Matilda," Laird Geoffrey greeted her. "I am pleased to see that you have risen from your bed and joined us for dinner. May I introduce Lord Mangan and his companion, Ashleigh?"

Jordan dropped into a chair and glared sullenly at Ashleigh. "I would much rather have had her in my bed last night than this cold fish of a convent girl," he grumbled. "I'm sure the Gypsy would have been much better sport."

"Indeed," the laird replied. "Ashleigh is quite beautiful, with her creamy cheeks and rosy lips against the backdrop of midnight tresses . . . a delicious combination. But stating thus at the table is poor manners, my son."

Ashleigh shrank against Mangan, clutching his arm for support while Mangan struggled to control his temper. "You owe both Lady Matilda and Ashleigh an apology," he stated. "Such rudeness is inexcusable."

Jordan shrugged. "My apologies, ladies," he replied carelessly, then took a draft from his cup.

"Yes, please excuse my son," Laird Geoffrey replied smoothly. "He is still young. Won't you sit down?" He waved for a servant to pour them cups of wine. Then, as if in afterthought, he motioned for the ladies to take seats. "Tell me more about these royal guards, for I find the situation intriguing."

"Perhaps we should not speak of this matter in front of Lady Matilda, for I am certain the details would be distressing to her," Mangan replied. "She came from a convent?"

Lady Matilda looked up. "St. Augustine's," she whispered.

Ashleigh's brows drew together. "I have heard of St Augustine's. My mother told me that she and her mother used to visit there when she was a child. She said it had a lovely apple orchard and the nuns would let her pick the best apples from the trees anytime she wanted."

Lady Matilda smiled tremulously. "Yes, that is St. Augustine's. The orchard is very old and quite beautiful. You remind me of another convent sister there named Glorianna. She had eyes like yours."

"Cease this prattle," Jordan interrupted. "Women's talk makes my head ache. I order you to speak no more unless I say you may," he informed Lady Matilda.

"Newlyweds," the laird said, as he leaned back and let his gaze drift over Ashleigh's face. "So you say you know the names of the vile men you accuse of murder, and now you seek justice. Tell me their names."

Ashleigh glanced at Mangan, whose face remained shuttered as he stared distrustfully at the laird.

"I know of Cormag and Eogan," Ashleigh replied. "They are from the village. The others are soldiers . . . Douglas, Tory and Curtis."

"And you want me to punish these men?"

"Yes. They should be held accountable for their crimes."

"Douglas," Laird Geoffrey called out to a man in the far corner. "You are responsible for maintaining my authority on the far side of the mountain. Is this the woman you suspect of witchery in the village?"

Ashleigh gasped rising to her feet. "That's him!" she cried. "That is one of the soldiers!"

"How convenient," the laird murmured, his lips thinning in a humorless smile. "You accuse the man who would point a finger at you. He told me of the trouble in the village, and I wonder if *you* have been doing mischief yourself. If so, you have caused the villagers to neglect their fields and herds, which in turn has affected my tithes. It would seem that you are the one who has committed a crime, not him."

Ashleigh opened her mouth to speak, but no words came out. Here was the man who had raped and killed her mother . . . who had brutally slain her father. She balled her hands into fists. A sour taste filled her mouth, and a red haze clouded her eyes. She wanted to kill him . . . to see his blood soak the rushes at her feet.

"Aye, milord," Douglas replied, as he stepped forward and smiled mockingly at Ashleigh. "She accuses me falsely in order to shift the blame from herself.

She evoked evil spirits upon the people and sent them
cowering in terror."

"Father Benedict?"

The priest stepped forward and spoke to Mangan.
"I warned you about coming here," he hissed. "Now
you will suffer the consequences of ignoring my
words. Did you really think I would not discover the
truth? Did you think I would be fooled by her Gypsy
tricks or your pious robes? You are no more a monk
than she is an innocent! You should have returned
to St. Ignacio!"

Ashleigh's hands wrapped around the knife laid out
beside her trencher as her gaze collided with Douglas's. "You . . ." she whispered as she walked forward,
her hand raised. "You killed them!"

Mangan leaped up and placed a restraining hand on
Ashleigh arm. "It is not for you to punish him," he
murmured. "His trial will be held before a higher
judge."

Douglas shrugged and glanced at his laird, who
shook his head mockingly. "Lord Mangan, you and
Ashleigh will be punished by my hand, which I assure
you will not be lenient. The Gypsy is found guilty of
trickery, and you are suspected of murder."

"Murder?" Mangan shouted as he pushed Ashleigh
behind him. "Who am I accused of killing?"

"The royal guards. Oh, and I suppose you killed
her parents as well."

"How dare you!" Ashleigh screamed. "He helped
me! 'Tis you and your henchmen who are murderers!"

Ashleigh darted forward and slashed Laird Geoffrey's arm with her knife, sending him scrambling
backward to avoid greater injury.

Within seconds the guards swarmed Ashleigh and

Mangan, gripping his arms and bending them up behind his back, and cruelly twisting Ashleigh's wrist until she dropped the weapon. Several converged to knock Mangan to his knees, while another then flung Ashleigh against the wall, where she teetered dizzily. A guard clasped her around the throat and pinned her to the wall while three other men pressed their swords against Mangan's neck.

He did not resist, but glared furiously at Laird Geoffrey. "How do you sleep, knowing you harm innocent people? Kill defenseless travelers? You will go to hell for your misdeeds!"

Geoffrey pressed his hand against his wound as his son helped him rise, then stepped in front of Mangan and kicked him with a booted foot.

"Stop!" Lady Matilda screamed. "What are you doing to them?" She rushed forward, but Jordan grabbed her hair and yanked her to a stop. "My father—" she started, but Jordan slapped her and she collapsed to the ground, sobbing.

"Your father will be dead by the next full moon," Jordan snapped. "And then I will take the throne!"

Matilda sobbed louder and covered her ears with her hands while both Mangan and Ashleigh stared at her in horror.

"Are you King Malcolm's daughter?" Mangan asked incredulously. He looked up into Laird Geoffrey's smug face. "You stole the king's daughter from her convent and wed her to Jordan? And then what? Do you plan to murder the King of Scotland so that you can claim the throne through your son?"

Douglas yanked Mangan upright and forced him to face Laird Geoffrey. "No," the laird replied. "The story will go thus: *You* ambushed Lady Matilda's caravan and sent mercenaries to murder the king while my brave son rescued the damsel in distress and wed her to save her reputation from complete ruin. Jordan acted with chivalry and will reluctantly take over the crown—under the careful guidance of his father—once it becomes known that the king is dead. Meanwhile you will rot in prison for the rest of your treasonous life."

"No one will believe you!" Mangan growled. "They know I am loyal to the crown. They will discover that I have been journeying on a quest." But even as he spoke, the soldiers' swords pressed against his neck and sent small rivulets of blood trailing down his throat. "You are raising arms against a warrior for God."

"A warrior so loyal that you left the battlefield?" the laird hissed. "Walked away from your family name and its holdings? So meek that you killed thousands of men with that very sword you still wear around your waist?"

Mangan's gaze grew guarded, and he glanced around the room in sudden comprehension. "You have been planning this villainy for a long time, and I conveniently came along in time to take the blame," he said. "How did you gain access to the convent?"

"Harold Dunkeld is tired of living in the king's shadow. His mistress also resides at St. Augustine's. It was a simple matter to gain access to one and then the other."

The laird checked his laceration, then gripped the front of Mangan's shirt and pulled his face close. "We both know you cannot dispute anything," the laird snarled. "You call yourself a monk. Can you prove your devotion? Can you tame the fire inside you that yearns to plunge a blade into my heart?" He shoved Mangan backward and sent him sprawling to the floor.

"Tell me. Will you rise up and fight, or will you trust in God to save you and your woman?"

"Mangan!" Ashleigh shouted. She struggled out of the guard's hold and rushed toward him, but Douglas gripped her arm as she raced past and he yanked her flush against his body. "What a familiar scene," he murmured against her neck. "A helpless man and his lovely lass . . . I guess you know how it all ends, don't you, sweetling?"

She screamed in terror, kicking and flailing, all the while seeing the laird lift Mangan from the floor and punch him in the ribs, then kick him in the groin to send him rolling on the rushes. "Mangan! Fight him! Fight him!"

Mangan gasped through the haze of pain, trying to keep his mind clear. He heard her voice, recognized her intense fear, but he would not fight to defend himself. He would not engage in battle just to beat his foe. He must use reason and let his fists remain at his sides.

If he was not going to give God his life, he at least owed Him his faith.

The laird kicked him again. Then he shook Mangan, banging his head repeatedly against the floor until the back of Mangan's head bloodied the rushes beneath him.

"If you kill me," Mangan managed to whisper, "you will have no one to blame." Mangan's gaze slid past the laird's face to Ashleigh's. Exotic eyes . . . clouds of black hair . . . his dark angel sent to watch over him. He smiled. How ironic that God had sent such a woman to show him his true path.

One must fully die before one could fully live.

Then the laird slammed Mangan's head against the

stone floor once more, and Mangan's eyes rolled up as he slid into unconsciousness.

"Mangan," Ashleigh whispered. "Wake up. Please . . . please wake up. I'm frightened of the dark."

He moaned and tried to open his eyes, but they felt like lead balls.

"Mangan? Can you hear me?"

He moaned again and this time managed to open one eye, but nothing seemed any different. It was still dark. He closed his eyes and pondered the situation.

"Mangan!" she said sharply. "I am getting annoyed with you! 'Tis time to wake up."

He sighed and opened his eyes again, realizing that the room must be dark and that was why he could not see anything. But he could smell her, and he felt her soft hands clasping his and her warm lap underneath his aching head. "I'm awake," he murmured, although the effort made his head swim with renewed pounding.

"They put us in the dungeon," she told him. "The laird told the guards to leave us here while he checked the defenses, but that he would be back to move me to a different place. A space with a bed."

Mangan sat up, although the spinning in his head made him feel nauseous. "How long have we been here?"

"An hour? Maybe more. 'Tis hard to tell time in this dark hole, but you have been sleeping for quite a long time."

Mangan rubbed his temples, then reached for her hand in the blackness. Up above him he saw an outline of a circular trapdoor that allowed a few thin streaks of light to penetrate the gloom. He sighed, wishing they had been put in a locked room instead, for then he could have tried to break the door. A deep hole such as this one made escape nearly impossible. "Did they harm you?"

"No."

Mangan squeezed her hands. "Thank God."

"They said they will torture you to get a confession. When they return, please tell them what they want to hear and then they won't hurt you."

"I will not shame my family name by lying." He stood up, pulling her with him. The walls were steep and the floor was small, reminding him of a dark well. "I will not confess to a crime I have not committed."

"Why not? Surely a small lie is better than days of torture."

"Lying is a sin."

Silence greeted his reply, and he pulled her closer and pressed his lips against her hair. "We must escape this dungeon. How did we get in here?"

"They placed me on a piece of wood attached to a knotted rope, then bade me to hold you as they lowered us down. I . . ." She paused in embarrassment. "You were too heavy, and I dropped you when we were halfway down."

"Ahhh. That is why my head pounds so much more than I expected."

"You should have fought them," she accused. "You could have—"

"I pledged never to raise my sword in anger, but only to lift it to defend the church and to fight for moral justice. Not only would I have lost my life should I have attempted to fight the guards, but I would have also lost my immortal soul." Mangan smiled in the darkness and captured her hand with his. "Besides, then how could I have kept my promise to protect you?"

"You have already done enough," she answered. "Seeing that man's viciousness . . . I do not want to become like him. I will get nothing from exacting revenge upon those men except a mean heart. It will not bring my parents back, and it will not bring me happiness. They should be punished, but not unjustly. Eogan and Cormag have already suffered, and the soldiers . . . they will face judgment one day."

"You are wise beyond your years, dark angel, but I made a pledge to help you, and I will honor that pledge. I will ensure that the men receive appropriate punishments, but will do so within the laws of man and God. I promise to help you find solace."

"I already have," she whispered. She lifted his other hand and placed it against her lips. Tenderly, as if she were afraid he would back away, she kissed his knuckles.

He shuddered.

"I am afraid of what the laird plans for me," Ashleigh said quietly. "He intends to rape me, doesn't he? Rape me like Douglas raped my mother."

Mangan pulled her close and pressed her head against his chest, his heart pounding. He had to protect her. He had to!

"Will you do something for me? Something very, very special?" she asked.

"Anything," he answered, raw pain in his voice.

"Will you make love to me?"

"God have mercy," he whispered. "Why do you ask that of me?"

"I do not want his hands to be my first. I want . . . I want to know the beauty of loving a man before I must endure the humiliation of submitting to a monster. My parents loved each other. I want to feel that love, too."

"Love is not the same as making love. I already love you. Your spirit . . . your vulnerability beneath the anger . . . I have feelings for you that reach beyond the heavens and touch my heart with music. I do not need to lie with you to prove my feelings."

"You feel things for me? You love me?"

"Aye," he replied huskily as he pressed his lips against her hair. "I think I began to fall in love with you that day I pulled you from the stream."

"Why? Why would such a man as you love a person like me? You are strong and righteous, while I am confused and . . . and a sinner."

"You are an angel. Even angels need guidance. In fact, the Lord's son forgave an adulteress and bade those who would castigate her to throw no stone against her because they, too, had sinned. God does not hate the sinner; He loves her and helps her find the way."

"What about you? Will granting me my wish cause you to commit an unforgivable sin? If what you say is true, will God understand?"

When he did not reply, she shrank back. "I know it is too much to ask. You are a monk and I am a poor Gypsy girl—"

"No. I am no monk. I never was. Brother Bartholomew knew that all along. That is why he would not accept my final vows. That is why he sent me on this quest. He meant for me to find out the truth before I swore an everlasting commitment. I realize that now. But, Ashleigh, I am not the man for you. I am tarnished deep within my soul. I have so much blood on my hands, I can never wash the stain from beneath my fingernails. My ears have heard too many cries for. mercy, and I have given none. You call the laird a monster, yet it is I who am the greater beast."

"Make love to me."

"Have you not heard anything I just said!" he cried. "I am a terrible man. I cannot return home, for I am ashamed; I cannot fight for my king, thus I am no warrior. I cannot live the life of a man of God, for I desire a woman's flesh—*your* body and *your* kiss. I am nothing!"

She slid her hands beneath his shirt and pushed it off his shoulders. She felt his warmth and reveled in the heat of his body. Using only her fingers as her guide, she slowly began to unlace his shirt.

"Are you deaf?" he shouted. "I am worthless! You should not sully yourself with someone as useless as I."

"I am not deaf," she whispered seductively, "but you appear to be so. Must I ask you again? You call me an angel, but why are angels upon this earth? What is their purpose?"

"To help mortal men follow the true path."

"I found you. Will you trust me to guide you?"

He groaned and gripped her shoulders in a punishing hold. "Why me?"

"I want you. I have wanted you since the day I saw you praying in the moonlight. We have been drawn to each other by an invisible thread that will not break, no matter how hard we each try to sever it." She leaned forward and kissed the small space on his chest that her fingers had laid bare. "Do you want me?"

"Yes," he breathed, his body trembling with the effort to hold back.

"Then will you make love to me?"

He waited. He tried. He bit his lip and squeezed his eyes shut and thought of all the reasons why he should say no, but in the end his will was not stronger than his desire.

"Yes," he whispered.

Chapter 20

He pressed her against the wall and brought his body flush against hers as he buried his lips against her throat and groaned. "You smell wonderful . . . like cinnamon and honey." He inhaled deeply, then licked her neck.

Shivers rippled down her body, and goose bumps spread across her arms. She sighed and wrapped her arms around his shoulders as she tilted her head. Her legs felt weak, yet she had no fear of falling. As long as his arms held her she was safe.

He fumbled with the laces on her dress, wishing that she had never donned the intricate attire. Beads tumbled to the ground, and the fragile cloth tore as he yanked her bodice open, wanting to feel her flesh against his.

She gasped as her breasts sprang free and the cool air caressed her nipples and made them tighten. His chest was firm, and the curly tufts of hair tickled her skin, intensifying the sensation. "Mangan," she moaned. "You feel . . ."

He grasped her around the waist and lifted her up toward his mouth. "I want to taste you," he told her fervently as shudders racked his body and made him hold her tighter. His tongue flicked out and touched the very tip of her nipple, and both of them gasped out loud. So intimate . . . so perfect together.

He swept his tongue in a circle, the sensitive taste buds exploring every bump and ripple of her areola. He wanted to lose himself in the beauty of her femininity; he wanted to memorize every inch of her body and emblazon her perfection upon his mind.

She pulled his head closer and wrapped her legs around his waist, showing him without words how much she wanted him. By opening her thighs she opened her heart, and by enclosing him in a dual embrace she wrapped him within her soul. As his mouth captured her nipples and he sucked, she quivered with unexpected bursts of pleasure. "Yes," she whispered as she arched her back and closed her eyes. "Heaven!"

He, too, closed his eyes and reveled in her taste, drawing her nipple deep into his mouth and rolling it around with his tongue. He felt the plump caress of her breast against his cheek, and he shifted one hand from around her back to push her other breast closer. He wanted both at once, and he dragged his mouth from one to the other, sucking and tasting pure ambrosia.

She wrapped her legs tighter and slid her hands around him so that her palms rested upon the hard planes of his back. Kneading like a cat, she dug her nails into his muscles and cried out with pleasure.

He growled deep in his throat, a feral sound of male dominance that reverberated around the small dungeon. He hated these constraining clothes on his angel; she should be in the woodlands, wearing loose-fitting Gypsy attire or nothing at all. Grasping the trailing laces with his teeth, he ripped her robe further, opening it to the waist, whereupon he pressed kisses upon her belly, worshiping her beauty and honoring her purity.

"You are a gift from God," he whispered. "A gift from the Lord most high. To love you is to love the earth and moon and stars."

Tears filled her eyes and rolled down her cheeks as joy spread throughout her heart. "This is love?" she asked. "This is how it feels to be with a man?"

He smiled and gripped the backs of her thighs. "No, you have not felt me yet, but you will, and you will scream with ecstasy. Only then will you understand the power of love between a man and a woman. As with Adam and Eve, we were meant to join together, and not even the promise of everlasting Eden was more powerful than the destiny of two souls learning that they need each other. There is no sin in loving. God knew from the beginning of time that man and woman would fall into each other's embrace. He designed our desires and inflamed our needs."

"Why?" she whispered. "Why would He do such a thing?"

"Because He loves us," Mangan replied. "He could have kept Eve innocent. He could have smitten the serpent and turned Eve's ear, yet He did not. He knew our human hearts would hunger for the joining that comes only from this." He lifted her higher so that the yards of fabric cascaded around him and her thighs draped over his shoulders.

She gasped and reached behind her, feeling for a stone handhold.

"Trust me," he whispered, and her hands slowly slid down the rough brick, and he felt the tightening of her legs around his neck.

She relaxed, bracing her back against the stone and

merely steadying herself with her hands. Her weight rested upon his shoulders and her calves rubbed against his back. As his breath teased the inside of her thighs, a strange tingling started at her private center and began spiraling upward.

He inhaled again, smelling the spicy sweetness of her being as he brushed his eyelashes against her thigh. So beautiful . . . so womanly. So perfect.

She tightened her legs, clasping him in an intimate embrace as her hips tilted upward, seeking something special. Her hands clenched on the stones, sending a small cascade of dirt and gravel tumbling to the floor, but neither of them took notice. All they heard was each other's breath; all they felt was each other's heat.

He wrapped an arm around her waist; then, using one finger, he stroked the crease between her leg and her quivering core. Silky hair . . . satin skin. He wanted to bury his face in her sweetness, but he held back. She needed this experience. She needed to learn the exquisite pleasure awaiting her, and thus he had to move slowly. His pleasure meant nothing; hers meant everything.

Her center was hot and swollen, yet still he used only the tip of his finger to dance around her blossoming rose. His cock twitched with need, and his mouth watered with desire, but it was her gasps that promised him bliss.

He found his way through the fabric of her garments, then bowed his head and let the joy of being this close to her wash over him. Her thighs around his shoulders . . . her body open for him . . . he could stand like this forever and regret nothing ever again.

She felt a budding desire pulse within her and she rocked forward, pressing her core against his forehead, anointing him with her dew. She shivered, feeling his pounding heart through the throbbing cords in his neck, and she knew without any doubt that he wanted her as much as she wanted him.

"Yes," she whispered.

His head lifted and he deliberately blew against her, parting her hair with the heat of his breath.

She cried out, the soft sound echoing off the walls. "Yes!"

His tongue flicked out and he touched her bud.

She spasmed, her thighs gripping him even as her muscles turned into molten pools. Heat . . . power . . . the intense feeling of the ultimate surrender . . . she felt everything in a flash of clarity that instantly tumbled into an abyss of desire.

He licked her again, keeping his tongue gentle and explorative, this time tasting the petal of her inner flower.

Streaks of pleasure swept through her core, dancing like brilliant fireflies against a blazing sunset. She arched upward, wanting more, knowing the promise was yet to be fulfilled.

His tongue dipped into her inner cavern, tasting her moisture, reveling in her arousal. At this moment he felt more powerful than the prophets, more transported than the disciples. By pleasuring her he was adding beauty and love to the eternal universe. He— *they*—were spreading peace and joy throughout the world by joining together despite the dark pit that threatened their souls.

Cupping her buttocks with one hand, he held her thighs open with the other and began laving faster, tasting each and every fold. She cried out louder as sparks burst behind her closed lids and her internal muscles started to pulsate. Something was happening . . . something was building to an earth-shattering climax, but the pinnacle teetered just out of reach, almost surmounted but just short of the final capitulation.

She jerked her hips and released her hold on the wall to grip his head and press it closer to her. Then, as he buried his head between her thighs and wrapped his lips around her bud, she screamed. His tongue flicked and stroked while he hummed in the back of his throat, sending vibrations through his mouth and onto her flesh. She screamed louder, her head flung back and her hair tangling against the rough stone.

He slid a finger into her, just deep enough to feel her maidenhead, then retreated slightly and twisted his finger to stroke an area inside her that sent bolts of pleasure through her body. He rubbed it with his finger as his tongue flicked and he sucked, his arm holding her writhing form. He felt her swell, felt her cavern ripple, then tasted the sudden drenching of her climax as her screams suddenly changed to ecstatic gasps.

She couldn't breathe . . . she couldn't think . . . she only felt the explosion his hand and mouth wrought within her. Wave upon wave of bliss . . . of pure paradise flooding over her like an endless ocean. This was heaven . . . this was exquisite happiness and earth-shattering ecstasy. Braced upon his shoulders, her thighs wrapped around his neck, she felt an arrow strike the loneliness in her heart and annihilate her fears, leaving in its place immense satisfaction and peace.

She collapsed against him, and he shifted so that her body slid down his front and he could hold her in a tight embrace. His angel. She had shown him. God had shown him. His path was her.

He was still a believer. He still worshiped the high spirit and wanted to live his life according to the moral codes of his religion. But he finally accepted that he could do so with a woman by his side. This woman . . . this angelic lass whose wild nature had pushed through his defenses and claimed his heart.

He gently laid her down upon his shirt to rest. He kissed her flushed cheeks, smiling at the lassitude that made her features soft and hazy.

"You are beautiful," he whispered.

"*That* was beautiful," she answered as her arms reached for him. "But is there not more? Do you not get to feel the delight that filled my soul?"

He smiled and stroked her face. "Aye, there is more, but it is an act that should be done only between a husband and wife."

She looked at him, her gaze flickering over his features, trying to decipher the meaning behind his words. "You said you would do that so the laird would not be my first."

"I do not intend for him to be your second, either. When you were on my shoulders your hands almost reached the top of the pit. If you stand on me you can escape."

She shook her head. "But I cannot lift you out once I have breached the top."

His smile grew, and he placed a kiss between her breasts. "I will survive if I know you are safe."

She frowned and grasped his hand with hers. "You must escape as well. I will find a rope and—"

"You will find your way out of the dungeon, recover your horse and leave this castle immediately. Do not wait for me. You must warn the king that there may be a plot to murder him. You must tell him that his daughter was forcibly wed to Lord Jordan and is now held captive within Castle Tiernay."

"How?"

"Go to St. Augustine's convent. It is directly east—just follow the sun as it rises in the morn. By horseback it should be no more than two days' ride. If you inform the nuns, they will relay the message."

"But by the time I find the convent and tell them, you will already be . . ."

Mangan pulled the torn edges of her bodice together and began to wind the laces around the frayed ends to pull them close as best he could. He smiled at her. "I told you, my existence is not important. You have already shown me more beauty in this life than I ever expected to find. Because of you I have made peace with my soul. What else is there? What other goal must I pursue?"

Ashleigh sprang to her feet and glared at him. "To live!" she cried. "To eat buttered bread and to drink fresh springwater! To . . . to . . ." She sputtered, suddenly afraid that he would not find living with her meaningful. Perhaps he had given her joy but did not desire to form a bond with her. She turned her back and gulped, unable to voice her sudden pain.

He grasped her shoulders and drew her around to face him. "Don't be angry, my angel." He touched the cross that still hung around her neck, then removed his ruby signet ring. Grinning ruefully, he handed it to her. "This ring has traveled far. It brought my cousin Istabelle and her husband, Ruark, together. Perhaps it will bring us back to each other. Take it and present it to the nuns as proof that the message comes from me. With this talisman, the king will listen to our tale."

She shoved his hand away. "I do not want it!"

He captured her hand and folded her fingers around the ring. "Please," he begged her. "Please do this. Your actions will not only ensure that the laird is punished and my life is vindicated, but also that the villagers are saved from becoming innocently involved in a battle for power. I have seen the fate of such villages, and the people are the ones who suffer most."

"Cormag and Eogan are villagers," Ashleigh reminded him. "They are not innocent."

Mangan stroked her face. "Remember, let God see to their fate. 'Tis not your duty. Now, come; we do not have much time. The guards will return shortly and there will be no other chance."

"You want me to go? You do not want me to stay with you?"

"I do not want you to stay."

Ashleigh took a deep breath and looked up at the wooden planks covering their cell. "It will be locked."

"No. I see no shadow of a bolt. This dungeon's security lies in its depth, not its locks."

"What if no one believes me?"

"They will." Mangan grasped her face between his two hands and kissed her on the mouth. "God bless you and watch over you."

She stared up into his eyes as she struggled to hold back tears. How had she plummeted from such bliss to such misery in only moments? She blinked rapidly, but nodded to indicate her acceptance. Then, bracing her hands on his shoulders and placing her foot in his clasped hands, she jumped up and reached for the trapdoor.

Chapter 21

Ashleigh fought her cumbersome skirts as she struggled to simultaneously push open the door and lever herself out of the hole. After the wooden planks twice banged her head and the skirts hampered her progress thrice, she finally made it out and rolled away from the edge. Panting with effort, she turned and peered down the hole and beheld Mangan staring up at her.

"I will find the rope," she whispered. "The same one they used to lower me down, and you will climb out."

He shook his head. "Hurry. Do as I instructed or all our efforts will be in vain. It is imperative that you follow the plan." He paused, knowing his next words were unfair, but needing to say them nonetheless. "I did you a favor. Would you deny me this one?"

Ashleigh's face tightened with hurt, and she moved away from the opening. She was uncomfortable in the borrowed garments and would have preferred to wear only her chemise than those clothes from Laird Geoffrey. Fumbling with the ties, she divested herself of the lovely overskirt and crouched in the thin linen underdress.

Lifting the hatch once more, she tossed her skirts

down the hole. "Use these to keep warm," she said as she gave Mangan one last look. "Good-bye."

"Good-bye," he replied. "Darling angel."

She lowered the planks in place and knelt on the stone floor. Rubbing her hands in the dust, then wiping them on her dress, she managed to make the white cloth dark and dirty in a matter of moments. She then rubbed her cheeks, nose and forehead. A light in the hallway made her freeze, and she heard voices approaching from down the corridor.

Thinking quickly, she pulled one long piece of lace from her chemise and tied an end to a filthy bit of straw she found on the dungeon floor. She had to distract the men long enough for her to slip around the corner, so she wrapped the bit of straw several times until it looked like a fat rodent with a long, skinny tail. Then she threw it over a torch bracket until it dangled to the ground. Nodding with satisfaction, she shrank back into the shadows just as the men entered the chamber.

"I be thinking the lass should be mine," Curtis complained. "I found them first."

"You *didna* find the girl," the other reminded him. "You only killed the man and woman, and never even saw the wench. It is because of that mistake that she and Lord Mangan are here at the castle. Douglas is furious w' ye for yer mistake."

" 'Twasn't mine alone," Curtis whined. "Douglas should have told us ta search the area. Besides, I don't know how she hid so well."

"The laird always gets first choice anyway," said the other man. "Ye should be grateful ye got to pound your prick into one o' them and not be yearning for more."

"Still," Curtis said, his voice dropping slightly, "we

could take a tiny taste o' her before we bring her up. No one would ever know."

"She would tell."

Curtis shrugged. "Who would believe her word against ours?"

The other man rubbed his chin and stopped to think over his companion's suggestion. A shadow to his left caught his eye, and he started to turn when a rat leaped from the floor and scrambled up the wall.

"Aagh!" the man screeched, and stumbled backward.

Curtis's eyes widened in surprise and he struggled to draw his weapon. "Kill it!" he shouted. "Mealy, disease-ridden filth! Only the sick ones come out in the torchlight. I'll nae be getting a disease from the likes of you today!" He shoved the other man and lunged forward, but the rat sped down the wall and jumped several times, as if it were planning an attack. Curtis squealed and swung his sword wildly, dropping the torch in his haste.

The torch rolled to the center of the room and landed on the wooden planks, where the dry wood and straw instantly began to smoulder.

Curtis gasped and pounded the trapdoor with his boot heel, trying to stifle the flames, while the other guard drew his short sword and made another lunge for the four-legged beast.

Ashleigh bit her lip and scooted backward as she played out her line, making the improvised rodent wriggle, then scurry up the wall once again.

"Eeeeeek! It can scale the walls!" The guard slashed at the rat, but only a few stray hairs appeared to fly off, and the bulk of the rat continued its terrifying race up and down the sheer wall.

Giving the lace one last yank, Ashleigh ducked behind the corner and dragged her contraption after her.

"It be gone!" the man shouted. "It went down the hall. After it, Curtis! After it!"

"Leave it!" Curtis yelled back. "That rat must be crazed with disease, for no normal rat could do what it did. Let it find a rat hole and die a terrible death, for I don't want anything to do with it."

Curtis's eyes began to tear with smoke and he sniffed, smelling the scent of burning leather as he tried to peer down the hallway, certain he saw the figure of a woman slipping around the bend. He wiped his eyes, then strained to see through the shadows until a searing pain made him leap from foot to foot. "Me boots!" he shouted. "Me boots are on fire!"

The planks groaned; then a shower of sparks cascaded down the hole as one snapped. Curtis's leg fell through the planks, scraping his thigh and causing him to crush his testicles against the neighboring board.

"Agh!" he bellowed, struggling to get free as the flames jumped from the planks to his breeches. "Me manhood!"

The other guard raced forward, but his added weight on the boards made another split in half, and Curtis's other leg fell through, and his entire body crashed on the center support. His eyes rolled up in his head, the agony so great he could not make a sound. The fire licked around him, burning through his clothes and singeing the hair between his legs.

He opened his mouth and reached for his companion, but the other man backed away in terror. "You'll be burned alive," he whispered. "Get up."

Curtis flailed, his useless feet dangling in the hole as his hands and face blistered and his torso became engulfed in fire. His jaw opened and he emitted an inhuman wail.

He stared down the hall, where the woman's figure suddenly reappeared. Her face was pale, and a shimmering light played above her dark tresses. "You . . ." he whispered. Then, with a thundering crack, the center plank snapped and he and the flaming boards plummeted down into the hole.

Mangan pressed against the wall as the body crashed to the floor. He stomped out the flames, then stared at the guard. The man's mouth gaped open and his neck was bent at an odd angle. His tongue had turned purple, and his eyes bulged. An expression of fear was frozen on his face, and his eyes peered out with lifeless horror.

Mangan looked up as the other guard glanced over the edge and beheld his comrade's broken body.

"Is he dead?" the guard asked.

Mangan touched the man's throat, then nodded. "Aye. God has punished him."

The man looked thoughtful, then unwound a rope from his waist and tossed it down the hole. "The laird sent us to bring you to him. I guess I'll be the one bringing ye, now." He glanced at the pile of skirts and assumed the lady was cowering in fear at the bottom of the dungeon. "The girl is to stay in the hole until the laird has time t' more properly make her acquaintance." The guard grinned, but his words fell flat and his grin faded beneath Mangan's cold stare.

Mangan gripped the rope and twitched it; then, as the guard braced himself, Mangan pulled himself up, hand over hand, until he was able to climb out of the hole and stare at the lone guard.

The man held his sword high and waved it at Mangan. "Don't be thinking to attack me," he warned.

"The door to the dungeon is bolted from the outside, and only a secret word will tell the exterior guard t' open it. Now, give me yer wrists and I'll put the chains on."

Mangan looked at the man's shaking hand and debated. He could easily disarm and kill the guard, but if what the man said was true, not only was he trapped within the dungeon halls, but so was Ashleigh.

He held out his hands, palms facing up. "I am a peaceful man," Mangan replied. "I will follow you amicably if you only ask."

"Aye, then," the guard grumbled warily as he clamped the iron bands on Mangan's wrists and held him by the chain.

Mangan smiled tightly, his eyes like cold emerald shards.

As they walked up the stairs to the first floor of the dungeon, then trudged down the long hallway, Mangan surreptitiously studied his surroundings. He could see that they were just below ground level, for several small windows opened a few feet above the courtyard, thus affording shafts of light. Three locked rooms contained prisoners and two stood empty, but one of the empty rooms held a raised feather mattress, clean bedsheets and a set of leather restraints.

He spotted Ashleigh crouched against the far wall of the furnished room, but she held a finger to her mouth.

"That be where the laird be takin' yer miss," the guard informed Mangan, not noticing Ashleigh's hidden form. "Who knows? If'n she behaves, she might even get a bed upstairs." He grinned, but his expression faded as Mangan's eyes narrowed and he blocked the man's view of the room. "Don't be blamin' me," the man complained. "You be the one who riled the laird. He was so angered, he cast Douglas out of the castle and bade him never to return."

"Forgive me if I don't care for a tour; nor do I care about the fate of a rapist," Mangan said sarcastically, then motioned to the door. "Shouldn't we be moving along?" Behind his back, Mangan pointed to the window.

Ashleigh nodded.

"Aye," the man grumbled, and yanked on the chains. They walked the final length of the hallway and the guard rapped on the door.

"What be the code?" a man on the far side queried.

"Tiernay," the guard replied, and the door was unbolted and Mangan ushered through.

"Quite an indecipherable code," Mangan drawled as he pretended to trip. He glanced over his shoulder and saw Ashleigh standing on the bed. Using the leather straps as a rope, she tossed one out the window. It must have caught and held on something, because with a small jump she clambered up the strap to the window ledge and pulled herself through the narrow aperture between two bars.

Sighing in relief, Mangan rose to his feet and nodded at the guard. "Pardon me," he said to the grumbling guard. No matter what happened to him now, at least he knew Ashleigh was out of immediate danger.

Ashleigh dangled half in and half out of the dungeon, then dropped to the courtyard. If not for the bed and the metal ring on the end of the restraint, it would have been impossible to breach the window.

She paused and scanned the area, stifling a shiver as she thought briefly of what might have happened on that bed. Mangan had passed her just after she had moved the bed to the far wall, and for a moment she had thought he was alone, but then she had seen the guard and had motioned for Mangan to remain quiet.

She looked up at the narrow window. He never would have fit through its bars. And he had been wearing chains.

Darkness had fallen, and her shoulders shook from both cold and a rising anxiety. She did not want to leave him. She wanted him here, by her side, escaping with her.

Wrapping her arms around herself, she tried to concentrate. He was not here, and she had to think clearly to do as he had asked. First she had to locate the stables and steal back one of her horses. Her second task would be to devise a plan to slip by the watchful eyes of soldiers guarding the front gate. She sniffed in irritation. Why did she always have to steal her own horses? It left little time to snatch other useful items from the unwary, like a cloak to cover her chemise and some food to fill her belly.

She spotted the dilapidated church and noted the open doorway. Perhaps she could find something of use in there. She and Mangan had already determined that the building was deserted.

She waited until it appeared that no one was looking her way; then she inched against the castle wall. Peeking around a corner, she made her way along until she was as close to the church as she could get without leaving the safety of the shadows. Scanning the area, she searched for the most sheltered route while also determining the positions of all the sentries. Three stood in close proximity to her, posted at even intervals along the upper ramparts. Between them were hundreds of birds huddled in sleep with their heads tucked underneath their gray and white wings.

Pigeons.

She groaned. Even if she could avoid the sentries, the birds would hear her passage and take flight, instantly alerting the soldiers to her presence. The church was only a few running strides away, but it seemed an impossible distance. Ashleigh ducked her head and fought a sense of defeat.

The birds shuffled, and a subtle wave of coos rippled throughout the flock, spreading an alert call.

Ashleigh's heart thundered and she slowly looked up, certain she would see a soldier staring directly at her. The birds lifted their heads one by one, and several hopped a few steps and fluttered their wings, but instead of peering down at her they were focused on the top of the church spire.

A soldier turned to look at what was disturbing the birds and he quaked. Silhouetted against the moon was a large black raven, its beak gleaming with forbidding promise and its large wings spread so wide, each feather appeared to stroke the midnight sky.

The soldier gripped a rock and flung it at the raven, and even though the rock fell short, it sent the pigeons surging up into the air, the combined noise of their vocalizations and their feathers drowning the sound of the rock's tumbling descent down the side of the church.

Taking the opportunity, Ashleigh dashed across the courtyard and pressed herself against the church. Bless her friend Cairdean!

The pigeons flew up and circled once, then landed back along the ramparts, cooing to one another and puffing up their feathered chests while Cairdean finished stretching his wings and folded them flat against his body. His head swiveled and his piercing eyes watched Ashleigh slip into the church. When she was safely inside, he swooped through a hole in the roof and flew to her outstretched hand.

"Why do you protect me?" Ashleigh questioned in the moonlit church. "Is there something in your beating heart that draws you to me? A long-forgotten memory? The sound of my voice, perhaps? Or is it as simple as mere curiosity? Are you only interested in food, shelter and stealing pretty objects? If so, why do you wait for me, watching with unending diligence until I reappear? Why do you help me?"

The raven stroked his long flight feathers with his beak until each one was perfectly in place.

Getting no response to her questions, Ashleigh smiled and rubbed her cheek against his newly cleaned feathers. "I'm cold," she said as bumps appeared along her arms and her delicate bones shivered. *I want your arms around me, Mangan . . . your loving arms holding me close, keeping me warm.*

Cairdean's head twitched and his black eyes stared into hers. Then, with a few quick beats, he left her arm and landed on top of one of a pair of closed cases on the church altar. Neither had been visible earlier, but Ashleigh observed scuff marks on the floor, indicating that someone had just recently pulled them out from underneath a covered table.

Curious about them, Ashleigh shooed Cairdean off the chest and rubbed the dust from the case's latch. The rusted metal crumbled in her hands. She crossed her arms and rubbed the cold from her flesh, hoping it would contain something to drape over her shoulders. Breaking the remaining piece of lock, she lifted the latch and peered inside.

She immediately beheld an old scepter, a chalice and a folded cloth. Her eyes lighting up, she lifted the cloth out of the case and unfolded it. She shook it free of dust, then, using her teeth, she tore a hole in the middle. With a yank she enlarged the hole enough to poke her head through, then used a ribbon from her chemise to tie the blanket around her waist. "It certainly does not look as fancy as that robe the laird gave me," she mused, "but it conceals my bodice and will keep me warm." Drawing her hair free from underneath the makeshift tunic and wrinkling her nose at the fabric's musty smell, she took a deep breath and turned her thoughts to gaining access to the stables.

A sudden shout from the sentries sent her diving into the shadows, where she strained to listen to their greeting.

"Messenger!" the guard declared. "From where do you hail?"

"Dunkeld!" the man replied, and shortly thereafter the guard descended, walked across the yard to the castle door and banged the large ring.

Grinding . . . the gate rising . . . a mumbled conversation, then a call to a groomsman to water and feed the messenger's pony.

Ashleigh tiptoed to the church door and peeked out. The gate was open and all eyes were upon the messenger and the laird standing silhouetted in front of the castle doorway. It was a perfect moment. She would be without her horse, but she could always steal some farmer's mule. How many chances would she get to slip out of the castle courtyard with such ease before the guards realized that she was not still imprisoned in the dungeon?

It would be so easy. She could slide along the outer wall, duck behind the horse troughs and dash through the open gate. Once outside she could either race for the trees or inch along the ground, hidden by the tall grass.

She would be free. She could do as she had promised Mangan and ask the nuns at St. Augustine's to bring her to the king.

Her heart thundered and she felt short of breath. Mangan had asked her to leave him behind and head directly for St. Augustine's. She had come this far. She had promised.

She glanced at the castle door and saw the shadows of several men flanked behind the laird. Just beyond them was the outline of a man in chains, kneeling on the floor.

Mangan.

He had sacrificed himself so that she could run free. He wanted to know that his life and death were not in vain. He was tortured by thoughts of the damage he had caused to so many others and wanted his final act to be one that saved his soul.

If she cared for him, she would leave and find the convent.

She glanced at the gate. It was still open, but the guards were starting to return to their posts. Within moments the gate would close.

Taking a deep breath, Ashleigh darted back to the courtyard and away from the open gate.

Chapter 22

Ashleigh heard the clank of the castle's closing gates on the far side of the courtyard, but she did not flinch, for her decision to remain and help the man who had sworn to assist her felt right within her heart. She could not run away and leave him when she knew he would not do the same to her.

Besides—she grinned to herself—everyone knew you could not trust a Gypsy's word.

The stable was dark, but Ashleigh felt her way along the stalls until she heard a familiar nicker. Recognizing Franco, she kissed the gray horse's muzzle, then searched against the opposite wall for her things. She needed the disappearing plate if she was going to gain access to the castle and rescue Mangan.

He would be angry, but she was willing to brave his anger as long as she knew she had done everything she could to prevent his unnecessary torture. Even this far from the castle she could hear the snap of a whip, and feared that Mangan was the recipient of the lash. The image of him kneeling in chains had been emblazoned upon her eyes, and had convinced her to do all she could to save him.

With a grim smile of satisfaction, Ashleigh found

the plate, unstrapped it from the saddle and tied it onto her back. Practicing a few times, she made sure the hinges were supple and the height was correct, then searched through her satchel to find one of the leather gourds she had retrieved from her father's wagon. She rolled it between her fingers, locating a small waxed piece of string that peeked out through the top, then searched Mangan's items for a flint. She tied an edge of her makeshift shawl into a pocket and placed the items inside. All she needed now was a sturdy rope.

After finding a lead line in the stable that would suffice, she was ready.

This time she crossed the yard far away from the church so that the pigeons would not notice her presence. Aiming for a servant's door, she made short, quick dashes from place to place, using her mirrored plate to conceal her approach. Several dark clouds covered the moon, making it easier to reach the castle undetected. Glancing upward, Ashleigh gave thanks for the warm blanket, certain that the clouds were heralding a coming rainstorm.

As she reached the door she heard the laird's angry voice. "Sign it!" he bellowed. "Sign your confession!"

She heard no reply from Mangan, but the laird growled with disgust. "You are a fool, Mangan. Sign the scroll and I will grant you clemency when my son becomes king. Your life or your pride . . . which is more important?"

"Sign it," Father Benedict pleaded. "Do what you must to survive."

"Would you sin to benefit yourself?" Mangan questioned Father Benedict. "Would you sacrifice your heavenly soul to maintain your bodily flesh?"

Ashleigh heard the thud of someone falling to his

knees. "Aye," Father Benedict whispered. "Faced with the same dilemma I would save myself. I am not as pure as I wish to be, for I am merely a man. The Father knows I have sinned, but He will forgive me. He will forgive you, too."

"No. I will sign nothing."

Ashleigh crept up the castle steps and held her mirrored plate before her as a shield. She took only a few steps at a time, then paused before moving again. She sneaked forward and peeked around the plate to count all the soldiers and memorize their locations. Her gaze swept the great room. One of the families in her Gypsy caravan did amazing tumbling feats, balanced along boards and swung from ropes. Perhaps she could imitate their antics from the upper rafters in this room. But to do so she would have to climb up onto one of the highest beams.

Barely ten steps before her knelt Mangan, his back bloodied and his head bowed.

Anger welled within her—a familiar, earth-shattering emotion that blacked out all thoughts but revenge—and yet she battled it back. Anger would not help her now. She had to remain focused and clear of thought. Compassion flowed into her, and she looked at Mangan more closely. A surge of pride made her lips curl up in a smile.

He was not slumped in defeat. His fists were clenched, and the cords of his neck were thick with tension. He was struggling to remain compliant, fighting to retain his dignity and honor as the laird tried to strip his will by inflicting pain. But the laird far misjudged Mangan. He was stronger than the laird could ever understand.

Ashleigh shuddered, knowing that Mangan's very strength would cause him more pain, for he would endure hours of torture while the laird tried to force his confession. It was imperative that she hurry.

Ashleigh spotted a set of stairs leading upward. As a young soldier carrying a hammer and anvil was brought in, another gripped Mangan's hair and yanked his head back. Ashleigh began backing up the stairs, the plate between her and the great room. The soldier had not even begun to shave, and Ashleigh hoped he would collapse under the weight of the anvil, but he managed to carry it all the way across the room before dropping it in front of Mangan.

Mangan glared into the eyes of the young soldier, and the boy involuntarily flinched at the force of his gaze. "Obey the laird!" the young soldier shouted, but his voice cracked and quavered. He held up his hammer and, after removing the chains from Mangan's wrist, placed Mangan's hand on the anvil. "Speak up now, or lose your finger," the boy warned. "Only by obeying his command, will the laird allow you peace."

Mangan lifted his lip in a snarl. "God is watching," he growled. "You are committing an unforgivable sin. I have trained at a monastery and found communion with God. To strike me is to strike a son of the true king."

The soldier paused, his gaze flicking toward the laird.

"Show him what the hammer will do," the laird commanded, but still the soldier hesitated.

"Is he a monk? . . . A man of God? He is not defending himself. How am I to torture a man who evokes the protection of God?" the boy asked, glancing at Mangan's impenetrable face, then back at the laird's. He finally looked to Father Benedict for guidance, but the priest turned his head away and did not speak.

"His vocation means nothing to me," the laird replied. "A man is but a man. Crush his finger and perhaps he will realize that God cannot protect him from pain. As soon as he hears his bones break, he will realize that he answers only to me."

Ashleigh froze in horror as the soldier slammed Mangan's finger between the hammer and the anvil, and the sound of crunching bone sent shards of pain into her heart. She gasped, then squeezed her eyes shut as tears instantly blinded her.

Mangan's body tensed and his breathing quickened, but his gaze did not waver. He stared at the soldier and slowly shook his head.

The soldier backed away, his face ashen.

"Tell me how you ambushed the king's daughter and killed her entourage," the laird demanded, "or I will have him break a finger each time you refuse to confess."

"But what if he did not do this deed?" the soldier asked, his hands trembling at the prospect of approaching Mangan again. "Perhaps he is innocent."

"Then he will have no fingers." The laird rubbed his chin in thought. "The girl," he said.

"The girl?" Father Benedict asked, looking at the laird in confusion.

"Bring me the girl," the laird insisted. "Perhaps Lord Mangan will be more inclined to answer when it is her finger on the anvil."

"I did it," Mangan said.

The laird raised his eyebrows and stroked his beard. "He confesses," he murmured with satisfaction. "And you killed the royal guards?"

"Aye," Mangan lied, his heart thundering. He must not allow the guards to retrieve Ashleigh, for once they discovered that she had escaped they would begin a thorough search, diminishing her chance of escape.

Mangan fell silent. The blazing spasms from his broken finger made him dizzy. He was trying to think clearly, but the throbbing made it hard, and worry about Ashleigh's safety clouded his thoughts. All he could concentrate on was the belief that the longer he kept the laird talking, the longer a lead Ashleigh gained. God willing, she was already galloping down the road and well on her way to safety.

"Break the next finger," the laird commanded.

The soldier trembled. "But he confessed," the youth whispered, accidentally dropping the hammer in the straw. He fell to his knees and started searching for it, his hands sweeping the stone beneath the rushes.

"I must ensure that he doesn't forget his confession," the laird replied while his lips spread in a vicious smile. "When I lead this nation through my son, I must be certain Lord Mangan does not recant, for it might raise awkward questions."

Reaching the summit of the staircase, Ashleigh folded her plate, tied it on her back and climbed up on a small table braced against the wall. Leaning forward over the ledge that separated the second-floor hallway from the vaulted ceiling of the great room, Ashleigh touched the edge of the rafter but was unable to wrap her hands around it. Stifling a moan of frustration, she leaned out farther, stretching from her toes and wishing desperately for just one more finger length.

The table teetered, and Ashleigh felt herself falling forward. *No!* she silently screamed as she pushed off with her toes in one final effort. Then, just as her palms slid along the rough edge of the beam, her fingers caught on a knot in the wood.

She dangled for an instant, her body suspended above the great room floor, then wrapped her other arm around the beam and pulled herself up. The makeshift shawl snagged on a splinter, ripping off several threads, and a thin shaft of wood embedded itself in the delicate underside of her arm.

Wincing, she managed to loop her legs over the rafter and press her cheek against the wood while her breathing steadied. As she pulled the splinter out of her arm, she assessed her situation. How angry her mother would be if she saw her daughter's escapades now! A tiny grin crossed her mouth. Her mother had been loving and protective, always warning her daughter about taking risks.

I guess I should have listened better. I miss you, Mother. She breathed through her nose and glanced down at Mangan, the laird, Father Benedict and the soldier with the hammer. *I miss you, Mother, and I hope you approve of what I am doing. He is a good man. He was willing to sacrifice himself for me. It is only right that I risk my life for him.*

The soldier gripped the hammer in his hand and approached Mangan warily. "Forgive me," he whispered. "I have no choice."

"You always have a choice," Mangan replied, but held out his hand and averted his gaze.

Ashleigh scuttled along the beam until she was directly above Mangan, then quickly tied the rope to the beam and withdrew the gourd. With no time to waste, she pulled on the tiny cord to loosen the bag and flung it down to the floor with all her strength. Even as it plummeted down, she quickly tied her hair around her nose and closed her eyes, praying that her trick would work.

The bag struck the soldier, broke open, then

bounced to the floor. A terrible smell burst forth, causing everyone in the great room to stagger back. Then a fine yellow dust swirled around the soldier and Mangan, nearly obscuring their forms before quickly dispersing outward.

The laird buckled over and gagged while Father Benedict dove underneath the table. The other soldiers in the room covered their eyes and noses as the dust filled their nostrils and coated their eyes, causing instant, excessive tearing. The soldier who had maimed Mangan flung himself on the ground and wailed, crying that God himself had struck him down.

As the room erupted in chaos, Ashleigh dropped the rope and scurried down. Mangan was doubled over with nausea and blinded by the yellow dust, so she gripped his shoulder and shook him hard.

"Grab the rope!" she hissed. "We have only seconds before the effects of the dust fade."

Mangan tried to peer up through his tears, his mind warring with his emotions. She should not be here, yet once again his angel was before him, offering to save his hide.

She shook him again as she frantically blinked the dust from her own eyes and tried to breathe through her mouth so she did not succumb to the nauseating effects. "Climb," she commanded.

"You first," he managed to whisper.

Having no time to argue with him, she gripped the rope wrapped her leg around the free end, and began her ascent. As soon as she was a quarter of the way up she felt the rope sway as Mangan began climbing after her.

"Open the doors!" the laird bellowed as he struggled to his feet and stumbled toward the front of the room. "Clear the air!"

Ashleigh reached the upper beam and swung up, then peered down at Mangan. His green eyes stared directly back at her, and he smiled as he climbed beside her. Then, as he pulled the rope up after them, he leaned forward and kissed her.

It wasn't a lingering, sweet kiss of gratitude, or a gentle blessing from a man of God; it was a blazing burst of passion, an instant display of possession, and even as his broken finger slid through her hair and gripped her close, his tongue dived inside her mouth and swept every recess, oblivious to everything but her.

Ashleigh tried to breathe, but his possession was complete. When she felt dizzy, it was his arms that held her secure.

"My angel," he whispered. "My wild angel, descending from the heavens to sweep me up into the clouds and away from my enemies."

She grasped his free hand and held it to her heart. "*Our* enemies."

"Aye." He nodded. "Our enemies." He touched her face reverently. "Where is my ring?"

Ashleigh pulled it from the folds of her skirt and handed it to him. "We must hurry," she said.

"Not yet," he insisted, holding her hand and pulling her back toward him.

Ashleigh tried to yank her hand free. "Now!" she whispered. "We have only seconds!"

"We have a lifetime," he replied as he slipped his ring on her thumb. "Wear this and be my wife."

"What? There is no time for this!"

"I won't move until you say yes."

"Yes, then! Now let's go!"

Directly below them, the soldier with the hammer rose to his feet, spread his palms upward and looked up at the ceiling. His gaze met Mangan's. They stared at each other for a long moment as Mangan let go of Ashleigh's hand and braced himself against the beam.

The soldier broke first and swung his gaze toward his laird just as a drop of Mangan's sweat fell and landed on the man's forehead.

The soldier lifted his hand and wiped his forehead, then trembled as he beheld his anointed palm.

"Come on," Ashleigh hissed as she scurried along the beam toward the stairs.

The soldier looked back up.

Staring into the boy's bewildered face, Mangan felt pity for him well up within his heart. The man was no more than a young child forced to obey the cruel commands of his master. He made the sign of a cross, asking God to forgive the youth's sins, and then gathered the rope and turned to follow Ashleigh.

The soldier saw Mangan's gesture and he fell to his knees, then dropped his head to the floor to pray.

"Where is he?" screamed the laird as he cast his gaze crazily around the room. "Where is Mangan?" He ran toward the soldier and yanked him up by the collar of his tunic. "Where did he go?"

The young soldier kept his gaze pointed downward as a secret smile flitted across his lips. "He went to the angels of heaven," he murmured.

The laird flung him back to the ground in disgust. "Search the castle," he commanded his soldiers. "He cannot have gone far. And bring me the girl! She is the only thing that seems to matter to him."

Chapter 23

Mangan and Ashleigh ran down the hall and dashed inside an adjacent room, quickly closing the door behind them. The room was draped in soft lilac and contained a delicate tapestry on the wall, but neither noticed the decor. Breathless from his kiss and thrilled that her plan had succeeded, Ashleigh spun in a circle with her arms flung wide. "It worked! My father always kept the gourd in his pocket when he played in crowds that appeared volatile. He said that if he smashed it against the ground, Mother and I were to close our eyes, cover our noses, hold on to his belt and run." She stopped spinning and pressed her hands against Mangan's chest. "Even so, I did not know how well it would work in such a large room. I feared that I would not be able to get you out before the air cleared."

He grasped her hands, flinching as his broken finger brushed against his own chest. "You should have obeyed me. You are supposed to be far away from here."

A sound from the other side of the room made them both spin around, and they saw Lady Matilda standing in the doorway of the adjoining master bedchamber.

"Quickly!" she whispered, motioning with her hand.

Mangan and Ashleigh glanced at each other, unsure.

"You are escaping, are you not? Then follow me. Jordan coveted your sword, so his father gave it to him before he put you in the dungeon. It is in his room." She turned and pointed to a table, where Mangan's sword had been placed.

Mangan strode forward and gripped the handle, hefting it a few times. "Once again you are in my hands," he murmured to the blade. "God either has a wry sense of humor or He is showing me His will." As Ashleigh came up behind him with a strip of cloth she had torn from a sheet and wrapped it around his broken finger, he smiled at her. If ever there was a woman who exemplified courage, it was Ashleigh.

Excitement energized him, and he gripped her around the waist and pulled her close. "Thank you, God," he whispered against her hair, then stepped away and scanned the room as shouts echoed from within the castle.

"The soldiers are coming," Matilda cried as she ran to the master chamber door and bolted it, then rushed to her adjoining door, closed it and wedged a chair against the handle before returning to aid Mangan and Ashleigh. "It will be only moments before they search these rooms. Go—hurry—and tell my father where I am," Lady Matilda insisted.

Ashleigh approached an arched window and peeked out into the darkness before ducking out of sight. "We can climb down," she whispered. "Torches light the ramparts of the outer stone wall, and a pool of light surrounds the open castle door, but just beneath the window it is dark."

"How far down?" Mangan asked, already looping the rope around the foot of the massive bed and tying it securely.

"I can't tell. I cannot see the bottom," Ashleigh replied.

"Come." Mangan waved to Lady Matilda. "You go first."

She shook her head and backed away. "I can't. I . . . I am terrified of heights, and I have never climbed a rope in my life. Please don't wait for me. Go! Escape and send my father for me."

They heard the sound of a door being flung open and several footsteps reverberating from a nearby room. Ashleigh's brows drew together and she bit her lip, not wanting to leave the lady behind.

"I will be fine," Matilda insisted as she quickly penned a note using the instruments on Jordan's desk. "Go to St. Augustine's and give this letter to a woman named Glorianna. She . . . she is my best confidante. It was her father who came to visit the convent and then opened the doors to Laird Geoffrey's men. Please, will you do this for me? She must know that I do not blame her, but place the blame on Dunkeld himself."

"Dunkeld?" Ashleigh asked, recognizing the name. Her mother had spoken of a man named Dunkeld whom she knew as a child. "How do you know—"

"We must go," Mangan interrupted. "We have only moments before they enter this room. I can carry you, Lady Matilda."

"No," she replied fiercely. "Go! I would slow you down and you would never escape. My safety is not as important as what you must do to save my father. You know I speak the truth. The kingdom must come first."

"Aye. You are brave, milady. I will not fail. I will send men to rescue you as soon as I am able, and I will protect your father even if it means giving my life to do so."

"Thank you."

Mangan bowed, then tested his knot around the bedpost. Finding it tight, he tossed the rope through the window and watched the end tumble into the darkness.

"What if there are soldiers down there waiting to catch us?" Ashleigh whispered.

"We will take that chance, for they most certainly will catch us if we remain here. Once you reach the end of the rope, relax your muscles, let yourself fall and roll upon impact."

Ashleigh yanked up her skirt and swung her leg over the ledge, then shimmied down the rope, expecting Mangan to follow directly behind her.

A sudden crashing sound made her pause halfway down. She looked up to where Mangan still stood facing the room, his back blocking the window.

"I found him!" a man shouted. Then she heard him lunge forward and the sound of his sword swishing through the air as Lady Matilda screamed.

She heard Mangan's heavier stride as he leaped out of the path of the man's swing. "I will not fight you," he stated. "I vowed not to fight another senseless battle; thus I will not engage you."

"Then prepare to die, for you are mine!"

Ashleigh had started to climb back up, her heart thundering, when she heard the man's footsteps race forward once again. Her face blanched as her head peeked over the window ledge and she saw the man aim his sword at Mangan's chest. Then suddenly the attacker went flying forward as he tripped over Mangan's outstretched foot.

Mangan jumped sideways and ducked beneath the

man's blade, then spun and glared at him. "You must learn to settle your affairs without violence," he cautioned. "If you do not you will be forever caught in the fire of damnation." He grabbed the man's tunic and flung him out the door, then slammed it shut and wedged a bar under the portal, since the bolt had already been broken.

He looked toward the window and frowned upon seeing Ashleigh's face. "Will you never do as you are told? I thought you were on the ground already."

"I came back for you," she answered angrily. "Why didn't you fight him? Don't you know how to fight?"

Outside the door they could hear the men slamming their shoulders against the wood and saw small splinters cascade downward as the door shuddered from the impact.

"Climb down!" Mangan shouted as he shoved his sword into its scabbard, squeezed through the window slot, and watched Ashleigh disappear into the darkness before gripping the rope to climb after her. His wounded hand throbbed, and he almost slipped when his palm wrapped around the rope, but the thought of tumbling down upon Ashleigh's head made him grip harder and thrust his pain aside.

He heard a splash, then an unladylike curse.

"Ashleigh?" he whispered. He reached the end of the rope and could barely make out the ground. It appeared they were on the east side of the castle, where the horse troughs were located, and Ashleigh had landed squarely inside one. With a grin he let go and landed in a crouched stance, then laughed at Ashleigh's affronted expression.

"You look like a drowned kitten."

Ashleigh shoved the wet hair from her eyes and

struggled to get out of the trough, but her hands slipped and she fell back in with a cry of distress.

Taking pity on her, Mangan reached in and hauled her out. "With antics like that we will never escape," he teased her.

She grumbled at him and pointed toward the stables. "Our horses are in there, but how will we get them out of the courtyard?"

"Listen carefully, and for once, do exactly as I say."

Ashleigh looked at him dubiously.

"Promise?"

She shook her hair back, casting water droplets across his face. "I promise," she mumbled.

"Go to the stable and gather my stallion and your two geldings. Put leads on two of them and mount the last; then wait for the gate to open. When it does, gallop at full speed and race out of the castle gates, stopping for nothing."

Ashleigh frowned. "Why will the gate open?"

"Because I will be on the other side and the laird will send soldiers out after me."

"How—"

"Stop asking questions and go." With that he kissed his hand and placed it on her lips. "Don't worry. Trust your husband."

She gasped, but he backed into the darkness and disappeared from sight. She considered running after him, then debated going to the stable. It was senseless. He would never escape and the gates would not open. Their best course was to hide within the grounds until an opportunity presented itself.

A breeze skated across her wet clothes and she shivered. She had been taking care of herself since her parents had died, but now Mangan was trying to protect her. She rubbed the ring on her thumb. Last time she had done what she wanted to do despite his instructions, and had managed to save him. If she disobeyed him again, would she manage to rescue them, or would her disobedience cause their demise?

Mangan scaled the wall, using the skill he had gained on many sieges to find foot- and handholds and climb quickly. The other side of the wall would be sheer, for the bricks were usually laid so that the outside edge of the wall contained the smoothest portion of the stone. His main hope was that he would be able to run along the passageway on top of the wall until he found a section under construction and was able to climb down to safety.

His sword clanked against his thigh as he levered himself over the top of the wall and pressed flat against the stone. Hearing no cry of alarm, he slid down onto the walkway and crouched in the shadows. Courtyard soldiers were searching the interior of the castle, and he prayed that Ashleigh was well hidden. She was a resourceful lass; he had faith in her abilities, but he was still anxious.

Shoving his concern aside, he concentrated on his position. Both to his left and right were sentry points with lit torches and armed soldiers. Unless he was willing to kill one of them, he needed to figure out a way to distract them.

By now the courtyard was ablaze and the laird was standing on the steps of the great hall bellowing orders to his men. Even from his position on the wall, Mangan could hear the fury in the man's voice and knew that he would show no mercy should he or Ashleigh be recaptured.

Mangan crept forward, recalling that the section of

the castle that was being reinforced had been visible from the road, thus closer to the gate. He remembered a wooden scaffold propped against the wall from which masons had been patching cracked stones. Unless the men had been unusually quick with their trowels, the scaffolding should still be in place.

A sentry was peering over the side of his station, watching the soldiers below. His crossbow was strung, and behind him was a ladder leading to the scaffold.

"Keep a sharp eye out!" called a plumed soldier from the courtyard below. "Kill upon sight!"

"Aye!" the sentry acknowledged, and lifted his crossbow to show that he was ready.

"He is a devious one," the plumed man replied. "A threat to our laird's plans. Under no circumstances should he escape!"

"Aye, Commander!" the sentry agreed, standing straighter.

The plumed man moved on, informing the next sentry similarly, while the man in front of Mangan gripped a torch and pointed it toward the courtyard so he could illuminate areas against the walls that were shadowed. He was frowning in concentration when a sound to his left made him spin around and drop the torch to pull his crossbow taut.

Mangan watched the rock he had thrown roll briefly along the walkway until it rolled out of the circle of torchlight.

The adjacent sentry called out, but the sentry in front of Mangan released an arrow, sending it shooting through the darkness toward the unexpected sound. A man's sudden gasp and the sound of his body falling to the stone made the sentry shout with victory, and he abandoned his station to race toward his victim.

Mangan padded toward the man's post, his booted

feet making no noise upon the flagstones. As he reached the ladder he heard the sentry's cry of distress.

"Hugh!" he cried. "I thought you were the prisoner!"

"I thought you were the prisoner," the wounded man gurgled. "I heard a sound . . ."

"So did I," the sentry answered. " 'Twas a stone that rolled along the walkway."

Mangan grabbed the torch and tossed it over the side into the courtyard to create another distraction, then swung down the ladder and began dropping from one level of the scaffold down to another.

The sentry above started shouting, and there was a flurry of activity as he called down to his companions, but by then Mangan had reached the ground and was running through the sheep lands to get out of range of the crossbows.

Once he reached the tree line and paused for breath, he turned to see alarm torches being lit along the entire wall and the gate slowly rising on its chains. A horn blew, casting its mournful sound across the valley, alerting all the outlying sentries to an enemy's presence.

Mangan looked around for a strong tree near the road, then quickly scaled it so that he was hidden in the branches.

The gate opened and a swarm of foot soldiers poured out of the courtyard and fanned out around the castle wall. There was a brief pause while the laird bellowed for his horse; then three steeds burst through the gateway and thundered along the road, narrowly missing the laird himself.

Clinging like a tiny burr to the mane of one of her gray mounts, Ashleigh was galloping across the road with the bravery of one of his own knights. She had done it!

Mangan held his breath as arrows cascaded around Ashleigh and the horses, and his hands clenched in helpless fury. If he could shield her with his own body, he would gladly do so.

He saw her jerk as an arrow grazed her shoulder, but her steed did not slow. Instead her hands reached higher on the horse's neck and her heels thrummed his sides as they careened toward him.

He whistled, the piercing sound reaching his stallion's ears just as Ashleigh glanced up in relief. The stallion veered to the trees, and Ashleigh angled her horse to follow. Slowing slightly, they galloped straight for him, and Mangan prepared to jump.

An outlying sentry suddenly leaped from his hiding place and raised a sword against the galloping horses.

Ashleigh screamed and yanked on the reins, sending her horse sliding on his haunches and whinnying in fear. The other gray shied sideways and crashed through the bushes, scratching his hide and tangling his feet until he fell heavily to his side. Mangan's warhorse reared up and struck out with his forefeet, smashing against the man's sword.

The sword slid along the stallion's leg, scraping across the flesh, but the impact was so powerful the man's hand became instantly numb and his weapon clattered to the ground. Mangan dropped down onto his stallion's back and squeezed his legs as the stallion reared again, this time striking the man's chest and sending him flying backward. As the stallion leaped forward to trample the fallen soldier as he had been trained to do, Mangan pulled on the reins and halted him.

"I spare your life," Mangan called out to the man,

glancing over his shoulder at the approaching men. So far only foot soldiers had passed through the gate, but mounted men would soon follow. "In return I ask that you draw no weapon against me or my family ever again." He stared at the sentry, his eyes piercing the man's soul.

The man cowered, shimmying backward and looking at Mangan in disbelief. His gaze slid toward his abandoned blade, but Mangan reached down and scooped it up, then flung it so that the blade was imbedded deep into the trunk of the tree. "I repeat, fight no more against me and become my friend, for I have given you the gift of life."

"Who are you?" the man whispered.

"I am Mangan O'Bannon, son of the Earl of Kirkcaldy."

"And I am Tory Rhoss, a man grateful for your gift."

Ashleigh shifted her trembling horse over toward Mangan. "He is one of them," she exclaimed. "He raped my mother."

Mangan swept his gaze over Ashleigh's face and form, relieved to see only a small injury along her shoulder but saddened to see the pain in her eyes. He lifted his sword and pointed it at the man, his heart pounding. "I will do as you ask," he told her. "I will kill him and avenge your parents' death if you will it so."

Ashleigh shivered and pulled the blanket she had used as a shawl tighter around her shoulders. It gave her an odd sense of comfort, and she shook her head. "No. Vengeance is behind me."

Mangan took several breaths, realizing only now that he had been holding his chest tight. "Very well. May God bless you for your mercy," he whispered as he sheathed his sword, then reached across the horses and touched her injured shoulder.

" 'Tis merely a scratch," Ashleigh told him. "My shawl is thick, and it partially deflected the arrow." She glanced over her shoulder at the sound of approaching hoofbeats. "The laird's mounted soldiers are coming." Her other horse clambered to his feet and shook his body, then pricked his ears toward the coming men.

Nodding, Mangan cast one last look at Tory, then sent his stallion trotting into the forest, hearing Ashleigh's horses following closely behind him.

They weaved in and out of the trees, using only the moonlight to light their way. Changing direction frequently, they managed to stay ahead of the soldiers and, bit by bit, lengthen their lead.

Several times they heard soldiers shout, and many times they heard them curse, until finally Mangan and Ashleigh had traveled far enough from the castle that they heard nothing at all. The moon traveled halfway across the sky and stars shifted in the cloud-strewn expanse before Mangan pulled his stallion to a stop at a sheltered glen. Protected on three sides by tall pine trees and on the forth by a solid granite boulder, the glen was a small oasis in the midst of a thick wilderness.

The call of a wolf pack echoed across the land. The hoot of a hooded owl punctuated the constant chirping of nocturnal crickets. They smelled the sweet perfume of pine needles and tree sap. Fireflies danced in the clearing, flashing on and off like tiny fairies.

They had done it. They had escaped.

Together.

As Ashleigh pulled up alongside Sir Scott and smiled at Mangan, he smiled back. Excitement thundered through him, and his heart raced with pleasure that they were alive and well. Ashleigh's dark eyes contained an inner light that illuminated the darkness just as the dancing fireflies cast a flickering glow throughout the glen. Her smile cut through his self-recrimination with the power of absolution. She accepted him. She cared enough for him to come back and rescue him. She did not care who he had been; she cared only who he was.

The enemy was lost behind him, a beautiful Eden lay before of him, and his wild angel stood beside him.

Chapter 24

Ashleigh sensed something different about Mangan. He emanated a newfound power, a surging aura of masculinity that made her both excited and nervous. Without his monk's robes he had ridden with confidence and pride. His shoulders flung back and his gaze steady, he exuded strength and self-assurance.

She shivered, aware that while his confidence was increasing, she was feeling less and less sure of herself. Since her parents had died, her focus on revenge had given her purpose. She had pushed aside sorrow in favor of anger, and helplessness in favor of vengeance. But now . . . now she did not know what to do or how to feel.

She had killed someone, and guilt churned inside her gut.

Mangan swung down from his stallion, then reached up to help her. She tried to turn to begin unbridling her horse, but Mangan held her firmly and forced her to look into his face. "You are not alone," he murmured.

Tears sprang to her eyes as she shook her head. "Why do you say that?"

"Because I sense that you feel lost and frightened."

Dizziness made her sway, and she clutched his shoulders for support. "After my parents . . ."

"I am sorry that they are dead, and I am even sorrier that I did not meet them, for they must have been incredible people to raise a daughter such as you."

Ashleigh pressed her cheek against his chest and wrapped her arms around his neck. "I do feel alone," she acknowledged softly. "I don't have anyone else."

"You have me," he replied as he took her left hand and clasped it in his, then pressed it to his lips. "Although it will never replace your own, I give you my family and my name. I pledge to protect and honor you; to place your needs above my own and to cherish you until the day I die."

Her tears fell as thunder rumbled across the far horizon.

He brushed the back of their clasped hands across her cheek and looked deeply into her eyes. "Do you weep from sorrow? Have I trespassed upon you and caused you pain?"

She shook her head and clenched her hand tighter around his. "I don't know what I feel. We just met . . . you were on a quest and I—"

"I have accepted that I am not destined for the priesthood, for God has chosen another path for me. I will serve Him in other ways, but I will do so in joy, not despair."

"I do not know my path," she answered.

The thunder rumbled closer, and a faint breeze rocked the treetops.

He smiled and kissed their joined hands. "You helped me find my path. Let me help you find yours."

A few drops of rain splashed upon their heads, and the fresh scent of the coming rain surrounded them. Ashleigh's pulse pounded, and she flushed even as her lips began to quiver. As his gaze dropped to her mouth and he gently combed his fingers through her tresses, she felt swift bursts of sensation trickle from her scalp and shiver down her throat. A fresh set of tears rolled down her cheeks, the remnants of deeply held emotion she could no longer contain.

He stroked her moist eyelashes with a fingertip, then touched it to his own lips. "I drink your pain," he whispered. "May you never feel loneliness again."

Several more raindrops pattered to the ground beside them, and the breeze rattled the tree branches as a storm cloud blew over the moon and the sky changed to darkly mottled gray.

Still her tears flowed. Soundlessly they poured from her limpid eyes and soaked her cheeks, mixing with the raindrops. She tilted her face up and closed her eyes, allowing the rain to wash over her face and his strength to cleanse her heart.

She pulled the old blanket over her head and flung it to the ground, wanting to feel the rain against her skin. A burst of thunder shook the landscape, but she welcomed it just as she welcomed his arms as they wrapped around her waist and pulled her close. Her torn bodice clung to her body, highlighting her nipples and caressing the rounded globes of her breasts.

The sensation thrilled her, and she opened her eyes to look into his hungry gaze.

He untied his shirt, drawing the laces through the eyelets with studied slowness, watching her mouth as it parted slightly and she panted with awakening passion. He bent and kissed the valley of her cleavage, licking the small pool of rain and tears that hovered there.

"I want you naked as God made you, your flesh uncloaked by the trappings of mortal man." He slid his hands up her back and caressed her shoulders, tracing the delicate lines of her collarbone.

She sighed and leaned harder against him, feeling a bulging tumescence pressing against her abdomen. She shifted left and right, rubbing against him, feeling the rasp of his partially undone shirt against her sensitive skin.

He slid his hands underneath the straps of her chemise and eased them down her arms, trailing their descent with his lips. Kissing her shoulder, he drew his mouth to the delicate fold in her inner arm and then to the sweet indentation at her wrist.

"Your broken finger . . ." she whispered.

His mouth returned to her shoulder, and he licked the bloodied scratch that marred her flesh from the arrow that had grazed her. "Tonight I feel only you. Tomorrow will be soon enough to worry about such things."

Thunder cracked, and a streak of lightning briefly lit the sky. The rain began to fall in earnest. Huge raindrops poured from the storm clouds, instantly drenching them in a warm, wet blanket.

Ashleigh blinked as she tried to clear the water from her eyes, no longer sure whether rain or tears blinded her, but she felt his strength against her, and it no longer mattered. She pulled his shirt off, flattening her palms against his hard chest and pressing her lips against his wet skin.

He shivered at her bold caress and bent down to grasp the hem of her clothing and drag it over her head. The wet material clung briefly, then slid off her body as if she were a wet sea-maid shedding her skin to reveal hidden secrets.

He groaned aloud at the perfection of her body. Beautifully sculpted hips, smooth belly, supple thighs . . . strong arms with long, finely toned muscles and a delicately curved back.

She slid her hands in his waistband and tugged. "You, too," she whispered. "I want to see the rain sluice off your shoulders and run in rivulets down the planes of your chest."

He yanked off his breeches and tossed them aside, then stood next to her, only a hairbreadth from touching her.

Energy sparked between them, an electric charge that shot down from the sky and melded with the intensity of their merging souls. It crackled, sending intangible shards across the tiny space that separated their bodies and fusing them into one towering pillar of passion.

He gripped her shoulders and pulled her flush against him. Wet, slippery and tingling with need, he slid his hands over her buttocks and the backside of her thighs, then kneaded her flesh, reveling in its soft firmness. As he stroked upward, his fingers trailed into the juncture between her thighs, then up the hidden valley between her buttocks and to the small of her back.

Their naked flesh touched.

Her nipples to his muscles . . . his cock to her belly . . . firm hands to wet skin . . . his cheek to hers. In wonderment their hands gently caressed each other, exploring and searching. As the rain slanted down around them, trickling off their noses and clinging inch by inch while sliding downward, they discovered a new universe.

She found rippling valleys and coursing rivers, while he found hard-peaked mountains and velvety meadows. Lightning cast a blue light above them, and thunder surrounded them like a powerful heartbeat. The swaying trees protected them from the wind, sheltering their small Eden yet surrounding them with the tinkling music of fluttering leaves and pattering rain.

She ran her hands along his shoulders, amazed by the thickness of his arms. They were arms that she could trust, arms that could hold the world at bay, arms that could enclose her in a loving embrace. She kissed a small indentation at the base of his shoulder where his muscle started; then she trailed her lips along his bicep. He shivered, and she knew that he was as affected as she. Emboldened, she kissed the other shoulder, then licked the pool of rainwater trapped within the crease of his elbow.

He covered her lips with his own, drinking her essence as he tasted the pure water that poured from the heavens, fresh and sweet. Her response replenished him, and he kissed her with a passion that contained no boundaries.

Lips slanted together . . . tongues intertwined . . . eyes closed in blissful surrender . . . They both clasped each other close, finding a merging of souls that was incomparable. Their bodies fit against each other, and their desire rose until they both felt the earth move as their emotions spiraled upward in a dizzying vortex.

He lowered her to the ground and laid her in the muddy grass. For a moment he just stared at her beautiful body sprawled beneath him. Her flesh gleamed and her hair glimmered with dark, wet highlights. As his gaze traveled lower, he saw her toes and fingers dig into the earth, and saw the soft mud ooze between the delicate digits.

She looked up at him with a mischievous grin, then took her muddy hand and ran a lazy trail along his chest, marking him with a mixture of rain and wet dirt. "You are muddy," she whispered.

He dug his hand into the ground and gathered a mound, then spread it in gradually widening circles on her upper chest until his fingers slid over and around her breasts. "So are you," he replied, then watched as tiny circles appeared as the rain peppered her skin and washed away his painting.

He slid his arm underneath her back and lowered himself half over her, keeping his hips to the side. Once again he kissed her, feeling her passion rise as her body arched against him.

Her muddy fingers gripped the back of his head and held him close, and she rose up slightly to cling to his mouth more tightly. "Take me this time," she begged. "Show me . . ."

"Aye," he growled as his mouth slid down her throat and found her nipple, washed clean with rainwater. He gathered it in his mouth and drew deeply, wanting to taste the milk of her womanhood.

She gasped and arched up again, feeling tingles shoot through her body and set fire to her blood. A primitive moan escaped her lips, and her open mouth accepted the falling rain as if each drop were part of his soul coursing down her throat and entering her body. She wanted him. She wanted more of him.

She raked his back with her fingernails, urging him without words, telling him with her passion that she needed to be closer.

He responded by sliding over her body and grinding his hips against hers. His thrusting member swelled and pulsed, wanting to bury itself within her wet haven, but Mangan held back. He teased her entrance with the tip, brushing back and forth until it found the tiny nub that lay hidden within her curls.

She gasped and held his shoulders. Heat from his caress battled the chill, making her flesh steam. Slippery from sweat as well as rainwater, she shifted back and forth in the mud, sliding her body against his harder and harder until her legs began to tremble with a rising tide of pleasure.

He lifted away from her, unwilling to let her slip over the edge without him. Even though she clawed his back in outrage, he made her pause. "Look at me," he commanded.

Her eyes opened and she looked through the rain into his eyes. Behind him were roiling thunderclouds and the tips of swaying trees, but within his gaze was something more powerful than even the forces of nature. His angled jaw . . . his wet hair plastered to his cheek and his corded neck. He was spectacular. Magical.

"By taking you, I claim you. No one shall ever trespass upon my soil nor reap my harvest. Once bound together, we shall never be torn asunder. Tell me you accept this, and accept me as your lord and husband."

Her black eyes shimmered, and the blue rim that surrounded her pupil grew brighter with emotion. As if frozen in time, she could not respond. The raindrops splashed into tiny pools, spreading into thousands of fragmented droplets before soaking the earth.

"The rain gives us life," she whispered. "It is the symbol of fresh beginnings, for it foretells the coming of new blossoms and green shoots. It is only right that we should promise each other within the embrace of the very water that comes down from the heavens and is responsible for the birth of all things. But, Mangan, how do you know your feelings? How can you be sure when we know so little of each other?"

He touched her face, his fingers trailing down her cheek with the raindrops. She had not said yes, but she had not said no, he told himself. She had already promised him while on the rafters, but he wanted her heart. Although he sought to make her understand that his arms would hold her enemies at bay and his name would shelter her, she needed to come to him wholeheartedly on her own.

"You are so wonderful," he whispered. "I know you are struggling against inner demons, and until you win that battle I can only stand beside you. I will be waiting for the day when you wake up in the morning and know that we are destined to be together. Then you will not doubt my feelings for you."

He kissed her lips, tasting her unique nectar. "I know *my* emotions," he murmured between kisses. "*I* have no doubts. You are my angel, and my home lies within the shelter of your wings . . . One does not need years to see into another's heart," he whispered as his lips touched her cheeks and the gentle slope of her jaw. "Up on that mountain . . . you saw into my core and handed me hope. I need no other proof, no other demonstration that you are the woman I want for the rest of my years."

She trembled as his hands slid down to her waist and lifted her closer. His power was overwhelming, and she wanted desperately to say yes, but part of her cowered in the dark, too afraid to accept his offer. "Don't leave me," she begged, her voice so quiet it was nearly drowned by the sound of the rain.

"I will never leave you," he replied just as quietly. "You may have yet to choose me, but I have already chosen you." He angled his body above hers and slid his cock against the petals of her opening.

Heat exploded between them, and Ashleigh cried out with reawakened passion. Words forgotten, she clasped her arms around his neck and pulled him closer as her thighs fell open in invitation. Thunder crashed and rain poured down in sheets, obscuring the closest trees and wrapping them in a wet, private cocoon.

He pushed against her, seeking . . . finding . . . slowly entering her. In one smooth stroke he thrust inside her as she tossed and turned, writhing in the muddy grass with uncontrollable ardor. His fullness stretched her. Her mind ceased to function as every part of her soul coalesced upon their joining.

His rod touched something within her, something thin but strong. She felt an instinctual fear, and her inner muscles clenched tight, gripping him with rippling waves. They both gasped and stared into each other's eyes as a shard of lightning lit the sky above Mangan's head.

He bent and licked her nipple, then kissed the hollow of her throat. "Take me," he commanded.

Her breathing grew heavier, and small shoots of pleasure vibrated within her, making her hips lift toward him. She wanted him . . . needed him deeper.

He complied, thrusting through her virginal barrier and driving deep within her core.

She screamed as he flung his head back and groaned. Her body clenched his tightly, bringing him to the brink of an explosion. They were one . . . melded together as God had created. Perfectly designed to encase each other in heavenly ecstasy.

"Feel me . . ." he whispered. "I am on my knees to you."

She opened her eyes and saw the pulse in his neck, saw his arms bulge as he held his weight off her small body. Sliding her hands down his back, she felt his buttocks bunch with the effort to remain still, and then his thighs that were bent in between hers and his knees that were dug deep into the wet ground.

"I feel you," she replied. "I feel you inside me . . . inside my body and soul."

He lifted slowly out of her, reveling in every inch as his length slipped through her tight folds until his barest tip remained within her. Then, as she arched up with yearning, he plunged back inside, firm and hard.

"This is me . . . me and you, together," he murmured. He stroked again, shuddering with the sweet sensation of their conjoined flesh.

"Yes," she cried, as her thighs held him close even as his body shifted up and down with every thrust. Each movement brought her nearer to some ephemeral point of absolute pleasure; she felt her inner pain slip further away, almost as if his power were strong enough to battle her demons, both real and imagined.

She clung to him, needing him and wanting him. Her eyelids fluttered as raindrops filled her lashes, and a soft smile spread across her lips. Something was filling the void within her . . . physical pleasure . . . emotional ecstasy . . . something even deeper and more meaningful.

She cried out as his thrusts increased in tempo and the tip of his cock rubbed against a secret pleasure spot buried deep within her. Fluid drenched her insides. She caught her breath, suddenly afraid, but he grinned and kissed her fears away.

"Feel me . . ." he reminded her. "Feel what I can make you feel."

The sensations changed as the rising tide spread from her core like lightning shooting up her belly and bursting within her mind. Thunder crashed, yet whether it was within her or from without, she did not know. It rolled and built, shaking her body, making her entire soul rumble with the force of a tumbling landslide.

She screamed again, a sound that was mixed with a plaintive whimper as her heart searched for something just out of reach.

He heard her . . . heard the change in her voice and felt the difference in her flesh. Blazing hot . . . slick and sweet. Her thighs clenched him with surprising strength, and her nails dug into his back, showing him how close she was to the ultimate precipice. He paused, holding himself up, watching her body squirm with unfulfilled desire; then he plunged hard, seeing her eyes glaze over with pleasure—pleasure his body alone could give her.

He bent his leg and tilted her body slightly to the side, allowing his cock to slide one tiny bit deeper until it pressed against the second barrier within her. Past that barrier was her womb, the beautiful place that gave life. Such a magical place . . . such an exquisite blessing contained within a woman's body. A place where a man placed his seed and claimed his woman eternally as his own. A place he wanted to fill with his essence and all the love he could offer.

Something deep within her burst in a cascade of shooting stars. She wrapped her arms around his neck and buried her head in his shoulder, shuddering, quivering, crying with such inexplicable pleasure that her mind separated completely from her body and left her core unrestrained. Pulsing, gripping . . . wave after wave of emotion and sensation. A climax that was stronger than the elements and more primitive than the very earth upon which they writhed. Her cry sounded like the scream of a wild jaguar, and her body bucked uncontrollably, caught in the throes of a pinnacle that reached higher than the heavens above.

As her body wrapped around him he felt his testes contract, shooting his pleasure into her core. His throat constricted; his heart stopped beating. Every fiber of his being centered on the point of their joining, on the sensation of her rippling warmth and on the intense release of his climax.

Endless . . . like death and birth combined . . . He felt her soul and wrapped it within his, cradling her and loving her. Rain poured down his face as he lifted his eyes to the storm. Lighting struck, sending streaks across the sky and electrifying his body.

Then his shout joined hers and his blood pumped, swelling his cock and stretching her even further as he filled her womb, claiming her forever.

They were joined. Two individual souls merged into one, promising without words to stand beside each other despite any who dared challenge them.

The sensations slowly ebbed, yet they remained close, unwilling to separate their bodies even as they continued to clasp each other in a tight embrace. Her wet hair lay splayed against the soaked ground, and rain beat against the length of his broad back, but they did not move. His head rested against her forehead. They breathed unsteadily while her hands trembled and her thighs fell weakly apart.

Out of the corner of his eye, Mangan spotted the old blanket Ashleigh had used as a cloak. Rolling both of them to one side, he reached across and pulled the blanket over them. Despite its wetness it afforded just enough warmth, and as he shifted his arm to form a pillow for her they both drifted into sleep, lulled by the sounds of rain and the comfort of each other's presence.

Chapter 25

Cairdean perched on the tree branch. He plucked a beetle from the bark and gulped it down. The feathered tips of his wings fluttered, and he swooped down to land next to the woman's naked form. The rain had stopped and the sun had risen, creating a crystalline iridescence to the forest foliage. A trickle of water traced its way down her exposed thigh until it dropped into a small pool of water on a fallen leaf.

He dipped his beak into the pool and drank, tasting the fresh rainwater mixed with the faint oil of the woman's flesh. He paused with his beak open, then cawed.

The woman rolled over and opened her eyes. "Cairdean," she murmured.

Cairdean spread his wings and fanned her, making her black curls flutter against her cheek.

She touched his shimmery feathers, marveling at the delicate wisps that made up such a powerful instrument of flight. "How amazing it must be to soar above the treetops and see the forest from on high. If only you were larger I would climb upon your back and let you take me up into the sky. But alas, humans will be forever bound to the earth."

Mangan opened his eyes and smiled lazily. "You speak to the bird as if he can understand you."

"His eyes . . ." Ashleigh said softly as she stroked the black feathers. "It is as if they speak to me. He has seen sadness just as I have, which is why we understand each other."

"How would you know he has experienced tragedy? He is but a bird with a small mind that can recall only good places to hunt and a warm nest in which to rest."

"Yet he follows me."

Mangan nodded, unable to refute her argument. "Men and women might fly one day," he finally said as Cairdean flapped his wings and flew up into the branches of a nearby tree.

Ashleigh twisted and looked at Mangan with amusement.

"Truly. We could design wings strong enough to lift a man above the clouds," Mangan explained.

"And why would we do that?"

Mangan looked up into the morning expanse. Glorious blue spread from horizon to horizon, streaked with shafts of sunlight. "God is up there." Then he gathered her in his arms and stared into her exotic eyes. "But today I do not need to climb into the heavens to be close to our maker, for His presence is all around us, all around you. When I am near you I feel heavenly joy."

She touched his cheek, surprised to see moisture collecting beneath his eyes. "You are a complex man. You were to be a monk, yet have become a lover. You worship God, yet you renounce the birthright God gave you. You mock my words to a raven, yet sense things about me with unique depth and understanding. And now, although you left the king's service, you send me to save him from a murderous plot."

"Are you any less mysterious?" Mangan replied. "Anger and pain filled your heart to overflowing, drowning all else within its wicked depths, yet you befriended a simple bird and called him a comrade. You had an opportunity to exact revenge upon Tory, yet you granted him mercy. And you came to rescue me. Lastly, when everything within you cries for a return of security and love, and I offer them both, you reject my proposal."

They stared at each other, each mulling over the other's words. It was all true, although hard to accept. From someone else the statements would have caused them to rise up in denial or lift their chins in defiance, but the bond of trust between them had already grown strong enough to withstand such honesty.

"What do we do now?" Ashleigh asked.

He smiled wryly. "We travel to St. Augustine's."

They rode in silence, using the trees as a shield against the laird's sentries. Ashleigh held her body straight and slender, the blanket that acted as her cloak draped behind her, covering her horse's haunch, and the black raven perched upon her shoulder. Mangan kept his sword drawn, ready to protect them should an enemy attack.

They came across one soldier, but instead of confronting him they stealthily circled and continued on their way.

Seeing the tension in Mangan's face and the clenching of his fist around the sword's hilt, Ashleigh finally asked a question she had been pondering. "Why do you carry a sword you do not use?"

Mangan ducked under a branch and remained quiet

for several moments, considering his answer. "If I tell you, I will be speaking of it for the first time."

"I will keep your confidence," Ashleigh replied.

He grinned. " 'Tis not your silence that makes me anxious, but my conscience."

"Tell me."

He sighed. "That last day . . . I stood amongst thousands of dead—some friend, some foe. The stench of their blood burned in my nostrils, and the cries of their agony reverberated in my ears.

"It was in France nearly two years ago," he continued. "It could have been near one of your Gypsy camps. I led my men to the battleground and berated the young boys who showed fear. I yelled and shook my sword in the air until bloodlust filled their hearts, and they rushed the field, convinced they were invincible. They fought with courage; then they fought with determination, and lastly they fought with desperation. So many died . . . so many mothers never saw their sons again. It felt so wrong . . . it was as if my soul died on that field with them."

Ashleigh reined in her horse and took his hand in hers.

"I must speak of it," Mangan whispered. "I must tell you everything, for if I do not, the secrets will rot within me. May I confess to you? Will you listen to my tale?"

Ashleigh nodded and squeezed his hand. " 'Tis a strong man you are," she replied. "Only a brave and honorable man can face a past he wishes to forget."

"I was born in a cave during a snowstorm. My mother . . . her voice is so beautiful she can calm beasts with her songs. She birthed me alone, trapped behind an ice wall. She protected me from the cold and cuddled me close to her heart while my father desperately tried to rescue us. He fought a bear . . . a huge male cave bear that was enraged by our presence, while my mother sang a lullaby to soothe the mother bear trapped within the cave with us.

"It was the strength of their love that saved us all. My mother named me Mangan after the bear. She always told me that even as a newborn infant I was stronger than the largest of all the wild beasts. I should have died that night—died of exposure—and my mother nearly bled to death. Meanwhile, my uncle fought with his wife and sent her body from high upon the castle ramparts crashing to the flagstones below. He only just saved his infant daughter, born moments after me."

Mangan shuddered, and Ashleigh urged her horse closer to his so she could touch his face. The forest embraced them, and sunlight shone down through the leaves. Far in the distance a river flowed with a natural, soothing rhythm.

"I was born into violence," Mangan summarized. "Throughout my mother's pregnancy my father and uncle battled for power, and my mother fought for my father's love, and even during the first week of my life my grandfather was poisoned. My cousin Istabelle . . . she responded by becoming wild and carefree. She embraced the violence of her birth and turned it to good use by becoming a pirate of the seas whose mission was to help those in need. I tried . . . I tried to be a warrior and defend my country, but I no longer see glory in killing."

Mangan pulled back and looked at Ashleigh. "I do not want to fight senseless battles, but fighting is in my blood. I am a good warrior . . . a renowned fighter. The king has heaped honors upon our family because of my skill and leadership. I survived the bloodiest of battles with only minor wounds, while most others have perished." Mangan closed his eyes briefly, then looked at her with shame. "I fight well because I like to fight. I kill easily because I enjoy the feel of my sword in my hand. My sword is my solace, for when I fight I forget my worries and live in the moment. I move on instinct and react without thinking, only afterward realizing how much devastation I have wreaked. Like I said . . . it is in my blood."

"Do you think your skill with a sword makes you evil?" she asked.

"I wonder if I am. I wonder if I am cursed for causing my aunt's and grandfather's deaths, for causing my father and his brother to feud . . . for being born when I was instead of waiting a few moments more before forcing myself into this world."

Ashleigh replied, "Just because you are a warrior does not mean you like to kill. Just because you wield a sword does not mean you want to maim. You are a good man, but not spared pain and suffering just because you care for the souls of others; on the contrary, you must merge your skills with temperance. You must accept your life and take from it what you will, glorying in the knowledge and experience you can offer others."

"That is what I have tried to do."

"No, you have rejected everything in order to protect yourself. That is not the same thing. Would you ask me to abandon my tricks because I was thoughtless enough to use them to frighten others after my parents were murdered?"

"It was a turbulent time for you. You were frightened and alone."

"Can you admit that you, too, felt frightened and alone? That standing in the battlefield amid all those dead bodies made you feel something you did not expect to feel? That you claim to blame the sword when, in fact, you blame yourself?"

A half smile lifted Mangan's mouth. "Did you study at the same monastery where I lived? You sound much like the abbot."

Ashleigh brushed her hands over his face, feeling the heat of the sun warming his brow. "The events before your birth were not of your making. Your swordsmanship is not a curse."

"I thought that if I became a monk, I would be cleansed."

"You are alive. You sought forgiveness for your actions, but piety does not mean you must relinquish life. Can you not be good and also be happy? Or do you think that you must avoid all pleasure in order to be devout?"

"I fear pleasure. I fear that I will be consumed by the fire of temptation and my judgment will become clouded and untrustworthy. If I allow myself to want something, how will I know when to stop? How will I know that I am using my sword for good, and not because I enjoy the sensation of power? 'Tis best that I avoid all temptation and thus make no mistakes."

Ashleigh rested her hand against his chest. "You once said I was a temptation. Do you regret meeting me?"

"Never," he replied firmly. "You have shown me a beautiful side of life. You have brought me joy, and I am everlastingly grateful for your presence. You have not led me away from my path, but toward it."

"You call me your dark angel," Ashleigh said.

"Aye."

"Are not most angels white?"

A long pause. A sigh. "Aye."

"Then you are my dark monk, a man who understands the populace more than other highborn men because you have lived with sorrow clouding your heart. You have seen the devastation wrought by war. You have felt the yearning of a mother for her lost son and seen the agony of a daughter for her murdered parents. Storms are part of living. If all were Eden, one would not know the difference between joy and misery. A man of the devil does not know these things. He does not feel guilt for what he has done; nor does he try to change the actions of others.

"You are not evil. Far from it. You are a man of deep spiritual understanding, yet still a man. Did you not take me to the heavens last night when your body covered mine? Such ecstasy is a gift from God. My magic tricks are also gifts. In fact, all that we have comes from the Father. Enjoying them is not sinful, but squandering them is. 'Tis one principle the Gypsies understand so much better than people in your society ever will. We dance, laugh, wear bright clothes . . . we enjoy life! You must enjoy *all* it has to offer. If you are good with your sword then use it, but use it wisely. Do not expect to be perfect. Be as you are."

Mangan turned to face her. Sunshine illuminated her face. Father Bartholomew had counseled him for hours, but never exorcised his demons. Mangan had knelt upon the altar stones and prayed from morning till night, yet never felt peace in his tortured soul. Even his own parents had watched with helpless confusion as he became more withdrawn and incomprehensible to all those around him, as the years brought him from pensive youth to stoic adult.

But Ashleigh's words made sense. They robbed his fears of their strength and let the gentle breeze wash them away.

"And you?" he questioned. "Are you ready to live again? Your words could be directed as much to yourself as to me. Do you yearn to pluck a sprig of hemlock and drown yourself in the stream, or are you ready to accept me in your life?"

"I want to live," she whispered. "I want to live with you."

Something blossomed between them . . . something nearly indescribable.

It contained the petals of acceptance. The stalk of forgiveness. And possibly the roots of love.

Chapter 26

The following afternoon they reached the convent of St. Augustine. Approaching from the south they passed a small cluster of cottages along a peacefully flowing river. Several small aqueducts diverted water toward a large apple orchard, its trees heavy with round green fruit.

The convent was a fortress built of whitewashed stone with an imposing cross high on the rooftop. Stone walls encircled the convent gardens, broken only by one iron-barred gate, which swung slowly open in the breeze.

A strange silence permeated the valley, and neither Mangan nor Ashleigh saw a single person. The cottages appeared to be empty, and no one was working in the orchard. Even the convent garden, lush with roses, sunflowers, daisies and lilies, looked deserted.

Mangan and Ashleigh dismounted and tethered their horses to a railing in front of the convent, electing to enter via the main entrance rather than take advantage of the open garden gate. Cairdean cawed and flew to the roof, where he perched on the cross, while Ashleigh's gelding, Francis, meandered over to a patch of grass and started to graze.

Ashleigh rapped on the door. No one answered, but the door swung open. After glancing at each other, they stepped over the threshold.

The convent was in complete disarray. Furnishings had been flung about, and plates and silverware were strewn across the floor. A clay pot lay in pieces where it had tumbled from the table.

His mouth tightening, Mangan drew his sword while Ashleigh stared around her in horror. "What happened?" she asked, not expecting an answer.

"She took them away," a woman replied.

Mangan and Ashleigh spun toward a hallway where an elderly woman stood. Although wrinkles marred her skin, she was still exquisitely beautiful. She had long, luxurious gray locks, and her blue-black eyes were strikingly vibrant against her pale skin. As she walked gracefully toward them, she swayed as if she were weak, but then she straightened and arched one eyebrow. "Why are you here?" she asked them.

"Greetings," Mangan murmured respectfully as he bowed to her. "We expected to find the convent inhabited. Where has everyone gone?"

"I told you," the woman replied as she glided over to a chair, righted it and sat down. She tilted her head regally, displaying the long length of her neck and the creamy complexion of her throat. Something about her looked familiar to Ashleigh, but too delicate, too ephemeral, as if a stiff breeze might sweep her away.

"Glorianna took them," the woman continued softly, her breath coming short and wispy. "After Matilda was taken Glorianna gathered everyone else and went into hiding. She feared that the men who had stolen Matilda would return and kill them all so that there would be no witnesses to Matilda's kidnapping."

"And did they return?"

"Yes. They came and murdered two men from the village and tossed them in the river; then they returned to dispose of the women, but by then Glorianna and the others had already fled."

"Who are you?" Ashleigh asked. "Why didn't you go with them?"

"Me? I am Laural-Anne MacLaren. I had no reason to leave, for Dunkeld's soldiers would never harm me. Harold Dunkeld loves me." She smiled, but an odd light flickered in her gaze and twin spots of color appeared on cheeks. She leaned sideways, then straightened with a jerk.

"Ma'am? Are you ill?" Ashleigh asked.

"Just a touch fatigued," Laural-Anne replied, but she sank against the chair back and took several deep breaths. She closed her eyes for a moment, then opened them and stared at Ashleigh and Mangan. "Who are you?" she asked again. "Why are you here?"

"She's feverish," Ashleigh whispered to Mangan.

"Aye. We must move her to a bed; then you can tend her while I search for others. We must find someone to care for her. I had expected to find soldiers here who could deliver a message to the king. Now we will have to make other plans."

"Very well," Ashleigh replied. She stared at the woman, wondering if the resemblance between her and her mother Mary was true or imagined. "I will wait with her while you find a bed."

Mangan searched the convent, coming upon several cells for the nuns and a few more spacious rooms where wealthy daughters had presumably resided. Returning to the front room he picked up Laural-Anne in his arms and carried her to the nearest bedchamber while Ashleigh followed.

Laural-Anne's head lolled back and her breathing became shallow. "I am dying," she whispered. She stared at Mangan as he laid her carefully on the bed.

Ashleigh opened a window covering and let sunlight fill the room, then turned toward the bed. Laural-Anne's shoulders were thin and frail, her eyes sunken and dark. The bright light was not as kind as the shadows, and her age became more apparent.

Mangan kneeled next to her and took her hand in his. "The Lord will claim you in His good time," he replied. "Until then you must accept each day as it comes."

The woman stared at Mangan's face for a long while. Her face was old and weary, and lines formed deep creases around her mouth. "I have nothing to live for," she finally answered. "I lost my daughter many years ago . . . and then I lost another."

"When did you last see your daughter?" Ashleigh inquired as she stood behind Mangan. Her heart thudded, and she struggled to keep her face passive. The woman looked so much like her mother. Could this be her grandmother? Could she be the one who had cast Mary aside because she wished to wed a Gypsy?

The woman closed her eyes and rocked her head. "The days glide away from me . . . I cannot remember anymore."

"What was her name?"

The woman's gaze slid up to Ashleigh's face, and a soft smile spread across the old woman's lips. "What a beautiful angel," she whispered. "Have you come to take me?"

Ashleigh's eyes filled with compassion, and she placed her hand on the woman's shoulder. Laural-Anne's hand covered Ashleigh's and she squeezed gently.

"Have you no one to care for you?" Mangan asked. "A family member, perhaps?"

"Dunkeld always promised to care for me," Laural-Anne replied. "But I haven't seen him in so long . . ." She sighed and shook her head. "He wanted to give me wealth. Then he wanted to give it to Glorianna."

"I have a message from Matilda for Glorianna," Ashleigh told her.

"My Glorianna . . . such a difficult child," Laural-Anne replied. "She made everything so complicated." She touched Ashleigh's clasped hand. "You would not do that, would you? You would be a good daughter."

Mangan rose. "I must search for others and restock our supplies." He bowed and exited the room while Ashleigh remained with the woman.

Laural-Anne closed her eyes in defeat. "They always leave." She turned her face away. "All men. They say they love you, but then they leave. Everyone leaves. There is no one left. I was Harold's favorite mistress and I bore him two children, yet he still left me all alone."

Ashleigh sat on the edge of the bed and stroked the woman's face. "You are not alone," she whispered. "Mangan taught me that no one is ever alone."

The woman opened her eyes and stared at Ashleigh as if seeing her for the first time. "Beautiful angel . . . have you come to take me? I long for peace . . . How am I to find my way?"

"I am here to guide you."

The woman's gaze swung back to her, and a flicker of hope touched her face. "Are you my daughter? Do you have Dunkeld blood in your veins?"

Ashleigh shook her head. "I am Ashleigh, a Gypsy with no other name, but my mother was called Mary. Did you know her?"

Laural-Anne gripped Ashleigh's cloak and pulled her close. "Beware of that man! He seeks to spread your thighs, not enfold you in his heart. He will not love you when your skin wrinkles and your hair turns gray. He will desert you like he has deserted others." She became agitated, and the spots of color in her cheeks spread over her face.

Ashleigh broke the woman's grip and leaned away. "Are you speaking of Mangan?"

"Aye, that man with you. He will betray you. I see the pain in your eyes. You fear abandonment. Someone left you, didn't they, whether they wanted to or not? Who was it? Your mother? Your father? A lover, perhaps? My advice, dear child, is to barricade your heart, for if you let it free it will bleed a thousand times over."

Laural-Anne coughed, and her chest rattled. Ashleigh stood up and helped her, but as soon as the fit was over she eased the woman back on the pillow and moved away to stare out the window at the gardens. Laural-Anne's words had cast a shadow over her heart, for she did fear abandonment. She knew it was childish, but she felt angry at her parents, almost as if she blamed them for their own deaths.

Ashleigh leaned her head against the window ledge. It was not her parents' fault, but whenever anger faded, grief arose. If only she had not loved them so much.

If she felt so much loss at their deaths, what would she feel if Mangan died? Or if he left her? Could she endure such a tragedy again? Maybe the old woman was right. Perhaps she should continue to guard her heart and not let her feelings for Mangan become too strong.

"Mangan will not leave me," she finally replied, but her voice lacked conviction.

"Of course not," Laural-Anne said soothingly. "He won't leave you because you are an angel, and angels don't do anything wrong." Her gaze bored into Ashleigh's back as the younger woman's body stiffened. "You haven't done anything wrong, have you?"

"No," Ashleigh answered, her voice harsh. *Except kill a man. Would Mangan leave me if he knew the truth?*

"He knows everything, doesn't he? All your faults . . . all your sins . . . but he still loves you."

"He does not know everything," she whispered.

"Do you love him?"

Ashleigh shrugged. "I don't know what I feel."

"You wear a signet ring on your thumb. Is it his? For if it is, he will remove it once he knows your secrets."

Ashleigh spun around and glared at the woman. "Why are you saying these things to me? You are trying to make me doubt his commitment. Just because you did not find happiness with your man does not mean you should ruin other people's joy."

"You sound just like her!" Laural-Anne exclaimed, suddenly sitting up and pointing her finger at Ashleigh. "When will you girls ever learn? Look around me. This is all you will have if you chase after elusive dreams. Dunkeld said he loved me, but he did not. I gave up everything for him, but he left me here to die! I warned Mary, I warned Glorianna and now I warn you!"

"You *are* my grandmother!" Ashleigh cried, aghast. "How could you have cast your own daughter from her home?"

"She lusted after a common Gypsy! She was a Dunkeld. She deserved better. Even as a bastard daughter, she could have done better."

"She had the best," Ashleigh replied coldly. "My father was a good man."

"Then where is he?"

Ashleigh glared at her, fury making her body shake.

As Laural-Anne smirked at Ashleigh, Mangan walked into the room, unaware of the tension between the two women. "I found the gardener," he said. "He stayed behind to tend his flowers and has consented to care for Laural-Anne for a small amount of coin. I am appalled that the other sisters left an ailing woman all alone."

"Maybe they did not want to take her," Ashleigh snapped.

"Are you all right?" Mangan asked, finally noticing Ashleigh's flushed face.

"I'm going out into the garden," she replied. "I need a moment."

He nodded, but his brows drew together in concern. "Would you like me to go with you?"

"No. I'd rather be alone."

"Stay here with me," Laural-Anne begged, drawing a raspy breath and falling back against the pillow, exhausted after her outburst. Her eyelids flickered shut, and she bent her finger to urge Mangan closer. "I need to tell you something. You look like a man who will listen."

Ashleigh exited the room and entered the garden, leaving Mangan with the old woman. She sat on a bench amid the flowers and took a deep breath. Only hours before she had felt safe. Now her stomach was tight and her mind was spinning. This was the woman who had hurt her mother, the same woman who had inadvertently caused her parents' deaths. If Mary had not come to Scotland to try to make amends with Laural-Anne, she would not have been in the glen with Laird Geoffrey's men. Romil would not be dead.

Ashleigh would not be alone.

But she wasn't alone; she had Mangan. She sat outside and listened to the soothing murmur of Mangan's voice as he spoke to her grandmother. Mary had been a wonderful mother, caring, compassionate, encouraging . . . How had she become such a beautiful person with a mother like Laural-Anne? Something must have changed during Mary's childhood to turn Laural-Anne bitter.

Cairdean swooped down and landed on a rose trellis. He cawed, and a shadow passed over the garden as a robin fluttered past. Ashleigh watched the robin's red-and-black wings reflect the golden sunlight as it circled the convent twice. Suddenly Cairdean burst into flight and began chasing the smaller bird. The robin cried out, then beat its wings and flew across the garden, swooping in between the blossoming trees with Cairdean close behind. Just as Cairdean was upon the robin's tail, the small bird twisted in midair and abruptly changed its path. Cairdean flew past, unable to follow the nimble maneuver. The raven called out again, but this time softer, and drifted lazily up into the sky.

Her mother had been the robin. She had changed directions and saved her own life from Laural-Anne's vicious clutches.

The door to the garden opened, and Mangan emerged.

Ashleigh rose and met him. "I want to leave," she said. "And I never want to come back."

"Ashleigh . . ." he started. "She said you were afraid to tell me something . . ."

"She is a foolish, mean old woman."

Mangan looked at her with an impenetrable expression. "Will you ever trust me with your secrets? If we are to build a life together we must trust each other."

Ashleigh turned away and stared at the rosebushes. "Do you love me?"

"Why do you ask?"

She turned back. "Why do *you* ask? That woman is my grandmother. She tried to destroy my mother's life, and now she is trying to destroy ours. Can we leave the past behind?"

"You told me I was brave to face my past. Are you less courageous?"

"I want to leave." She whistled for Cairdean and pushed open the iron gate, then untied Franco. As she mounted she saw Mangan come out after her. He appeared subdued, but he untied his stallion and mounted beside her.

"I do love you," he told her. "With all my heart."

Ashleigh swallowed and looked aside.

He reined around and started his horse down the hillside.

"Where are we going now?" Ashleigh asked, clucking to her horse.

He glanced over his shoulder and slowed his stallion so that she could catch up with him. He had left his homeland for the monastery, but his quest had led him full circle. His father the earl had tried to call him home after he had left the king's service, but Mangan had refused. His emotions had been too raw to share . . . to painful to divulge to anyone except God. Now, during his mission for the abbey, he had discovered a plot against Scotland's leader, and he was the one person who could warn the king of Laird Tiernay's murderous intentions.

He had left the battlefield seeking celibacy, yet found a woman to love for eternity. He needed redemption; Ashleigh needed understanding. Mangan's father could assist in saving the king, and Mangan's mother could comfort Ashleigh.

"We are headed for the one place where both of us will find help," Mangan answered, knowing he spoke the truth. "My home, Castle Kirkcaldy."

That night they camped next to a fallen tree covered with velvety moss and tiny fernlike sprouts. A small pond lay nestled in the forest, fed by a crystal-clear stream that trickled over a series of brown and beige rocks. Ashleigh wet the small washcloth she still carried, then wiped the travel dust from her face and neck.

As Mangan started a small, smokeless fire, Ashleigh hung the bit of cloth on a branch to dry, then arranged her blanket and his bedroll against the log so they could relax in comfort. Cairdean's eyes watched them, but he seemed more agitated than usual. He continually shifted along the branch, his beak dipping up and down and his wings fluttering. He plucked at the washcloth until Ashleigh was forced to shoo him away.

"What do you suppose makes him stay with you?" Mangan asked.

"He understands me."

"I'd like to understand you."

Ashleigh smiled sadly, then broke off a piece of flatbread and held it out to the raven as a conciliatory offering. He swooped down and took it from her hand. "I don't understand myself," she replied. Cairdean suddenly turned his head and peered at the lake, where a large, elegant white bird glided just above the water. The swan landed gracefully and arched her long neck, then dipped her beak into the water. As she drank, small droplets trickled down and splashed into the pond, causing ripples to spread in concentric rings until they gradually dissipated.

Ashleigh turned toward Mangan. "Are you angry with me for not . . . ?"

"Not telling me your hidden worry? For not telling me that you love me, too? No, sweet angel," he answered. "You are as lovely as that bird. When you finally accept me, heart and soul, we will be bonded for life, just like swans."

Mangan gathered Ashleigh close and leaned back against the log. In silent harmony they watched the bird's feathered majesty, marveling at her effortless movements. The tip of her tail feathers turned upward in a saucy curl, and her black eyes were shadowed by a dark gray fringe. As she swam, her neck reached forward and back in rhythmic motions, and a small wake flowed behind her. The glorious sunshine that had beaten down upon their backs all day faded to a pleasant warmth, and soft beams filtered through the leaves and sparkled on the water.

He smiled and pushed a curl behind Ashleigh's ear. "You are so beautiful," he murmured. He touched his finger underneath her chin and leaned forward to brush his lips across hers.

She glanced down, suddenly shy.

He kissed her again, softly, barely touching her mouth.

Her lips tingled and a blush spread across her cheeks. A shiver ran down her spine, and she pulled away slightly.

He stroked her back, calming her, telling her without words that she was safe.

She looked up and stared into his eyes. So green . . .

so mesmerizing. She touched his eyelashes. They were long and luxurious, so lovely against his masculine face. As her hand trailed down his cheek, she felt the stubble of his beard and wondered when he shaved. She had an impulse to ask him, but his mouth captured her finger and all thoughts fled her mind.

He suckled, his tongue tracing the unique swirls of her fingertip.

Her breath shortened and she began to feel lightheaded. Sun rays danced across her face, and a soft breeze rustled through the leaves. She stroked his lips with her wet finger, exploring even as her body sank back against his arm for support.

"Tell me that you are happy . . . right this very moment," he whispered against her delicate hand. "That is all I want from you."

"I am happy. I feel . . . at peace."

He pulled her up against his body and kissed her more fully, his tongue touching her lips in silent invitation. He had kissed her before—rushed, guilt-ridden bursts of uncontrolled passion—and he had taken her body in a stormy explosion of desire. But this was different.

Such tenderness. Such sincerity . . .

Her mouth opened and he felt her heat flood his soul. Diving his tongue within her, he tasted her essence. His tongue danced with hers as they met and challenged each other in an intimate series of unrehearsed steps. She was innocent . . . her experience limited to what she had done with him. He was skilled, yet only just freed from the constraints of a year of celibacy, thus his heart raced unnaturally fast and his fingers trembled like an untried youth's.

Their lips parted briefly, but the need to taste each other was so strong they instantly merged again, sinking into each other's arms and reveling in each other's lips. The warm sun rays brushed against their closed eyes, and their hands reached for each other, embracing and worshiping.

His hands squeezed her shoulders while her fingers dug into the hair at the back of his neck. She moaned deep in her throat as his lips slid down her neck and traced butterfly kisses along her collarbone.

"My angel . . ." he whispered. "Open your wings for me."

She sighed as he stroked her hair and twisted his fingers around one curl, then pulled her head back to bare her throat. Using his tongue he tasted her flesh, then shifted upward and gently nibbled her earlobe.

Ashleigh took a quick intake of breath, then smiled as a tiny laugh bubbled from her lips.

He grinned, and a glint of mischief sparkled in his eyes. Darting quickly, he thrust his tongue into her ear and swept it around in a rapid swirl.

Ashleigh giggled and tried to pull away, but he held her tight. "You can't escape," he growled with false fierceness before blowing on her moistened ear.

Ashleigh's eyes narrowed, and she slid her fingernails down his back as he tensed in suspicion. Then her eyes widened with glee and she dug her finger into his armpit and wiggled it.

He jerked back and tried to regain to his feet, but she grabbed his ankle and toppled him backward, then scrambled on top of him and pinned his arms to the ground.

"What are you going to do now?" he asked, amused.

She shifted, sitting on his hips as she brought her knees up in front of her; then she stretched her toes out and buried them in his exposed armpits once again.

He laughed aloud and twisted to and fro, trying to avoid her persistent wriggling, but her agile body rode him with ease, and she laughed with him, delighted to find a weakness in his powerful body.

"Stop!" He gasped.

Instead of stopping she started tickling the palms of his hands while she continued her toe attack, and he struggled even harder to elude her clutches. With a sudden upsurge he bucked his hips and tossed her to the ground as he easily freed his arms and reversed their positions.

Her cheeks flushed and she stared up at his suddenly serious face. He leaned over her and kissed her palms, then trailed kisses all the way up her inner arm until he reached its juncture with her torso. There he paused, and Ashleigh tightened with anticipation. Would he kiss her or tickle her?

The moment extended and her heart pounded. Her mouth opened and she panted, unsure what she wanted from him. Something deep in her belly rippled and rolled, and her thighs trembled.

His head lowered and she yanked against his restraint, trying to break free. She felt as if a bubble welled up in her throat, then burst as she gasped with pleasure. Moisture dampened her thighs as he raised her wrists higher above her head.

She felt exposed . . . vulnerable . . . and heady with desire.

He licked her, then caressed her body with his heated breath.

It tickled, yet she moaned and arched upward, moving her hips against the thrust of his tumescence, and he shifted positions to kiss her again, both of them needing to blend their mouths and souls together.

They kissed long and slow, drinking each other, rolling over so that he no longer straddled her but they lay side by side with arms and legs intertwined. A subtle change flowed through them as desire blossomed into something more. Their kisses became less passionate and more loving. The sense of urgency that had driven their earlier encounters drifted into leisurely contentment.

His hands slid along her hip, teasing her with his light touch while she traced the firm muscles of his upper arms. He found her earlobe again, and this time his touch sent shivers through Ashleigh's frame as she responded by nibbling his throat and kissing his jaw. Soon she cuddled up against him and tucked her head into the crease of his neck, fully relaxed. Her passion was not just for his body; it was for the sense of peace his presence brought her.

He smiled and rested his chin on her head and looked across the pond at the swan, which still glided over the water with effortless poise. Far above, Cairdean remained perched on the gnarled tree, his beady eyes scanning the forest with piercing intelligence, watching over them, protecting them. Graceful . . . elegant . . . beautiful and powerful . . . black and white.

Man and woman, together forming one whole.

Chapter 27

The next morning a light mist whispered through the trees, gently dissipating as the sun rose. A rainbow spread across the sky, its pale multicolored blessing framing the pond with its magical presence. Blue, violet, orange . . . yellow . . . the colors shifted and merged, so that one could not define exactly where one band began and another ended.

Mangan rolled on top of Ashleigh, kissing her beneath the rainbow. They made love gently and sweetly, exploring each other's bodies with the awe of new lovers. A delicate caress here, a lingering kiss there. Long after the mist burnt away and the rainbow faded into memory, they melded their bodies and hearts with exquisite tenderness.

Eventually they packed their belongings and began the two-day journey to Kirkcaldy. They traveled fast, alternating short bursts of speed with distance-covering trotting, slowing the horses to a walk only when the woods became too thick or the horses too tired.

They talked as they rode, learning about each other as their steps drew them closer to their destination, but even though Ashleigh answered his questions with queries of her own, a kernel of anxiety remained in the pit of her stomach. No matter what she revealed, it was superficial compared to the burning secret she still hid. Laural-Anne had warned her that Mangan would reject her if he knew the worst that she'd done. Even though Ashleigh knew that the woman had deliberately instilled doubt in her mind, she could not take the chance that her grandmother was right. It was safest to bury her guilt and never reveal her deed—even if to do so meant guarding a piece of her heart against Mangan.

They reached Kirkcaldy valley two days later, late in the afternoon. Like all newcomers to the castle, Ashleigh was struck by the vision of golden bricks casting a shimmering glow from the castle walls.

"Is it made of gold?" she asked, amazed by the sheer beauty of the structure.

"The earth in this valley is tan and filled with tiny white crystalline flecks; thus the bricks appear golden." Mangan smiled with a trace of wistfulness. "It has been a long time since I was home. There is no place like it."

Ashleigh heard the sadness in his voice as well as the carefully hidden anxiety. "Do you fear your father's reaction to our arrival?" she asked him.

He nodded, his gaze guarded. "Last time we communicated I told him that I was relinquishing my birthright and that he should select a new heir."

"Did he?"

"I don't know."

Ashleigh stared down the slope at the majestic castle. If someone were next in line to inherit Kirkcaldy, she doubted he would gracefully concede the position just because Mangan had chosen to come home.

"Will there be strife?" she asked.

Mangan glanced at her face, then took a deep breath. "My mother had no other children. My closest relative is Istabelle O'Bannon, the girl born to my uncle moments after my birth. As I explained to you before, the succession was . . . complicated at that time. I hope my return will not further disrupt the family. It might be best if I do not ask to be reinstated."

"But you are the rightful heir."

He clucked to his horse and began the descent into the valley. "I will not shed blood over it. My sword will not be used for political gain. I may have realized that becoming a monk was not my destiny, but I have not wavered in my principles. If my return causes complications, I will accept the consequences and not request my reinstatement."

When they finally clattered over the drawbridge, Ashleigh drew comfort from Cairdean perched on her shoulder. She raised her chin and brushed aside the locks of hair that fluttered around her face, tucking the strands behind her ears with hands that trembled from nervousness. She would stand beside Mangan no matter what reception he received.

Just as they dismounted the great doors to the castle were flung open, and a lovely middle-aged woman with tight black curls and a rich green velvet dress dashed down the steps and launched herself into Mangan's arms.

"Mother!" Mangan grinned in relief as he hugged her close. "You look gorgeous, as always."

The woman stepped back and glared at him. "And *you* look terrible. Where have you been?"

"Traveling," he answered with a teasing glint. "May I present my wife, Ashleigh. Ashleigh, my mother, Lady Matalia O'Bannon, your new mother-in-law."

Matalia swept the younger woman with an assessing gaze, noting the black raven clinging to her shoulder. Her brows rose, but she inclined her head in greeting. "I see there have been some changes in your life," she said dryly. "Let us go find your father before we say more, shall we?"

Mangan reached for her shoulder and halted her before she could turn around. "Will he be angry?" he asked.

Matalia cupped her son's face. "Disappointed. Confused. But never angry. He will be pleased to see you . . . and will welcome your wife." She smiled and picked up her skirts to ascend the stairs, obviously expecting Mangan and Ashleigh to follow.

"Perhaps you should speak to him alone," Ashleigh suggested, an odd lump forming in her throat. Seeing Mangan's mother made her own loss achingly sharp, and she had to look away in order to maintain her composure. "I am not certain I am prepared to meet your parents just yet."

Mangan kept his face expressionless while his thoughts tumbled over one another. What did she mean? Did she still doubt her love for him? Did she not want to be introduced to his family because it symbolized commitment? Or had his instinct to bring her home to his mother been correct? Perhaps all she needed was Matalia's warm love to mend the final fragments of her broken heart.

"This is my home," he replied. "My parents are good, kind people. They will want to meet my wife."

Ashleigh bit her fingernail. Not only did it hurt to remember her parents' final moments, but it also reminded her of her own sinful deed. What would his parents think of her if they knew that her palms were stained with blood?

Matalia reappeared at the top of the stairs and looked at both of them with concern. Ashleigh shook her head and started to turn toward her horse. "I'm sorry," she mumbled. "I'm not good enough for you. You deserve so much better." A sob caught in her throat, and she waved to encompass the castle and its inhabitants. "All of this is too much for me."

Mangan gripped her arm and halted her, then stood directly behind her and bent his head so that his lips were close to her ear. " 'Tis I who must apologize. If you are not comfortable meeting my parents, I will not force them upon you. We will leave."

She sank back against his chest and closed her eyes in misery. "No. That is not what I mean. I wish I could tell you something . . . something about myself that I would give anything to make untrue."

"There is nothing you should fear telling me. Speak, and absolve yourself of guilt."

She shook her head. "I cannot."

Her reticence tried his patience. "Cannot or will not? Why don't you trust me?"

Ashleigh twisted away from him and looked at him with a hurt expression, but before she could answer Lady Matalia hurried down the stairs and took Ashleigh by the hand.

"Come along, dear." She tugged on the ragged blanket that Ashleigh still used as a cloak. "It is getting dark, and we have already dined, but I just arranged for a platter to be sent up to your chamber." Casting her son a reproachful look, she pulled Ashleigh up the stairs and through the great doors.

Once within the golden walls, Lady Matalia immediately ushered Ashleigh up another set of stairs toward a bedchamber. Ashleigh looked back as Mangan entered the great hall more slowly, then paused just beyond the threshold as an older man rose from an ornately carved chair placed in front of the fireplace.

"Father," Mangan greeted him, then bowed respectfully.

It could only be Brogan O'Bannon, the Earl of Kirkcaldy, Ashleigh surmised. He stared at his son from across the room. "Why have you come to Kirkcaldy?" he asked. "The last missive from Brother Bartholomew said that you were on a quest and would return only once you had found the true meaning of faith."

"Indeed. My faith is strong, and I have embraced God's plan for me. The path is not always easy, and I have stumbled upon many obstacles, but God sent an angel to guide me to where I am meant to be."

"And where is that?"

"Home. With you and Mother and the people of this land. I want to see my children born under this roof and watch my mother cuddle her first grandchild. Father, will you welcome me home?"

Brogan opened his arms and embraced his only son.

"How did you meet my little boy?" Matalia asked.

Ashleigh glanced up quickly, intimidated by Mangan's beautiful mother. She had no idea what to say. Should she tell Matalia that Mangan had saved her life when she was so overcome with despair that she had tried to kill herself? Should she say he had captured and confronted her about her trickery in the village? Or should she say that they had met alongside a road and he had promised to help her even before he knew her problems? What of her parents? Should she say simply that they were dead, or should she say that they were tortured and murdered while she huddled behind a disappearing plate?

Matalia watched expressions flit over Ashleigh's face and felt compassion for the young woman. She looked lost and confused despite the elegant raven perched on her shoulder. There was something fragile about Ashleigh, something at odds with a woman who could command the obedience of such a bird and had evidently broken through her son's emotional reserve.

Matalia opened the door and walked across the room to stare out through the window slits, keeping her back turned toward Ashleigh. "It doesn't matter, you know."

"Doesn't matter?" Ashleigh asked as she stepped into the room and looked around. It appeared to be Mangan's room, for a child-size wooden sword and shield stood in the corner near the fireplace.

"Whatever you don't want to tell him. I learned a long time ago that love is a powerful weapon."

"I don't understand."

"I don't know Mangan anymore. He is my son, but he left ten years ago to lead the king's army. He came home every now and then, but he was so distant . . . the battlefield had changed him." She sighed and turned to face the younger woman. "I miss my little boy. He used to laugh and play with me, but now he is a grown man. I accepted his decision to become a monk, was even pleased when he found sanctuary, but today he arrives without any warning and presents me with you." She smiled and opened her arms. "I hope you will like me, Ashleigh. I already respect and admire you, and have a thousand reasons to thank you."

She gave Ashleigh a brief hug, then walked to the bed and turned down the covers. "You look exhausted, my dear. You must be overwhelmed, and I am only making matters worse by talking on and on. Rest and we will converse later. You have brought me much joy. Not only has my son returned, but I have gained a daughter as well.''

She placed a kiss on Ashleigh's left cheek, carefully avoiding the black raven on her other shoulder, then left the room and closed the door.

Ashleigh stood in the empty room, her heart beating so loudly she could hear it echoing between her ears. Cairdean's presence brought her some solace, but Mangan's absence made her heart ache. Even Lady Matalia's kind words made the hurt worse, for they reminded her that she had once been someone else's daughter. Mary's daughter.

And Mary was dead.

Battling tears, Ashleigh lifted Cairdean off her shoulder and placed him on the window ledge, then took off her cloak, peeled off her clothing and slipped underneath the covers. The linens were crisp and clean, and the ticking was soft and comfortable. Rolling over so that she faced the wall, Ashleigh closed her eyes and cried herself to sleep.

Mangan came up to the room several hours later. He shut the door behind him, then walked quietly across the floor to stare down at her. He touched one of her curls splayed across the pillow. Dull throbbing filled his head, and he rubbed his temples to try to ease the pain. He had not had a headache in so many days, he'd forgotten how much they hurt.

Ashleigh's magical fingers had swept them away before, but he was afraid to ask for her help tonight. She did not trust him, and one could not love unless one trusted.

Trust, hope, forgiveness and acceptance. Faith, hope and love. Or—he grinned wryly to himself—as he had said as a child, *God, love and milk make you strong.*

He had faith. He had love. He had hope. But they needed trust.

He sat down in the chair, leaned forward and rubbed his forehead with his palms. Should he let her go? Was it selfish to hold her to a vow she did not want?

He looked at her through his fingers. Even the light coming through the window felt like piercing arrows in his eye sockets, but he could not tear his gaze away from her. She was so beautiful, her skin pale against the pillow, her delicate ear surrounded by a cloud of tousled black hair. He could already trace her jaw from memory, as each curve was indelibly etched into his mind. He could hear her voice even when she was not talking . . . feel her purity even though she had her back turned toward him.

How could he live without her?

She stirred, turned over and her eyes fluttered open. Lifting her head she stared at him in silent contemplation. "I saw your father welcome you home," she finally said.

"Yes. He told me about his time abroad before he came to Kirkcaldy to fight for his inheritance." Mangan dropped his hands and sat back, then closed his eyes. "He said that all great men question their lives at one time or another, and that he believes I have become a great man."

"So all is well?" Ashleigh asked.

Mangan was silent. Was all well? He had told his father about Laird Geoffrey, and an armed contingent had already been dispatched to warn the king, who was residing in his summer castle in the south. His father had insisted on leading the small army, knowing that his status as earl would command the most respect with the king, especially since they were accusing the king's own cousin of a dastardly plot. Brogan had also sent a call to all his vassals, demanding that they provide armed and mounted warriors to join the O'Bannon men.

If all went as Mangan expected, the king would send his army to Tiernay and rescue Matilda, order her marriage annulled, and punish Geoffrey and Jordan for treason. No doubt there would be a great battle, and many lives would be lost. One day, Mangan prayed as he bent his head in contemplation, men would be able to resolve their differences without bloodshed, but until that day, the feudal laws of Scotland would prevail.

"It is a beginning," he finally answered Ashleigh as he lifted his head. "But there may be more trouble before all is settled. Prior to my father's departure he penned a letter to my uncle Xanthier informing him of my return. Xanthier and his wife, Alannah, had a son named Aaragon ten years ago, just after I joined the army, and my father was forced to name him Kirkcaldy's heir when I renounced my birthright."

Ashleigh swallowed and glanced down at the coverlet. "Will Xanthier and Aaragon accept your return?"

"I am not certain. As I told you, my father and uncle fought over Kirkcaldy, but my father won, since I was born moments before my cousin Istabelle. Xanthier has never attempted to reignite the feud, but he is an enigmatic man. I am not certain he will relinquish this castle a second time, especially if it is for his son."

"But what if *you* have a son? Will he lose his birthright? Won't he want Kirkcaldy and expect to lead his own people?"

"Do you mean if *we* have a son?"

Ashleigh glanced away and clutched the coverlet tighter.

Mangan stretched and shifted his legs, closing his eyes once again as he leaned back in the chair. He could not bear to look at her, not when only a few days ago he had completely believed in their union. Something had changed at St. Augustine's. The bond of trust had been stretched taut and its fibers were fraying. Ashleigh held a secret, and unless she told him they were at risk of losing everything.

Chapter 28

Late that night, Mangan slipped into bed and pulled Ashleigh close. Under the cover of darkness he kissed her, his sense of desperation making his hands and lips rougher than usual. He trapped her beneath his body, using his legs to separate her thighs; then he bent his knee and rubbed it against her as he devoured her mouth and plunged his tongue deep into her throat.

She struggled only briefly, then gasped as his unparalleled desire inflamed her passion and she arched up against him, raking her nails down his back in a primitive mating ritual of possession.

He bit her neck, leaving bright red spots, then shifted down to her nipples and sucked on her until she cried out with a mixture of pain and pleasure. The sound sent blood pounding through him, and his cock swelled until it doubled in thickness and its length jutted forward to press insistently against her belly.

The need to dominate her, to show her that he was lord and master, made him groan with repressed agony until he flipped her facedown and raised her hips high in the air. The smooth double moon of her buttocks nearly made him explode, as did her muffled moan and the heady scent of her arousal.

Gripping the front of her thighs, he lifted her buttocks upward and thrust forward, seeking and finding her inner sanctum and plunging his length deep inside her. He bucked against her, his testes pounding against her sensitive nub, raising her desire in an escalating torrent that matched his.

Both of them panted, their breath heating the room even as their combined sweat dampened the linens. He slid one hand up to her breast, squeezing it, feeling its fullness as it swayed back and forth with their movements. Heavy and succulent . . . filling his hand to overflowing.

Her arms grew weak, and her cheek pressed against the pillow while she held her buttocks up high. Being so exposed made her heady with desire. His powerful grip, the rippling musculature of his thighs against hers . . . She screamed as light burst behind her eyelids and the room spun in wild circles around her head.

Each thrust pushed her further, flung her deeper into a universe of ecstasy more powerful than before. Screaming until her voice was raw, Ashleigh tossed her head back and forth and her hair tangled in wild ringlets around her face, yet still he demanded more.

Deeper, deeper, deeper . . . harder, harder, harder . . . until his punishing grip on her began to tremble and his muscles began to quiver. Blood drained from his head and he fell forward on top of her back while his hips thrust one final time and he yanked her by the waist until every bit of their merging flesh became seamless . . . there was no man and woman; there was only one.

His voice joined hers, a shout that shook the bedposts and caused the logs in the fireplace to tumble to the hearth.

They hung together in eternity . . . their souls clinging to hope, searching for the peace they had shared for all too brief a time. Then he exhaled and collapsed upon her just as her body melted into limpid muscle and exhausted flesh, and their minds separated, became guarded and unsure.

He turned her around and nestled her body against him, but both sensed the tension in the other, although neither dared confront it.

Over the next fortnight Ashleigh spent more time with Mangan's mother than with him. She and Matalia went for walks together, and Ashleigh watched with amazement as the older woman sang beautiful songs until all the animals in the forest paused to listen. A pack of wolves lived in a nearby glen—three old wolves, one gray, one black and one red, along with three generations of younger pups ranging from robust adult to squirming puppy. Matalia sang to them every day as they lolled in the grass.

As they grew to know each other, Ashleigh felt safe enough to discuss with Matalia the horror of her mother's rape and the loneliness of parents' absence. Clasped within the older woman's embrace, she cried, vividly recounting the terrible day and her agony for weeks thereafter. Telling the tale finally leached it of its power, and with Matalia's support Ashleigh took the final steps toward healing.

Still, she could not tell Matalia of the murder. No matter how kind and understanding Matalia appeared, or how often Mangan's sorrowful gaze fell on her, Laural-Anne's warning echoed in her thoughts. Ash-

leigh could not admit her sin to anyone, for she feared
the loss of her only security. Her secrecy placed a
strain on her relationship with Mangan, but she felt
helpless to release it. No matter how she turned the
problem over in her mind, she could find no way of
admitting her awful deed without losing him forever.

Cairdean stayed nearby, and Ashleigh spent solitary
twilight hours sitting by the lake with the raven
perched on her shoulder, his beak always facing the
setting sun regardless of which direction she sat. His
agitation had not calmed, and Ashleigh was surprised
he remained with her, since it seemed as if he were
being drawn westward.

She shifted positions, and Cairdean spread both his
wings and batted the air, his breast feathers ruffling
in the breeze as he, too, moved so that his beady eyes
could continue to stare raptly into the distance.

Ashleigh was honored by Cairdean's presence, and
he gave her a small kernel of hope, for he knew the
truth, yet stayed with her even when she could not
look at her reflection in the lake without seeing her
own guilt staring back at her.

"Do you forgive me for injuring you?" she asked
Cairdean one evening. He stretched out a wing tip,
gently caressing the tears from her cheeks. An unspoken communion whispered between them . . . an indescribable bond that confounded yet reassured
Ashleigh. "What do you see when you look at me?"
she asked him. "Are you lonely, too? Is there someone or something over that horizon that calls to you?
My friend," she whispered, "do you see something in
me that I have yet to discover in myself? Can you tell
me what to do?"

Cairdean opened his beak and made a soft coo, flew

up into the air and swept over the treetops in a westward direction, then slowly turned in a large arc and returned to perch on a rock beside her.

Ashleigh looked up when she heard a twig snap and beheld Mangan leaning against a tree.

"How long have you been standing there?" she asked.

"Only a few moments."

"Why didn't you make your presence known?"

He shrugged, then pushed off the tree with his shoulder and ambled toward her. "You and my mother have gotten along well together."

Ashleigh nodded. "She is a talented woman."

"Aye, that she is. Do you like it here?" he asked, and she wondered at the break in his voice.

"It is a lovely castle," Ashleigh replied as she cast her eyes downward.

"I came to tell you that my father sent word that the king's men have laid siege to Tiernay Castle. My cousin Istabelle's husband, Ruark Haagan has a comrade, Seth, who is handling the negotiations. He is a good man. I met him at the abbey while he was recuperating from a wound. Perhaps he will convince Laird Geoffrey to release Matilda and avoid a long and costly fight."

"Good," Ashleigh replied.

"Ashleigh," Mangan said softly as he fell to one knee beside her. "You are tearing my heart with your silence. Talk to me, for if you do not we have no marriage."

Ashleigh rose and glared at him. "I never wanted to wed you. You forced me to say yes when we were on the rafters, but a coerced acceptance is meaningless."

"But—"

"Just leave me alone!" She yanked the beaded chain from around her neck and flung the cross at him.

Mangan rose, and his eyes grew cold as he picked up the cross and placed it over his own head. "Very well. Stay here and stare at the water and wait for the sun to set, as you have done night after night. But know that for every day you do so, you waste a day of your life in which we could be happy together. You are the one who told me to live again, yet you are deliberately killing our love."

Ashleigh picked up her skirts and ran away from him, his words reverberating in her ears. She was a killer! She was a murderer! She raced along the lakeshore, not caring whether Mangan followed her. Mud splashed her bare feet, and sharp stalks of pond grass cut her calves, but she did not stop. She ran as fast as she could, wanting desperately to escape her guilt. Her breath grew labored and yet still she pressed on. After reaching the other side of the lake, she scrambled through bushes, tripping over logs and ducking under branches, until finally, exhausted, she fell to the ground and sobbed.

A hand descended upon her shoulder.

"I'm sorry, Mangan," she cried, her tears blinding her. "I should have told you. I murdered a man. I killed Branan with a knife, and I watched him bleed to death before my very eyes. God forgive me, but I have committed the worst of all sins!"

"How fascinating, but I don't care who you killed. All I care about is how you ruined my life," a man's voice mockingly replied.

Ashleigh gasped and looked up into Douglas's face.

She tried to scramble to her feet, but he twisted his hands in her hair and pulled her up against his body. "It seems that I've seen a face like yours before," he

said with a chuckle. "I wonder what I did next . . .
Ah, yes, I remember. I tossed her dress up and sank
my cock into her sweet, tight core."

Ashleigh swayed dizzily, and spots flashed before
her eyes. Everything came rushing back. The blood . . .
the crunch of the man's sword against her father's
bone. Her mother's cry of agony . . . Mary begging
her to stay hidden . . . stay hidden behind the plate . . .
even as the men tore her clothes and fell upon her
body.

"No!" Ashleigh screamed. She yanked back in desperation, ripping a hunk of hair from her scalp, then
spun and stumbled away from Douglas in panic.
"Leave me alone! No, please . . ." Terror raced
through her, and her mind flung her back to the clearing on the mountain. It was all happening again, every
moment repeating itself in with excruciating detail.

She had to escape!

Ashleigh dashed through the trees as Douglas raced
after her. He shoved leaves and branches aside and
bounded over rocks as he rapidly gained on her fleeing
figure. "I'll catch you!" he shouted. "You rejected
your man and now you have no one, just like me!
Because of you I lost everything, but if I bring you to
him, Laird Geoffrey may forgive me." He caught her
shoulder and shoved her to the ground.

As she fell, she rolled and glared up at him. "Tiernay Castle is under siege. Soon he will be captured
and punished before the king."

"Auch!" Douglas bellowed as he struck Ashleigh
across the face. "You did this! If only I had found
and killed you that first day!"

Ashleigh struggled to get free, but Douglas was too
strong. He gripped her arm and hauled her upright,

then slammed her against a tree. "Don't think you're going to get it easier than your mother did," he snarled. "I will keep you for days until you plead for the release of death." He drew off his belt, bent Ashleigh's hands behind her back and lashed them together on the other side of the tree. Then he pulled a knife and held it to her throat.

"Stop!" Mangan shouted as he burst through the trees. "Lay a hand on her and you will die!"

"Ha!" Douglas replied. "I know your tale, Lord Mangan. You turned coward and will not raise your sword against another. Tory told me that you granted him mercy, and the fool actually admired you for your leniency. Both of you are idiots. A strong arm and a merciless heart make a man powerful!"

Ashleigh kicked Douglas's shin but he instantly responded by slapping her across the face. As Mangan surged forward, Douglas pressed the knife against Ashleigh's throat. "Don't be stupid," he growled. "One move and her blood will spill as easily as when she robbed that peasant's life force."

Mangan stopped, but he drew his sword and lifted it to the darkening sky. Thin trails of orange and gold reflected off the blade's sharp edge, but Mangan's gaze remained unrelenting on the man who held his woman hostage. "You will not leave this clearing alive."

"And how do you expect to smite me?" Douglas mocked. "Do you think your God will strike me with a bolt of lightning?" Douglas stepped away from Ashleigh, then pulled his own sword and pointed it at Mangan. " 'Tis you who will not be leaving this glen."

"Mangan!" Ashleigh pleaded. "Go. I already caused the death of one man. I could not bear to be the cause of yours. Go!" Ashleigh screamed as Douglas began to advance. "Please! If ever I ask you for anything, I ask you now. Go and save your life! I am not worthy of your sacrifice."

"Don't worry, my angel," he told her gently. "I will keep you safe. I promise." Then his face grew grim. "Confess your sins and repent," he commanded Douglas. "We can avoid bloodshed if you admit your misdeeds and ask for forgiveness."

Douglas laughed. "I confess nothing and want no forgiveness. If it is confession you demand, the girl should be the one asking for redemption, for 'tis she who committed murder."

"Why didn't you tell me?" Mangan asked Ashleigh from across the clearing.

"I did not want to lose you," she replied. "You are so good and righteous, I knew you could not accept such fault in the woman for whom you had sacrificed everything. You left the monastery because of me . . . and I am a murderer."

" 'Twas after he raped and murdered your own mother before your eyes," Mangan replied. Then he turned toward Douglas. "Ashleigh did not know her mind. But you knew you were terrorizing the villagers and causing them pain and suffering, yet you still did it to ensure their cooperation in the wedding of Lady Matilda and Lord Jordan. Was their silence worth the death of two innocent travelers? Of the royal guards and a lady-in-waiting? You cared nothing for the trauma you inflicted upon their families, or the horror your revolt would have caused this nation."

"I am still guilty," Ashleigh whispered. " 'Tis true. I killed Branan."

Douglas shrugged. "None of that matters. Before the sun fully sets, Mangan, you will be dead, and I will have days in which to enjoy the delicious fruits of your woman's flesh.''

Ashleigh trembled and shook her head mournfully. "I will never be forgiven." she whispered.

"There is one way to prove to you that God forgives you," Mangan said quietly. "I ask for a trial by swords, with God's hand to decide the victor."

Douglas laughed. "You want to fight me to show your woman that God forgives her? You are a fool several times over. I will win because I will show no mercy, whereas you have grown soft."

"Do you accept?" Mangan asked.

"I will kill you regardless." Douglas hefted his sword and took a step toward Mangan.

"Then you have no reason to refuse my request. Is there not one small part of you that would be pleased if you win? For if you do, it is because God has forgiven all your sins. Wouldn't you be pleased to have God's blessing on all that you have done?"

"I don't care what God thinks," Douglas replied, but his mouth twisted in contemplation.

"Are you certain?" Mangan asked.

"If I win, it means that God stands behind me?" Douglas asked in disbelief.

"Aye. But if I win, Ashleigh is forgiven and may face the new day with a cleansed heart."

"Then I accept the trial by swords," Douglas replied.

Ashleigh paled. "Mangan," she whispered. "You have not fought in two years. Please do not do this for me. I . . . I love you. I don't want to see you die."

Mangan's gaze took in her smooth cheeks, her long black tresses and her unusual eyes. "I have waited a long time to hear those words," he murmured with a smile. "I will not die. Trust me, and trust in God's mercy."

"But you swore not to lift your sword. I do not want you to fight to save my soul at the expense of your own."

"I told you I love you. You are my wife in body and soul. I accept your faults, as I hope you accept mine. We have all done deeds of which we are not proud, but as long as we always turn back toward God, we are forgiven."

"Did you know?" she asked. "Did you know about Branan?"

"I suspected."

"Why didn't you confront me?"

"I wanted you to trust me. You cannot be forgiven until you learn to forgive yourself. I love you. I love every bit of you, dark angel. You saved me; now let me save you."

"But—"

"There is nothing more powerful than that which is between two faithful lovers, except the love of God himself. I said that I would never lift my sword for unnecessary violence or for an unjust cause." He kissed the flat of his blade, then looked up to the heavens and offered a quick prayer. "I ask in your name, O Lord," he whispered. "Guide my hand and infuse my body with strength, for I fight for the woman I love."

Then he faced Douglas of Tiernay. "Let the trial begin."

Chapter 29

They stripped down to their breeches and boots, although Mangan left the cross around his neck. Then he made a large circle in the dirt with his shod foot. "No matter what happens, you are not allowed to leave the circle," he informed Douglas. He drew a line with the tip of his sword across the middle of the circle. "Once either one of us crosses this line, the trial cannot be stopped except by death."

" 'Tis not I who will die within the circle's boundaries," Douglas replied.

Ashleigh's arms ached, and her back was raw from the bark of the tree, but she did not notice the pain. "Please," she whispered. "Please prevail, Mangan. Not for me, but for youself."

She knew that Mangan's frame was lithe and firm, and his chiseled abdomen rippled with strength, but Douglas was massive, his biceps alone as thick as Mangan's thigh. She watched helplessly as they both held their broadswords with the ease of well-trained warriors, and warily sized each other up.

Douglas stretched and swung his broadsword a few times to loosen up his muscles. Mangan knelt down, closed his eyes and took a silent moment to pray. The setting sun beat down upon them, causing small beads of sweat to trickle down their bare chests even though they hadn't begun to fight. Mangan's cross hung between his pectorals, a stark reminder of the seriousness of the coming fight.

Without warning, Douglas lunged forward and swung his blade across the circle's center and toward Mangan's bowed neck.

Except Mangan was no longer there.

Douglas spun around to see Mangan balanced easily on the pads of his feet on the far side of the circle, his sword raised and ready. "You seek to win by cheating?" he asked coldly, his piercing gaze sending a shiver of fear up Douglas's spine.

"The laird should have broken your thumb instead of your finger," Douglas snarled. "But even so, you will find you lack control and have grown weak."

"But my heart and soul have clarity of purpose, while your innards are full of evil intentions."

"You are a fool if you believe God cares about this battle. 'Tis a fight of power and strength, like any other." He darted forward and swiped the ground at Mangan's feet in an attempt to maim him, but again Mangan eluded him by jumping up and spinning away, his sword still perfectly balanced in his hand.

"You are afraid to attack," Douglas mocked. "Your conscience hinders you, monk. Once, you were a great warrior, but now you are incapable of killing." He swung and this time sliced a bloody streak across Mangan's side.

Ashleigh screamed and struggled against her bonds, desperately wanting to stop the fight.

Mangan retreated and carefully circled his enemy.

"I've drawn first blood." Douglas smirked. He lunged to the left, then swung his blade to the right, again nicking Mangan's skin. "Your time in the monastery has made you slow. Surrender now and I will kill you quickly."

"Please stop this!" Ashleigh begged. "I will accept my punishment. Don't kill my husband!"

Mangan stalked Douglas's frame as the soldier claimed the center of the circle and swung his blade over his head. The blade whizzed by Mangan's face, and he barely ducked in time to avoid being decapitated. His cross flickered in the sun, momentarily blinding Douglas, and Mangan was able to leap forward and meet the man hand-to-hand.

Mangan shoved him backward, then punched him in the face while simultaneously gouging him in the abdomen with his elbow. As Douglas stumbled, Mangan retreated and waited for the man to recover.

"You fool," Douglas hissed. "You had your chance, and you did not have the stomach for it. Only one of us will walk out of this circle, and it will be me." He charged with his blade aimed at Mangan's heart.

Mangan raised his sword, and the two came together in a clash of metal that echoed throughout the forest. As their blades slid against each other with a sickening wail, a wave of nausea made Mangan stumble.

Douglas pressed his advantage, gathered his strength and swung his blade with all his might.

Mangan barely raised his sword in time to deflect the attack, but he fell backward even farther until his heel stood on the circle's line.

"You have nowhere to go," shouted Douglas as he surged forward for the final thrust.

Mangan saw movement out of the corner of his eye and he glanced up. Cairdean hovered behind Ashleigh's ashen face like a pair of dark wings upon her shoulders. The sunlight glittered in between the strands of her black hair, forming a halo of golden sunshine. His wild angel.

Power surged through him, and he rolled to the side, barely avoiding being cleaved in half by Douglas's broadsword. Mangan sprang to his feet and lunged forward, smashing his sword against the soldier's with nearly supernatural force.

The blades vibrated with the impact and Douglas stumbled back as Mangan advanced. Mangan twisted sharply, disengaging their weapons, then lunged forward and raked his sword's tip across Douglas's chest.

" 'Tis you who must surrender, for the force of righteousness is far stronger than the corrosion of hate," he warned Douglas.

Douglas recovered and warily circled Mangan. He surged forward, but Mangan easily deflected his blow, then countered with his own attack. Both men began to sweat heavily, and the scent of maleness permeated the forest.

Ashleigh strained against her ties, stunned at the transformation of Mangan from solitary monk to wild warrior. His chest was covered in a fine, wet sheen, highlighting every powerful muscle, and his eyes were lit with an inner fire that blazed across the clearing and seared her heart.

Mangan ducked as Douglas struck again. Then, using two hands, Mangan swept his broadsword up, tracing another thin, bloody streak up Douglas's torso from his belt to his neck, making a red crucifix upon Douglas's flesh.

As Mangan's power grew and his sword flashed faster and closer, Douglas began to shift backward, his face betraying his fear. Lifting his sword in desperate defense, Douglas flinched as the swords clashed.

Barely able to keep Mangan's blade from striking a lethal blow, Douglas was losing strength even as Mangan's energy surged.

Ashleigh caught her breath, awestruck by the mighty skill of her champion. Shivers rippled up her back as his arms pulsed and swelled while he pressed forward, swinging his blade with savage strength. He was no longer a man of peace, but a warrior for God, his intensity casting a wavering glow around his body that was only dimmed by the flash of sunlight on his sword.

Mangan swung, locking Douglas's sword with his, and for an instant, both sword tips pointed heavenward. As Ashleigh's eyes grew wide, Mangan's body appeared to pause and gather strength, and then his muscles uncoiled in an explosion of force. His sword bore down on Douglas's, bending it, making it quiver beneath Mangan's deadly attack.

Then, suddenly, Douglas's sword wavered and snapped at the hilt. As the blade tumbled out of the circle, a stunned Douglas was left holding only the handle. He looked into Mangan's fierce gaze and fear welled up from the pit of his stomach. He staggered out of the circle while Mangan strode after him.

"No!" Douglas shouted. "It can't be!"

Mangan drew a deep breath and the light of mercy entered his gaze. "Repent and I will grant you life," he said as he lowered his blade.

Douglas dropped the useless hilt of his broken sword. "I repent," he whispered.

Nodding, Mangan turned his back on Douglas and moved toward Ashleigh in order to free her, when suddenly Douglas withdrew a short sword from under his tunic and lunged at Mangan's back.

As Ashleigh screamed, Mangan ducked and fell to

his knees, then, holding the sword in both hands, stabbed it behind him from underneath his arm. Douglas's own momentum carried him forward onto the blade, impaling him clear through the heart.

Douglas's body quivered as Mangan's weapon penetrated his chest and went out his back. He stumbled, then toppled to the ground as bloody foam gurgled out of his mouth and he clutched at the protruding blade.

Mangan turned dispassionately to look at him, knowing that Douglas's death had been unavoidable. Still, he knelt next to the dying man and made the sign of the cross over his head. "You have one last chance to confess your sins and be forgiven so that you may ascend to eternal bliss."

Douglas opened his mouth, but could not form any words. He stared at Mangan—stared deep into the man's dark green eyes; then his eyes glazed over and his head lolled to one side.

Mangan went to Ashleigh and freed her from her bonds, then knelt with her beside the fallen man. Mangan rested his palm against Douglas's forehead and spoke a blessing for his departed soul. He asked for forgiveness for taking his life. All was quiet as his calming voice spread throughout the clearing, as even the birds and animals seemed to fall silent.

Mangan prayed in his own way and for his own desires, but he also prayed for the people of Scotland. Some needed peace, some forgiveness, some food for their families. The power of the moment stretched . . . built from a newly formed foundation that would never shatter. Love, faith and hope had conquered all.

He and Ashleigh rose and turned to each other. His angel smiled back at him and opened her arms.

Chapter 30

Several months after the trial by swords, Father Benedict arrived at Castle Kirkcaldy to inform Ashleigh that Laural-Anne MacLaren had died.

The threesome sat in the great hall while Matalia and Brogan, who had recently returned from the successful siege of Laird Geoffrey of Tiernay's castle, left them alone to speak.

"I owe you my gratitude for speaking to the king on my behalf," Father Benedict began. "Without your support I would have been convicted of treason just as Geoffrey and Jordan were. Thus I came today to give you a message. But first, why did you protect me from punishment? I was as much to blame as the others, for I knew that Matilda was being abducted and wed without the king's consent."

Mangan leaned forward and stared into Father Benedict's eyes. "Did you take Christ's blanket from St. Ignacio's monastery?"

Father Benedict averted his gaze. "I was afflicted with such a desire to possess it . . . I could not control my impulse. I knew my sin was terrible, and I tried to exorcise my demons, but they followed me from church to church. Every place I went I took something. A chalice, a scepter, a lock of hair, a blanket . . . It wasn't until I entered the chapel on the mountain that my need to possess things was overshadowed by my need to help people. The villagers asked for my guidance, and they offered me respect when I deserved none. Because of them I sold some relics to gain funds to help the peasants and hid others in Laird Geoffrey's church. Then I burned the church and resolved to forget about the relics' existence."

"Is the blanket still there?" Mangan asked.

"Alas, I cannot remember what items I sold, and all else was destroyed during the siege."

Mangan sighed and placed a hand on Father Benedict's shoulder. "The world has forever lost some sacred relics, and you will have to live with the knowledge that their loss was due to your actions. But I am not the one who will judge you in the end, and there is time for you to make amends. There is always time, if you are truly ready to admit your faults to God. I asked the king to pardon you because I hoped that you would find a way to repay those you hurt."

"You would have made a good priest," Father Benedict replied.

Mangan placed an arm around his wife. "Ah, but I make a better husband."

Father Benedict rose. "I came to deliver a message. The old gardener at St. Augustine's called for me to offer last confession to Laural-Anne. She was Harold Dunkeld's longtime mistress and common-law wife, and many believe he loved her more than he loved anyone. Laural-Anne herself came from a well-born family, but she was cast out when she eschewed a legitimate marriage for an unlawful one. Early in their relationship they had one daughter named Mary, and Dunkeld was in the process of arranging a marriage between that daughter and one of his most powerful allies when Mary ran off with a Gypsy lover.

"The incident caused Dunkeld to lose prestige, and he was forced to banish Laural-Anne to a convent in order to appease the jilted lord. However, later that same year, Laural-Anne gave birth to another daughter and named her Glorianna."

Ashleigh caught her breath. "Glorianna is my aunt?"

"Aye. She is living in a cottage on the edge of the western Highlands and is nearly exactly your age. Laural-Anne's last request was that I tell you where she is so that the two of you could meet." Father Benedict bowed his head. "I believe that this was one of the only selfless acts Laural-Anne ever accomplished and I encourage you to find Glorianna. I fear for her, for Dunkeld has made it no secret that he is also looking for her."

"Why?" Ashleigh asked.

"Because she is his daughter, and he wants her back under his control. 'Tis whispered that she can control beasts with her mind, and Dunkeld seeks to harness her power for his own nefarious use."

"Dunkeld was not convicted of treason along with the Tiernays?" Mangan asked.

"He fled before the king's men could capture him, although he has been spotted several times since then. The soldier, Seth, has taken Lady Matilda into hiding until Dunkeld is taken."

"Matilda asked me to tell Glorianna that she did not blame her for the kidnapping, but I was never able to complete the task. We must find her," Ashleigh told her husband. "I want to find my aunt."

Mangan bowed to Father Benedict. "Thank you for your message. My wife is gratified to learn that she has a blood relative in Scotland when she thought she had lost everyone. May God bless you on your own journey."

"And also on yours."

Their search was long and hard. Electing to travel lightly, they decided against a wagon and guard, and rode on horseback for many weeks until finally they reached the western Highlands just as the summer leaves were turning red and orange. With apparent excitement Cairdean guided them onward, his loud cawing echoing over the hills with increasing stridency. Soon the raven would not even stop to eat, and Ashleigh began to wonder if they were getting close.

A thin trail of smoke in the distance suggested a cottage nearby, and since Cairdean was headed directly toward it, Mangan and Ashleigh decided to stop there and question the owner. After weeks of traveling they were both tired and would appreciate a warm bed and a soft pillow.

Cairdean flitted from branch to branch, his feathers ruffling with extreme agitation and his tiny head swiveling to and fro as he peered through the trees at the clearing around the house. He then swooped down and landed on Ashleigh's shoulder, where he clung tightly.

Mangan and Ashleigh dismounted, stretched, then clasped hands as they approached the cottage.

The door opened, and a dark-haired young woman stepped outside. "I have been waiting for you," she said as she gracefully descended the steps and walked down the path toward them. "Welcome."

"I am Ashleigh O'Bannon, and I am searching for my aunt, Glorianna. Are you she?"

"I am Glorianna, born of Harold Dunkeld and

Laural-Anne MacLaren." She withdrew a locket and showed it to the pair.

Ashleigh gasped. "My mother used to have a locket identical to yours! It was burned with our wagon after her death."

"Both lockets belonged to my mother, Laural-Anne, and they came from Harold Dunkeld, whose clan ruled Scotland well before the present Caenmores. They were gifts given to her at the birth of both her daughters."

Cairdean cawed, and Glorianna smiled and held out her hand. The raven rose from Ashleigh's shoulder and glided to the other woman, immediately perching on her shoulder. Glorianna cooed at the bird, and Cairdean sang back, then nestled his head against her throat.

Feeling light-headed, Ashleigh gripped Mangan's hand, "You know my bird?" she asked the woman. "Did he befriend me because of you?"

Glorianna stroked Cairdean's head, then whistled toward the forest. A golden lynx emerged, its large pointed ears framed by thick clumps of gray fur and its long tail twitching back and forth above the grass. "Yes," Glorianna replied. "I sent him to find you." Glorianna walked over to the lynx and scratched under his chin. Cairdean remained on Glorianna's shoulder. He kept spreading and folding his wings.

Ashleigh stared into Cairdean's eyes from across the field. "He is my friend. Without his companionship I would have lost hope."

Glorianna smiled and stroked the bird's back. "Yes, he is a good friend. I have been lonely without him."

Ashleigh smiled back. She had Mangan now. It was only fair that she relinquish Cairdean to one who needed him more.

Ashleigh let go of Mangan's hand and walked over to her aunt. The lynx hissed and backed away into the forest, but Cairdean remained on Glorianna's shoulder. "May we stay awhile?" Ashleigh inquired. "I would like to talk with you."

"Yes. I expected you would. I prepared something for you." She glanced at Mangan. "For both of you."

She led them through the trees until they reached the edge of a rocky cliff that plummeted downward to where a ribbon of water ran through the verdant valley. Far across the valley was another cliff, its rocky shelves made of alternating red and gold granite. Occasional bursts of white flowers bloomed against the cliffside, having found small patches of dirt from which to sprout and blossom.

Mangan and Ashleigh stared across the valley in awe.

"I worried for your safety when I sensed that my sister, Mary, had disappeard while en route to St. Augustines," Glorianna said. "Since her sudden disappearance occurred just after Matilda's kidnapping, I became wary and withdrew to this mountain. Mary was much older than me, and I am greatly saddened that I was never able to meet her. Ashleigh, you are the only one I have left except for my animal friends." She stroked Cairdean's back and smiled softly at his twittering response. "You and Mangan both began a journey that took you to unexpected places, but once I learned of you I wanted to be part of one special moment in your life. Come." Glorianna walked along the cliff edge until they reached a beautiful arched trellis. Made of branches skillfully woven together, it seemed a symbol of man's and nature's best intentions transformed into artistic harmony. A multitude of autumn flowers had been entwined within its mesh.

"I made this wedding arch for you," Glorianna said, then plucked two rings from the center of a morning flower whose petals lay open to the sunshine. "These are symbols of unity that I forged in my own hearth. They are made of pounded gold, and each contains an engraved message."

" 'Eternal love,' " Mangan read.

"Wear them, and remain strong together. Place them upon each other's fingers and pledge your life to each other."

"Do you come to me, heart and soul?" Mangan asked Ashleigh. "Are you ready to trust me completely and wed me beneath this wedding bough?"

"I do. I am," Ashleigh whispered, sliding the ring upon Mangan's finger. "I will remain true to you. I will love and honor you. To me you will always be my warrior monk. Will you accept me as your wife, with all my faults and all my strengths?"

"I will," he replied, placing the ring upon her left hand, "for you are, and will always be, my wild angel."

Epilogue

Matalia was smiling and thinking of Mangan and Ashleigh together, the long life that stretched before them, as she carefully folded the last of the old garments Mangan had left behind at Kirkcaldy. He had asked her to send his monk's robes back to the monastery, along with a missive he had sealed and attached to the inside of a trunk he had provided for that purpose.

She touched an old blanket that Ashleigh had worn as a cape when she first arrived, fingering the soft fringe along one edge. It was a baby blanket from long ago, and was so worn and tattered it should probably be thrown away. She also came across a tattered piece of material that looked like it had been used as a rag.

"Matalia," Brogan called as he came up the stairs and stepped into the room. A teasing look made his lips turn up as he reached for Matalia's hand.

She absently placed the blanket in the trunk to be returned to the monastery while tossing the rag in a pile to be burned, then turned toward her husband. "Yes?"

"Will you come to bed with me?"

"Always, husband. Always."

Also available from
Sasha Lord

In My Wild Dream

She is Kassandra, a fey dreamer who is innocent
of society's rules and too reckless to follow them
anyway. In her nighttime visions she sees a
powerful Scottish laird with whom she is
destined to share a passionate bond...if she can
save him from a hooded murderer. For him,
she will travel to the king's court, risking ridicule
and confronting treachery in her quest to claim
the man of her dreams.

THE LAST HEIRESS

BERTRICE SMALL

**The much anticipated conclusion to the
popular Friarsgate Inheritance series**

A dazzling tale of passion, intrigue, and
seduction, set against the glorious backdrop of
King Henry's sixteenth-century court,
The Last Heiress stars Elizabeth Meredith, the
youngest Bolton daughter, who will risk
everything to protect her beloved Friarsgate.